PRAISE FOR *SHADOWHOUSE FALL*

"I turned pages so quickly I got paper cuts." — NPR

"Older knows that today's young people are just as magical as his characters." — *Teen Vogue*

★ "Older paints a compelling picture of contemporary life for black and brown teens in cities: Afro-Latinx Sierra and her friends deal with police harassment and brutality, both on the streets of Bed-Stuy and at school, themes that feel especially timely and relevant. . . . Older excels at crafting teen dialogue that feels authentic, and props to everyone involved for not othering the Spanish language. This second volume features a tighter plot and smoother pacing than the first, and the ending will leave readers eagerly awaiting the further adventures of Sierra and her friends. Lit." — *Kirkus Reviews*, starred review

★ "With the same keen eye for the power of art and a sly commentary on the insidious nature of racism and white supremacy—as well as a deft handle on zippy teenage banter and cinematic pacing—Older delivers a fantastic follow-up to his bestselling *Shadowshaper* (2015), which not only intensifies the stakes of the first book but expands the scope of his well-wrought, vivid world building. . . . The expanding cast of well-rounded characters, clearly choreographed action, and foreshadowing of installments to come will have fantasy fans eagerly awaiting more of this dynamic, smart series." — *Booklist*, starred review

★ "Exciting. . . . Older has upped the ante with this second installment." — *School Library Journal*, starred review

"A stunning sequel that will leave fans clamoring for book three." — *Shelf Awareness*

"Beautifully rendered. . . . Older has a knack for evoking cultural particularity and evading stereotype, a talent evident in characterization and in dialogue." — *Latinxs in Kid Lit*

SHADOWHOUSE FALL

SHADOWSHAPER
CYPHER
BOOK 2

DANIEL JOSÉ OLDER

SCHOLASTIC INC.

For Sam

Text copyright © 2017 by Daniel José Older
Map copyright © 2017 by Tim Paul

This book was originally published by Arthur A. Levine Books,
an imprint of Scholastic Inc., in 2017.

ISBN 978-1-338-33178-3

10 9 8 7 6 5 4 3 2 1   19 20 21 22 23

Printed in the U.S.A. 40
This edition first printing 2019

Book design by Christopher Stengel

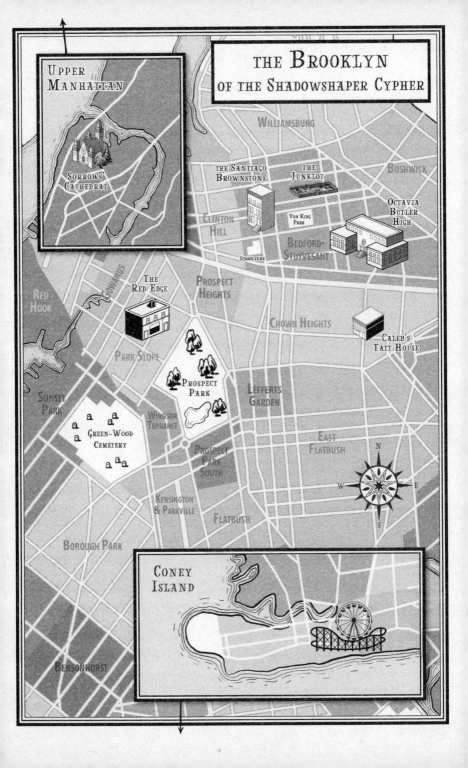

ONE

Sierra Santiago closed her eyes and the whole spinning world opened up around her. A brisk wind whispered songs of the coming winter as it shushed through browning leaves and then whisked along the moonlit field, throwing Sierra's mass of curls into disarray. Up above, the first round of overnight flights leaving JFK cut trails across the cloudless sky. Traffic whirred along just outside the park walls, and beyond that the shuttle train sighed and screeched to a halt; doors slid open; weary passengers collected their personal belongings as instructed, adjusted their earbuds, and headed off into the night.

But that was the simple stuff. Sierra had learned to expand her senses out farther than any normal person. It wasn't easy, but when she quieted her mind and the spirits were close, she could hear the city's clicks and groans halfway across Brooklyn. Tonight wasn't about meditation or the ongoing urban symphony, though. Where were her spirits?

As if in response, a vision sizzled into view in her mind's eye: There in the forest, not too far from her, a figure crouched. She could make out the silhouette leaning against a fallen tree, see the person's fast-beating heart telegraph frantic pulses out into the chilly night. The person scratched something onto the tree and looked around for nearby spirits.

I see you, Sierra thought, tensing her face into a smug smile. *Whoever you are. Now who else is out there?* She let the image go and immediately another appeared: in the field she sat on the edge of, a figure lay facedown in the grass, breathing heavily. After a few seconds, the person hunched up on their elbows and peered into the darkness. *Okay.* Sierra nodded. *Got it. What else?*

The next vision appeared so suddenly it almost knocked her over. Dark trees whipped past, and someone was panting. Running and panting. Sierra felt her own heart thunder in her ears. The other views she'd seen had been through spirit vision: a cadre of shadows she'd come to think of as her own Secret Service detail. But this was different — it was someone alive. Or some*thing* . . . Branches whisked out of its way as it bounded across the forest. *Which forest? Was it . . . was it close?* Sierra tried to scan for clues, but everything was moving too fast.

Spirits, Sierra beckoned. *Find this . . . thing.* She didn't remember having stood up, but she was on her feet. A wave of dizziness rushed over her as the half dozen views of

Prospect Park swimming through her mind veered suddenly skyward and then turned toward the shadowy fields and forests below.

All but one.

Whatever it was kept storming through the forest, panting, its whole body tensed with intent. It was . . . it was hunting. Sierra felt its hunger deep within herself; saliva flooded her own mouth. Flesh would be torn, a panicked heart would race and then falter and finally fail in this monster's jaws. The thing lunged, and Sierra's eyes popped open as a hand landed on her shoulder.

"Gotya!"

Sierra screamed and spun around, elbows first. She hit something soft and jumped back.

"Ow! What the hell, Sierra?" Big Jerome stood there rubbing his chest and pouting.

"I . . . Jerome . . ." Sierra scanned the field behind him, the forest beyond. Nothing. "I don't know . . . what happened."

"I do: You were so surprised I actually won a practice round you damn near cracked a rib."

"No . . ." Sierra rubbed her eyes. A branch snapped in the woods she had been facing. She turned, probed the darkness for movement.

"Sierra?" Sierra's mom, María Santiago, called. "¿Qué pasó, m'ija?" She walked up next to Jerome. "I was hiding and then I saw this guy barrel past and actually reach you and I knew something had to be going on."

"Whoa," Jerome said. "Mrs. Santiago with the snark. If you hadn't tangled your chalk spirits with my twig monsters at the last training run, neither of us would need extra practice."

"Mind your manners, jóven," María snapped. "What's a twig monster supposed to do anyway? Set itself on fire and dive-bomb the bad guys? Come on, man. Anyway, you didn't 'shape anything this round to win, you just ran through the field like a lost moose! That doesn't even —"

"Shh," Sierra said, her eyes still on the forest.

María scowled. "Sierra, don't you —"

"*Shh!*" Sierra hissed. "Something's out there."

If María asked a bunch of annoying parenty-type questions instead of being quiet, Sierra was going to scream. A year ago, that's what her mom would've done, but since embracing the family legacy and becoming a shadowshaper four months back, María had let go of some of her extra-eyeroll-worthy mom habits. She sighed, probably scrunched up her face, but said no more.

Sierra exhaled. Squinted into the forest. If her kinda-sorta-maybe-sometimes boyfriend Robbie had shown up like he was supposed to, at least she'd have another skillful shadowshaper to face this down with. But of course, he was once again a no-show.

Her spirits had swooped back down into the park and were springing along through the underbrush. The charging, starving whatever-it-was was gone. At least, she couldn't see through its eyes anymore. Maybe it was right there at the edge of the darkness, watching her.

Sierra narrowed her eyes and steeled herself. She had done enough running away over the summer, when she first learned about the magical art of shadowshaping and her family's legacy. It had only been a few months, but she wasn't that scared little girl anymore. She wasn't even just a shadowshaper — her dead abuela had passed on the mantle and made Sierra into the next Lucera, the beating heart of the shadowshaping world. She was still figuring out what all her powers were, but one thing she had promised herself was that she wouldn't be that freaked-out, screaming girl in all the horror movies. No more running away. She took a step toward the dark forest.

"Uh, Sierra," Jerome said. "What're you doing?"

"There's something in the trees."

"I get that. Why are you going *toward* it?"

Shadows rose up around Sierra, tall, long-legged spirits that would leap into her drawings and lash out if needed. Their gentle hum rose in the night air, filled her with that familiar mix of ferocity and calm, like a loving hurricane within. She pulled two pieces of chalk from her hoodie pocket and held one in each hand. "Stay where you are, J. I got this."

"But —" Jerome started. María must have calmed him with a hand on the shoulder, or probably a gentle slap. She knew better than to try to stop her daughter in one of her gung-ho moments.

Sierra reached her arms out to either side and strode into the shadows. She scraped the chalk along the trees around her as she walked, then tapped the marks once with her fingertips. The forest night closed in around her. Even with the spirits heightening her vision as they slid along in smooth, sparkling strides, it seemed like a blanket of darkness had been thrown over the whole world. She could run — she could always run — but she would never run. She would find out what this was and fight it if she had to. The chalk scratches sped along the tree trunks, flashes of color, and then disappeared in the gloom up ahead. They weren't the best weapons to have — nowhere near as strong as a painted mural, for example — but they'd be able to keep an enemy busy till she could work out something better.

Hopefully.

And then, very suddenly, Sierra stopped. She wasn't alone. The certainty of someone else there, a presence, tickled along her shoulders and the back of her neck.

"Don't be afraid," a girl's voice said as Sierra spun around.

"Mina?"

Mina Satorius was a grade above Sierra at Octavia Butler High, but she looked fourteen. She had big eyes and her strawberry blond hair was ponytailed, with bangs at the front and a spindly curl framing her face on either side. She stood in the middle of a clearing, wearing a plaid shirt over a tank top and a sweater tied around her waist. Despite what she'd just said, Mina herself looked terrified — eyebrows creased with worry, bottom lip trembling slightly, arms wrapped around her slender frame.

"What are you doing out here?" Sierra asked. Her towering shadows emerged in a circle around Mina; their gentle glow pulsed in time with Sierra's own heartbeat. Shimmering chalk marks appeared on the trees, poised to flush forward and attack.

"I'm . . . I . . ." She looked like she might collapse into a puddle any second. Sierra resisted the urge to walk up and hug her. Something had been out here hunting, something ferocious. It was hard to imagine Mina could have anything to do with that panting monster whose eyes Sierra had seen through, but . . .

"Spit it out, Mina. We're not safe here."

"I know," Mina said. "That's what . . . that's what I'm here to say. A warning."

The shadows around Mina rustled, seemed to whisper to each other. Mina glanced up, her eyes widening even more. She had the spirit vision, Sierra realized, just not very advanced. At least, that's how she made it seem.

"You have a warning for me, so you hide out in the woods and wait for me to come to you? You couldn't send a text or something? This is creepy."

"No, I know, I . . . I was gonna come out and talk to you, but then I felt it nearby and . . ."

"Felt what, girl? Come on, now."

"The . . ." She sighed. "Here." With a trembling hand, she held up what looked like an old playing card.

Sierra didn't move. "What's that?"

"It's from the Deck of Worlds. Take it."

Sierra shook her head. "My mama told me not to take freaky magic cards from strange white girls I meet in the woods."

"Sierra, I'm . . . I'm not here to hurt you. I know you've had problems with the Sorrows before, but —"

"You're with the Sorrows?" All the shadows tensed and took a step forward. Sierra clenched her fists. "Get out of here. Leave. Don't talk to me in the hallway. Don't talk to my friends. And definitely don't let me catch you skulking around these woods while I'm working with my shadowshapers."

"It's not like that, Sierra, listen —"

"I listened. I heard what you said. Get out of my sight before I let these shadows loose on you."

Mina shook her head, took a step backward. "You don't understand," she whispered, placing the card in the soft forest soil at her feet. "But when you do, come find me. I'm not . . . I'm not your enemy, Sierra. Take the card. *Don't* leave it there. You need to . . . you need to take it." She turned around and ran.

Sierra took a step toward the card.

"Sierra?" María called from behind her. "¿Estás bien, m'ija?"

"Sí, Mami," Sierra said. "Ya voy."

She crouched down to get a better look. An archaic, faded drawing was scrawled on the front of the card. It showed a white wolf with blue glowing eyes, its jaws open and lips pulled back into a snarl. Gleaming castle towers spiraled toward a stormy sky in the background. *El SABUESO de la LUZ* was scrawled across the top in elegant, medieval print. On the bottom it read, *The HOUND of LIGHT.*

Sierra stood up. The spirits flushed around her as she backed away from the card, then turned and walked quickly out of the woods.

TWO

"The hell was that all about?" Jerome asked, huffing and puffing to keep up with Sierra.

"I'm not . . . I'm not really sure," Sierra said. Prospect Park had always felt like a sanctuary to her, an escape from the cruel, busy city, and later a safe place to shadowshape in peace. But now, she exhaled with relief as they crossed out of its dark embrace and into the bright, bustling roundabout at Grand Army Plaza.

"What do you mean you're not sure?" María demanded. "What happened?"

Sierra leaned against the stone wall at the edge of the park and shook her head, panting. "A girl I know from school was there. Mina."

"You mean Snap Crackle and Pop Mina?" Jerome asked. "Huh?"

"Mina, that tiny white chick that usedta kick it with Little Jerome?"

"I guess," Sierra said. "Why y'all call her Snap Crackle and Pop?"

"She always used to read books about serial killers in seventh-grade homeroom. Like, every day, it was another one. So you know . . ."

"Serial, cereal . . . You guys are terrible."

Jerome shrugged.

María crossed her hands over her chest and scowled. "¿Y qué carajo hacía en el parque a esa hora de la noche, coño?"

"I dunno, Mami. I mean, someone could easily wonder what *we* were doing in the park at this hour too . . ."

"We were practicing our cultural heritage. ¿Y qué?" María had emerged from a lifetime of denying shadowshaping to become its most militant advocate.

Sierra sighed. She didn't dare mention that Mina was somehow lined up with the Sorrows — her mom would lose her mind and spend the rest of the night freaking out, and anyway, Sierra wasn't totally sure what to make of it all yet.

At a creepy, abandoned churchyard down a sidestreet on the northern tip of Manhattan, three golden shrouds held court. They called themselves the Sisterhood of the Sorrows, and Sierra had jacked up their shrine last summer to find out where a deranged anthropologist named Dr. Wick was hiding. They weren't happy about it, but considering that they'd helped Dr. Wick incapacitate her grandfather and nearly destroy the shadowshapers, Sierra didn't really care how they felt. Then again, they'd vowed revenge, and she'd spent more than a few sleepless nights wondering when they'd come collecting.

Or if they already had. A strange man had attacked her at the beginning of September. He'd had some kind of supernatural stuff going on, that much was clear. Bennie and Sierra had fought him off but they never did figure out who sent him.

"You coming home, m'ija?" María was already heading up Eastern Parkway toward the train.

"No, Mami, Juan has a show tonight at the Edge and we're already by the Slope. You're not coming?"

"Sierra." María's voice tightened, her eyes narrow. A few seconds passed, during which Jerome became very interested in his phone. "I don't want to . . . I don't want to go through it again. What happened this summer. I don't want to wonder if you'll make it home alive every time you leave the house."

"I know, but I'm not gonna let one random girl showing up in the woods make me miss my brother's show. Nothing's wrong. It was just weird is all. I promise."

María stared down her daughter for a solid five seconds, then relented. "Wake me up when you get in."

"Okay, Mami."

"And Jerome, if anything happens to her that doesn't happen to you, you get to explain it to me. ¿Me entiendes?"

"Yes, Mrs. Santiago. I'd take death at the hands of a horrible phantom before having to explain shi — anything to you. I swear."

"Good." She turned around and walked off into the night.

"Your moms is a trip," Jerome said. They walked into the quiet avenues of Park Slope, the park safely behind them. "Like, I kinda wish my moms was as cool as your moms, but then again I don't, because your moms looks like she'd whip ass with a quickness and mine acts like she would but really, her bark is like way worse than her bite, ya know?"

"My mom's alright," Sierra said. María Santiago had rejected shadowshaping entirely when she was Sierra's age. Grandpa Lázaro and Mama Carmen were the two most powerful 'shapers around, but after their daughter's refusal to even acknowledge the family magic, Lázaro had fallen back on his machismo ways, insisting that shadowshaping was a men's practice. Sierra still hadn't brought herself to fully forgive him for keeping her in the dark about the family legacy her whole life. Anyway, he was laid up on the top floor of their brownstone now, wasting away and incapacitated from an attack by Dr. Wick.

"You were lying when you said that nothing's wrong, though, right?" Jerome said. "Cuz . . . I get the feeling something's wrong."

"I'm not sure," Sierra admitted. "I'm really not."

"And wasn't Robbie supposed to show up tonight? Where he at?"

Sierra heard the snarl in her own voice before she had time to smooth it out: "That's a terrific question."

Sierra would normally never go to the Red Edge. The first and only time she'd gone in was the first time Culebra played there and the night that strange man attacked her, right there in the alley behind the club in fact, and that was quite enough for her.

Besides, she wasn't even seventeen yet, and even if she had a fake ID, the unimpressed-to-death bouncers outside would surely see right through it with their x-ray vision and then have her arrested or something. But more importantly, the place oozed with creepy excess and awkward-fake-schmoozy small talk. Sierra had passed it plenty of times on the way to her favorite comic book store in Park Slope, and there were always one or two uncomfortable-looking black or brown folks in the corner surrounded by tons of white folks, chattering away.

But it was Wednesday night, and Sierra's brother Juan had managed to get his salsa-thrasher band, Culebra, a weekly gig playing the Red Edge's back room. This meant that on Wednesdays and Wednesdays only, the place transformed into a raucous, multicultural smashpot of punk rockers, hip-hoppers, poets, graffiti artists, and the occasional random old Puerto Rican guy who would wander in off the street. Sierra felt right at home.

"Where y'all been?" Bennie demanded. Sierra's best friend stood outside the Red Edge with her hands on her hips and one eyebrow raised over her glasses. "The show's already half over!"

"Girl," Sierra said. "I don't even know where to begin."

"That random girl Mina from AP Chemistry was chillin' in the woods," Jerome said, leaning in for his hug. "Like, for no apparent reason."

Bennie scrunched her face at Sierra. "Mina Satorius? For why?"

"She said she wanted to warn me about something," Sierra said.

Bennie frowned. "'Bout what?"

For a second, Sierra was deep in the dark forest again; the horrible panting filled her mind. Was it a memory or another vision? She shook her head. "I don't know. She tried to hand me a card."

"Like a business card?" Jerome asked. "The woods a weird-ass place to network."

"Looked like one of those tarot cards Tee messes with, but . . . it was different. I've never seen one like it before. Had a wolf on it, or a hound, I guess."

Bennie pulled out her phone. "You want me to get all the 'shapers together? I think Izzy's abouta go on stage, but . . ."

"No," Sierra said. She already felt strange telling Jerome and Bennie what had happened and she didn't know why. She told Bennie *everything*, especially now that she had become a shadowshaper too. But something clenched inside Sierra every time she tried to talk about the girl in the woods. "Let's just go in and have fun. We're safe for now, and anyway, I don't wanna miss Izzy's set." She made herself smile, but Bennie's narrowed eyes let Sierra know she wasn't fooled.

"Alright, girl, whatever you say."

Sierra glanced up and down the block one last time — it was late and most of the fancy bistros and Thai restaurants of Park Slope were shut down for the night. A few taxis idled on the block, ready to collect the drunken after-party stragglers; a police car rolled past, then a bicyclist.

No spirits — they were probably all inside enjoying the show — and definitely no giant hungry monsters.

Sierra took a breath and walked in.

Culebra was in full swing when Sierra joined the crowd. Juan stood at the front, strumming a ferocious *wukka-wukka* against muted strings on his Stratocaster, every once in a while exploding into a fury of static and then pulling back. Beside him, tall, dark-skinned, and dreamy-eyed Pulpo hit long, resonant notes on his bass as he sang into the mic: *"Duerme, soñar, duerme, soñaaaaaar."* He'd cut off his locks since Sierra saw him last, and now rocked a close-cropped cut that suited his big, beautiful head. Ruben slid into a cool hip-hop march. His brother Kaz patted out a fierce rhythm on the congas; they called him Dirtyhands and it was clear why — the drums seemed to be whispering tantalizing secrets into the autumn night. Then Izzy strolled out from the shadows, her white tank top already sweat-soaked from moshing, her fitted cap tilted just so, and her tightly wound braids pulled back in a ponytail.

"Impervious on the mic!" Izzy yelled.

"*YAAAA!*" the crowd screamed back, and she let out a goofy grin, taking it all in.

"What it do, Park Slope?" Izzy looked off to the side at nothing in particular, her mouth slightly open, and let the cheers wash over her. "The King is in the building, feel me?"

"*Duerme,*" Pulpo crooned. "*Soñaaaaaar.*" Juan's wa-wa strut growled into overdrive and the drummers responded; cymbals crashed and then the snare blasted twice like a gunshot and Izzy leaned into the mic: "I don't sleep to dream / don't make a peep, don't scream / Cream! Screw the money, get the honey / eff the bills eff the pills put the pump in let it fill / Think I won't, well I will / I came to kill I came to kill / Don't believe me check the bill / I done delivered all the death to the crimson tide krill." She took a breath, smiled, then yelled, "Now rock!" And Culebra unleashed sonic carnage on the Red Edge.

"Sierra!" Tee yelled, making her way through the thrashing crowd.

"Hey girl!" They hugged, then Tee leaned against the bar between Sierra and Bennie. "You guys ain't gonna dance?" she yelled over the pounding guitars and her girlfriend's frantic rhymes.

Sierra shook her head. "Not in the mood tonight."

"What's wrong?"

What indeed? Sierra felt like if she had to try to explain something she herself didn't even understand one more time, she'd explode. "I don't even know."

"I hear that," Tee said. "I'm not really in a dancing mood myself, just here to support my baby."

"She's killin' it tonight," Bennie said.

"It's all she knows how to do." Tee grinned. "I've literally never seen her half step even a random freestyle on the corner. She was born to slay. And you know I'm not just saying that cuz she's my girl."

"Oh, we know," Sierra said, finally allowing herself a smile. Here, in this crowded, sweaty club with her brother's music screaming all around her and two of her favorite people beside her, it was easier to ignore the growing unease creeping along her bones.

"Ah, I meant to tell you," Tee said, leaning into Sierra's ear. "Bumped into that chick Mina earlier — remember the one who worked on the newspaper with me over the summer?"

Sierra closed her eyes. *Crap.*

"What?" Bennie yelled. "Did you say Mina? Sierra, isn't that —?"

"Yes," Sierra growled.

"Y'all saw her too? She was standing outside the park, looking like a freak, but you know, she does that — you ever notice that? Chick'll just stand places and like, not do anything. Weird-ass. Anyway, she gave me this."

Sierra didn't have to look; she already knew what it would be. And she just wanted it to be gone.

"And it was really strange," Tee went on. "Felt something . . . I dunno, something inside myself when I took it. Like . . . something lit up? Or shuddered? Hard to explain."

"Sierra," Bennie said, "you might wanna look at this?"

Up on the stage, Izzy was yelling something and it didn't sound like part of the song.

"Uh-oh," Sierra said. Culebra's fierce ruckus clattered to a halt.

"You heard what *I* said; I got a mic," Izzy yelled. "I wanna know what *you* said, with ya no neck-having linebacker-lookin' ass. Seriously, where's ya neck, man? Anybody seen it?"

Tee's eyes got wide.

"Oh word?" Izzy's voice boomed over the club. She threw the mic down and hurtled headfirst into the crowd.

"Every! Damn! Time!" Tee snarled as she shoved through the sweaty concertgoers. "I swear!"

Sierra and Bennie sighed at the same time and then leapt into the crowd after their friend.

THREE

"The hell was that all about?" Tee demanded as the four girls fastwalked around a corner and down a quiet side street.

"That big musclehead white dude said the n-word!" Izzy said. "That's messed up. *I* don't even say the n-word and I'm black!"

Bennie rolled her eyes. "I'm not cool with him saying it either, but he was singing along to your lyrics, Iz! How you gonna say you don't say it?"

"That's no excuse! That's King Impervious up there, it's a persona, you know? The King says stuff I would *never* say. And anyway, that's not the point. I can say it. You can say it. *That* dude can*not* say it."

"You hadta mess him up, though?" Tee said. "Or more to the point, you have to mess someone up *every* show? Like literally every single show?"

Izzy shrugged. "It's like my signature. People come to expect it."

Tee stopped walking and slapped her hand against her face. "Please tell me you're kidding, babe. I beg you."

"I'm kidding! Sheesh! I just get wound up sometimes, ya know?"

"*Sometimes!*" Tee scoffed.

"It's always the short ones," Bennie said.

Sierra stifled a laugh.

"Ay, di King!" a gravelly voice called from behind them.

Izzy froze, her hand inches away from swatting Bennie. "Desmond!"

A middle-aged man in a blazer and whitewashed jeans came hurrying up the block with an envelope in his hands. "Yuh cut out before mi pay yuh, girl."

Izzy looked at the pavement. "I thought you were gonna be mad."

"Mad? Fi wha?"

"The fight?"

"A joke yuh a mek? Di YouTube video gone viral already. Next week, it a go bring double di amount a people. Here." He handed her the envelope and smiled at Sierra, Bennie, and Tee. "Whaa gwaan, ladies?"

"Desmond." Tee crossed her arms over her chest. "Do not be encouragin' her shenanigans. It might be good publicity, but it ain't safe. Who knows who she beefin' up out there?"

"Nah, nah, you right," Desmond conceded. "But I would've done the same ting if da yute de did sey dah word de round mi."

"Desmond," Tee growled.

"Alright!" He clapped once. "Mek mi go back een before mi get ina trouble." He nodded with a wild grin and then took off back toward the club.

"You really caught all that?" Bennie asked.

"Mostly, yeah," Izzy said. "My grandpa's Jamaican, and he only speaks in Patwa now that the dementia's set in."

"Desmond is the real MVP," Tee said.

"You should see him when we in the studio," Izzy said. "He gets so worked up when a song is hot, you worried he gonna bust a blood vessel. Stays up all night fixing all the little production details, then passes out for like two days straight. And this music thing is just his side gig, he's a lawyer during the day."

"Hey, where's Jerome?" Sierra asked.

"He hung back to talk to some chick," Bennie said. "Said he'd catch up with us."

They reached the corner; across the street, Prospect Park seemed to reach out with its tendriled darkness. "Tee," Sierra said. "Let me see what Mina gave you."

"Oh, right! Hang on." She dug through her pockets and pulled out a card the same size and shape as the one Mina had held out earlier. On the front, a medieval knight in black armor held a flaming sword over his head as a city burned behind him. *KNIGHT of SHADOWS,* it said.

"Freaky," Izzy said. "This some shadowshaper-type mess, Sierra?"

"I don't know what it is," Sierra said. "She tried to give me one in the park earlier when I was running a practice session with Jerome and my mom."

"You didn't take it?" Tee asked, eyeing the card.

Sierra scrunched up her face. "I don't trust her, and . . . you never know with this kinda stuff . . ."

Izzy swatted the card to the ground and hugged Tee. "Is she contaminated?"

"If I am you shouldn't be grabbing on me like that! What if I'm contagious?"

"I'm going down with you, baby! We in this together!"

Sierra rolled her eyes. "You guys gotta chill. I don't think it's contaminated; I was just being overly cautious. Now I'm thinking maybe I should've taken it. She swore up and down she wasn't my enemy."

"What enemy worth her salt wouldn't?" Bennie pointed out.

"True, but she seemed sincere. What'd she say to you, Tee?"

Tee picked up the card and held it under the streetlight. "Well, first of all, she was being mad coffeeshop cryptic."

Sierra raised an eyebrow. "Coffeeshop cryptic?"

"You know," Tee said. "The way Izzy gets when she spends too much time sipping mocha-frappa-whatevers at the spot on Bedford and writes bad poetry — no offense, babe."

Izzy glared at her. "How you gonna say some real offensive shit and then — you know what, never mind. Imma take the L on this one."

"Wise woman," Bennie said.

"Anyway!" Tee yelled. "Mina was like, 'There's a play in the works!' And I was like, 'A school play? It's October, son.' I mean — I kinda knew she didn't mean that but I felt like messing with her, cuz how you gonna roll up on me out of nowhere talkin' 'bout a play in the works? No 'Hey, Tee,' no 'Do you need help studying for that bio quiz next week?' I don't, by the way. But yeah! So, she was like, 'No, someone's bouta make a play.' And I was like, 'Well, who, girl?' And she said she didn't know, but it was gonna be messy and then she said *the Deck* was back in play, she said it like that too, got all whispery: *the Deck*. And I was like, 'Inspectah Deck?'"

Bennie gasped. "You did *not* ask that white girl if she was talking about Wu-Tang, Tee! Tell me you did not!"

"Okay, no," Tee admitted. "That woulda been funny, though, right? I mean, she's from Staten Island, so . . ."

"ANYWAY!" Sierra said.

"Anyway, she said the Deck was back in play and who wielded the cards wielded the power, something like that, and she didn't know a whole lot but she trusted me — I mean, we bonded a bunch over the summer and she's cool, but I had no idea she was involved in any of this. Anyway, she said she wanted the shadowshapers to be okay, so she was giving me this even though she shouldn't, and if I could figure out who it was, who this Knight of Shadows dude is, then it could help us not get destroyed? Or something like that."

Sierra cringed. She should've taken the card. Even if she didn't trust Mina, at least with the card they could try to figure out better what all was going on. And if Mina was telling the truth, she'd be able to maybe control whatever monster was lurking out there, or whatever the Hound of Light was.

"What's wrong, Sierra?" Tee asked.

"We need the card Mina tried to give me," Sierra said. "There's someone . . . something . . . lurking . . . I can see through its eyes sometimes, the way I can with spirits, and . . . it's looking for something. Or it was earlier tonight. I think it might be the hound that was on the card? I don't know — none of this makes sense to me."

"Can you see where it is right now?" Bennie asked.

Sierra looked back and forth between her friends' scared faces. Whatever happened, they were going to have to go back into the park and get that stupid card. And the thought terrified her.

She took a deep breath and closed her eyes. "I'll try."

The dark forest came rushing toward her. Trees brushed past and that same heavy panting filled the air. The creature was moving faster. A frantic heartbeat thundered through Sierra's ears. Then a wide-open field spread out beneath the moon. It was Prospect Park's main lawn, the one they'd been practicing in earlier that night.

Sierra's eyes shot open and she almost toppled over, gasping. "It's going for the card!"

"And you want to —" Izzy said, frowning.

"We have to get there first." Sierra hopped over the stone wall and ran into the park.

For a flickering second, Sierra wasn't sure if she was seeing her own vision or the thing in the forest's. They'd cut through the small field by the half-shell stage, crossed the cement bike path, and raced into another woodsy area. Sierra's panting mingled with the heavier, feral breaths of whatever-it-was, and when she blinked, a different area of woods surrounded her.

"Sierra!" Bennie yelled as the ground rushed up out of nowhere. Sierra caught herself midstumble and kept running.

"Can't . . . stop . . ." she panted. "It's close."

And then the spirits were there, everywhere, pulsing and swarming through the trees around them. The forest became crisp, each blade of grass and trembling leaf suddenly sharp, perfectly clear. Sierra leapt over a boulder, skidded her landing as the ground inclined downward toward the open field.

They were going to make it. The card was on their side of the park; the whatever-it-was still making its way through the woods off to the edge of where they were, from what she could tell. Still . . . it wouldn't be far behind when they arrived, and she had no idea what to do with the card when she got it.

If it was still there . . .

A guttural howl shattered the stillness of the night. Sierra froze. The sound seemed to rip out into the world from deep inside of her. But she wasn't howling. She looked around. Her friends were still running. They hadn't heard it. The terrible sound trailed off, and in the stillness that followed, Sierra wondered if she'd heard it at all. Then it came again, louder this time, and Sierra dropped to her knees with shock. It was inside her, relentless and mournful.

She had to get that card.

She was up and running before the second howl finished. She bounded past her friends, the shadow spirits carrying her along like an impossible wind. They lifted her up, elongated each stride until she was fast-floating across the dark park. And then she was back at the small clearing where Mina had been standing just a few hours ago. Sierra's heart went into overdrive as she gaped at the empty spot of soil where the card had been.

"Make a circle facing outward," she called when she heard her friends arrive. "Get ready to 'shape. Something's coming."

They complied without a sound, and Sierra dropped to her knees and rustled some of the fallen leaves around, trying not to let the tremble she felt inside reach her fingertips. She grazed something stiffer than the crinkly leaves, grabbed it, and then let out a grateful sigh. "Got it!" she yelled. The pale blue eyes glared back at her from the face of the card.

"Good," Tee said. "Cuz whatever it is is here."

Sierra spun around. Something huge and dark lurked in the shadows just beyond where Bennie, Tee, and Izzy stood. A rainbow army of chalk arrows trembled in the trees around them, ready to strike. Other tall shadows waited on either side. A low growl sounded — it was wet and slobbery and horrible. Also, somehow familiar.

Sierra held the card up, trying to stop her hand from shaking. She looked past it at the creature in the woods. It took a step forward, and Bennie, Tee, and Izzy stepped back. "Attack?" Tee asked.

Something prickled at the edge of Sierra's mind, like a twinkle of light caught in the corner of an eye. Something about that familiar growl. "Wait," she said, knowing they'd all be cursing her out silently.

The beast took another step forward and then burst into the moonlight toward Sierra.

"Cojones!" she yelled as the huge dog leapt into the air and collided against her in a furry tangle of jowls, hot breath, and paws. "It's you!" She braced for the inevitable slobber bath, but Cojones just stared at her, tongue lolling out the side of his slightly open mouth. "That's weird," Sierra said, scratching the dangly black folds of his neck.

"Man, I ain't seen Cojones since everything went down over the summer," Izzy said.

"I was cool with that, though," Bennie put in. "I almost damn peed myself just now. Nobody put this beast on a leash?"

"You alright, Sierra?" Tee asked.

"I am now," Sierra said, pushing Cojones off her and getting up. "Feel like I just found a long-lost friend!" Sadness quickly dimmed her flush of joy. Cojones was Manny's dog, and Manny was dead. The self-proclaimed Domino King of Brooklyn had been a good friend of Sierra's family and one of the original shadowshapers. Sierra had spent long hours at the Junklot he owned, painting a huge dragon mural and laughing to herself while Manny and his buddies took turns verbally ethering each other to the rhythm of clacking domino fichas.

And then she'd found Manny's mostly lifeless body sprawled out in the barber's chair that he used for thinking in the basement newspaper office. So many other things had happened in those couple days — there were so many losses and so much danger — Sierra felt like she'd barely had a chance to mourn. Manny's death still snuck up on her out of the blue sometimes, a sudden visitor who was neither announced nor invited.

"What's this?" Bennie gingerly pulled something from under Cojones's spiked collar. "Uh-oh."

"What is it?" Sierra asked. Bennie passed her the card.

SHADOW HOUND, the script said on top. The creature in the picture was even more terrifying than Cojones: a hideous, snarling demon dog with a limp, child-sized figure hanging from in its fanged, blood-splattered jaws. A fiery plain stretched around it. Sierra felt her stomach plummet.

"The hell?" Tee said.

"Literally," Izzy added.

"If Cojones is the Shadow Hound," Bennie said, "that means . . ."

"This one" — Sierra held up the card Mina had tried to give her, the Hound of Light — "is still out there."

FOUR

"Hold up," Bennie said as they approached the edge of the park. "Who's that with Jerome?"

They had backed out of the woods, eyes glued to the darkness, and then fastwalked across the moonlit field. Sierra kept slowing to check in on what the creature that had been tracking her was seeing: First it was just trees and shadows, and then it all seemed to dissolve into a cloudy emptiness. Anyway, no one wanted to slow down, so they made quick time to the entranceway, until Bennie held up her hand and they all squinted through the trees to where Jerome stood with his arms raised.

"I didn't do nothin'," he was saying, so loud it sounded like he hoped someone else would hear him. "I was just standing here!"

"Shit," Tee whispered. "He with the cops."

"Just standing there, huh?" The officer's voice seethed with sarcasm. Sierra couldn't make out his face through the trees, but it looked like there were two of them. "Minding your own business."

"Yessir," Jerome said.

"Man, I thought stop and frisk was s'posta be over," Tee said, ignoring Izzy's scoff. "We gotta go help him."

"Help him?" Izzy shook her head. "You high? What we gonna do?"

Bennie's hand wrapped around Sierra's and squeezed tight. Bennie's brother Vincent had been killed by cops three years ago, and her eyes still got a faraway look every time she mentioned him. Sierra squeezed her hand back.

"Turn around and keep your hands in the air," the other cop said to Jerome. "You have any sharp objects in your pockets? Anything I could cut myself on?"

Jerome turned around, raised his arms. "No, sir."

"Tee," Sierra said. "You come with me. Izzy and Bennie hang back. Keep your cameras ready."

Bennie shot her a grateful glance and wrapped her arms around herself. Sierra and Tee walked out of the woods to the path and then out of the park.

"Why are you sweating?" one of the cops said.

"Um . . . because I'm being randomly stopped by two guys with guns on the street."

"Ha, a joker, huh? Or you got something to hide?"

"He's with us, Officer," Sierra said, stepping with Tee onto the sidewalk, her arms raised. "We was just hanging out in the park, and he —"

"Whoa whoa whoa!" The cop frisking Jerome, a young white guy with a sharp chin and mirrored sunglasses, stepped back quickly, hand on the grip of his holstered gun.

The other one, tall and pot-bellied with light brown skin, shook his head, smiling. "Alright, Stevens, I got this. You girls do know the park is closed at this hour, right?"

"We didn't know," Tee said, her voice cold. "No sign."

"You being funny?" Stevens said.

"Nope, just being true."

The officers exchanged dubious glances. "We could drag all three of you down to the station," the tall one said. "Give your parents a call. How's that sound?"

"Sounds wack," Sierra said.

"You have IDs on you?"

Sierra and Tee nodded.

"Drugs?"

They shook their heads.

An uncomfortable moment passed. "You going straight home?"

Hell no, a voice inside of Sierra yelled. *And why should we?* "Yep," she said, managing a smile.

"Is this even legal?" Tee said. Sierra's gut clenched.

The tall cop's eyes narrowed. "Look —"

"Actually, it's a gray area," a voice said. The door of the cruiser closed and Sierra looked over. A burly guy in a business suit with thinning blond hair walked toward them.

"Oh, this guy again," the tall cop muttered. "Thought he went to get us coffee."

"Wayne Garrett," the business-suit guy said. "I'm with the Volunteer Lawyer Corps. Just on a routine observational run with these fine officers here." His smile screamed used-car dealer, but Sierra was relieved to have someone else there anyway. "How y'all doing today?"

"Not so hot," Jerome said.

"Crappy," Izzy added.

"Wack," Tee agreed.

"We were much better before you decided to butt in," the tall cop said. The officer in sunglasses didn't say a word.

"Well, look," Wayne Garrett said, "unfortunately — or fortunately, depending on how you look at it" — he winked at Sierra — "the law is still trying to work itself out when it comes to random stops. But one thing is certain: There needs to be some reason for a stop. The police don't actually have the right to search you unless they have what we call 'reasonable suspicion' that you've committed a crime. Or if you give them permission, of course." He gazed at Jerome, Tee, Izzy, and Sierra. They stared blankly back at him. He chuckled. "Did you?"

"Uh-uh," Tee said.

"Hell no," Izzy said.

"Nope," Sierra said.

"Not a chance," Jerome said.

Garrett looked at the two officers. "Guess that's that, then."

"Alright," the tall cop said. "All three of you, go on then."

Sierra exhaled, trying not to look too relieved.

"Stevens," Tee said.

The white cop looked up. "Excuse me?"

"That's your name." She squinted at the shield on his uniform shirt. "And 2876 is your badge. Got it. Thanks."

He took a step toward her. "Oh, so you *do* want trouble?"

"Easy," the other officer muttered.

Tee glanced at him. "And you are?"

"Sergeant Toderick, badge 781, and good luck with your complaint." He placed a hand on Stevens's shoulder. "Y'all have a nice evening."

Stevens just stared from behind his mirrored sunglasses. Garrett waved amiably as the four started to walk away.

"You good?" Sierra asked Jerome once they were out of earshot. She glanced back: Stevens gazed into the park while Toderick said something into his radio. The lawyer must've already gotten into the car.

Jerome nodded and wiped sweat off his face. "Almost shit my pants, but otherwise I'm good."

The cruiser zoomed past, even its headlights darkened.

"I'm not," Tee said. "Ain't a goddamn reason we should be going home or have to say we are or any of that! We ain't criminals. We ain't do nothin' but be. We can't be without getting the third degree?"

"You right," Sierra said.

"They asking all those drunk white kids in the Slope what they're up to on this fine night? Huh?"

Jerome and Sierra shook their heads. Tee spat.

"I'm just glad to be out that mess alive," Jerome said. "Where Bennie and Iz?"

"Up there," Sierra said. They were coming up on the bright lights of Grand Army Plaza; Bennie and Izzy sat on one of the benches, their faces lit up by their phone screens.

"Y'all okay?" Tee said.

Izzy shook her head. "Just lit up Hoozit with a rant about it, so I'm good."

"The hell's Hoozit?" Jerome asked.

"It's like Twitter but not for old people," Tee said. "Iz got like four million followers on there."

"King Impervious do," Izzy corrected. "And it's more like forty thousand. And now they mad as hell."

"Well done, babe," Tee said, dapping her girlfriend and blowing a kiss.

"Ah!" Jerome yelled, skittering back a few steps from the park. "What is — back!"

Cojones emerged from the shadows, panting — maybe even smiling, Sierra thought, eyeing his massive jaw. "Oh, sorry, J." She patted her thigh and Cojones pressed happily against her leg and plopped his butt down on the pavement. "You don't remember Cojones?"

"I'd been trying to forget," Jerome said, venturing back to the group.

"If that dog gonna roll with us," Izzy said, "we gotta call him something cooler than Nutsack."

Sierra let the wave of sorrow pass over her — Manny

had named him Cojones, knowing that the other old guys at the Junklot would yell it as a curse and inadvertently summon the overenthusiastic guard dog. "Yeah," she said. Izzy did have a point. Manny's uninhibited belly laugh echoed through her.

"Cojo," Tee said. "Sounds like Cujo, which is, you know, appropriate."

Sierra scratched behind the dog's massive ears absentmindedly. "That works."

Bennie had her arms wrapped around herself again.

"You alright?" Sierra asked quietly.

Bennie shook her head, nodded, shrugged. "Walk me home?"

"Of course!"

They hugged their good-byes to the others and told each other to stay safe and text when they got home. Tee yelled, "Thanks, moms!" while Izzy put her hands over her mouth and beatboxed and Jerome did the robot.

"That was a *lot*," Sierra said as they passed the majestic Brooklyn Museum with its fancy modern glass awning over ancient stone pillars.

Bennie shook her head, frowning.

"You wanna talk about it, B?"

Bennie sighed. "I just . . . It's not just about that, I

just . . . I thought . . ." She shook her head, looking up the wide stretch of Eastern Parkway.

"Spit it out, girl."

"When you first told me about the spirits and all that, I was skeptical. I mean, duh, that's my job as a scientist, right? But I saw how serious you were and I went with it — whatever, there must've been *something* to it, I figured. And then the more you talked about it, the more I believed in it, what you were saying, and then . . . then you brought us into it, that night on the beach, and . . ."

They stopped walking. Cars rushed past. An ambulance idled in the roundabout beside the museum, two medics sleeping soundly inside.

"I thought he'd come," Bennie said. "I thought he'd show up. I learned how to see the spirits, and there they were, and I kept looking for him, some sign of him, you know, in those shadows, and . . . nothing. I went to his mural, and you know I hate going by there. I waited. I squinted, did the 'soft eyes' thing you taught me to see the spirits." She sighed. "Nothing."

"Damn," Sierra whispered.

"I just thought . . . I hoped . . ."

Sierra nodded. She'd wondered the same thing a few times, whether Vincent would show up. Besides her grandmother Carmen, the original Lucera, Sierra didn't have any other dead relatives that she'd known personally. But Vincent . . . Some spirits just didn't make it to the other side. Or maybe he was off somewhere else, keeping an eye on things in another part of town. "I wish I knew what to say," she said. She wrapped her arms around Bennie. "Besides that I'll keep an eye out for him."

Bennie laughed but it sounded like she was about to cry. "Thanks, Sierra. I'm alright." She stepped back from the hug, wiped her nose. "Just . . . you know."

"Yeah."

"What's up with Robbie anyway? We ain't seen him in a minute."

Sierra rolled her eyes. "Ha . . . I wish I could tell you. He's just so . . . I dunno. Flighty?" They headed across the Parkway, Cojo trotting along beside them.

"I mean," Bennie said, "he did spend the first couple days after meeting you disappearing."

"Yeah, but he had good cause! There were corpuscules after us, and he thought he was saving me by getting them to chase him."

"Girl, I guess."

They rounded the corner of Washington where Vincent had been shot and all conversation faded away. They never spoke about it, that moment of silence, it just always happened. Tonight the emptiness felt especially heavy.

They stopped in front of Bennie's stoop and Sierra shrugged. "Thing is: Robbie's an amazing dude. And he gets me, you know, on the 'shaping tip, the way no other guy would. And when we're together everything's really cool. But . . . he only texts me back half the time. He's always busy painting or handling some of his own 'shaping stuff and . . ." She threw her hands up. "Bah!"

"Guess the downside of dating the hot mysterious enigmatic dude is that he's mysterious and enigmatic, huh."

"Right? I don't even know if we're really dating. Need to find me a regular ol' hot unenigmatic guy to roll with."

"If you find one, see if he has a hot unenigmatic brother."

Sierra snorted a laugh. "We gonna work it out. All we've been through together already — we gotta." She hugged Bennie and then turned toward home. Cojo followed a few seconds later, panting happily.

"Yo, Sierra," Bennie called. "Seriously: People always tell you who they are. At some point, you gotta listen."

Twenty minutes later, Cojo stopped short at the corner of Sierra's block. "What is it, boy?" He wasn't growling, just staring directly ahead. A figure stood in the shadows in the middle of the block. He was tall and thin. Sierra narrowed her eyes. "Robbie?"

He spun around, stepped into the streetlight, and smiled. Sierra rolled her eyes. "You're too cool to text a girl back but not to show up unannounced at any ol' hour of the night, huh?"

Robbie's smile slid to one side of his face and then faded. "I've had my phone off mostly. And sometimes I just . . . forget."

"So romantic." Anger surged inside Sierra. She closed her eyes, let it go back to a simmer.

Robbie looked distraught. "I know . . . that didn't sound good. But you know I'm not a phone person really, Sierra. I . . . I'm better face-to-face. Doesn't ever really feel like it's you when it's just words on a screen."

Sierra couldn't decide if it made it better or worse that this was undeniably true. Robbie sucked at technology. Sierra did too, a little, and at first they'd bonded over both still having crappy flip phones when everyone else had gone all fancy. But then she'd finally upgraded — sorta ("Welcome to the early 2000s," Bennie had groaned) — and gotten the hang of things, while Robbie had stayed stubbornly in the 1990s. "I've heard this before," she said, sounding colder than she meant to. "Doesn't change the unanswered texts staring back at me on my phone." She felt petty and then guilty and then angry all over again. Cojo, apparently understanding this wasn't going to be just a quick chat, lay down beside her and rolled onto his back, legs spread, gigantic tongue lolling out of his huge, slobbery mouth.

"I thought maybe we could take a walk or something," Robbie said.

"It's almost two a.m., Robbie."

"Okay," he said, his shoulders sagging. They stood less than five feet away from each other, but it felt like a whole ocean stretched between them.

"Who . . . who are you?" The question came out of her without warning. Bennie's fault, she thought.

"I'm Robbie," he said brightly. "I'm Robbie!" As if it was that simple.

"I mean, who are you to me, Robbie? What are we?"

"Oh." He crossed his arms over his chest and stared up at the night sky for a few seconds.

Sierra bit her upper lip, tried not to sigh.

"I don't know," he said. "I'm sorry. That's the most honest answer I can give. I'd say we are what we are, because that's true, but I know that's really vague and will only piss you off."

Don't tell me what will piss me off, Sierra wanted to yell, but he was right: It would've. She pushed the thought away.

"That's not good enough," Sierra said. "*This.*" She cast her arm at the dark night around them, the ridiculous time, the street they stood in the middle of. "This isn't good enough." It felt great, it felt awful.

Robbie nodded. "I'm sorry. I'll try to do better." He nodded at Cojo. "Nice dog." And then he turned and walked away.

Sierra's whole body shook. She didn't know if it was the tension of the conversation or just how tired she was or the terror of the night — all of that put together — but suddenly every nerve seemed to wake up inside her and be screaming at every other nerve, like those old ladies who would lean out the window and yell gossip to the old ladies in the next building over.

She exhaled, walked over to the stoop, and plopped down on the third step. Cojo leapt up, hurried over, and then flopped back down on the pavement in front of her, splayed obscenely out again for all the world to see. Sierra rubbed his belly. Tired as she was, something about her house felt uninviting somehow.

"I just need a minute to take it all in," she said to Cojo, or the night sky, or maybe no one at all.

Robbie had felt like such a splash of freedom once: someone Sierra's own age who understood this wild new magic she was a part of, someone who loved drawing as much as she did. Plus he was cute as hell with those long tattooed arms and that shy smile, the way his locks swung easily around his face when he walked or got animated with a new idea. They'd shared all the excitement and trauma of facing down Wick and his throng haints, and Sierra had thought it would form an easy bridge between them. Instead, Robbie seemed to fade away as the summer nights grew long and then short again. By the time the autumn winds whooshed through Bed-Stuy, he had become an occasional meetup, an awkward conversation, a few kisses, and many unanswered texts.

The front door opened, scaring Sierra half to death, and María walked out, her face sullen.

"Mami." Sierra stood up. "What is it?"

María motioned for her to sit back down. "I . . . It's your abuelo, Sierra." She sat next to Sierra. Stared past the parked cars out into the empty street.

"What? What happened?"

She shook her head. "Se murió."

"He's . . . he's dead? But . . . just like that? I don't understand! Don't we need to call an ambulance or something?"

María sighed. "He had a do not resuscitate order. He didn't want interventions or hospitals. He died just how he wanted to — at home, in his sleep."

The initial shock faded and Sierra was left with something even worse: emptiness. Shouldn't she feel something? Anything would feel better than this ugly void that seemed to open up around her heart. María put her head on Sierra's shoulder. "He was a messy, complicated man," she said. "But I loved him anyway."

"Should we go inside?" Sierra asked. She breathed a tiny sigh of relief when María shook her head.

"I just want to be out here with you right now," she said. "What's Cojones doing here?"

"Long story."

For a long time, they were quiet. Then, just when Sierra thought her mom had drifted off to sleep, María said, "I will miss him, but I know it was time. I feel it." Tall shadow spirits began gathering on the block, their long strides carrying them gracefully toward the brownstone.

"They're paying their respects," María said.

Sierra smiled, but inside felt only empty.

The sun began to rise.

FIVE

At the house that morning, the slow, mindless bureaucracy of death took hold as first cops, then firefighters, and finally paramedics came to fill out their paperwork and check off all the necessary boxes. Sierra sat blinking into her hot chocolate at the kitchen table, half dazed from barely sleeping and wondering where all her sadness was hiding. One of the cops kept asking if she was okay and saying he was sorry for her loss while María fussed with Lázaro's ID cards. The phone kept ringing. Her father Dominic came home from the graveyard shift at the hospital where he worked security, gave Sierra a big hug, and then fell into chummy small talk with the cops.

"Should I come home?" Sierra's oldest brother Gael asked over a staticky satellite line from Afghanistan. It had taken them like eighty tries to finally reach him, as always, and like Sierra, he sounded more worried about their mom than sad about Grandpa Lázaro passing.

"I don't think so," Sierra said. "We got it. Gonna do the

wake and whatnot in the next couple days, so you prolly wouldn't make it in time anyway."

"Yeah." His voice sounded a million miles away in more ways than one. "You alright?" he asked after a pause that could've been from technology or deep thought.

"Yeah," Sierra said, echoing him in word and tone. "Just tired and weird."

"Heh, tell me about it."

"Anyway, I'm not the one on a military base in the middle of Helmand Province. *You* alright?"

Gael chuckled. "I'm probably safer than you right now, kiddo."

"Ha, I doubt it," Sierra said, but she wasn't so sure.

Tee glared at Officer Fenwick. "You know we're never the ones who shoot up schools, right?"

Sierra, Izzy, and Bennie all groaned at the same time. "Can you give it a rest, babe?" Izzy said. "Just once? We're already late."

Officer Fenwick just rolled his eyes and waved the metal detector wand over Tee's body. "Turn around, young lady." He was old, his long jowls jiggled when he shook his head too fast, and he clearly just wanted to make it to retirement and be on his merry way.

"Y'all not even real cops," Tee muttered.

"Nor would I want to be," Officer Fenwick said with a chuckle. "This is quite enough excitement, thank you very much."

Tee softened. "Don't you get bored of scanning us every morning?"

"Only as bored as you must get giving us attitude every morning."

Sierra was in no mood for the daily tit for tat between Tee and school security. She'd slipped off to school before the madness of phone calls and notifications really turned full tilt, before the morgue guys came to collect the body. She didn't go upstairs to say a last good-bye — it would've felt like a lie — and she still hadn't shed a single tear.

And now she stood in the line to get metal detected and searched along with all her other classmates, just like they did every morning, except today every delay and clatter seemed specifically designed to irk her. She hadn't even had time to grab a coffee on the way to school, and *that* irked her most of all. And Bennie hadn't met up with them outside like she usually did so they could all brave the humiliation of the metal detector together, and *that* irked (and slightly worried) her.

And now Tee was getting into it with Fenwick, and *that* —

"Hey, there's Bennie!" Izzy called out. Sierra turned; Bennie was at the front door, waving. And there, just a few people behind Sierra in the line, was Mina Satorius. She looked more than a little freaked out. Her big eyes got even wider when she saw Sierra look at her.

"There a problem, Fenwick?" Officer Branson had shown up. Everybody groaned. Branson was just a few years older than most of the students, and he clearly enjoyed having power over everyone around him.

"No problem," Fenwick said. "I got this."

"The problem is this whole system," Tee spat.

We gotta talk, Sierra tried to mouth to Mina. Mina tilted her head, confused.

"You're cleared to go, Trejean," Fenwick grumbled. The line pushed forward.

"AP History," Mina whisper-yelled.

It was their third-period class, and Ms. Rollins let them sit wherever they wanted. They could pass notes if nothing else. Sierra nodded.

"We see y'all," Izzy said, emptying about eight dollars' worth of coins into the plastic dish and then setting off the metal detector anyway. "Cuz I spit hot steel when I rhyme," she explained. The wand Fenwick waved over her let out an urgent bleep.

Another collective groan went up from the line.

Second period was Mr. Bantam's AP Chemistry class. Bantam was a short, stocky, and overcaffeinated little guy with a blond ponytail and reddish beard, but even his singsongy antics and matter-of-fact storytelling couldn't defeat Sierra's utter lack of sleep. She nodded off, jolted awake when Bennie bounced a crumpled-up piece of paper off her forehead, nodded off again. In her dreams, she walked down a never-ending corridor that may have been her home and may have been school, and everyone she'd ever known was there, walking in and out, getting the place ready for Grandpa Lázaro's birthday party, but where was Lázaro? And suddenly the electric tone was blurting out and Sierra rubbed the sleep from her eyes and got her stuff together.

Mina was already there when Sierra stumbled into their third-floor classroom. Sierra slid into the seat next to her as Ms. Rollins wrote the names of the Founding Fathers on the chalkboard. "You okay?" Mina asked.

Sierra shook her head. "Fine. Listen, you need to tell me what's going on with the Sorrows and these cards."

"Did you pick up the one I left you?" Mina looked like she was about to burst into tears.

"Yeah, but . . . you can't just give out these cards and not explain. Something's . . . There's something after us. Or after the card. There was something else in the woods last —"

Ms. Rollins cleared her throat. "Okay, class, we'll be beginning now, if Miss Santiago here is done talking."

Sierra bristled. How was she supposed to know to be quiet when class hadn't even started yet? She shot Rollins a defiant glare but swallowed the snarl trying to work its way across her face.

Rollins smiled at Sierra and then addressed the whole class. "Turn to page 304 and let's discuss the Bill of Rights, shall we?" She was in her late twenties, with curly brown hair pulled back in a tight bun and an alarming tattoo of a naked Japanese woman being eaten by a sea monster on her right arm.

Izzy's hand shot up. "Wouldn't it be more accurate to call it the Bill of Rights for White Dudes, technically?"

Perfect. This would be the distraction she'd need to be able to find out what she could from Mina.

"That's funny, Isake," Ms. Rollins said. "And in a way you're right, but —"

"There's always a but," Tee said. "'Slavery was terrible, but!' 'Sucks we killed the Natives, but!' We heard it all before, lady."

"Girl," Jenny hissed, "shut up and let the teacher teach."

Sierra nudged Mina. "Tell me what's going on," she whispered.

Ms. Rollins's voice wavered as she tried to raise it above the din. "If you would let me finish, I could explain . . ."

"We always let y'all finish," Big Jerome said, "and y'all always come with some rationalization-type justification shit."

"Language, Mr. Watkins. And how did I become *y'all*?" Ms. Rollins demanded. Her smile had vanished entirely. "I am me and no one else. You can't judge what I haven't even said yet based on what your other teachers have done. That's not how this works."

"That's how it works for us," someone yelled from the back. "Why should it work different for you, miss?"

Mina leaned close to Sierra. "I don't know much, I swear. But . . . the Sorrows say the Deck of Worlds is back in play. Something you did set it back in motion."

"Something *I* did?" Sierra said too loudly.

"Sierra!" Ms. Rollins said. "You will pay attention or you will carry on this conversation you're so intent on having with the headmaster. Is that clear?"

Sierra nodded.

"Now, class. I appreciate your concerns about how slavery is handled in these texts, I do. And — not but, *and* — in order to have an intelligent discussion about it, you have to let me talk so we can —"

"What you mean intelligent?" someone demanded. "We intelligent."

"And you always talkin'," Little Jerome said. "How 'bout you let us talk on this?"

"From what body of knowledge are you talking?" Ms. Rollins's voice got sharp. "What exactly can *you* tell *me* about early American history and slavery? That's a serious question, not rhetorical."

"I don't know what you did," Mina whispered. "I just know the Deck is in play, and that means that some forces will be trying to make moves to get control of it."

Sierra pulled a scrap of paper out of her notebook and scribbled on it: *Who has control of it? How does one even get control of the Deck of Worlds?* She folded it and stretched her arms to either side, dropping the paper on Mina's desk.

"I am perfectly willing to have a reasonable discussion with you," Ms. Rollins announced as if it was a major concession. "Key word: *reasonable*. I will not have chaos in this classroom. And, to be totally honest with you, my job is to prepare you for the Regents and SATs, so you can go to college and have a full range of career choices available to you." Mina scribbled something on the scrap of paper. Folded it back up. "That's how the system we live in works, like it or not."

"System based on slavery," Tee grumbled.

"Having said that" — Rollins looked like the effort of ignoring Tee might cause her head to explode — "I am happy to move the slavery discussion up a few days so we can have it earlier. I think that's a fine idea. Sierra!"

Sierra had snatched the note off Mina's desk and froze midway through unfolding it.

"Why don't you share your take on this conversation with the whole class, since you feel so compelled to pass notes back and forth."

Sierra glared up at Ms. Rollins. "Since you asked: I think you're being defensive. No one wants to represent a whole bunch of other people, but the truth is, we have to do that all the time, and as much as you want to be treated as an individual, we still see all the other teachers who have shut us down and don't want to talk about things that matter to us. So when you try to tell us to be reasonable, we're looking at the fact that it's slavery we're talking about, possibly the *least* reasonable thing to happen in this country, and so all these people whose great-grandparents directly benefited from it telling us to be reasonable about something so unreasonable doesn't sit well, and we're tired of being told how to respond."

The room was very, very quiet when Sierra finished. She realized her hands were trembling slightly, so she put them under the desk.

Ms. Rollins took a deep breath, her eyes wide. "You can finish reading that note in the headmaster's office."

A general mutter of disagreement rose from the class-room, which Rollins silenced with a fearsome glare. Sierra rolled her eyes, stood, and shoved her notebook into her bag. "Shouldn't've asked if you didn't wanna know." She started toward the door.

"And for the record, my grandparents emigrated here from Russia and Poland in the forties and didn't receive a dime from slavery."

"That was s'posta be a mic drop?" Izzy whispered loudly. "Cuz . . ."

Sierra was halfway out the door when Mina stood up. "If Sierra's going to the headmaster's office, so am I," she declared. "I literally passed the note to her, if that's what you're sending her for. Because you can't just send her for saying something that made you uncomfortable."

"Fine," Rollins said. "Be my guest. Everyone else, turn to page 304 and we'll get started."

The door slammed behind Mina and their sneakers squeaked and echoed against the linoleum halls as they walked side by side toward Mr. Korval's office.

Nobody really knows how the power of the D.O.W. works.

Cards latch to someone and merge, connection is formed — > power

. . . lets talk after class, 2 much 2 write

Sierra stared at the folded scrap of paper. At the front of the classroom, Mr. O'Leary's phone let out a little jingly noise and he cursed, staring intently at the screen.

Korval had rolled his eyes when Sierra and Mina tried to explain why they were there. "Go to O'Leary's classroom," he grumbled. "He's got off this period. And think about what you've done."

"What did we —?" Sierra started, but Korval silenced her with a twitchy glare.

"I don't care, Ms. Santiago. Something, apparently. Whatever it was, think about it. Or get your homework done. Surely Ms. Rollins assigns homework amidst all that rigorous debate."

"Yes."

"So do it."

Mr. O'Leary had just smiled and waved them toward two seats in the back of the room without looking up from his phone.

"So this card you gave me," Sierra whispered. "There's someone this card is latched to?"

Mina nodded. "But we don't know who."

"And they're, like . . . the Hound of Light? Like, that's who they are?"

"Think of it like, the Hound of Light passed on its heritage from generation to generation, not through blood but through the card. It's a role, and this person, whoever they are, is connected to that role somehow. They fulfill it."

"I think I get it." Sierra's grandmother had explained a similar idea when she'd passed on the role of Lucera to Sierra, although that had been carried on through generations of her family. "And so the card Tee has — the Knight of Shadows?"

"Look." Mina leaned in close. She wore a long, loose sweater that draped to either side of her chair like a cape, and some kind of citrusy perfume seemed to form a fruity haze around her. "I wasn't supposed to give y'all the cards. The Sorrows think something bad is about to happen. They want to activate the Deck. They sent me to get it started by finding who the cards would latch to. They didn't want the shadowshapers involved, though."

"Who are you to the Sorrows anyway?" Sierra tried to keep the sneer from her voice and failed.

Mina shook her head, her eyes glued to the floor like it

might slip out from under her at any moment. "I know it's weird. They're like . . . My mom died when I was pretty young and my grandma's a certifiable maniac, and the Sorrows kind of looked out for me, they were like my spiritual protectors. I know they're kinda messed up —"

"Kinda," Sierra muttered.

"That's the thing, I don't know how . . . There's a lot I don't know."

"You girls good?" Mr. O'Leary asked, standing and brushing crumbs off his shirt. "I'm going for a soda."

Sierra and Mina glanced at each other. "We're cool, Mr. O'Leary, thanks," Mina said. He smiled and left the room, already back on his phone.

"And this Hound of Light," Sierra said. Her voice trailed off. Mina seemed genuine, but there were too many unknowns still, and if Sierra had learned anything in the past few months of dealing with the spirit world, it was that things were almost never what they seemed. She pocketed mentioning the visions she'd had in the woods. "It's connected to the Shadow Hound?"

"The Deck of Worlds has suits — Shadowhouse is one of them: you guys. The House of Light is another. The Sorrows are part of the House of Light. They run it, actually."

"And they're trying to get their house in order." Sierra shook her head. The Sorrows had granted Dr. Wick powers and turned him loose on Sierra's family, then they'd betrayed him when he was no longer useful. They were power brokers, and ruthless at that. "For whatever mess abouta come down the pipes. And they don't want you to give cards to the shadowshapers. Shadowhouse. I see how it is."

"I'm not sure if it's quite like that," Mina said. "But I see how it can look like that. The House of Light, the Sorrows, they're all about order. They feel like they are the best ones of all the houses to maintain order, since the Deck kinda started with them and they've been holding an uneasy peace for generations."

"Peace," Sierra snorted. "Didn't feel like that this summer."

Mina met her eyes. "I know." Her face curved into a severe frown. "There's a lot I don't know, but I'm doing my best to figure it out, and I know the Sorrows' peace really just means peace for them. When everything went down with you in June, I . . . I heard about it, and I guess I'd always known there was *something* messed up with the Sorrows, but I never knew what. The Sorrows have always been very guarded and secretive. They speak in vague riddles mostly and keep the details hushed. And they're usually all about power and light and love, and then suddenly one night they're losing their whole entire shit about a girl, *a girl of the shadows,* they keep whispering, and I didn't know it at the time, but it turned out it was you, and I *know* you, or kinda anyway, and so many of their plans hinged on what happened with you, what you did. They never said they were out to get you, but I could tell from how they spoke about you that something was off. It didn't seem fair or right, all that being on your shoulders. Then you

57

smashed their relic and they really lost it, obsessed, and all they could talk about was how Little Lucera would learn her place and just wait . . ." She sat back, eyes far away. "I guess the whole thing kinda collapsed around me, all I'd dreamed up and believed, all *they'd* led me to believe, about who they were. I've been trying to figure out the truth ever since. Haven't had much luck, but I know I gotta do something. I know I'm in a position to keep this from getting worse, somehow, and I want to . . . I want to do what I can. I still don't know what that is entirely, but I know if they distribute all these cards and link them to folks, things are gonna get much, much worse for you guys."

Sierra wasn't sure whether to scream at Mina or thank her. The girl had taken a huge risk for Sierra, if she could be believed, but she didn't seem to grasp the urgency of the situation. How could she *not* see that the Sorrows were probably preparing to wipe out Sierra and her crew? Then again, she may have saved all their lives. Sierra rubbed her hands over her face, then stood up.

"Where you going?"

"I gotta see 'bout some stuff. Sounds like things may be about to get really bad. For us."

"What about O'Leary?"

"He don't care. Tell him I have a family emergency," Sierra said as she walked out the door. She tried not to think about how many ways it was true.

SIX

Old furniture and stacked boxes packed the hallway on the fourth floor of the Santiagos' Bed-Stuy brownstone. They were already clearing out Lázaro's place, Sierra realized, as she stepped gingerly between an old sewing table and a rusted file cabinet. At the far end, her metal ladder waited.

Sierra had come to think of it as hers since she first started going up to the roof, a few weeks after everything went down over the summer and she'd suddenly found herself at the head of a whole strange fellowship of urban sorcerers. She'd been standing outside of Lázaro's door, trying to figure out what to say to him even though he probably wouldn't understand any of it anyway. She'd come up blank, just like every other time, and then she'd noticed the ladder, mostly hidden behind a coatrack. It stretched up from a little corner inlet, and she'd completely forgotten about it. A gorgeous panorama awaited her at the top — it felt like discovering that a beautiful painting had been hidden under an old curtain in a room you'd lived in your whole life. Bed-Stuy's rising and falling brownstones and towers spread out around her. Farther off,

Manhattan twinkled in the growing darkness. On the roof, no one could find her, no one could bother her, not even the creeping sense that she was supposed to say something to the ancient, incoherent man who'd denied her her own family legacy and almost gotten her killed.

And now, Sierra thought, stepping onto the squishy asphalt and taking in the marvelous array of rising and falling buildings around her, it was too late.

Spirits flitted through the red-and-orange sky like leaves blown on the October wind. They dipped and darted over the brownstones and housing projects, swooped around the towering glass palaces, and dove into the crooked alleyways. Sierra smiled. The world had become so much more alive once she'd learned to see the dead. For a few moments, she just stood there, let herself be a spectator to the ever-unfolding drama of city lights and spirits. She wondered if Lázaro's ghost was out there, or if he'd just faded into the ether of the universe and would never be seen again. She wasn't sure which she preferred.

The Deck of Worlds is back in play, Mina had said. *Something you did set it back in motion.* The night Sierra defeated Wick, she'd channeled hundreds of spirits through herself, melded her own desire for victory with theirs, and weaponized the combined energies into a force more powerful than anyone in the spirit world had known in generations, maybe ever. Of course there'd be repercussions. On top of that, she had no idea what effect desecrating the Sorrows' precious sculpture garden might have had. It seemed like when it came to spirits, any tiny thing could snowball into some gigantic mess: the butterfly effect on steroids.

She knelt down and pulled the Hound of Light card from her pocket, placed it on the roof. Then she zipped her hoodie against the autumn night breeze and closed her eyes. "What set this in motion?" she said out loud. "And how do I stop it?" If stopping it was even the right thing to do . . . Sierra wasn't quite sure. Something bad was coming, or at least the Sorrows thought so. Or wanted her to think they thought so. She shook her head, tried to clear it, then opened her eyes.

And almost jumped back in shock.

A shimmering, hooded figure sat across from her on the rooftop. Usually, spirits would show up a little more gradually when she summoned them with a question. They'd float at the edge of the rooftop, dance and deliberate, then one or two would venture forward, Sierra would draw some figure to 'shape them into, and they'd take it from there. But this one sat perfectly still a few feet in front of her. At her sharp intake of breath, the spirit looked up, then pulled the hood back from its head.

Sierra gasped again.

"Vincent?"

Bennie's brother let one edge of his mouth rise into a sad half smile. *Hey.* He had a wide nose and narrow eyes with long lashes. The same scant goatee circled his mouth, and he wore the same fitted Yankees cap he always used to have on.

Sierra wanted to jump forward and wrap her arms around him, but she resisted. Hugging spirits usually didn't work out so well, and she wasn't sure how he'd take it. "You . . . I . . ." Sierra said. "Where've you been?" She cringed. "I'm sorry — that was rude as hell."

But Vincent was laughing. *No, it's cool. It's a good question.*

"Bennie's been . . ." She let her voice trail off. There was no right thing to say.

I know. Vincent's smile vanished. He looked off over the Brooklyn rooftops. *I know.*

"What . . . what happened?"

I didn't . . . I still don't . . . remember anything. Try to look back on my life and I got nothin'. It's gone.

"Then how you here?"

They told me. He nodded toward the spirits swirling through the night sky. *Told me everything. How I died, the rallies afterward.* Sierra remembered the protests that broke out in front of the 79th precinct after Vincent was killed. She'd begged her parents to let her go but they refused; she was too young. Juan, of course, had managed to cajole their oldest brother, Gael, into taking him while they were out running an errand.

They told me about my family, Vincent said. *But they're not mine. They're not my memories. Just stories other people told me. I've been by to see them, but . . . I don't know them.* He looked away, then seemed to force himself to meet her eyes. *I don't remember you either, Sierra. It's all what they've told me.*

"Bennie needs you," Sierra said slowly. "Or . . . she misses you, I should say. I know you don't remember, but . . ."

I know. But I don't know how to see her yet. Talk to her, I mean. I . . . I can't.

A moment passed. "That's not why you came to see me, though," Sierra said.

Vincent shook his head. They both looked at the card. *The Deck of Worlds,* he said. *There's something happening in the spirit world. It's like a realignment. Like cats suddenly feel like they gotta pick sides, but no one even knows what side is what yet. Folks eyeing each other with suspicion suddenly who once were best friends.*

"The Sorrows are preparing for something."

I don't know a lot about the Deck. Seems no one really does. But I'll do what I can to find out.

"What should I do?" Sierra asked. "I don't even know what side *I'm* on."

Vincent chuckled, then scowled. *Word. None of us do. Look, Shadowhouse . . . that's us. That's what side we're on, if we're on any.*

"That's the shadowshapers?"

The Sorrows seem to think so, for what it's worth. And if they come for us, that's who they'll be coming for.

Sierra felt her insides clench. Her friends, her family. They were targets once again. She couldn't protect them all, not even with the vast powers that came with being Lucera — powers she didn't fully understand yet. "Imma gather the 'shapers. Get the new ones on point with combat 'shaping. Track down some of the old ones, whoever's still alive. We need to be ready for whatever comes."

Vincent squinted, closed his shining eyes. *I'll put together some'a my peeps too. We gotta get organized.* He stood up. *Tell Bennie . . .* But then he just shook his head.

"You tell her," Sierra said. "When you ready."

Yeah. He took a step back, toward the edge of the roof. *I was there that night, over the summer.* When she took on Wick, Sierra realized. She nodded at him. *You did something that night. I dunno 'bout settin' off no Deck of Worlds, but I know you did something for us, Sierra. And that shit matters most of all. We'd never wielded that kinda power before; we'd never moved as one before, man. We needed that. I dunno what'll happen next, but that night? That had to happen. Feel me? Whatever happens next is us moving forward.*

Sierra shoved her hands in her pockets. "Thank you," she said, but they didn't seem like the right words.

Vincent smiled and faded into the night.

"You remember this?" Sierra's brother Juan held up a frayed cardboard box, the words CONNECT 4 barely visible over a picture of the yellow-and-blue plastic contraption.

Sierra rolled her eyes. "Only chance for having any fun at their place on Myrtle once Abuelo decided it was time for his nap."

"Man . . ." Juan tossed it onto a growing pile of junk in Grandpa Lázaro's already cramped apartment and went back to picking through a trash bag full of random knickknacks.

Sierra stared at the photograph in her hands. In it, old Lázaro stood smiling beside Professor Wick, the man who would one day betray and nearly kill him. Off to the side, the shadowshapers were looking surly. Someone had written their names beside each one in elegant script. This was from back when they were the all-boys club Lázaro had insisted they be. Lucera, Sierra's grandmother, had sensed danger before she went into exile in the sea; she'd enchanted the photo so that each of their faces would be smudged out by an inky fingerprint if they were murdered. Wick's attack had taken its toll: black labyrinthine splotches covered more than half the shadowshapers' faces.

Five remained untouched: Delmond Alcatraz and Sunny Balboa, two genial old men in caps and button shirts who worked in a barbershop on Marcy; Caleb Jones, a huge, light-skinned dude with a red fro and tats all up and down his arms and neck; Theodore Crane, an older white man, hunched over with a pinched face; and Francis True, who wore a track suit and Stetson hat, and had big bushy eyebrows and the slightest hint of a smile.

She glanced at Manny the Domino King's face, or what she could make of it beneath the dark fingerprint, and sighed, fighting back the sadness. He had been the one to ask her to paint the mural on what turned out to be Wick's hiding place. And then Wick had killed him and sent his corpse to attack Sierra.

"What's wrong?" Juan asked. Sierra hadn't even realized she was clenching her fists.

She grimaced. "Thinking 'bout last summer is all. I'm alright."

Of the living shadowshapers, Sierra had only met Delmond and Sunny — they used to cut her hair when she was a kid. They'd come to Manny and a few of the others' funerals and offered genuine smiles and condolences, but it was clear neither wanted anything to do with shadowshaping.

"You ever meet any of these cats?" Sierra held up the photo. "The ones that're left, I mean."

Juan squinted at it. "Who's that huge dude with the Ronald McDonald fro? That Caleb?"

"Caleb Jones," Sierra said.

"That dude was no joke. He's like one of the premier tattoo artists in the world, I think. Has a little studio over in the Hasidic part of Crown Heights. He was cool. Kinda serious but cool. And there's Delmond and Sunny, of course, knew them. Who's that little old white guy?"

"Theodore Crane."

"Oh, that guy! Right. He was a historian — or is, I guess, if he's still alive. I mean like a spirit-stuff historian. Only met him once, but Abuelo always talked about him like some wise old scholar, said he had all the data 'bout what was what in the larger community, whatever that is."

The other houses, Sierra thought. *Old Crane will know about the Deck.*

"I think I remember that dude in the track suit," Juan went on. "He was, like, the bodyguard from what I remember. Badass."

"Any idea where any of 'em are now?"

He shrugged. "Nah. Everyone kinda faded when Laz and Lucera fell out."

Sierra still bristled inside when she thought about how Lázaro had brought her brother in on the secrets of shadowshaping and not her. It didn't help that Juan was never really invested in it, didn't seem to care much about it or use it. The spirits showed up when he played his thrasher salsa, did their thing, and that was pretty much that. She tried not to grumble about it too much, but the truth was, it had nearly cost her her life.

Maybe Old Crane would be more forthcoming with his knowledge, if she could find him. Surely Lázaro had his info somewhere around here. "Alright, man." She put the picture aside and dug back into the cardboard box she'd found it in. There were a bunch of Spanish books about Puerto Rican history; some envelopes full of bills and assorted boring paperwork dating back to the eighties; a couple letters, handwritten in Lázaro's elegant script, that all seemed to be about absolutely nothing in particular; and . . . a spiral-bound notebook. Sierra's pulse quickened as she opened it.

Towers of numbers teetered up and down the lined pages. Equations. This was where the old man worked out his income tax statements, Sierra realized. "You know, for a mysterious leader of an underground occult fraternal order," she growled, "Abuelo's paper trail is boring as hell."

Juan laughed without looking up from the stack of papers he was going through. "What did you think you were gonna find? A . . . oh, man."

"What?"

He just shook his head.

"Juan?"

He raised his eyebrows and held up a piece of white paper folded in half with little cartoons scribbled on it. "I made this for his birthday when I was like . . . eight."

"You alright?"

"Yeah," Juan said, but he looked like he was blinking away tears.

"Yo, Juan?" a deep voice called from the floor below them. "You there?"

"Up here, Pulpo!" Juan yelled. "Fourth floor."

Sierra felt her tummy give a little lurch. "Pulpo's here? Why?" She was wearing an old T-shirt and long cargo shorts and flip-flops. A bright red headwrap kept her gigantic fro at bay, but only barely.

"Um, cuz he's our bass player and we have rehearsal."

"Yeah, but you guys usually rehearse at — Oh, hi!"

Pulpo poked his head into the room, smile first. "Whaddup, Juan." He saw Sierra and brightened. "Oh, hey, Sierra!" He did brighten, right? It wasn't just Sierra's imagination? "Sorry to hear about your grandpa."

"Thanks, man," Sierra said. "We're managing."

"You coming in," Juan said, "or you just gonna stand there lookin' like a moose head on the wall?"

Pulpo already towered over most people around him, especially extra-short Juan, but in Lázaro's cramped apartment, he looked like a mythical giant. He wore a dark purple T-shirt that was still lighter than his dark skin; it was just tight enough to show his pecs but not enough to look like he'd had to squeeze himself into it. And he had arms. Arms with muscles that did a kind of bulging, flexy thing when he moved them. Bennie and Sierra had decided he was probably dumb as a box of cereal a long time ago. It was partly because he never seemed to have much to say, but mostly wishful thinking: If he was dumb, he could just stay in the hot-but-dumb category where he was safe, a lovely figure to admire and nothing else.

The sides of his face, Sierra noticed, still bore the off-colored remnants of the wicked acne Pulpo had had as a preteen. The locks must've covered them up before. She smiled, remembering the scrawny, long-limbed goofball with braces who used to follow her brother around everywhere and talk about video games with a solemn awe.

"Sierra?"

"Huh?"

"I said, it was good seeing you at the show last night."

He had *seen* her? She'd been in the midst of the crowd in the dark club all night. "Oh!" She giggled, cringing inside. "Of course. I always come support you guys."

Who was this ridiculous person she had become? This was not the Sierra that Sierra knew and loved. And anyway, she and Robbie were . . . something, sorta. Maybe not.

As if on cue, Sierra's smartphone let out a blip, and there was Robbie, texting her a random *hey* as if he hadn't been impossible to get a text back from for the past two months. Exes — or whatever Robbie was to her — really did have special psychic powers when you were in the presence of someone new and sexy, apparently. Sierra rolled her eyes, pocketed her phone.

"We trying out this new song?" Juan asked.

"Sure," Pulpo said. "But I don't wanna interrupt if y'all need to get this done."

He didn't have to be polite too — that was just over the top. Juan had once made Sierra swear never to date a musician. She'd been about to point out the obvious problem with his statement when he cut her off. "We're all charm and skill," he'd said, looking dead serious, "but just horrible people deep down inside, trust me."

And he was probably right, Sierra thought as she went back to digging through Lázaro's stuff. Juan would make self-effacing jokes, but this wasn't that. This was from some sad part of his twisted heart, and he had meant every word. And for all she knew he was referring specifically to Pulpo. She scowled.

"See you later, Sierra?" Pulpo said.

Footsteps came up the stairs as Juan stood and dusted himself off, then Tía Rosa's screechy cackle rang out. She appeared in the doorway next to María, gaped up at Pulpo, and then frowned at Sierra. "Oh."

"What are you guys doing up here?" Sierra asked. She'd finally stood up to her aunt's casual bigotry over the summer, and her Tía Rosa had been reserved around her ever since. Sierra was pretty sure her mom had given her some talking-tos as well.

"We were just going to take your grandfather's stuff to the church drop-off center," Rosa said. "These strapping young men can give us a hand."

"No," Sierra said. "You're not."

Rosa cocked an eyebrow but didn't reply.

"We're still sorting through all this. His body isn't cold yet. You're not giving away his stuff."

Rosa looked at her sister. "Do you have any idea how much you could get for this apartment right now? Can you really afford to wait around for who knows how long when —"

"Bye, Rosa." Sierra's voice left no room for argument. She waved, squinted once, and then went back to digging through boxes.

Rosa let out a gargled "oh" and then retreated. María stood at the door for a good thirty seconds before Sierra looked up. "I know your tía can be a lot, Sierra, but you don't have to be mean to her."

"Mean? Mami, she was about to give away all Abuelo's stuff. All his . . . you know."

"I don't want to argue," María said, already backing down the stairs. "I just need peace in the house right now. ¿Oíste?"

"I hear you, Mami," Sierra mumbled.

"Whoa," Pulpo said when she was gone.

"Welcome to Casa Santiago," Juan said.

Sierra tried to figure out if Pulpo's expression was admiring or just shocked. She thought she saw the slightest hint of a smile creep around the edges of his mouth. She shrugged, pulled an old photo album out. "She pisses me off daily."

"C'mon, man," Juan said. "Let's get this song figured out."

They left, chattering nerdy music stuff on their way down the stairs. Sierra exhaled.

SEVEN

"And, 'shape!" Sierra yelled.

On the darkened basketball courts in front of her, Tee, Izzy, Bennie, and Big Jerome dropped to a crouch and raised their left hands. Tall shadows converged around them. Tee was the first to slap the hulking chalk gorilla she'd drawn on the ground. It sprang to life across the courts, a brilliant flash of green. Izzy was next — her orange sea serpent started out slowly and then launched after Tee's gorilla while Bennie and Jerome still huddled, waiting.

"Man!" Jerome grumbled. "This sucks."

"I don't even see any —" Bennie started to say, then she chirped with glee as a shadow rolled up on her and vanished. She slapped her picture, a skeletal lizard, and sent it tottering off toward Tee's and Izzy's spirits. Jerome just started slapping the ground, sending little chalk clouds up around his rapidly fading shark.

Meanwhile, Sierra had to jump out of the way as Tee's and Izzy's creations tumbled toward her. Izzy's sea serpent had coiled all the way around the gorilla and was snapping at its face, while Bennie's lizard stumbled along behind them, taking feeble swipes at nothing in particular.

"You like that?" Izzy yelled, staring at the thrashing chalk monsters. "You want some mo'? I got mo' fo' ya."

Tee didn't respond, just glared at the ground, her hands open, palms down in front of her.

"I got some'a *this*," Izzy laughed as the serpent snapped its jaws. "And *this*!"

"Yo, Iz," Sierra said. "Try not to wake up *all* of Bed-Stuy. We don't need the cops on us again."

"For real," Jerome said. He'd given up and just sat himself down to watch the action.

"Some'a this too," Izzy went on. "And how 'bout a little —"

Suddenly, Tee's green gorilla snatched the serpent by its neck and smashed it twice across the face.

"Oh, shit," Izzy gasped. The serpent's coils went slack and the gorilla heaved it up into the air and then whipped it out, shattering Bennie's skeleton lizard into dust. Spirits scattered to either side and disappeared into the night.

"Aw, man!" Bennie yelled. "You didn't haveta go and do that!"

"My serpent," Izzy moaned.

The gorilla lifted the limp sea creature over its head and pulled, ripping it cleanly in half and tossing each side off into the darkness.

"Damn," Sierra said.

Tee chuckled.

"I'm breaking up with you," Izzy pouted.

Tee took a step toward her, arms out. "Aw, babe, c'mon, it's all games."

"Don't *babe* me, Trejean. Imma go get a soda. Anybody besides this traitorous pet killer want anything?"

"I'm good," Bennie said.

"I'll take an icey," Jerome said.

Sierra raised her hand. "Hold up, y'all, we almost done, just give me a sec." They gathered around, and for a moment Sierra felt the weight of their expectant faces peering at her out of the darkness of the schoolyard. It was a chilly night, the kind of cold that reaches its fingers right through your hoodie and scrapes frost against your bones. The spirits loped in a wide semicircle around them, and Sierra wondered if Vincent was nearby, watching his sister, trying to figure out how to talk to her. She hugged herself, exhaled a steamy breath.

"This whole thing with the cards," Sierra said. "From what I gather, it's serious business. I don't know what's coming, but everything points to something bad. Either the Sorrows themselves are making a move on us, or something even worse is, something we don't even know yet."

"That wolf thing?" Big Jerome asked.

"Maybe. I just know we gotta move real careful right

now. Like, everyone needs to be on point all the time. That's why I asked you all out here tonight. We gotta get our skills up."

"I'm tryin'!" Jerome said.

"I know, man, I know. We'll get you on point. But beyond that, I need folks to try and figure out what your strongest 'shaping form is. Like, I paint, so my spirits move strongest through the paintings. It might be sculpture or, I dunno . . . something else. Or maybe it's chalk, and that's cool. But try some stuff. Think on it. Figure it out. Sooner rather than later, aight?"

"I can't even get chalk right," Jerome said. "How am I s'posta figure out my special skill?"

"Maybe that's the problem," Tee suggested. "You have to click with another medium."

"I guess." He didn't sound convinced. "By the way, since we're all here, we gotta start figuring out Halloween stuff. Cuz that whole zombie abolitionist rappers thing really didn't work last year." He glared at Izzy.

"My Zombie Frederick Doug E. Fresh costume was poppin'." Izzy shrugged. "And no one told you to go in whiteface!"

"Who's that?" Bennie said. They all spun around. Someone was walking toward them across the dark yard.

Sierra tensed, reaching for her chalk, then let out a sigh. "That's the second time you've looked sketchy this week, Robbie."

He shrugged, waved at everyone. "Comes with the territory, I guess?"

"About those iceys," Tee said.

Izzy put her arm over Tee's shoulder. "Yeah, we hittin' the bodega."

"Later, Robbie," Bennie said, walking backward. "C'mon, Jerome."

Sierra shook her head. "My subtle-ass friends."

Robbie laughed but his eyes stayed sad. "I texted you."

"Yeah. Finally. Then you showed up late anyway." She hated the quiet nag in her voice, the way this whole conversation made her feel needy, when really she just felt far away.

He brushed a lock behind his ear. "I'm sorry 'bout Lázaro. He was . . ."

"Don't say he was a great man," Sierra said. "I don't wanna hear it. The wake is tomorrow and it's gonna be full of people lying and carrying on."

"I wasn't gonna say that. But in ways he was, even if in ways he wasn't."

"That what you came to say, Robbie?" Sierra's voice sounded even more vexed than she felt. She wanted to pull the words back inside herself, run away from this entire conversation and hide out on her roof for the rest of the week. Or year, maybe.

"I just . . . No, Sierra, it's not." He scrunched up his face, looked off at something in the distance. For a second, Sierra thought he was going to tell her to run and hide like he'd had to do so many times back when they first met. But no, this was a whole other kind of creepiness seeping between them now. They just had no idea how to talk to each other.

Robbie looked at her suddenly, sharply. Stepped closer. "I came to say I want you, Sierra."

She caught her breath, met his eyes.

"I know I suck at showing it. I know I'm bad at . . . at *this*. And I know I seem unreliable and wack when things get tight, and I've messed up. And a lot of that was because I didn't know what I wanted, which I realized was really because I had what I wanted all along and that had never happened before. I didn't know what that looked like, even. So I didn't see it, but I felt like I should see it, it was right in front of me, and part of me knew it and was like screaming at the other part of me to realize it. But that other part of me was terrified, because what's scarier than getting what you want, right?"

"Getting it and then losing it," Sierra said quietly. She felt her eyes welling up with tears, sniffled to make them go away.

"Well, yeah, that," Robbie said. "And that's what I was afraid of. Like . . . you get me. Who else gets me? No one ever has. Not like you do. Not all of me."

Without warning, they were hugging. Sierra wasn't sure who initiated it, it just seemed to happen. She took in his familiar smell, the gentle scratch of his locks against her cheeks. A month ago, hell, last week even, she would've done anything to hear him say those words to her. Now . . . they felt like pebbles thrown into an empty well.

"Can we . . . can we try this for real?" Robbie said.

Sierra swallowed a sob. It would be so easy to say yes, pretend everything was fine. Gravity seemed to tug her that way; she could just melt into his embrace and stop clenching and overthinking.

She stepped back. "I don't know," she said, but it felt like she was saying good-bye. "I just don't know."

Cojo caught up with her on Bedford Avenue. The gigantic hound just fell into step beside her like it was the most natural thing in the world. She could almost hear him humming in a slobbery baritone as he trotted along. The thought brought a smile to her face, what felt like her first in a while.

"I don't know, Cojo," Sierra said. "These boys don't make no sense to me." She walked a few more steps. "But if I'm being honest, I don't make much sense either. Let's be real." She was talking to a dog. Whatever. "I been wanting Robbie to come around and be my man for months. And now he does and I'm like, *I don't know, man.* I mean . . ." She stopped on the deserted corner. Cojo stopped too, cocked his head sideways at her. "I *don't* know. So what else was I supposed to say, right?"

Cojo seemed to almost shrug as he turned and kept walking toward her house. "Wait up!" Sierra called.

A fresh October breeze swooshed through the Brooklyn streets, blew Sierra's fro back, and sent her hoodie whipping behind her as she walked. The trees whispered a scream as it passed, and Sierra couldn't help but think of the howl she'd heard the other night in the park. Cojo stopped short, those massive lips curled up in a snarl, and his low growl seemed to fill the whole world around her. Sierra wasn't sure, but it looked like he was glowing slightly, radiating a greenish light.

"What is it, boy?"

She scanned the area. A hair salon, a dive bar, and a furniture shop sat side by side, all darkened and shut down for the night. Across the street, there was a mosque and a liquor store, also dark, and a dimly lit bodega.

Sierra closed her eyes, but no spirits seemed to be nearby. Then the image hit her like a splash of cold water. It was a dark street, not far from where she stood. The creature — the Hound of Light, if that's what it was — moved along through the shadows of brownstones and trees. Sierra sucked in her breath. It was close; she could feel it. She opened her eyes, glanced around the street where she stood, but nothing moved except Cojo's trembling muscles.

She closed her eyes again, trying to make out the street. The Hound of Light was running now, past parked cars and a dumpster, and then suddenly everything went dark.

"Ah!" Sierra gasped, falling suddenly out of the trance and almost collapsing. Cojo broke into a run, bolting up Bedford Avenue and around a corner. "Cojo, no! With me!" she yelled, taking off after him. She turned onto the quiet residential block and saw the massive black hound standing beneath a lamp in the middle of the street, glaring at something farther down the block.

Nothing moved. Dim pools of light illuminated wooden doorways and gates, front stoops, and gardens. "C'mon, Cojo," Sierra said. "Let's get out of here." He snarled one final time and then hurried after her.

Sierra made it home, exhausted and shaky, and patted Cojo as he settled onto his spot on the front steps. She made her dreary way upstairs and collapsed on her bed. Tomorrow at school she'd pry more info about the Deck from Mina. She'd figure this out, whatever it was. Tomorrow.

Still in her clothes, she fell into a fitful sleep.

EIGHT

"I know what Imma call my memoir," Tee announced in the metal detector line the next day.

"*I, Tee*?" Bennie tried. "Get it? Like IT but not."

"I get it," Big Jerome said. "But Tee don't have nothing to do with information technology, so like . . . no. She should call it *The AudaciTee of Dope*."

"Cuz she's dope," Izzy said. "I like it."

Sierra, once again exhausted and coffeeless, ventured a guess: "*Tee-Rex: A Life*."

Tee scoffed. "Y'all tried, though. Callin' it *A Tee Grows in Brooklyn*."

"Take off your jewelry, young lady," Officer Fenwick said. "You can write your memoir later."

"Whatever." Tee pulled her metal bracelets off and clanked them into the plastic bucket.

"A kid ain't got no business writing no memoir anyway," Fenwick said. "Y'all ain't lived yet, not really."

A groan of annoyance rose from the line as he waved the wand over Tee. "Next."

Sierra rolled her eyes. "Y'all comin' to the wake tonight?'

"Of course," Jerome said, holding up a suit bag he had slung over his shoulder. "Brought my best suit so I wouldn't have to go home and change!"

"We'll be there," Tee said from the other side of the metal detector.

"Take off your bracelets, young lady," Fenwick said to Sierra. "And your belt."

Sierra repressed a snarl.

"You didn't notice we talking about something important?" Izzy snapped.

"Safety first," Branson declared from the security desk. "You're not even supposed to be chitchatting in line, but we let you, so don't get cute."

"Ain't nobody chitchatting," Izzy said. "We talkin' 'bout a wake."

Sierra threw her bracelets and belt into the plastic bucket. "Anything else? You want my bra in there too?"

Branson raised his eyebrows. "I mean . . ."

"Ew!" Izzy, Tee, and Bennie yelled at the same time.

"She was being sarcastic, you pervert," Tee shouted. A couple other kids in the line started yelling too.

"Keep it moving, everyone!" Fenwick growled. "Calm down! Ms. Santiago, please step through the machine and keep it moving."

Sierra shot Branson a death-glare, stepping through the machine. He shrugged and went back to his paperwork. She put her jewelry back on, willing the lava pit not to overflow inside her.

"C'mon, Sierra," Tee said. "Let's get to class. We'll all be at the wake tonight, don't worry."

"Alright, everyone," Ms. Rollins said as the bell toned and kids got settled at their desks.

Sierra woke with a start and rubbed her face. She'd gotten to class early so she could get a word in with Mina and then knocked out waiting for her.

"I realize I was testy with you guys yesterday," Ms. Rollins went on, "and that wasn't exactly fair."

"No shit," Izzy muttered.

"And I don't usually do this — I never do this, actually — but: I'm sorry. I apologize. This one's on me. I shouldn't have lashed out and I shouldn't have sent Sierra to the headmaster's office. What she said was true, I got defensive." She wrapped her hands around themselves, then sighed and pushed them behind her back. "But I want to make it up to you, if you'll let me. We're going to take all the time we need to discuss slavery and civil rights and everything else we need to. We're going to make sense of this, *together*. And that means that I have to listen to you. And that's my promise, right now: I will listen to you. Not just about history or slavery — whatever you want to talk about, I want to be there for you. Okay?"

Sierra tried not to roll her eyes. Ms. Rollins seemed genuine enough, and it was rare a teacher deigned to admit they were wrong, let alone apologize. Still, Sierra was worn out and couldn't find it in herself to get excited about this change of direction.

"Of course, we have to teach the test still. You guys have to pass, and do well. Doesn't do anyone any good if I lose my job at the end of this year, does it?"

No one seemed too sure, so she kept going. "But amidst that, we can still get into the discussions we need to have. Sound good?"

Murmurs of approval.

"Okay, good! Let's begin. I think Mina made a salient point yesterday when . . . Where is Mina?"

Sierra hadn't even realized the seat next to her was empty. She gazed at it, then locked eyes with Bennie. Bennie shook her head and shrugged.

"Has anyone seen Mina Satorius in school today?"

The class was silent.

Mina didn't appear for the rest of the school day. Sierra sat in the mostly empty lunchroom — her seventh-period study hall teacher, Mr. Salvator, let them study anywhere they wanted once they'd checked in — and tried to keep her mind focused on the physics equations scrawled across her notebook. Miss Rita, the older lady who ran the cafeteria, had snuck her a Styrofoam cup of black coffee, and Sierra sipped it gratefully as she swung back and forth between hoping the final bell would just ring already and dreading what would come next. The wake would be full of relatives in stuffy suits saying random, incoherent things about a man they barely knew — a man *she* barely knew, really. A million sweaty handshakes and muttered condolences, wretched small talk, wack little snacks.

And where was Mina?

Sierra peered around the vast lunchroom on the off chance the girl just happened to read her mind and magically show up, but the place was deserted. The only sounds were the drone of the dishwasher and Miss Rita humming to herself as she tidied up the kitchen. The image of Mina's empty chair in AP History unsettled Sierra. Had something happened to her? Or did she vanish on purpose, because things were about to get really bad? Had she lied to Sierra?

She took out the Hound of Light and the Shadow Hound cards and put them on the table beside each other. Something seemed to click in her mind, but it was nothing Sierra could put words to. They looked right, paired off that way. A kind of balance formed between them. Still, both were frightening; a kind of haze of terror seemed to surround them — Sierra felt it in her gut whenever she took them out. (If the Shadow Hound didn't make her think immediately of Cojo, she'd probably be even more freaked out by it.)

Sierra squinted at the face of the childlike figure in Shadow Hound's jaws. She frowned. It looked more like an adult's face — those blue eyes eerily calm considering what was happening and somehow familiar. She shuddered, staring harder at it. Where had she seen that face before?

"Sierra!"

Sierra looked up, her heart thundering in her ears, then exhaled. Jerome stood in the lunchroom doorway wearing his shiny gray suit, posing. "How I look?"

She grinned at him, packing up the cards. "Like a dapper devil, J. You tryna pick up some wake booty?"

Jerome's smile disappeared. "I would never!"

"Uh-huh. Let's get out of here, seventh period pretty much over anyway."

Cojo sat in his usual spot outside the great pillared entrance-way of Octavia Butler High, panting. When Sierra and Jerome walked out, he leapt up, turned a circle around himself, and let out a monstrous bark of excitement.

"If that dog wasn't on our side," Jerome said, keeping a few feet away as Sierra held Cojo back from jumping on him, "I would pretty much just give up the ghost. It'd be a wrap. Cojo equals game over for whoever up against him, that's it. Godzilla vs. Cojo? My money on Cojo."

"Word," Izzy said, sauntering up with Tee. "Majin Buu would get that ass beat in a one-on-one." She had on a pin-striped blue suit and a Stetson hat and carried a cane with a skull on top.

"Either way, we already look like the damn Scooby Crew enough without a huge dog hanging around." Tee wore a silky violet dress and had put her hair up into a pompadour.

"Whoa," Jerome said. "How you gonna outdapper me though?"

Sierra couldn't hold back her grin. "Y'all look *slick*! When did you even have time to get all dressed up?"

"Home Ec is for losers," Tee said. "You know Miss Gray don't really give a damn and can't see past the rim of her glasses anyway. Just raised my hand and said I needed to use the bathroom soon as class started."

"And?"

"Got a pass, went to the bathroom. And stayed there till I looked like this. Technically, I did need to use the bath-room, so . . ."

"And I just walked out," Izzy said. "Like *kablam*." They took a mini-promenade down an imaginary runway together, arm in arm.

"You don't think we look *too* slick for a wake, do you, Sierra? We don't wanna be disrespectful or nothin'."

Sierra shook her head. "Please. We're gonna need whatever slayage we can get up in there. Now I gotta figure out what the hell Imma wear."

"You find Mina?" Tee asked.

"She wasn't in any of her classes today," Jerome said. "I checked." He paused. "Uh . . . in a non-creepy way, of course."

"Can't believe she missed Rollins's stunning reconciliation speech," Izzy chuckled.

Tee shrugged. "I thought that was pretty genuine, actually. She owned her shit and said she was willing to listen. That's all we can ask, really."

"I guess," Izzy muttered.

"Hey," Sierra said. "Y'all gonna help me get dressed for this wake or what?"

NINE

"Lo siento tanto," a tall, middle-aged woman in a ridiculous hat whispered, shaking Sierra's hand. She shook her head, brow furrowed, and the little bells on her hat jingled. "Lo siento."

"Gracias," Sierra said. She'd borrowed one of her mom's black dresses — a simple, elegant number that kept everything contained and, she hoped, wouldn't beckon too many wandering eyes. The woman moved on to Juan, who was nursing a pink, pungent fruit drink that Sierra was 99 percent sure he'd spiked.

"Lo siento tanto," the woman said.

"Thanks," Juan said. "Nice hat."

"Juan!" Sierra whispered, once the woman had moved on down the line.

"What? It was!"

"Sierra girl!"

Sierra turned, almost yelled: "Uncle Neville!" She reached up to wrap her arms around his neck. "You're

90

back!" Her godfather had been gone for more than a month. As long as she'd been alive, Neville had vanished periodically with no explanation given and everyone just learned not to ask questions.

"How you holdin' up?" Neville said quietly enough for Sierra to know it was a real question, not more bullshit small talk.

She nodded her head in his shoulder, realizing with a start that for the first time since Lázaro had died, she actually had tears welling up. "I'm okay," she whispered, feeling anything but. She wiped the tears quickly on Neville's blue suit and smiled up at him. "Thanks for coming back."

"Shoot, you know me and Láz go way back. I couldn't miss this. Whoa, who's this?" Neville's mouth was already a little on the extra-large end of things, and now it got even wider as he broke out into the biggest smile Sierra had ever seen on him. "Fancy meeting you here!"

"Hey, y'all!" Nydia Ochoa said. Nydia ran the anthropology archive at Columbia University and had helped Sierra research and then fight Wick over the summer.

"Nydia!" Sierra went from Neville's arms to Nydia's. The librarian smelled like fancy perfume and . . . Uncle Neville. Sierra held Nydia at arm's length and inspected her carefully. "Nice . . . tan."

"Thanks!" Nydia's smile was also gigantic; her big teeth shone against her shining brown skin.

"It's October."

"Hey, Juan." Nydia leaned in, kissed Juan on the cheek. "Sorry for your loss, man."

"Thanks," Juan mumbled, suddenly awkward.

"Yeah," Nydia said, "took a couple extra vacation days on top of our Columbus Day holiday. Figured, Columbus killed my ancestors, I deserve more than one day off to recover from living in a country that still thinks he's worth a national holiday, am I right?"

"You right," Sierra said, glancing back and forth between her and Uncle Neville.

"What?" Nydia said, giggling slightly.

"Nothin', girl, you do you." Sierra dapped her and then turned back to the line of guests. She found herself looking into an ancient pair of eyes.

"You don't know me," the little old white man in the green plaid suit said. He reached out a shriveled, trembling hand, supporting himself on a walker with the other. "But I was a good friend of your grandfather's. I'm . . . I'm so sorry he's gone."

Sierra took his warm hand in hers, squeezed it. Then his face clicked into place in her mind. "Oh! You're Theodore," she said. "Theodore Crane? The metalworker?" One of the few surviving shadowshapers from the original crew and perhaps the only one who would know about the Deck.

He brightened. "Lázaro mentioned me? I'm honored."

"Well, not exactly," Sierra admitted. "It's that —"

"Oh!" Crane's eyes went wide. "You're the new . . . Oh, my. I didn't know."

Sierra nodded, very slightly. "I've been wanting to talk to you, actually."

"Certainly, my dear, whenever you like."

"Do you . . . We can't talk now, but do you know about the Deck of Worlds?"

The old man's face seemed to crinkle in on itself, suddenly grave. "It's in play, then? Of course it must be, for you to ask me about it. The Sorrows must be anxious." He looked up at her, his eyes sharp. "I stay at the St. Agnes Home out in East New York. I'm not worth much these days, I'm afraid. Just an old man made of many memories. But come find me. Come soon, Sierra. Don't delay. We must speak." He hadn't let go of her hand, and now he squeezed it a little too tightly.

"I will," Sierra promised. "I will."

"And this must be Juan!" Old Crane crowed, finally letting go. "It's been years, my boy!"

"Sure has," Juan said, shaking his hand and leaning down to accept a sclerotic little hug. After the old man teetered along, Juan threw back the rest of his drink and burped. "I can't take much more of this, sis."

"I feel you," Sierra said. "I been cringing since I woke up this morning." At least she'd found one of the old shadowshapers, though. Tomorrow, she'd go to St. Agnes, maybe bring Bennie along. Old Crane would help them. And if he had shown up to the wake, maybe some of the other original 'shapers would too. She craned her neck above the crowd of mourners. There! A bright red fro bounced along above all the other heads. The man turned, and sure enough, Sierra recognized Caleb Jones, the famed Crown Heights tattoo artist. She took a step into the crowd and then stopped, her way blocked by two highly manicured women in their early thirties, one of them extremely pregnant.

"Terrible loss," one of them cooed.

They were cousins on her dad's side, Sierra was pretty sure.

"Yeah," Sierra said, trying not to scowl.

"Very sad," the other said. "And after all he's been through."

Sierra cocked her head. "Been through?"

"Just" — the woman frowned severely — "the mental illness and all. Very sad. You know."

"Actually, I don't know," Sierra said. "You mean his stroke?" It wasn't a stroke, technically; it was the trauma of a spirit attack by Wick, but that was beside the point.

"No," the first said. "The . . ."

"Never mind," the other snapped. "It doesn't matter now."

"Say what you gotta say," Sierra said, keeping her tone even.

"It's fine. Never mind."

"Atención, por favor, amigos y familia," María called

from the doorway. Her voice didn't waver; she even managed a slight smile. Her grief would be an intimate, long-standing engagement, Sierra realized, not a spectacle. "Thank you all so much for coming. We will now proceed into the chapel."

Tía Rosa poked her head in. "You heard, everybody? Come this way, please! Okay?" She clapped twice. "Okay."

The two cousins smiled almost identical smiles at Sierra and made themselves scarce.

"Let's do this," Sierra said, but Juan was across the room, refilling his drink.

Father Carasquillo droned on and on as the line inched Sierra closer and closer to Lázaro's open casket. The mourners murmured around her; Sierra could feel the unceasing whisper-tide of bochinche sweep across the chapel: *What were those crazy shadows the old man always spoke of? When did he lose it? Was it when Mama Carmen passed? No, surely before that. She'd been loca too, you didn't know? ¿De veras? Claro que sí.*

Sierra bristled, then forced it all out of her mind. She would pay her respects. She would grin and bear it, then she'd be gone. Somehow all her friends had gotten ahead of her in the line and were already sitting in the wooden pews, looking uncomfortable. All Sierra wanted was to hang out with them and at least be able to pretend that everything was normal.

Then the family in front of her — a middle-aged couple and their grade-school kids, all in black — moved away from the coffin, and there was Lázaro, his brown skin pale and waxy, his cheeks sallow. Sierra approached, feeling a hush fall on the room. All eyes must've turned to her. *Y esa, la nieta, tan loca como el viejo. She always was . . . strange, no? And that big, nappy hair, tsk. Dressing for a wake must've been easy, though, all that black she wears.* Sierra shoved it all away. Focused on her grandfather's emaciated face, almost unrecognizable after the embalmers had made a CGI monster out of him.

She knelt on the step stool. They'd dressed Grandpa Lázaro in a pin-striped gray suit and Stetson hat. He looked well pressed and dapper. Sierra waited for the flood of emotions she should be feeling to well up in her. She'd loved Grandpa Lázaro her whole life, even if he'd gotten distant and quiet as she got older. Just because he'd hidden the most important aspect of his world from her, and his secrecy had almost gotten her killed, didn't make all those earlier years irrelevant. She looked at his shriveled old corpse and felt nothing. *Or did it?*

Maybe it wasn't what he'd done or what he was, sexist old fart or not, but *her*. Maybe it was Sierra's heart that was slowly becoming overgrown with weeds. She saw Robbie's face in the darkness of the schoolyard, his eyes pleading, finally open to her after so long being remote. All she'd felt was empty. Had she built a wall inside herself?

The people behind Sierra coughed politely and she looked up. She'd lingered too long. Devastated, they all probably thought. Unable to cope with the loss. She sighed, stood, and took her seat between Juan and her dad in the front row. Dominic put his arm around Sierra's shoulders and she leaned into him, closing her eyes, and willed the whole weird world away for a few perfect moments.

———————

"And so," Tía Rosa chirped, what felt like three hours but was probably only forty-five minutes later, "we must remember always the charitable, honest, kind soul that was Lázaro Corona. A father, a son, a brother, a friend." She smiled like an ill iguana at the mostly dozing audience, nodded at Father Carasquillo. "And let me tell you something else we all loved about Lázaro."

Sierra must've knocked out for a bit there. She wiped her eyes and looked up from her dad's shoulder just in time to see Juan stumble up the steps and pause on the maroon carpet beside the podium. Rosa's speech came careening to a halt. Juan squinted out at the chapel, broke into a perfect moonwalk, spun once, and then mamboed up to the microphone as gasps and mutters broke out across the room. Rosa stepped out of the way, her face bright red. Sierra sat up and rubbed her temples.

"Look," Juan drawled, his voice blurting sloppily from the cheap PA system. "Imma let you finish, actually! Psych! I'm not! You talked long enough, for like an entire lifetime, Tía."

"I —" Rosa stuttered. "Pero . . ."

"Nah." Juan shook his head a few too many times, then stared at the back of the room like he was trying to will it to slow down. "Vete. My turn."

Rosa frowned and stepped off the dais, grumbling to herself.

"None of y'all really *knew* Láz," Juan said. "Not me, not my sister Sierra or Gael. But most *definitely* not that lady that just spoke, okay? Tía Rosa trashtalked my abuelo for as long as I can remember, so don't let her come up here and suddenly flash that tyrannosaurus-with-lipstick-ass grin talkin' 'bout" — Juan's voice suddenly leapt four octaves and he affected Rosa's Puerto Rican accent — "*He was charitable! Honest! Kind!* Stop." He shook his head. "Just stop. He didn't let us in, not really. Even the ones he did, like me, he didn't. And my sister, his own granddaughter —" Juan looked directly at Sierra, his eyes rum-punch bleary, his frown sharp. "He just locked her out like she was a stranger. And why?" Sierra felt like her ears were on fire. "Why? Because she's a girl. This is kindness? This is charity? C'mon, now, peopleses. It's like not 1912 anymore, and that shit wasn't cool then either, to be honest. Let's be adults about this. Old Laz was a good dude to some; he was trash to others. And some'a the ones he was best to, like my florally named auntington here, were the *worst* to him when he turned his back. Am I right? Some'a y'all *still* trashtalking the man. *At* his own wake." He furrowed his brow, shaking his head. "What would Jesus do? Not this, my people. Not this."

Commotion erupted in the chapel as the mourners finally had enough.

"Get down from there," someone yelled.

"Who you think you are?"

"¡Desgraciado!"

Sierra felt herself moving up the dais steps before she'd even decided to stand up. She didn't really know what she was going to do; all she knew was that she'd never loved her brother more than at that moment, and she wanted to shield him from whatever mess was about to ensue. Someone moved alongside her as she fastwalked toward the podium — someone tall.

"Pulpo?"

"Actually, my name's Anthony," he said, moving around to the other side of Juan and flashing a winning smile down at Sierra. He was wearing a dashing three-piece suit. Of course he was — it was a wake, but still . . . Sierra'd only seen him in his old T-shirt rock band uniform. She tried not to gawk. "It's a long story."

"Word?" Sierra wrapped an arm around Juan's shoulders and together, she and Pulpo — no, Anthony — walked him away from the mic. "Imma haveta hear it some time. Under less, er, pressing circumstances."

"What'd I say?" Juan drawled, finally succumbing to the rum punch. "What'd I even .... say?" His head slumped forward.

"Back exit," Anthony muttered. "Got the Culebramobile parked out in the alley."

"Brilliant," Sierra said. She arched her neck around and made eye contact with her dad to let him know she had the situation handled. He nodded once, then went back to calming down Tía Rosa. Sierra headed for the back door with Juan and Anthony. She wasn't totally sure why she was smiling so hard, but there was no way to stop it.

TEN

"You sure you good?" Sierra asked, peering in the driver's side window of Anthony's van and trying to ignore the striking smell of his cologne. And the shape of his stubble beneath his cheekbones. And his big, delicious lips.

"Yeah, Imma drop him off at your house. I'll take care of him, don't worry."

"Blurba," Juan muttered from the passenger seat. His eyes were closed and his head leaned against the window.

Anthony shook his head. "Won't be the first time."

"Damn. I'm sorry, man."

He smiled, and his whole face seemed to light up with those dimples and shiny teeth. Sierra almost flinched. "I'm good, I said! He's done way more for me than I could ever repay him for. This is nothing. And stop worrying. You got bigger problems to worry about."

Sierra's face fell — did he know about everything going on with the Sorrows? How . . . Then she realized he meant her ridiculous family and dead grandfather and almost guffawed her relief. "Alright, man, get out of here. And thanks."

101

She hopped down from the window and banged the side of the van twice with her palm as she walked back toward the loading dock. "Not gonna watch him drive off," she said, then turned and did it anyway. She thought she caught him glimpsing her in the rearview, and then he revved around a corner and was gone.

Sierra turned back to the funeral home and caught her breath: Someone huge was standing in the loading dock. Backlit by the neon door lamp in the dim twilight, the man looked like a shadow spirit for a moment. Then a flicking noise sounded, and a tiny flame illuminated his light brown face and furrowed brow. Caleb. He lit a spliff hanging out of his lips, pulled deeply, and then released a cloud of dank, pungent smoke into the darkening sky.

"Sierra María Santiago," Caleb said, leveling his eyes with Sierra's as she approached.

"The one and only. Caleb Jones." She stood beside him, facing the cement driveway that led out to Lafayette Avenue and feeling oddly comfortable.

"I hate funerals." He passed her the spliff and she took a little hit. It caught in the back of her throat and sent into her a coughing fit. She shook her head, handing it back.

"Been a minute?" Caleb said with a curt chuckle. He held out the plastic cup he'd been holding.

Sierra took it, drank heartily, spat it out. "BLAH! You and Juan with the spiked punch! Can a girl get a break?"

Caleb laughed with abandon now, a low-rolling, joyous rumble.

"And yeah, been like eight months," Sierra said, "and I really only smoked once or twice back then, so yeah."

He finished laughing and nodded. "Hm."

"And I hate funerals too. And wakes."

"Old Crane said the Deck of Worlds is in play."

"Yeah, you know about it?"

Caleb shook his head, running a hand over his red fro. "Not as much as Crane. But I know you better get those cards, all of 'em, and get 'em quick."

"Why?"

"Historically" — Caleb took another drag, let it out — "whenever the Deck has come into play, and it doesn't happen often, people die."

"But who . . . or where do the cards come from?"

Caleb shrugged, glaring out across the driveway. "Some powerful sorcerer created them a few generations back. They're somehow wrapped up with the Sorrows and their power, but it's all kind of hazy and lost to history. Like I said, Crane the expert, but what we do know is that the Sorrows are always trying to 'get complete' — whatever that means. Whenever they roll up on the scene, they're whining about the Deck and getting complete." He scowled, offered Sierra the spliff.

She shook her head. "I'm good."

"Anyway, I don't think anyone's ever put all the cards

together in one place, because cats always stealing one, running off, passing it along through generations of different families. But the Sorrows stay trying to put the ones they got into play, deploy them, so to speak. Dunno how that all works, though."

A school bus stopped at a light, filling the section of street they could see beyond the gate with dirty yellow. The growl of its diesel engine rumbled through the air and then seemed to linger even after the bus had pulled off. Sierra frowned. It wasn't the engine that was growling now; it was a deeper, fiercer sound. She squinted into the darkness and realized something stood in the shadows by the gate. She stepped forward, her heart thundering.

"Hey, y'all," Izzy said, walking out onto the loading dock. "What it do? I hadta dip out of that mess, everyone being annoying and stressed out." The door closed behind her, and the growling stopped. Sierra saw two eyes flash in the darkness.

"Cojo!" Sierra said. "What is it?"

The hound didn't run up to her like usual; he turned back to the street and resumed his low, terrifying growl.

"Y'all playing with that satanic dog again?" Izzy said. "Listen."

"I'm Caleb Jones," Caleb said. "You one of the new shadowshapers, huh?"

"Oh snap, you the tattoo dude? What up, my man!" Sierra heard them exchange a dap and then what must've been an awkward hug, considering how tiny Izzy was beside Caleb. "I'm Izzy."

Sierra followed Cojo's bristling gaze out to the street, but all she saw were parked cars, a few empty stoops.

"King Impervious Izzy? I'm a fan." Caleb somehow managed to sound completely unenthusiastic in spite of his words, but Izzy didn't seem to mind.

"Word? Thanks, man. I hear great things 'bout your tat work."

Sierra closed her eyes and immediately fell into the strange, blurry world of the Hound of Light. It was a street nearby. The street was still except for a few swaying trees. The creature wasn't moving, just staring. Sierra tried to make out where it was, but everything was a little blurry. Looked like brownstones. Parked cars. Where, though? Was it the same block she was on? Her eyes flew open as she stumbled back a few steps.

"You guys . . . something's nearby. I think it's the Hound again . . ."

Caleb was beside her in seconds. "The Hound of Light?"

Sierra nodded, appreciating how quickly the tattoo master jumped into action. "I can . . . I think I can see what it sees. I have been anyway. And it looks like it's close."

Cojo suddenly launched into the street with a growl and took off down the block.

"Cojo!" Sierra yelled.

"Wait." Caleb's voice was quiet but sharp.

"What?"

"You don't know what you're running into. It could be —"

"This thing has been trailing me for two days, Caleb. I don't know what it is, but I'm not running from it."

"I get you." Caleb glanced up and down the street. "But at least 'shape something first. I'll follow Cojo. You and Izzy send some spirits out and split up. You can see through the spirits' eyes, right?"

Sierra nodded as Izzy came up beside her.

"Can you 'shape, Iz?" Caleb asked.

"Not that well, but I know how to mess someone up."

He gave a curt nod. "That may help." Then he took off down the street after Cojo.

"You trust him?" Sierra said, crouching and taking the chalk Izzy handed her.

"Yeah, I kinda do, actually," Izzy said. "I don't know why, I don't usually trust anyone."

"Crouching sucks in this skirt." Sierra scribbled some badass red ninjas with katana blades on the sidewalk. "You sure it's not just cuz he likes your rhymes?"

"Ha. Yeah, I'm sure. Something real about him. I'll keep my eyes open, though."

"Good."

Three tall shadows loped down the street toward them. They were bent over slightly and seemed to shine with a slight golden hue. Sierra squinted at them, lowering her hand. Her shadows sometimes radiated hazy colors, but never gold. Were these three related to the Sorrows somehow?

Before she could stand, the spirits launched into her, sliding through with that familiar icy flush that sent her stumbling onto the pavement over the drawings. As she touched them, the red ninjas slid to life. They scrambled up the block a few feet and then doubled back, closing quickly on Sierra and Izzy, blades raised to strike.

"What the hell?" Izzy yelled, stepping back.

Sierra stood her ground, arms raised. The first figure flew up into the air and lashed out, slicing her cheek. She yelled; the second ninja was already leaping across the open air in front of her. A shrill burn erupted across her face as it screeched into her.

"Back!" Sierra yelled as the third leapt. She shrugged her shawl off and swung it, trying to ignore the vicious sting blossoming along her forehead. The third chalk ninja splattered into the ether.

"Sierra!" Izzy hollered. Sierra spun around. The first two red ninjas had Izzy cornered, swiping at her as she swung back at them. Behind her, another shadowy spirit was barreling down the street toward them. Sierra recognized the figure, even with its face hidden beneath a hoodie: Vincent. She ran forward, splattering one red ninja just as the other leapt at Izzy.

The graffiti! Vincent yelled, launching into the air past Izzy. Sierra saw the big, bubbly shape spray-painted on the gate beside her. She raised her arm just in time for Vincent to splash into her, then smacked the gate. The abstract image bustled to life and rattled off the gate, spinning into the advancing chalk form. Both colorful shapes tumbled into the pavement, tussling viciously until Vincent's painted form swung a bright tendril out and scattered the red ninja into dust.

Sierra and Izzy stared wide-eyed as Vincent's shadowy, panting form rematerialized out of the graffiti.

"The . . . spirits . . ." Sierra gasped. "They turned on me . . . and they were glowing gold."

"What is going on?" Izzy said.

I don't know, Vincent said. *But I got a crew. There not many of us yet, but you can trust us.*

"Sierra, is that . . . ?" Izzy whispered.

Sierra nodded. Glowing hooded forms were materializing in the street around them.

I call 'em the Black Hoodies, Vincent said. *They were killed like I was . . .*

By the cops, Sierra thought, completing his trailed-off sentence. There were five of them, counting Vincent. Two were tall, one very wide; one looked to be just a child. Their faces were all obscured beneath their hoods.

What can we do? one of the tall ones asked in a deep, melancholy voice.

"The Hound of Light is near," Sierra said. "Caleb is after it. So is Cojo. We gotta find out what's going on."

Vincent nodded, threw a glance at his crew. *Let's move.*

ELEVEN

The streets of Bed-Stuy reeled below — the pinkish haze of streetlamps glinting off parked cars and puddles, the blinking bodega signs and dim bougie bars. The child spirit, Tolula Brown, her name was, swooped low along a narrow residential block, brownstones whizzing past on either side, and then swung up above the rooftops and around a project tower. Sierra watched from the ground, her eyes closed, seeing all that Tolula saw. Vincent stood nearby, keeping guard.

Izzy had ducked off after Caleb and Cojo, the two taller spirits following close behind like bodyguards, and Sierra had taken a moment to shove away the roiling terror of being attacked by her own 'shaped spirits. That had never happened before — not as far as she'd heard — and it left a nervous tremble in her hands.

It was a relatively warm Friday night, and now that the rain had tapered off, small groups of revelers hit the Brooklyn streets to enjoy one of the last nights of the fading autumn. None of them appeared to be giant, ancient beasts, but then, maybe the Hound of Light was disguised somehow. Tolula swung low again, rounded a corner onto Marcy Ave, and grazed past an oak tree. *Maybe the Hound is a human,* Sierra thought.

Then she saw people moving quickly out of the way of something, raising their arms and yelling. Tolula dipped even lower, slowing her flow. Something huge and black thundered along the avenue: Cojo. Caleb's towering, red-topped form sprinted along not far behind.

What are they chasing, though? Sierra thought. *And where's Izzy?*

Sierra opened her eyes and ran, Vincent swooping along beside her. "Think they're getting close," she panted. Vincent nodded. She hated being so far away from everything as it was happening: the downside of being able to see through spirit eyes. She bolted up Halsey at a steady jog, swung left and right across the street, and was soon huffing and puffing toward Marcy.

At the corner, she stopped and checked. It was the Hound of Light's vision she tapped into this time. It hurtled down the middle of a dark street; she could hear it panting. Was it chasing something? Running away? She tried to make out the street but it was all a blur. Still . . . it *looked* like Bed-Stuy — some part close by, Sierra thought.

She blinked her eyes open, ran another block, and paused again, catching her breath. It was one of the tall spirits that followed Izzy she tapped into next. Izzy stood with her back to the spirit, fumbling desperately in her suit jacket pocket.

The street around her was all darkened houses, but Sierra thought it might be Madison, where she used to walk on the way to elementary school with Juan. Just a few blocks from where she stood. Izzy yelled, "No!" as she pulled chalk from her pocket, but her hands were shaking and the chalk flew out into the street.

Sierra watched in horror as a huge gold-tinged shadow loomed up over Izzy — Izzy, who could barely 'shape and was now without chalk. She had to get to her.

Sierra was about to open her eyes and run like hell when Izzy's voice filled the air.

"A tyrant, ultra-violent, unstoppable, undroppable, a monsta / thought ya had her now ya lost her," Izzy spat. Her voice started shaky — she backstepped as she rapped — but it got stronger with each rhyme. "I'm a slammer, demon duchess / like MC Hammer you can't touch this / I'll crush this, you luckless, number one on the suck list." Sierra felt the tall spirit whose vision she shared strengthen as each line dropped. Long, shadowy arms stretched out and darkened, solidifying with the strength of Izzy's lyrical prowess. The spirit splayed her fingers, reveling in this sudden power.

Sierra's whole body thrummed with the spirit's exhilaration. What a feeling, to take form, to bristle with this sudden ferocity, this life!

"Unbroken I'm no token / I dismember ya, then I be smokin' your embers as you croakin', chokin'."

The two tall spirits stepped up either side of Izzy,

glistening and solid. The gold-tinged one facing her stood perfectly still, then launched forward. "You'll be shattered, ripped up and tattered / splattered, from here through the stratosphere / I know no fear, ya hear?" Izzy's tall guardians met the attack head on, closing with each other in front of Izzy. The gold-tinged spirit was crushed between them, evaporated with a squeal.

Izzy and Sierra let out simultaneous yelps of victory and then Izzy leaned against a tree, panting. "I did it," she whispered.

Sierra shook her head, blinked her eyes open, and glanced around. Sweat ran down her back, glistened against her brown skin. She was still wearing her stupid funeral dress and uncomfortable flats, and the Hound was still out there, somewhere nearby, but at least Izzy was okay for the moment.

A police car zoomed by, lights flashing. Then another. She looked at Vincent, who had been scanning the street for enemies. He shrugged.

Tolula, she thought, taking off down Marcy. *Where they at?* She blinked her eyes closed long enough to make out a dark expanse; rooftops peered out over the tree line in the distance. Von King Park, where Sierra had played as a little kid. Caleb and Cojo were sprinting up Tompkins Ave toward it. The glare of the police precinct lit the whole street.

Sierra ran harder, pulling out her phone.

"Sierra!" Izzy yelled after one ring. "I just . . . I just . . ." She sounded like she was running too.

"I know," Sierra said, gasping out a laugh. "I saw it . . . It was amazing, Iz!" She held the phone away from her face and exhaled loudly. "You're a hero! Listen, head to . . . Von King. Caleb and Cojo . . . there."

"Already going that way," Izzy said. "Sierra, I'm a shadowshaper!"

Sierra felt tears edge up into the corners of her eyes. She smiled at the phone. "Hell yeah you are! Now meet me at Von King, southeast corner!"

The intersection was empty when Sierra ran up, sweaty and breathless. She leaned over, hands on her knees, and let the air return to her. Von King was only a block or two in either direction and mostly wide-open playing fields, with a small, sunken amphitheater in the middle. If Caleb and Cojo were in there, they shouldn't be hard to find. She was about to close her eyes when Izzy ran up.

"Sierra! Over there!" Izzy didn't even stop running, just pivoted off to the right and headed down Greene Avenue along the side of the precinct.

Red-and-blue lights splattered their pulse across the buildings at the far end of the block.

"Dammit," Sierra whispered, stumbling into a run.

* * *

"What . . . what happened?" Sierra asked, stopping beside where Izzy and Caleb stood behind yellow police tape. Cojo sniffed her one time before returning to his position, pointing and growling at the intersection.

"Cojo led us here," Caleb said. "We rolled up just after this went down. Looks like a police cruiser hit a girl."

Sierra put a hand on Cojo's collar, holding him back, and gazed past the police tape. Throngs of uniformed men clustered around an NYPD squad car halfway up on the sidewalk. Cops were everywhere — taking pictures, taking notes, looking burly and unimpressed. Some thick, stressed-looking guys in suits milled around squinting at people — detectives, Sierra guessed. And there, in the center of it all, a slender white girl lay crumpled on the wet pavement, blood smeared around her.

Sierra gasped. Was that —?

"Coming through!" a cop yelled from behind them. "Get out the way, let's go!" An ambulance rounded the corner, lights and sirens blasting, and pulled up at the intersection. Two guys jumped out, grabbed their bags and a backboard, and hustled over to the girl.

"The hell happened?" one of the medics asked the sergeant escorting him across the street.

"Girl just ran out in the middle of the street," the sergeant said. He was portly with a mustache and a suspicious squint that looked like it had become part of his face. "Our cruiser swerved but sideswiped her anyway; ended up on the sidewalk." He nodded toward the vehicle. Sierra saw cops leaning into the windows, talking to the driver and passengers. It sounded like one of them might be crying. "They're fine, I think, just upset. But y'all might wanna get another bus to check 'em out." The sergeant gave a what-you-gonna-do shrug and ambled out of the way.

One of the medics said something into his radio, then they crouched by the girl's body and carefully rolled her over.

"Mina!" Sierra yelled, ducking the police tape and sprinting into the intersection. An officer shouted and reached out to stop her but she dodged out of the way. "That's my friend!" The medics were strapping Mina to a backboard. "Mina, can you hear me? What happened?" Sierra yelled, trying not to get in the way as they lifted her onto the stretcher. Blood stained her pale face and yellow shirt, but it didn't look like anything was broken. Mina's eyes blinked open groggily when she heard Sierra's voice.

"Sierra?"

"You gotta stand back, miss," one of the medics said. "We're gonna take care of your friend."

"Mina? Tell me what happened!"

"The Deck," Mina mumbled.

"Miss, step away, please." The medics began wheeling her off.

Mina flailed her arms, eyes suddenly wide. "Wait!"

"Young lady," the medic said. "Calm down."

She grabbed at the plastic brace around her neck, moaning. "Ugh! Stop!"

"Young lady!"

Sierra ran alongside the stretcher. "The Deck, Mina. What about it?"

"The amphitheater," Mina gasped. "The amphitheater in the park. Get it! Get it now!"

They reached the ambulance, its bright rear lights throwing ghastly shadows behind them, and the medics loaded Mina in. One hopped inside with her and slammed the door as the other hurried over to the front cabin.

Sierra threw her arms in the air. "What . . . the hell?"

"What she say?" Izzy asked when Sierra walked back over to the police line.

"She said the Deck's in the park amphitheater. Gotta be Von King, right?" She nodded toward the street they'd just come from.

"Cojo and I came through the park," Caleb said. "If it was her scent we were following, she must've too. Which would've given her time to dump the cards there, if she was afraid she was gonna get caught."

"But why would she tell me where she hid it?" Sierra said. She looked up at Caleb, his wide, freckled face, his stern eyes and furrowed brow. What if Mina was hiding the Deck from him? Had she said too much?

Cojo was still growling, his wrinkled, slobbery snout pointing sharply into the street. "Come on, Cojo," Sierra said, pulling his collar. "We gotta go get that Deck before someone else does."

They headed down the block at a quick jog, the shadowy forms of Vincent's Black Hoodie squad stretching ahead of them.

Von King seemed especially dark this night. They entered cautiously, Caleb and Izzy scanning either side, Sierra in the center casting her vision into the spirits' eyes. A few rows of seats lead down to a small shadowy stage ahead of them.

"Where would she hide it?" Izzy said. "She was prolly in a hurry, so it's not like she coulda dug and buried it, right?"

Sierra made a face. "I guess? Let's see what we turn up."

They spread out: Caleb headed to the stage, Izzy walked the aisles, while Sierra checked the small wall on the edge of the amphitheater. Something about what Izzy had said prickled at her subconscious. *Prolly in a hurry . . .* That made sense, if Mina was being chased or chasing something, which seemed to be the case. And if she thought she'd be caught, like Caleb said, she'd try to stash the Deck and then either go get it later or let someone know. It was risky, but apparently less so than letting the Deck fall into the hands of whatever was chasing her.

The short wall was painted with happy dancing figures and a few graffiti tags. Some trash lay strewn about, but no creepy cards.

Not like she coulda dug and buried it. Of course she couldn't, Sierra thought. *Unless.* She scrunched her face, trying to tease out the thought. Unless Mina was the Hound.

Sierra opened her eyes wide and then slammed them shut. *Where was the Hound right now?*

Everything was dull gray. A metal bar stretched across Sierra's vision. Then the whole world trembled. A big brown face appeared. "You're gonna be fine," the face said.

An ambulance. Sierra's eyes shot open. The Hound of Light was in an ambulance.

"You guys," Sierra said. "I think . . . the Hound . . ." She shook her head. The Hound wasn't a hound at all, it was a . . . girl?

"What is it, girl?" Izzy snapped.

"Check the grassy area around the theater," Sierra said. "Look for freshly moved dirt."

"You think . . . ?" Izzy gasped. "Damn."

Caleb ran up the stairs out of the amphitheater and pulled out his phone, using its light to search the grass. *Maybe in a little* too *much of a hurry,* Sierra thought. Then she growled at her own paranoia, swinging her own phone light along the pavement toward the grass. If Mina *was* the Hound of Light, though . . . Nothing made any sense. Sierra crouched beside one of the small hedges by the theater, peering into the shadows beneath the leaves. Why would Mina give her the Hound of Light card if she *was* the Hound? Unless it was somehow controlling her and she was trying to get rid of it . . . Or maybe it wasn't the Hound whose vision Sierra had been seeing all along. Maybe Mina was something else entirely . . .

Something lay barely concealed beneath fallen leaves under the hedge. A little package, it looked like. Sierra grabbed it, her heart racing, and restrained a gasp; tiny, tingling eruptions danced up her arm and into her chest.

"Find anything?" Izzy called.

"Nope," Caleb said from the grassy area not far away.

"Nah," Sierra said. She hadn't, for all she knew, and she had no idea who to trust anymore. She unwrapped the red string holding the fabric closed, caught a glimpse of a picture — a masked man in front of a stormy sky. Slid the card to the side to reveal another, then another.

The Deck of Worlds.

Sierra tucked it into her jacket pocket and stood.

"Got nothing," she said, trying to keep her voice from shaking. "And I dunno how long we can be out here pushing dirt around. Mina coulda been delirious, coulda been lying . . . Who knows?"

"I got nothin'," Izzy said, taking the steps out of the amphitheater two by two to stand beside Sierra. "Caleb?"

"I feel y'all," Caleb said. "But if the Deck is here, we gotta find it. Imma keep looking. Y'all head home. I know you got family stuff to handle, Sierra." He stepped out of the darkness and the park lanterns threw his humongous shadow forward, illuminating a halo of gold around his red fro. "My condolences, by the way. I know he was a complicated man to be close to, believe me, but death is still death. Even for us ghost-handling folks."

Sierra didn't know what to say — it was the most genuine word of condolence anyone had given her, and here she was lying to him. "Thanks," she mumbled. "You shouldn't stay out here, man. There's clearly some foul spirits around." She held off telling him about the red ninja attack, and was glad Izzy didn't mention it either.

"Heh, I'll be alright," Caleb said. "Can you make it to Old Crane's tomorrow?"

"Yeah," Sierra said. "Gimme your phone."

He passed it, one of those huge, fancy touchscreen ones that might as well be a flatscreen television. Sierra typed her number in and pressed CALL, then hung up when she felt the vibration in her pocket. "We'll hit you up when we headin'."

Caleb smiled, pocketing his phone. "Alright, and let me know when y'all make it home."

Sierra nodded, backing away with Izzy. Cojo ran up beside them as they turned and headed out of the park. "Stay safe, man," Sierra called, over the dog's enthusiastic, panting snorts.

Something about the empty, darkened funeral home left Sierra uneasy. Or maybe it was the Deck in her jacket pocket, the weight of that secret and that strange flash of power she'd felt when she touched it. Either way, she wanted to get off the streets and home fast.

"You text the crew?" Sierra asked Izzy. "Oh, man! My phone's been on silent this whole time!" She pulled it out and cringed at the anxious messages from her mom and dad wondering where she was.

"Yeah, Imma head to Tee's," Izzy said. "The rest went home."

Sierra punched in a quick *Im OK, be home soon* text to her parents and hit SEND, feeling like a jerk. She looked up at Izzy, whose eyes were wider than usual, brows raised expectantly. Sierra was about to ask her why when she remembered, and smiled wide at her friend. "You did it," she said, hugging Izzy close to her. "You found your magic."

"In retrospect, like, prolly shoulda guessed that I'd be a lyric-shaper. I mean, duh, right?" She shook her head in Sierra's shoulder. "Thanks for bein' patient with me, though."

"Of course!"

Izzy turned and started down the street. "Now Imma go make Tee practice with me and whup her ass into next week, ayyyy!" She ran off, chuckling.

Sierra's smile lasted a few blocks, then the confusion of so many threads and shadows crept in. A whole cadre of spirits had fallen into step with her as she and Cojo strolled through Bed-Stuy. She was alive, so at least there was that. A text came in from her mom: *We're out to dinner. Be safe please.*

Vincent's hooded form appeared beside her, and Sierra greeted him with a solemn, "Hey."

You okay?

"Man . . . I don't know who to trust."

Caleb been with the shadowshapers a long time, Vincent said. *But you right to be suspicious of everyone and everything.* He shook his head. *Twisted times.*

"I hate lying," Sierra said. "And . . . those spirits that turned on me tonight. That's . . . that's never happened before."

I know . . . and I dunno know what that was. We tryna look into it, Si. I'll let you know if anything turns up.

"Can you look into Caleb too? Poor guy's out there checking for the Deck still, far as I know." Tolula Brown's little shadowy form flitted up ahead of them. "She could do it?"

The child spirit nodded, spun a pirouette in the sky, and flew off toward the park.

"Thanks!" Sierra called. She turned to Vincent. "You gonna talk to B or what?"

Vincent closed his glowing, shadow eyes and made a face. Sierra remembered that face — the begrudging "I guess so" look he got when the Jacksons asked him to watch his little sister. He'd act like it was such a burden, but then all three of them would end up playing video games for hours and having a great time. Those moments were just with Sierra and Bennie now, though. Vincent had lost his entire past along with his life. *I'm just . . . Guess I'm scared is all.*

He sighed. *I will, though. I promise.* He started to fade into the night. *Soon.*

"Uh-huh," Sierra said. "You better."

━━━━━━━━━━

"Hey!"

Sierra jumped away from the shadowy stoop where the voice had come from, arms raised for the oncoming attack. A kid about her age in a three-piece suit stepped out of the darkness. She squinted at him. "Little Ricky?"

"Uh — didn't mean to startle you."

"What are you doing . . . dressed like that?"

The last time she'd seen Little Ricky he'd been throwing game with some other fellas on the block. He usually sported sagging jeans and a fitted cap. He shrugged, putting his hands in his pockets, and looked away. "I just . . . I cleaned up."

"So I see."

Little Ricky met her eyes. "I wanted to say — sorry I was creepy to you over the summer. You said no and I was a dick about it."

"Sarcastula," Sierra said.

"Huh?"

"That's what you called me."

"Oh, ha, damn."

She just looked at him.

"I mean, we knew each other when we was little kids," he went on. "And I guess it kinda hit home. That you're a person and everything."

"Not just an ass and a pair of legs walking past."

Ricky brightened, realized Sierra wasn't smiling, solemned back up. "Yeah, that."

"Yeah," she said. "Okay, man."

"And anyway, I'm getting my GED. You know, going the straight path."

Sierra forced a smile as she started to backstep down the block. Something about Little Ricky still creeped her out. "That's great, Ricky. I'm happy for you."

He looked stricken. "Wait. I just — I wanted to see if you wanted to go out some time."

Sierra shook her head. "I can't, man. It's complicated." She resisted the urge to apologize.

"I want . . . I want to be part of what you're part of, Sierra."

She stopped, eyeing him. *Did he know?* "I gotta go, man. It's late."

"Sierra . . ."

"I'm glad you gettin' it together, Ricky. Good luck."

She turned and walked quickly away.

TWELVE

Sierra walked into the house, kicked off her flats, and sighed. Her dress and stockings had been squeezing too tight all evening; she felt like a mound of flesh shoved into a tiny sleeve. She shrugged off her jacket, pulling the Deck of Worlds out of the pocket, and headed toward the stairs.

And then froze.

Someone was moving around up there. Her eyes darted around the kitchen for something she could use to 'shape with or defend herself.

"Easy, Juan, easy," the voice came from upstairs.

Sierra almost burst out laughing at her own paranoia. Anthony. In all the excitement, she'd forgotten he'd taken Juan home. She felt that jittery lump rise inside herself and walked quickly up the stairs so it didn't have time to grow any bigger.

"Get it out, man, get it out."

The bathroom light cut a bright triangle in the dark hallway. Sierra peeked in through the open door. Juan was leaning over the toilet, returning all those creepy little funeral-home finger foods to the world. Anthony stood over him, rubbing his back. Juan heaved and coughed, then something else splashed into the bowl.

Sierra leaned against the doorframe, raised an eyebrow, and said, "You come here often?"

Anthony looked up, startled, and then smiled. "Only when duty calls, alas."

"Maybe we should make sure my brother gets puketastically smashed out of his mind more often, then," Sierra said, then she scrunched up her face. Did she really just say that? Was that any way to flirt? Anthony just looked perplexed for a second and then Juan gurgled, "I heard that," and Sierra and Anthony burst out laughing.

"Seriously, man, I got that," Sierra said. "You don't have to —"

Anthony waved her off. "It's no thing. Told you it's not the first time." He shook his head, still smiling.

"Well, at least let me keep you company, then," Sierra said, stepping into the room and perching her butt on the edge of the claw-foot tub.

Juan burped.

"Thanks," Anthony said. "How was the rest of the service?"

I don't know because I had to cut out early so I could chase a phantom hound creature who may actually be a teenage white girl who then got hit by a cop car. "Oh, it was cool. You know how wakes be." Did he? Was that something people even said? Sierra tried not to roll her eyes at herself.

Anthony nodded. "Yeah."

Lying to him felt crappy, even a tiny, meaningless lie like that. "I actually took off pretty soon after you did . . . Something came up."

"Oh, I hope everything's alright?" Anthony said, then he frowned. "I mean . . . Sorry, that was a stupid thing to say after your grandfather's wake."

"Oh!" Sierra said, smiling because finally he was acting as awkward as she felt. "No, I'm okay about my granddad, actually. I mean — that sounded cold. I mean, everything's not alright —"

"Oh, damn."

"But not because of the wake." Sierra shook her head. "It's hard to explain. Let's talk about you! Anthony's not a Spanish name — what flavor Latino are you, bruh?"

He laughed — a full-throated, unself-conscious kind of laugh, his big white teeth glinting in the bathroom light as he leaned back. Sierra squirmed inside of herself. "I'm not. Mom's people are from North Carolina, Dad's from Chi-Town."

"My dude! Your nickname's Pulpo, which you still owe me a story for FYI, and you sing *in Spanish* in a salsa-thrasher band. What cross-cultural shenanigans are these?"

Anthony was still laughing, waving his hands around like he was trying to explain while she talked. "Listen!"

Juan let out a gurgle and rolled away from the toilet, slumping against the wall and smacking his lips a few times as his head lolled against his chest. Sierra and Anthony looked at each other and burst out laughing again. Sierra was pretty sure none of this was actually *that* funny, but somehow it was.

She stood, eyeing her brother. "We better get him into bed. You get the shoulders, I take the feet?"

"Sure," Anthony said. "Why's that thing you're carrying glowing?"

Sierra looked down at her hand and almost yelled. She was still clutching the Deck of Worlds, and it was indeed pulsing with a faint light. "Shit," she whispered. Then she looked up at Anthony. All the joy seemed to have seeped out of the room in just a few seconds. "Just something someone gave me at the wake."

"Weird. You know what it is?"

Sierra shook her head, frowning, then said, "Yeah," distractedly. "I guess. Just some, you know, wake . . . gift. I'll go put it away, then we'll bring Juan over."

Another lie. Just a tiny one. Surely for Anthony's own good — he didn't need to be mixed up in all this . . . whatever this was. Still: It felt like wringing out a dirty towel inside herself. She hurried down the hall to her room, stashed the Deck under her pillow, and came back to the bathroom.

"I'm sorry," Sierra said. "That was weird. I do know what that is, I just can't exactly talk about it." She focused on the tiled wall behind Anthony, her hands crossed over her torso.

"That's cool," he said. "You barely know me, even though we've known each other for like . . . how long now?"

Sierra had had a crush on Anthony since he'd started coming around with Juan when she was twelve. "Four years," she said, hopefully not too quickly. "Almost five now."

"Right. Weird, right?"

"Very," she said, relieved to be talking about anything besides her own secrets. "Juan's never . . . said anything about our family to you?"

"Lots of stuff," Anthony said, then quickly: "Nothing bad though! 'Cept about Rosa, I guess."

Sierra snorted. "No, I mean . . . Okay, cool."

He raised an eyebrow. "Why, y'all got dark secrets?"

Sierra laughed, playing along. "You have no idea, bruh. Come help me move this drunk-ass." She knelt down, grabbing one of her brother's feet under each arm. Anthony got behind him and wrapped his big arms under Juan's armpits. Sierra tried not to think about what it would feel like to have those arms wrapping around her from behind.

"Lift on one, two, and three," Anthony said, heaving Juan easily into the air while Sierra pulled his legs up. "Seriously, though, I've always just been kind of in awe of your family."

"Word?" Sierra said. She kicked the bathroom door the rest of the way open and they maneuvered into the hallway.

"Oh, man, you guys are like . . . legends! First of all, Gael was always that cool older brother dude, even if he was a little uptight, then he goes off to Afghanistan, so: hero. Then this drunken degenerate here" — Anthony nodded down at Juan.

"Blurga mo faz faz," Juan mumbled.

"Is probably a musical genius, and I don't use those words lightly."

Sierra pushed her butt into the door of Juan's room, shoving it open, and they carried him in without bothering to turn on the light.

"And you," Anthony went on. "I've seen your artwork."

Sierra tried not to let her pulse quicken, but . . . there they were in a dark room together, never mind that Juan's unconscious body hung slung between them.

"And you know, you've got this kind of magic thing about you," Anthony said.

She laughed, feeling herself go flush all over. "I'm sure I don't know what you mean. Here." They lined up beside Juan's bed, using only the crooked light from the hallway as a guide.

"I'm sure you do." For a moment, they just stood there. Did he see some flicker of Lucera coming through? Did he feel the power of all that legacy churning inside her? Or was he just being beautifully corny? Sierra hoped it was the latter.

"C'mon, this little guy heavy," she said. They deposited Juan on the bed and Sierra tucked him in.

"Bashmooga," Juan said gratefully, smacking his lips with satisfaction.

"Bashmooga," Sierra said.

"I usedta tag." Anthony's voice came from somewhere behind her in the dark room. But low.

"Excuse me?"

"The cross-cultural shenanigans. I'm answering your question."

"Oh! Well, by all means, carry on, then." Sierra felt her way to the other side of the room until Anthony's hand found hers and pulled her down beside him on Gael's bed. They sat side by side, their legs touching, their elbows touching. Sierra's pulse thundered in her ear, no matter how much she tried to get it to calm the hell down.

"My tag was a squid."

"What kinda ridiculous —?"

"I know, but I loved animals as a kid and for whatever reason . . . I dunno!" He shrugged with mock defensiveness. "Everyone was doing letters and little words that didn't make sense anyway, so I was like, you know . . ."

"Lemme put a squid up in the mix!" Sierra let out a belly laugh.

"Basically, and then —"

"Wait! You're telling me how you got your nickname, aren't you? But . . . Pulpo is octopus, not squid."

131

Anthony shrugged, his delicious arm moving up and down against hers and sending friction all throughout her body. "I'm not that good at drawing."

"Oh my God!" Sierra yelled, blurting out another burst of laughter. "You're killing me! That's actually the worst nickname origin story in the history of things having names, man!"

"But it's mine," Anthony said, his voice raspy with his own laughter.

"Okay, so you *say* you're black American, non-Latin, but you sing in, like, flawless Spanish, man."

He shrugged again. Sierra tried to think of more things she could say that would make him shrug. "What's that even mean though? I took Spanish in middle school and when I was at Butler — Ms. Fernandez, by the way; she was the bomb."

"So did Bennie, but she wouldn't be able to find the bathroom in a Mexican restaurant."

"Your brother and Gordo help me with pronunciation — you know Gordo a pronouncing-shit jefe."

"Ha! As long as it's not shit in English."

Sierra was positive if she just pushed off her arm, she could flip her whole body over onto his, land face-to-face and straddling him, kiss him hard on the mouth, and then let the sweet gravity of the moment catch hold of her.

She was also pretty positive her parents would be home any moment. And her brother was knocked out on the next bed, even though he probably wouldn't wake until tomorrow afternoon. And there was Robbie to consider. And the Deck. And the Hound. And Mina's blood-splattered body laid out in the middle of the intersection.

And and and.

The room suddenly felt very dark, very small. Sierra's breath caught in her throat. Just like that, all the joy of the moment slinked off once again as the whole world crowded in. "Anthony?" Her voice sounded small, choked in the newly silent room.

"Hm?"

Had he fallen asleep, just like that?

"Tell me something."

"What?"

"Anything. Something about yourself. Something all your adoring fans don't know."

Anthony scoffed. "Adoring fans. What they love is that music Juan writes. I'm just the conduit."

"That's cute, man, but I'm pretty sure if *I* tried to sing 'Deus Ex Smackinya,' the reaction wouldn't be the same."

"Alright, whatever. Um . . . something about me, let's see." He adjusted himself on the bed and Sierra felt herself sliding into his body; her head landed softly on his shoulder as his arm wrapped around her back.

"I'll tell you something nobody really knows about. Nobody 'cept, like, Juan and my parents, basically. And Gordo. But it's not funny."

"Okay," Sierra said. "Promise I won't laugh."

"I get, like" — he took a deep, shaky breath, lifting Sierra's head with his shoulder; she felt his pulse quicken against her ear — "really bad panic attacks? Sometimes."

"Wow, really?"

His chin moved up and down against the top of her head as he nodded. "Like, *really* bad, sometimes. I mean, I mostly have 'em under control now, I guess, but . . . still feels like any ol' minute one could just show up and blow my whole world to hell. Just like that. You know?"

"I had no idea, naw. You seem so . . . Ugh!" Sierra shook her head. "Anything I say next will be wrong. Sorry. I'm sure that's what everyone says to people who have anxiety — *Oh, you seem okay, you seem okay!* Or, *You seem so normal!* That's pretty wack."

Anthony half laughed. "It's alright. I get it, I do. It *is* wild, because I know you'd never know it unless I told you or you saw it. And people wanna be like, *Oh, just take some deep breaths and you'll be okay,* but they don't understand there's actually no air to breathe when it's happening, and no room in my lungs. It's like seeing someone with a cut and going, *Oh, just stop bleeding, you'll be okay!*"

"Damn. I never thought of it like that."

Downstairs, the front door opened and Sierra heard the bustle and chatter of her parents coming in. She knew she should jump up, rush around trying to make it look like she hadn't just been sitting in a dark room with a hot guy, but she didn't have it in her to break the moment. She felt like she held a little part of Anthony's spirit cupped in her hands and if she moved, it would blow away.

"I've only told four other living people that," he whispered.

"Thank you," Sierra said. "For trusting me. Even though you barely know me. Even though you've always known me."

She could feel his smile pressed against the back of her neck. "Thank you for listening."

"¿Sierra?" María's voice rang out from downstairs. "¿Estás aquí, m'ija?"

"We should probably . . ." Sierra said.

"Yeah."

"Alright."

"Okay."

Neither moved.

"¡Sierra!" Frustration tinged María's voice now; she was probably already fed up with Sierra for that disappearing act at the wake.

"I'm coming, Mami!" Sierra yelled. "Be right down!" She stood, grudgingly disentangling herself from those loving arms. "I'm glad we finally got to hang out after all these years," she said.

"Me too." His voice was almost a whisper.

"You getting up?"

"Gimme a sec. Go hold 'em off for me."

Sierra clicked the light on as she left and hurried downstairs.

"You okay, Mami?" Sierra said, hugging her mom and planting a kiss on her cheek.

María had been crying but she nodded, sniffling. "It was a good ceremony."

Sierra laughed, feeling herself get choked up at seeing María's red, watery eyes. "It was a *terrible* ceremony."

"It was a terrible ceremony," Dominic agreed, taking his wife's coat and hanging it up beside his.

María chuckled into Sierra's shirt. "Okay, yes, it was. But I'm glad we did it. Well, we had to do it. How's Juan?"

"He's upstairs. Anthony's up there taking care of him."

Dominic raised his bushy brows. "Who?"

"Oh!" Mistake number one. "Pulpo."

"*That's* his name?" María said. "All this time, who knew?" She kicked off her heels and walked into the kitchen.

"Sierra did," Dominic said, now with just one eyebrow raised.

"Yep, he was here helping Juan puke his guts out when I got in. Just a few minutes ago." Mistake number two.

Dominic grunted something, eyeing Sierra. "Thought you'd been home longer than that."

"How was dinner?" Sierra asked, following her mom into the kitchen.

"Worse than the ceremony," María said. She took her

hot chocolate stash down from the cupboard and put some water to boil. "Your tía's boyfriend was there."

"Déjame, mi amor," Dominic said, taking the mugs from her and ushering her into a chair next to Sierra. "Yeah, we coulda used some backup, Sierra."

"I know. I'm sorry. Something came up with one of my friends."

María put her hand on Sierra's. It looked so small and wrinkled suddenly. "Everything okay?" Their eyes met. *Shadowshaping stuff?* María's face asked.

Sierra nodded very slightly. "Yeah, it's cool. Just, you know, drama."

Dominic made that grunting noise again, something like a snort, and poured the hot chocolate mix into three mugs. He'd never asked Sierra about shadowshaping, but she was pretty sure he knew *something* was going on and had elected to trust that his wife had it handled.

"Not for me, Dad," Sierra said. "I'm turning in soon."

"Hey, Mr. and Mrs. Santiago," Anthony said, coming down the stairs. "Juan's in bed. He'll be alright."

"Not when I'm through with him," Dominic grumbled.

"Thank you for taking care of him, Pulpo," María said with a knowing smile. "Or should I say, Anthony?"

"Oh, it's no problem at all," Anthony said. He pulled his suit jacket on and then leaned over to kiss María on the cheek. "Sorry for your loss, Mrs. Santiago."

"You don't want to stay for hot chocolate?"

Anthony shook his head, shooting a glance at Sierra. "I'm good, thanks, though." He shook Dominic's hand. "Sir."

"Anthony," Dominic said with a smirk.

"Oh, haha, yep, that's me!" He walked back over to where Sierra sat and craned down to wrap her in an awkward hug. "Later, Sierra. Glad we got a chance to spend some time together finally."

Aaand mistake number three. Sierra smiled through her cringe. "It was fun. Thanks for taking care of Juan."

"Anytime!" He waved and headed out.

As soon as the door closed, Dominic shot Sierra a look. "Just got home, huh? Got a chance to spend some time together, huh?"

"Dominic," María chided.

"Your timetable don't add up, young lady."

"Whoa, look at the time!" Sierra said, getting up from the table. "Whew! I'm tired! Good night!" She blew kisses from the stairwell and then hurried up to her room, closing the door against her parents' murmured discussion.

The Deck.

Sierra let out a long breath and then hurried over to her bed and retrieved the package, which was still glowing faintly. Her hands trembled as she pulled out the cards and laid them in a thick stack on her desk.

The REAPER was written across the top card. It showed a robed man with a grim face, slicing his scythe across terrified masses of tiny naked people.

"Fantastic," Sierra whispered.

She placed the two Hound cards and the Knight of Shadows on top of the Deck, then splayed them all out in a messy arch beneath the light of her desk lamp, each card peeking out from behind the next. Ten of the twenty-five cards were blank — it looked like they'd been hastily painted over with dark red watercolors. The rest had eerie figures on them: an old crone called *La CONTESSA ARAÑA* worked a spindle with six long arms. ("The Countess Spider," Sierra said out loud. It was the only card without an English translation.) *The EMPTY MAN,* a figure with no face, stood at a window, glaring in at a family huddled together.

She found the *SISTERHOOD of SORROWS* card: three golden phantoms hovering in an inverted triangle over a mountainous forest, the red sky stretched wide above them. Down the sides, it read *OUR LADIES of the LIGHT* and *NUESTRAS SEÑORAS de la LUZ.*

Grim faces stared out from the other House of Light cards: a warrior, an old wizard, a sly masked man, and of course, the white wolf, the Hound of Light. But their narrowed eyes spoke of determination and grit; they were reluctant killers in a broken world. Sierra glanced at a few of the Shadowhouse cards and was met by the wild, frenzied eyes of maniacs.

She shook her head, stacked the cards, and folded them into their package, then clicked off the desk lamp. The faint glow from the Deck filled her room with an eerie gold tinge.

The Sorrows.

Sierra wanted to throw the Deck out the window. That glow . . . That's what the world became when the Sorrows drew near. They had helped destroy the original shadow-shapers, and now they were inserting themselves back into Sierra's world, into her room! She wanted the Deck gone, out of her life, but of course, it wasn't that simple. It was never that simple, she thought, changing into a pair of Gael's sweatpants and an old T-shirt. Getting out of those tight funeral clothes felt amazing. She pulled the pins from her hair, wrestled it under a silky headwrap, and lay down, replaying her conversation with Anthony over and over to avoid thinking about the creepy golden glow.

THIRTEEN

Caleb was waiting for Sierra and Bennie the next morning when they came out of the train station in the far reaches of East New York. A little shimmering form sat on his shoulder and broke into an excited jig when the girls got closer.

"Tolula!" Sierra yelled, then she scrunched up her face at Caleb.

"Mmhmm," he said, squeezing one end of his mouth into an unimpressed scowl. "I gather you found the Deck last night."

"How . . . But I . . ." Sierra let her voice trail off. "Great job spying, Tolula. And Caleb, I'm sorry. I didn't know if I could trust you. That's all."

He waved her apology off with a grim smile. "It's fine. You can, but you didn't know that. I don't want the Deck anywhere near me, to be honest, let alone to hold it. I'm happy studying it from afar; the shit creeps me out."

"I hear that," Sierra said.

"And you actually saved me a night of searching by

sending Tolula here — once I realized I was being stalked, I figured you'd probably found the Deck and dipped."

"I mean . . ."

Caleb sent his voice a few registers up. "'Nope! No Deck here, everyone! Guess we all better go home! Good night!'"

Bennie punched Sierra's arm. "Girl. You never could lie for shit. Someone wanna fill me in, though?"

Sierra had spent the train ride retelling the chase to Von King Park while Bennie ate a bunch of nasty bodega candy and then started in on her coffee. But she'd left out the part about Vincent showing up — hadn't mentioned his crew at all, in fact, just kind of rendered them as general spirits and left it at that. She hadn't mentioned the convo with Anthony either, although she wasn't completely sure why. Somehow she just wanted to enshrine it somewhere quiet in herself. If she told the story, it'd be bantered about, turned into a thousand jokes, and then it might somehow seem . . . lesser. Besides, both Vincent and Anthony had entrusted her with secrets, and she meant to keep them.

"Tolula was one of the spirits that showed up last night to help us," Sierra said. Not a lie. "I asked her to keep an eye on Caleb here, which I take it she did for about two seconds before he turned her."

Tolula stood up on Caleb's shoulder and raised one arm like she was going to say something, then just shrugged and patted his red fro with a ghostly little hand.

"I take it that means Tolula approves of Black Power Elmo here," Bennie said.

Sierra laughed. "Guess so."

Caleb looked like he was about to say something, then just shook his head.

The little ghost paused, her gaze landing on Bennie for the first time. Her eyes got wide — with recognition, Sierra realized.

"Hi!" Bennie said, waving and flashing a big, cheesy grin. "She's adorable!"

Tolula looked at Sierra, who gave a tiny shake of her head, and then she smiled and sat back down on Caleb's shoulder.

"Shall we?" Caleb said. "Old Crane's anxious to see you."

Smiling faces stared out from the walls along the corridors at the St. Agnes Center for the Elderly. They were a little too smiley, Sierra thought, gazing at one of the photos — a white-haired couple walking arm in arm through the park — like they were trying to prove just how happy they could be. Plus, the picture had to be from like the mideighties or something.

"You comin'?" Bennie called from the end of the hall, where she and Caleb were waiting in front of one of the rooms.

"Yeah, yeah," Sierra said. She walked past an empty aquarium with an apologetic, faded sign on the front promising more fish "in the next sevril days," more smiley photos, and some posters for Bingo Night, '70s Dance Night, and a Night of Entertainment by "the Legendary Cowboy Buck Chuck," which didn't sound promising. All the night-time events started at three in the afternoon.

Bennie was shaking her head when Sierra walked up. "I see you judgin', girl."

"I ain't say nothin', B!"

"Wait till it's our turn. Cowboy Chuck Buck gonna be the highlight of ya whole entire week."

"It's Buck Chuck, I'll have you know."

"Y'all done?" Caleb said in that dry, impossible-to-tell-if-he-was-kidding voice.

"I think so," Sierra said. "We done, B?"

Bennie flipped a lock of hair behind her shoulder. "Been done."

"Outstanding." Caleb knocked three times on the wooden door in front of them.

"Ay," Old Crane's crinkly little voice sounded from inside.

Caleb pushed it open, and Bennie's and Sierra's eyes both went wide. At first, the whole room seemed to be a spar-kling array of silver. Then Sierra realized they were spoons. Hundreds and hundreds, maybe thousands, of spoons. Each one dangled from the ceiling by a thread and spun ever so slightly, glinting with the incoming rays of midday sun from the wide window at the far end of the room.

"They got coffee in the rec room?" Old Crane croaked from somewhere within the spoon universe of his room.

"I'll check," Caleb said. "You want anything, girls?"

"Coffee," Sierra said without taking her gaze off the spoons. "Black with two sugars."

"Remember it's nursing home dirt water," Old Crane said. "Not Bustelo."

"No sugar," Sierra amended.

"I'm good," Bennie said, also staring unabashedly into the room.

Caleb walked off.

"Come in, come in, young shadowshapers," Old Crane chuckled. "Those spoons won't hurt *you*." Sierra thought it funny how he emphasized the *you* slightly, like . . . who would they hurt? But she quickly forgot all about it as she found herself immersed in a dangly ocean of silver.

It was strangely peaceful, like floating somehow. Both girls were smiling when they emerged on the other side and found the little old man sitting at a wooden table.

"Please sit, my dears." He waved at two plastic chairs. "Bennaldra Jackson, I presume?" He reached out his crooked hand to her and Bennie smiled and shook it.

"That's me."

"Pleasure to make your acquaintance. Pretty, right?"

Bennie looked confused for a second, then looked

around. "Oh, yes, beautiful. Must've taken a long time to hang 'em all up."

"Ages. Caleb helped me, though, he's a good lad. Tall."

By *helped*, Sierra imagined Crane meant *did everything*. "Any reason in particular you have a million spoons hanging from the ceiling?"

"Decoration," Crane said, his face dead serious. A moment passed, then he gurgled and let out a high-pitched wheeze. Sierra was about to go find a nurse when she realized he was laughing.

"Imagine!" Crane managed between hacking screeches. "Ah . . ." He caught his breath. "No, no, I jest, of course. This is protection, young shadowshapers. But we'll speak of all that another time. Caleb seems to believe you have acquired the Deck of Worlds. Did you bring it?"

Sierra thought now would be a good time to discuss what exactly a million dangling spoons would protect against, but she let it slide. "I did." She pulled the package from her jacket pocket and placed it on the table. That faint glow still pulsed slowly from within the wrapping, making the whole thing look like an ultraviolet, cube-shaped heart.

Crane nodded and smacked his lips a few times. Sierra wasn't sure what would give him away as someone who couldn't be trusted with the Deck — it was probably too late anyway — but he seemed cool and collected. "As long as he don't go all *My precious* on us," Bennie had said on the train ride over, "I think he'll be alright."

Sierra unwrapped the Deck.

"Spread it," Crane said, in almost a whisper. "Please."

She wasn't sure if his hands were shaking from the excitement of the Deck or if that was just normal for him. She pushed over the stack of cards and arched them across the table, just as she'd done the night before in her room.

For a few moments, Crane just stared at them, nodding ever so slightly. Then he rasped, "Interesting."

Bennie looked at Sierra, then back at Crane. "What is it?"

"The latent houses," he said, picking up one of the all-red cards with some difficulty. "They're making a play for emergence."

"Meaning?" Sierra said.

"Coffee," Caleb announced from the doorway.

"Sierra, dear," Crane said without taking his eyes off the card he was holding. "Would you kindly help Mr. Jones make his way through the silverware forest? He always spills when he tries to do it himself."

Sierra locked eyes with Bennie as she stood. Bennie gave the slightest of nods and kept a sharp watch on the old man. The spoons sang a soft tinkle as Sierra moved through them, sweeping clusters aside so Caleb could pass.

"There's a house trying to come through," Crane said as Caleb put down three steaming Styrofoam cups. The magnificent body paint reaching up Caleb's huge arms made Sierra think of Robbie. She shoved the thought away.

"Figured," Caleb grunted. "Can you see which?"

" 'Fraid not." Crane had the card all the way up to his squinted eyes. His breath came in long, ragged wheezes in the quiet room. "Beast, maybe? House Echelon? *That* would be interesting."

"You're gonna have to speak English for the young 'uns," Caleb pointed out. "They're looking impatient."

Sierra and Bennie had their glares turned up to ten without even meaning to. They tried to adjust before Crane gazed up at them but didn't quite make it. He rasped out a congested chuckle. "My apologies. You girls have every right to be annoyed. The Deck is my area of study, you know, and I get caught up. Young Caleb only understands because he lets me drone on about it so."

"You gonna tell us what these houses are?" Sierra said.

"They're like suits in a regular card deck," Crane said. "Aces, spades, etc."

"But with nuclear weapons and a hundred years of pent-up rage," Caleb added.

Sierra gaped at him. "Whoa."

"Um . . . that escalated quickly," Bennie said.

"Look." The old man held out the blank card. Bennie stared at it dubiously.

Sierra took it, held it up to her face. "Oh, snap! There is something there." She could just make out what looked like a figure rising out of some viscous liquid — and maybe a church or something in the background, or a city — all hinted at with straggled lines, barely visible against the crimson mire. "So it . . . emerges? How?"

"It's part of the Deck's sorcery," Crane said, taking the card back. "The Deck only represents the world around it, really, and enhances it. So whatever house this is that's making a play for emergence, they have a pretty fair shot at it, given these lines."

"And if they *emerge* or whatever," Bennie said, "then they'll be . . ."

"Fully visible on the cards. And powerful."

"But what houses are these?" Sierra asked, separating the drawn-on cards from the Deck.

Crane chuckled under his breath. "Yours, Sierra."

"Mine?"

"Well, Shadowhouse is, of course. Also represented: the House of Light — the Sorrows. And these five." He separated the Reaper, la Contessa Araña, the River, the Empty Man, and Fortress. "These are called the Five Hierophants. It's the trump suit. Always showing. They belong to no house but their own. Very powerful — the power brokers. There was an uneasy detente for a while, when no one house was on top, but Shadowhouse is Dominant right now, and has been ever since you became Lucera and stacked your deck."

"Stacked my . . . ?"

"When you initiated a whole new cadre of shadow-shapers," Caleb explained.

"The old regime of shadowshapers had fallen almost entirely off the grid," Crane said. "Caleb, bring me the *Almanac*, please." Caleb pulled an old leather-bound tome off the shelf behind him and placed it on the table. "The shadowshapers weren't a concern," Crane went on, "particularly after Wick wiped away half of them." He opened the book, thumbed gingerly through the pages. "Then Lucera passed on the mantle to you, and there was a moment when the Sorrows thought maybe they'd have a chance to take over as the Dominant house." He stopped on the entry titled, "Subdominant: The House of Light." It showed the Sorrows card over a brief summary. "This is the *Almanac of the Deck of Worlds*. It was written over a hundred years ago by the creator of the Deck and then endowed with magical powers that allow it to continuously update over time as the Deck shifts."

"Old-school wi-fi," Bennie whispered.

"When you initiated more 'shapers *and* got the Deck, Sierra, the *Almanac* updated and . . . you became a threat."

"But —" Sierra said. She and Bennie traded a glance. "I never . . . I don't know anything about this. This isn't my world, my magic. I don't . . . I don't want to play."

Crane nodded sadly. "Unfortunately, it's not up to you. To any of us. The Deck . . ."

MURDER! an icy whisper shrieked. Sierra and Bennie jumped, glancing out into the forest of dangling silver. The

spoons wavered as if a winter zephyr had suddenly insinu-
ated itself into the room. *Murder most slow . . . most
meticulous, yesssss?* Slithery hisses sounded around the first
voice, snickering, cackling, seething. *Murderrrr . . .*

"What the hell?" Sierra gasped.

Caleb looked spooked too — he'd pulled a Sharpie out
of his pocket like a shank.

Old Crane shook his head. "It's okay, children. Caleb, if
you would kindly slide me closer to the spoons there? I'm a
bit fatigued."

MURDER!!

"Uh." Caleb raised one eyebrow.

"It's fine, I assure you I can manage. The whisper wraiths
have been pestering me for the past week or so. A few assassination attempts is all. Nuisance, really."

Bennie and Sierra had backed all the way against the
window and were each holding chalk, ready to 'shape.
"A few assassination attempts, though?" Sierra sputtered.
"What's the deal, man?"

. . . Sssssssslowww . . . trembling . . . death, yessssss?

"Caleb, if you would . . ."

Caleb frowned, then gingerly slid the old man's chair
along the tile floor until he was within reach of the first row
of dangling spoons.

Sssssssslowly . . . Death will come . . . sssssslowww . . .

"Yeah, yeah," Crane chortled shortly. "What is life if not

death coming slowly? Quiet yourselves now, vile demons." He swung an arm wildly, sending the spoons clanging into each other.

The whispers erupted into a scream as one. The spoons all trembled, vibrating like a tiny earthquake was blasting through them. Sierra stood frozen against the window.

Ssssssssoooooon!! the whisper wraiths shrieked. The spoons vibrated harder, then something seemed to give in the air around them, a breaking point, and the whispers faded. The spoons fell back to their gentle dangle. Old Crane slumped.

"Crane! Crane?" Caleb leaned over the old man's crumpled body, pulling him upright. "Sierra, get a nurse."

"Bah!" Crane snarled, his eyes shooting open. "What use is a nurse to a man of magic? I'm fine, Caleb. You should know better. The conjure work takes it out of you, more so in these waning years of life, young friend. They can keep throwing themselves at me, these pathetic cowards, and keep smashing against my defenses. Such is life. Now." He looked up at Sierra and Bennie. "You two should probably be on your way, yes?"

"But . . ." Bennie started.

"The whisper wraiths will be back, I'm sure, but don't fear for me. I'm more than capable. Take the Deck." He collected it into a stack with remarkable agility, his wrinkled hands moving more like a slick Vegas dealer's than those of an old man in a nursing home. "I'm sorry we didn't have time to get into more, but listen: With Shadowhouse Dominant, the others will be coming at you. The Sorrows will be looking to form an alliance with whatever house is emergent. Each card is connected to one of your people, Sierra. Find them, link them, form the bond between the Deck and Shadowhouse, and it will help you hold power. Those whom the cards choose will be able to lend you their power as well, since you are the head of Shadowhouse. You must be unified. The Sorrows will be relentless in their attacks. They will not stop until they've killed everyone you care for and resumed dominance for the House of Light."

"But . . . how do I . . . ?" Sierra didn't even know where to begin.

"Figure out which card fits who," Crane croaked. "Besides the Master or Lady, there is a Warrior, a Spy, a Hound, and a Sorcerer in each suit. And take it from there. You will need your troops in top form — the Deck will get them there."

"I don't want any of this," Sierra said. "I don't want to be Dominant, I don't want to play this stupid game. I just want my shadowshapers to live in peace."

Crane put his chilly, shriveled hand on Sierra's. "I know. I know. It's not fair. But you don't have that luxury. You inherited a position that is the envy of many, and that comes with consequences, I'm afraid."

"Which . . . which card is me?"

"Our Lady of the Shadows, of course, or the Mistress of

Shadows, as she's sometimes known." Crane flipped through the Deck, retrieved a card, and passed it to Sierra. "The Lucera card. Head of Shadowhouse."

The monster depicted made Sierra flinch. The Mistress of Shadows hung suspended over a thrashing ocean. Lightning tore through the dark sky behind her. She wore a shredded gown. An elaborate blue-and-orange skull mask covered three quarters of her face, its deathly grin matching her own vicious smile. Rows and rows of razor-sharp fangs lined her gums, and a forked tongue slid out of one side. The Mistress's skin shone with a deathly gray hue, and her hair exploded around her in wild silver locks that seemed to writhe in the throes of the ocean wind. It looked more like La Llorona, the mythical phantom who had murdered her own children and wandered the world haunting kids' nightmares, than like anything Sierra would want to be.

Sierra stood. The hand holding the card trembled and the image seemed to waver in front of her eyes. "I don't . . . I don't like it," she heard herself mumble. "This isn't me." She shook her head and the whole world spun.

"Si, you okay?" Bennie said.

"Yeah. Let's get out of here." She looked down at Old Crane, letting the nausea recede. The world became crisp again. "This isn't me," she said. "It's not. This game — I don't accept it."

"Luceras never have," Crane said. "Your grandmother felt the same way, but hers was a time when the Sorrows had even less footing than they do now. A time of relative peace. Unfortunately, it doesn't matter if you accept it or not, my dear. The egg that falls from the nest doesn't have to accept gravity, but in the end, the result is the same, I'm afraid."

Sierra picked up the cards and tucked them into their pouch. "I don't . . ." She shook her head. Nothing she could say mattered, it seemed. As far as the old man was concerned, anyway, she was trapped in a game she wanted nothing to do with.

"I'm sorry, dear. I wish I brought better news. Take these, all of you." He pulled open a drawer in the table and removed a plastic case with orange earplugs. "They're unused, I assure you. The whisper wraiths are intent on disturbing my peace today, it seems. I doubt they'll trouble you, but better to be safe. Once you leave the premises, you'll be perfectly fine."

Sierra, Bennie, and Caleb shoved the little rubber plugs in. Sierra knew she should thank Old Crane, but all she wanted to do was snarl at him and walk away. Everything seemed grimmer now that they'd spoken, and while it wasn't his fault, she couldn't help but resent him for it.

Still — no one else had been quite so forthcoming with her, and that's what she'd always asked for. She took his warm, small hand in hers. "Thank you, Mr. Crane," she said, finding a smile. "I appreciate your help."

"Of course, dear. You carry a great weight on your little shoulders. Anything I can do to help, do let me know. You can reach me through the front desk, room 307. I don't get out much" — he rasped out another bronchial wheeze that Sierra realized was probably a laugh — "so I shouldn't be hard to find."

"Well, that was unsettling as hell," Bennie said as the A train rumbled back toward Bed-Stuy.

Sierra shook her head. "The whole entire Deck can kiss my whole entire ass."

They'd made it out of St. Agnes without being jumped by any whisper wraiths. Now the A train seemed dim and gloomy; its roars and screeches burned through Sierra's ears as they pulled in and out of station after station.

"Wish I knew what to tell you," Caleb said, shaking his head and looking even more sullen than usual. "But the old guy knows what the hell he's talking about, unfortunately."

"Feel like I'm supposed to be happy," Sierra said. "Shadow-house is Dominant, whatever that means. I'm like . . . the head of it? But all I can think of is that creepy Our Lady of the Shadows card and its skull face and . . . Ugh."

Caleb shifted in the seat so he faced her directly. "Listen, I know. But also — consider that there's a new power in you now. It's not the same as shadowshaping, even though it's connected. It's like, the shadow is within you and it's yours. You can do what you want with it. It's your power."

"Like what?"

"Give me your wrist," Caleb said. Sierra held out her arm. He took out a Sharpie and drew a single line just below her palm while Bennie watched with eyebrows raised. "Shoot it."

"¿Qué?"

"Imagine you 'shaping, but without the spirits. Just call it up from inside of you."

"Oh, just call it up. Right. No problem."

Caleb stared at her.

"Okay, okay! Sheesh." She focused on a model smiling out of a shampoo ad across from them. Then she closed her eyes and tried to look inward. Was it shadowy in there or was that just the darkness behind her lids? She couldn't tell. She opened her eyes and shoved her hand forward, flexing. The black line shot off her skin like a bullet and cut an unruly mustache across the model's face.

"Well, damn," Bennie said. "Look at that."

Caleb nodded sagely. "Each card gives its power to the person it connects to. So, the Warrior receives extra physical strength, the Hound can track folks, the Sorcerer, I think, is responsible for healing and initiation, and the Spy can track down foes. The Master card of each suit — that's you — can potentiate their powers and borrow them."

"Pretty cool," Sierra admitted. "But I'm still creeped out by the whole thing."

Caleb stood. "As you should be. This my stop. We'll get back over there soon and find out what more we can from the old guy, alright?"

Sierra nodded and gave him a dap as the train screeched to a halt and the doors flew open. "Alright, man. Stay safe out there." He waved at Bennie and was gone.

"Man . . . I dunno," Sierra said as the train pulled off again.

"Thing is . . ." Bennie said.

"I know, I know." Sierra affected Old Crane's rickety voice. *"Gravity doesn't give a damn if the egg believes in it."*

"So you gonna do what he said?"

"Match the cards to shadowshapers? I haven't decided yet. Can't help but feel like I'm playing right into someone's hands. Not Crane necessarily, just . . . the Deck's? I dunno."

In the dark windows, Sierra watched her ghostly reflection stare back at her, and tried not to think about the monster floating over the ocean hidden in her pocket.

FOURTEEN

"You good, Sierra?" Tee asked as they waited in the metal detector line on Monday morning.

"Yeah." Sierra shrugged unconvincingly, then shook her head. "Nah." She'd spent her Sunday trying to track down Mina, calling area hospitals and getting the runaround, all the while failing to ignore the Deck. Her dad had popped his head in to check on her as the sky grew dark. He'd smelled like aftershave and had his uniform pants on and a hoodie, and all Sierra felt was guilty that she wasn't spending time with her family when they needed her most. Dominic had asked the same question as Tee, but Sierra had managed to maintain her lie through his doubtful stare, then he'd shrugged and kissed her forehead and headed off to work, and Sierra nearly burst into tears.

"I feel you, sis," Tee said, lowering her voice. "Izzy had me up all hours trying to make sure she can shadowshape like a pro. That whole thing with the gold-tinged phantom had her shook, between you and me. I mean, I'm glad I could help, but I'm *spent.*"

"Damn," Sierra said.

"Anyway, is it the whole losing your grandpa that you're not totally sure you cared about thing, or the whole creepy cards thing, or the seeing Mina right after she got wasted by the cop car thing?"

Sierra burst out laughing and had no idea why. Whatever, it felt good, and she wanted to hug Tee for the unexpected gift. "All of the above, I guess."

"What kinda wack therapist are you?" Izzy demanded, poking her head between them. "Are you upset because your whole life's a hot mess, or because no one likes you, or because everyone hates you, or because dinosaurs are about to eat your whole family?"

"That's *not* what I said!" Tee yelled.

"I mean, basically."

"I didn't mind," Sierra said. "And anyway, she was spot-on with all of 'em. Tee can be my therapist any time."

Izzy rolled her eyes. "Whatevs. Cojones the only therapist I recognize. Cojo be knowin'."

"How a dog gonna be your therapist?" Big Jerome demanded from farther back in the line.

"Because he don't talk back. Just listens. That's all anyone really needs. And if a bad guy comes, he'll eat him. Boom. What therapist got ya back like that, I ask you?"

"She has a point," Bennie chimed in.

"My actual therapist," Sierra said, popping open the lid

of her coffee and inhaling deeply, "is the barista at Bedford Grind House. She's a monster."

"She kinda cute too," Tee said.

Izzy groaned. "Aka she has a pulse."

"Next!" Fenwick hollered. Tee stepped up to the metal detector and started taking off her bracelets. "You know, young lady, if you would just wear less jew —"

"If you promise to wear deodorant," Tee said, "I'll wear less jewelry. Deal?"

The line erupted with hoots and laughter.

Fenwick just shook his head and waved her through. Sierra passed Tee her coffee and took off her own jangling bracelets.

"Any time now, Ms. Santiago. The whole line is waiting to get to class."

"If you were really worried about people getting to class on time," Sierra said, "you'd take out these useless machines and just let us go into our own school without feeling like criminals."

For a moment, Fenwick's whole face seemed to crumple. Sierra thought he might cry. Instead, he just nodded, pulling himself back together, and waved her through.

"What's going on with Fenwick today?" Sierra whispered to Tee as they waited for the others in the mezzanine. "He gone soft on us?"

Tee shook her head. "Man, I dunno, but it's weirding me out. I almost feel bad clapping back at him."

"Let's not get ahead of ourselves," Sierra said as Fenwick waved Izzy through the metal detector with a surly grunt.

"Trejean, are you with us?" Ms. Rollins said, just as Sierra was reaching across the aisle to wake Tee up.

"Huh?" Tee said, blinking her eyes open and wiping drool off her face. "Yeah! I been with ya. The Treaty of Versailles, 1919!"

Ms. Rollins chuckled. "Correct date, but you're about four modules and two centuries ahead of the rest of the class."

Tee dapped Sierra and smiled. "Cuz I got it like that."

"And that was the third time you've fallen asleep this period. Something going on?"

"Nuh-uh, just tired, Ms. Rollins. My bad."

"Yeah, you can tell me all about it during study hall next period."

The class let out a chorus of *oooh*s.

"Now, now, I'm not sending Trejean to detention, I'd like to point out. Trying something new here, okay? You can spend your free period in here with me, alright? No letter home, no conversation with the headmaster. We'll see how that works."

"Great," Tee said, still squinting in the bright classroom lights. "I'm with it."

Sierra tried to ignore the empty chair beside her where Mina usually sat. At least this time she had *some* idea where the girl was, for better or worse. She snuck a glance at her phone. One message. It was from a 917 number she didn't recognize.

Auditorium, the message said simply. *Whenever you have a moment.*

It was so polite! Maybe it was Mina? Or . . . a trap. Or Mina setting a trap. She considered texting back to ask who it was, but instead just slipped her phone away and looked up at Ms. Rollins.

"Where were we, guys?" Ms. Rollins asked. "Ah yes, the good ol' US Constitution!"

Sierra stood at the back of the Octavia Butler High auditorium. A velvet carpet ran down the center aisle, bracketed by row after row of uncomfortable wooden seats where Sierra and her friends had squirmed on their first day of high school while Korval had given them the "Look to your left, look to your right" speech.

The vast hall was completely empty, except for someone who must've been sitting at the grand piano on stage. A gentle melody sounded, tentative like someone walking on tiptoe, and low. Sierra walked a few steps down the aisle, marking the wooden seats with chalk as she went. Behind her, a small battalion of spirits stood waiting. She felt strangely at peace. The melody seemed to gather confidence and grow hopeful as it reached its end, then it cycled back to the top note and became shy again, a lost lover, a desperate suitor.

She tapped each chalk line as she made it, felt the spirits seep through her. Then she nodded ahead and watched them slide along the carpet toward the stage. She kept her pace even and let the piano notes swirl around her as the remaining spirits longstepped across the rows of seats, closing in on the hidden pianist.

"Sierra?" Anthony's head poked up from behind the grand piano and the melody stopped.

A huge smile blossomed across Sierra's face without permission. "Anthony?" She waved the spirits off, keeping her hand below where he could see. "What are you doing here? More importantly, why'd you stop playing?" The room seemed suddenly empty without that gentle song prancing along through the air.

Anthony held up his hands. "Sheesh! Tough crowd!" He sat back down and resumed playing. "I stopped playing cuz I heard someone come in, and I was hoping it was you."

"You texted me?" She climbed the stairs up to the stage and sat down at the piano next to Anthony, enjoying his familiar smell, the chance to be close to him.

"Yeah, got your number from your brother. Sorry, shoulda asked."

"It's cool," Sierra said. So cool. All the troubles that had been swirling around her slipped away. The boy must be magic. "You know the words to that little number or you just gonna keep playing the bass line over and over?"

"Ha. I was trying to make sure I had it right. Wait, let me get the right hand in there." He bounced his fingers over some keys midway down the piano, chiming in with curt, playful chords in between each downbeat. It sounded like ska.

"*It's been a long time,*" Anthony crooned in his rich vibrato. "*Something something on my mind.*"

Sierra laughed. "I'll take it!"

From somewhere, the bell for next period toned. The world of cold linoleum halls and a million bustling teenagers seemed a hundred miles away.

"*And now I see . . . something something here with me.*"

"Best lyrics ever, though, seriously."

"Help me out on the chorus," he said, squinting at the keys in concentration.

"Oh, no, man, I can't sing. You'll never look at me the same way, trust."

"Do it!" Anthony laughed. "I promise I won't care. Here it comes!"

"*Stir it up,*" they sang together. "*Li-ttle da-rling'.*"

"That wasn't so bad!" he said. "Really."

"Just keep playing while I hide my face."

He let the notes cycle back to the one, that single note

sliding into the next, then darting back, tumbling forward again and then unspooling into a happy strut up the keys.

Sierra tried not to swoon. "So, you just decided to show up at my school and brighten a girl's day? How did you even get past security?"

"I usedta go here, you know. I'm cool with Fenwick and them. Actually, to be honest, I used to sell Fenwick weed back when I was doing that kinda thing."

"Weed? Fenwick?" Sierra busted out laughing. "That's classic! I shoulda known."

"Mmhmm." Anthony kept playing and Sierra just closed her eyes and let the notes sweep over her.

"Can I ask you something?" she said.

"Anything."

"What do you do? When it happens . . . The panic?"

"Oh." He stared at the keys and for a few seconds just tumbled along the gentle bass line.

"Sorry," Sierra said. "I shouldn't've . . ."

"No, I'm glad you did. I am. It's just . . . Doesn't mean it's easy to talk about."

The notes tinkled to a stop. Sierra cringed. She'd broken the moment.

"But I'll try," Anthony said. "Usually I just lock myself somewhere and try to wait it out. I don't like to . . . No one really knows. 'Cept your brother. If he's around, he helps me."

The idea of Juan as a healer — not just any healer, but

the *one* person in the world Anthony could go to — was a whole new side of him. "What does he do?"

"Just stays with me. Hard to explain. It's grounding, to have someone you know won't judge you just be there. That's it, really. Then we're cool, business as usual."

"Do you guys have a secret code?"

"Huh?"

"Like, when it's happening. Like, do you walk past him all smooth and whisper 'Pandabutt' all cool like? And then he knows?"

Anthony let out a belly laugh and it echoed up and down the auditorium. Sierra wanted to curl up inside it. He laughed like someone who had never known shame.

"You could hit me up sometime," Sierra said as Anthony started playing again. He watched his own fingers on the keys, smiling now. "If Juan isn't there, I mean. If . . . if you feel safe doing that."

He met her eyes. "Maybe I will."

TEE!

Sierra glanced around. Spirits ran out of the shadows of the auditorium, all breaking for the far door.

TEE! TEE!

The song stumbled to an abrupt end. "What's wrong, Sierra?"

Their call bleated urgently inside her head; it rose up from all around the school. Two school security officers sprinted past the windows to the hallway. Sierra stood.

Caleb had said the cards could gift someone their powers; had Tee somehow . . .

TEE!

"I gotta . . . Something's happening. I gotta go." She ran to the edge of the stage, then turned and looked Anthony full in the face. "I'm sorry. I know this seems weird . . . It's . . . I'll call you?"

He smiled sadly. "Please."

TEE!! A collective outcry, louder than the others.

Sierra jumped off the stage and ran.

FIFTEEN

Sierra charged down the corridors, the spirits sprinting in long strides beside her. Another security officer ran past, then two more. *What the hell had happened?* Students pressed their faces against classroom windows.

She rounded a corner and saw Tee, her back pressed up against a glass display case, a circle of five school cops around her. Everyone was yelling. Ms. Rollins's classroom door hung half off its hinges, a huge dent in the middle, the glass shattered. Ms. Rollins herself stood nearby, waving her hands around and crying: "This is not what I meant to happen! Everyone just calm down! Calm down!"

No one paid her any mind. Tee had a wild look in her eyes; she was cradling her right hand like she'd just . . . Sierra looked back at the door. Had she . . . ? But how could she? "Tee," she yelled. "Tee, it's me! What . . . what happened?"

"Get back!" Officer Fenwick yelled. "Everyone back!"

Tee locked eyes with Sierra, shook her head. "I don't even . . . I don't . . ."

The card.

Caleb had said when a card locked with someone, it granted them the physical powers associated with the image. Had the Knight of Shadows somehow given Tee superhuman strength?

A few more students ran up, watching and yelling at the school cops.

"Everyone back! Calm down!" Fenwick shouted. "Calm the hell down, goddammit!"

Pitkin, a short kid in Sierra's year, pulled out his cell phone and started filming. The school cops looked back and forth at each other like they were about to bum-rush Tee.

"Tee, be cool!" Sierra yelled. "Don't fight them!" As far as she knew, they already thought Tee was some superhuman monster. If she actually could overpower them, it would only go worse for her.

"Be cool?" Tee yelled. "You see these guys being cool?"

"I know, I know, but trust me, just —"

At some unseen signal, three of the cops blitzed, grabbing Tee in a messy, chaotic embrace.

"Hey!" the whole crowd of kids yelled at once. Sierra felt the breath leave her body just watching it. Tee came down hard, one arm pinned behind her back, the other wrapped around one of the cops. Two fell on top of her.

"Mace!" one of them yelled.

Sierra screamed, "No! Tee! Don't . . . Tee!"

Suddenly, Izzy was beside Sierra. Her eyes were closed, her hands steepled in front of her face, her lips opening and closing around silent words. Rhymes. Shadows gathered on either side of her, began to materialize.

"Izzy, no!" Sierra yelled. "Stop!"

Izzy opened her eyes and glared at Sierra. "They're attacking my baby, Si! I gotta . . ."

"I know," Sierra said, "but what you gonna . . . what . . ." She shook her head — no words made sense. And then something heavy and solid rammed into her from the side and she was shoved out of the way as a school cop barreled past, swinging at Pitkin.

"Gimme that!" Officer Branson snarled. "Turn that shit off!"

Pitkin kept filming, running backward.

"Turn it off, I said!"

Pitkin tossed the camera to one of his buddies just as Branson lunge-tackled him.

"Get off him!" Pitkin's friends yelled. A few more officers joined the fray.

A sharp tanginess suddenly filled the air. Blinking back tears, Sierra and Izzy turned to where the officers were still holding Tee down. A nasty orange haze hung over the fray, and Sierra watched through the stinging gloom as a school cop blasted a final shot of pepper spray in Tee's face.

"No!" Sierra and Izzy both yelled, running forward. Two school safety officers blocked their way, shoving them back. Somewhere, Ms. Rollins was still wailing that she hadn't meant for any of this to happen. A form came hurtling out of the throng of body parts on top of Tee — one of the cops. He skidded across the floor and lay sprawled out half-way down the hallway.

"Tee, don't fight them!" Sierra yelled. The other officers stared after the one who'd been tossed.

"Cuff her!" Fenwick yelled. "And get her out of here! And who used that Mace?" Everyone was squinting through the nastiness.

"Iz!" Tee yelled, tears streaming down her face. "Babe!"

"I'm here, babygirl! I'm right here!"

The cops heaved Tee to her feet and started shoving her toward the stairwell.

"Iz! What's happening? Where they taking me?"

"We gonna find out, babe. We gonna come get you! Don't worry, okay? I'll call ya mama and them!"

"Stay back!" Fenwick yelled. "Everyone clear the hall!" Sierra and Izzy and a few other students followed them down the corridor, and then the cops holding Tee went down a stair-well and were gone. The remaining cops scooped up Pitkin and dragged him off too as students jeered and cursed at them.

Sierra turned to see Ms. Rollins standing behind her. "I didn't . . ." she moaned. "I didn't mean for any of this . . . to happen." She shook her head back and forth, watery eyes staring off at the dispersing cluster of students.

"What happened?" Sierra demanded, trying to control the growl in her voice. "What did you do?"

"We were talking . . . I asked her why she couldn't stay

awake in class and . . . I told her she could talk to me." She looked at Sierra, her bottom lip quivering. "You know you guys can talk to me, I always say it. And I mean it. But there's also certain things I *have* to report, it's not up to me. We're mandatory reporters, you know."

"And?"

"She was talking about seeing spirits. Like, ghosts. Dead people, Sierra."

Sierra's fists tightened.

"When a student admits to an untreated psychological disorder, which hallucinations are a symptom of, I have no choice but to —" She looked suddenly past Sierra. Izzy stood there, eyes closed, whispering into her steepled hands again.

Sierra pushed Izzy's hands down. "Not now, Izzy," she whispered. "We gotta figure out what happened and get Tee back. *That's* not gonna help us."

Izzy grunted and fell back, still muttering to herself.

"You called school safety on her," Sierra said to Ms. Rollins.

Rollins nodded and blew her nose into a wet tissue. "But I didn't . . . I didn't think . . . How could I . . . ?"

"If you had even the slightest clue how shit works," Sierra growled, "you wouldn't have to think, you would *know* that that wasn't gonna go well for anyone and that you didn't *have* to call security on a perfectly . . ." She ran out of words. She was too angry to speak. "Forget it. Where did they take her?"

Rollins looked up like it had never occurred to her to ask such a question. "Oh! I mean . . . Woodhull, I suppose. That's the closest city hospital with a psych ward."

"A psych ward?" Izzy yelled. "Are you out of your goddamn mind?"

"Now listen." Rollins's voice veered from broken to hyper-reasonable in seconds flat. "There's no need to —"

"We're out," Sierra said, pulling Izzy along with her as she stormed off. "Thanks for getting our friend locked up and Maced. Good to know we can tell you anything."

"I didn't . . ." Rollins started, but her voice just trailed off.

"What the hell, Sierra?" Izzy yelled as they burst out the front doors of Octavia Butler High.

"Iz, the Deck —" She flailed her arms around uselessly — where to even begin?

Izzy glared at her. "What about it?"

"I think the card Mina gave Tee the other night —"

"The Knight of Shadows or whatever?"

"Right — I think it somehow gave her supernatural strength. It's how the Deck works. That's why she could hurl that security guard across the hallway."

"Good!" Izzy yelled. "She gonna need it. Shoulda hurled them all!"

"And then what? She'd be headed to prison, not a psych

ward. Or *dead*. You know that! You saw how they were attacking her."

"How else she gonna defend herself if she don't have superhuman strength? They were coming at her like that before she tossed any of 'em. They don't care! We just animals to them, Si."

"Iz . . ."

"And now they takin' her to Woodhull, *they say*. If she even makes it there alive. Nah, we gotta get there and make sure she okay. And we gotta figure out how to get in once we there. We can't . . . That's my . . ."

All Izzy's rage dissolved into tears and she buried her head in Sierra's jacket and bawled.

"I know, Iz, I know . . . I'm sorry," Sierra whispered, rubbing Izzy's back.

"Hey!" They both turned to see Mr. O'Leary storming out of the front doors behind Branson and two other school safety cops. The officers were carrying something between them that Sierra couldn't make out. "Come back here! That boy is hurt," O'Leary yelled. "You can't . . . He needs medical attention."

A crowd of students bustled after them, yelling and cursing. The cops kept walking, and now Sierra realized they were carrying Pitkin's slumped-over body. His arms were handcuffed behind his back and blood speckled his forehead and pink button-down shirt.

"You guys filming this?" O'Leary said, taking out his own cell phone and raising it.

Bennie and Big Jerome and a few of the other students had been recording; more started now. Sierra and Izzy ran over as a chant rose up: "Free Pitkin! Free Pitkin!"

An NYPD cruiser pulled up to the curb, and the mustached sergeant Sierra had seen the night Mina got hit stepped out, frowning at the scene. "What's this?"

Two more cruisers screeched up behind him, lights flashing.

"This student attacked us and resisted arrest, Sergeant Valdez," Branson said. "He gotta go to the precinct."

"He's injured," Valdez said. "He's bleeding. You can't bring him to us like this, you know that."

Branson flinched. "*I'm* injured, Sergeant. He was just scuffed up while resisting —"

A tense argument ensued, the cops growling at each other in lowered voices as students gathered around, yelling, and more officers arrived to hold them back. Sierra noticed shadow spirits skirting around the edge of the crowd with long strides; a few of them had black hoodies on, but she didn't see Vincent.

Finally the students let out a cheer as an ambulance rolled up; the medics collected Pitkin, and an officer jumped in to ride along. They sped off toward Woodhull, sirens wailing. Sergeant Valdez shook his head at the whole situation and squeezed back into his cruiser.

A light rain began falling.

"This the shit I'm talking about," Izzy said, wiping her eyes. "This . . . We gotta get to Tee, Sierra. *Now*."

"I know, I know, let's go."

"To Woodhull!" someone shouted. "Wood-hull! Wood-hull!" The chant picked up and spread. Sierra looked around, mouth hanging open. The crowd had quadrupled around her. Angry students spilled out into the street, talked heatedly about other times this had happened, updated what was happening on their phones.

"Guess we ain't the only ones going there," Sierra said as the crowd lurched into motion, screaming as one: "Pit-kin! Pit-kin!"

"Yeah, but they ain't going there for Tee," Izzy said. "This is messed up."

"What happened to Tee?" Bennie panted, running up beside them with Jerome.

"That's what started this whole thing!" Sierra said. "Ms. Rollins got her to open up about the spirits and then called security to take her for a psych eval."

"Daaaaaamn," Jerome growled. "That's low."

"Ugh!" Bennie yelled.

Sierra started pushing toward the front of the crowd. "We gotta let 'em know."

The Wild Seeds, Butler High's marching band and step squad, had ganked their coach's megaphone and were leading the charge as the steppers fell into a hot routine at the front of the line.

"*Free-dom! For Pit-kin!*" Trey Washington hollered through the megaphone as the crowd echoed. Trey always looked way too old for high school, like he'd maybe been kept back a decade. He had a little goatee and was bulky for a basketball player. But Sierra had demanded his ID once and he'd been born a few months after her. "Most people get fake IDs to pass for older," Izzy had said. "You weird on all counts, dude." Today he was in his element, a born leader. Once the crowd fell into a steady rhythm of "Free-dom! For Pit-kin!" Trey blurted out improvised lines in between the chanting. The drumline picked up at the very back of the march — they'd run back to their lockers to get their stuff just as everyone took off toward Woodhull, and were only now catching up.

"Yo, yo, yo!" Sierra yelled, running up to Trey. "Bruh, it's not just Pitkin, man. Tee got hauled off too!"

"Yo, Trey doing his thing right now!" a tall kid named Gary yelled. "Fall back, girl!"

"You fall back," Izzy snarled, getting up in his face. "*Gary.*" She spat his name out like it tasted nasty in her mouth. Bennie and Jerome came up beside her.

Trey put down the megaphone and leaned in to Sierra. "What'd you say, sis? It's loud up here!"

"I said, you need to give Izzy the megaphone for one hot sec! Tee got roughed up too! It's not just Pitkin!"

"This some bullshit," Gary huffed, staring down Izzy.

"*Free-dom! For Pit-kin!*" the crowd yelled.

Trey thought for a sec, looking out at the crowd, and

Sierra felt herself tense all over. Even though he was a cool guy, she hated that they were dependent on this one dude giving up the mic to let everyone know about Tee. It wasn't fair. Finally, he shrugged and handed Izzy the megaphone. "Tell 'em 'bout it, sis."

Izzy took it without looking at him. "Yo, stream this to Hoozit." She handed Sierra her phone.

Sierra boggled at it. "Hoozwhat?"

"Gimme," Bennie said, rolling her eyes. She immediately clicked open an app and held the phone up horizontally to Izzy's face.

"Thanks, girl." Izzy smiled. "I dunno what I was thinking."

Before Sierra could respond, Izzy raised the megaphone. "Yo yo yo! Everyone hold up a minute, yo! Hold up, hold up!"

The drumline at the back shut up as the march ground to a halt. "What the deal?" someone called angrily.

"Yeah, what's going on?"

"Let's go!" Gary yelled. He tried to keep moving but came back when he realized he was all by himself.

"Alright, now that y'all calmed down," Izzy said into the megaphone, "listen up! My girl Tee got roughed up by the school safety grunts too, okay? That's what started this whole damn thing!"

Folks hissed.

"Okay! And listen, y'all: They *Maced* her! Okay?"

Boos erupted.

"Like . . . I don't even know if you allowed to Mace somebody if you a school safety officer."

"You're not!" Mr. O'Leary yelled.

"Thanks, Mr. O. See, you not! So I'm saying: Yeah, we want freedom for Pitkin! But we gotta raise up Trejean's name too, you feel me?"

Most of the crowd erupted into cheers, though a few dudes up front were still grumbling, Sierra noticed.

"An' if you got a problem with her cuz we gay, come see me. The King'll sort you out!" Izzy flashed a winning grin. "And remember if you come at the King, better come correct."

"Tre-jean!" the crowd yelled as the march picked up again. *"Pit-kin! Free-dom!"*

Sully Bradwick appeared at the front of the crowd. "What can I do, Sierra?" he yelled over the chanting.

Sierra looked out across the crowd. Besides Sully and Mr. O'Leary, it was still almost all black and brown kids marching. "Text all the white kids you know," Sierra said. "Tell 'em to get out here."

"Okay!" Sully said.

"You gotta tell the whole world that white kids ain't cool with this shit either," Jerome said. "Let 'em know!"

"On it!" Sully said.

"Tre-jean! Pit-kin! Free-dom!"

Up ahead, Woodhull's concrete, prison-like façade loomed.

SIXTEEN

"I'm afraid that's all confidential information," the lady at the front desk of the psych wing said flatly.

Sierra stepped off to the side and closed her eyes. Outside, the chanting and drumming blazed on in a muted growl.

"You can't even tell us if she here or not?" Izzy said. "Like, a yes or no?"

"I'm afraid not."

"You don't look afraid," Bennie muttered.

"Excuse me?"

The pristine linoleum corridors of the Woodhull psych ward flew past in Sierra's mind's eye. Two of the Black Hoodie spirits, little Tolula Brown and a woman in her twenties named Alice, whizzed around corners and up stairwells, searching each name tag and sullen face for Tee.

"All we wanna know is if she here," Izzy said. "Can you, like, wink twice if she is and wipe your nose if she ain't? That way you ain't *really* saying one way or the other, feel me?"

"I'm afraid," the lady said again, "that won't be possible."

Most of the psych patients looked more stressed out than anything else. A few yelled, some talked quietly to themselves, but it wasn't the eccentric madhouse most movies showed. One whole wing had people strapped to their gurneys, staring up at the blank ceiling. Sierra shuddered.

"Let's do a hypothetical," Bennie tried. "Can we do that?"

"By all means."

"Let's say our friend was taken out of Octavia Butler High over in Bed-Stuy for a psych evaluation because a teacher thought she was hallucinating. Would she be brought here?"

"In theory, there is a strong probability that would be the case, yes."

"What floor and room would she theoretically be brought to?" Izzy asked.

"Nice try," the receptionist said.

"What if she got Maced?" Jerome asked. "She'd still come here?"

The swirl of linoleum hallways and worn faces suddenly ground to a halt in Sierra's mind. *What is it, Alice?*

A face, came the reply. *Not Tee, but . . . someone else.*

The view circled back, then into a mostly bare patient room. Just a bed with an old man sitting on it, reading. Alice swooped down to give Sierra a clear view.

"Oh, no," the receptionist said. "In that case, the patient would have to be cleared in the ER first, *then* come here."

"Boom," Jerome said. "You're welcome. Let's go."

"Thanks for your help," Izzy said to the receptionist. "I guess."

Sierra gasped.

"What is it?" Bennie said.

She shook her head. "I gotta . . . I gotta . . . You guys go without me. I'll catch up. I gotta see 'bout something."

"Sierra, really?" Izzy growled.

"Yes. Trust me. I'll be with y'all in a sec."

Izzy rolled her eyes and headed off toward the elevators. "You aight?" Jerome asked.

"I'm fine, man, thanks," Sierra said. "Just go 'head."

"I'm staying with you," Bennie said. "Jerome, go with Iz, we'll catch up."

He scowled at them, then shrugged and followed Izzy to the elevators.

Bennie and Sierra stepped away from the reception area, ducking into a little waiting room. "What is it?" Bennie asked.

"We going in, B. You'll see when we get there."

"But . . . how? This place on lockdown."

"You forget we shadowshapers? C'mon."

Getting past the front desk turned out to be pretty simple: Sierra unleashed a few chalk goblins and sent them to wreak havoc in the staff lounge. A few minutes later, a coffeepot exploded and the microwave started beeping out the melody of "When Doves Cry." The receptionist glared at them, pushed a button, and then hurried around the corner to see what the commotion was. A security guard followed soon after.

"Uncle Neville would be proud," Bennie said, dapping Sierra.

"He would be if he wasn't busy getting busy with Nydia O."

"Say what?"

"Just a hunch. Anyway, c'mon!"

They rounded the hallway where the security guard had come from, turned another corner, and came up against a set of locked double doors. A little keypad sat on the wall, blinking softly.

"Damn," Sierra said.

"I'm gonna . . ." Bennie started. "I wanna . . ."

"What?"

"Imma try something, okay? Don't make fun of me if it doesn't work."

Sierra stepped back. "I would *never*! Usually. Anyway, do it quick, girl."

A spirit longstepped down the corridor toward them: Alice. She was tall and walked with her hands tucked into her hoodie. Bennie glanced at her, then pulled out a Sharpie. "Okay," she said, breathing heavily. "Alright." She drew a thick black line on the gray wall beneath the keypad, then crossed it with three smaller lines and sketched a spiraling circle at the bottom.

Sierra cocked her head at it but didn't say anything.

Bennie glanced back at Alice, nodded, then raised her right hand and put her left one against the symbol. Alice covered the last few steps between them in seconds, dove forward, and vanished into Bennie. Bennie shuddered, and then her drawing shot upward into the keypad.

"Yo," Sierra whispered.

Bennie shook her head. "Hold up, that wasn't even the — just . . . wait for it." The keypad suddenly let out a mechanical burp and then sparks sizzled out of it. "Whoa!"

The door flew open.

"Yo!" Sierra gasped.

Bennie shrugged with mock nonchalance. "I been practicing at home some."

They caught glimpses of patients as they passed rooms on either side of the corridor: a man watching TV, another scribbling frantically at his desk, someone in a wheelchair looking out a window at the gray sky over Brooklyn.

"Here," Sierra said.

Bennie gaped at the name on the door. "Sierra!"

"I know. I know. And yes, I'm sure. He might know something about the Sorrows or the Deck. We gotta try."

They peered in the window. Dr. Jonathan Wick sat on his bed, staring at his hands. His emaciated body was still ravaged from the inner thrashing the spirits had dealt him at Sierra's bidding. He was in his thirties, and had looked it when he first started coming around the shadowshapers, learning their magic from Lázaro. He'd had a big mess of brown hair and a young face, a gentle smile. Now, he sat hunched over himself, a line of drool dangling from his toothless mouth.

Sierra felt a pang of guilt. She had done this to him, turned him into a gaping shadow of himself. But he had killed and kidnapped people she loved, had tried to kill her. She shook her head, scowling at her own thoughts. "Does your shadowshaping work on mechanical stuff too or just electronics?"

"Maybe? Lemme see." Bennie sketched another quick symbol. This one looked more archaic — jagged, ornate lines crossed the center and gear teeth protruded from the circle. Tolula Brown swam down the hallway toward them.

"You ever notice how all these spirits be wearing hoodies recently?" Bennie said.

Sierra shrugged, hating herself for keeping secrets from her best friend. "I guess."

Bennie touched the drawing and raised her hand as Tolula dove toward her. The symbol spun in a figure eight along the wall and then slid into the lock. It clicked.

"You're a genius," Sierra said.

Wick looked up, his sunken-in eyes twitching.

"Greaggghh," he gurgled, falling backward on the bed and trying to scramble away.

"Wick!" Sierra hissed, stepping into the room with Bennie. "Relax! We're not here to hurt you. Close the door, B."

The door clicked shut and Wick turned to face them. He wiped saliva from his lips with the back of his hand and let out a long, shivering sigh. "You did this," the broken anthropologist seethed. "Now you've come to m-m-m-mock me in my pathetic state. Bah!" He glared at his hands again.

"I —" Sierra tried to push back the tide of guilt rising up in her. She hadn't come to mock him, and she *definitely* hadn't come to be lectured on morality by a killer. "We're not here for that. We need to know about the Deck of Worlds."

Wick snapped his head up, focusing his twitchy eyes on Sierra. "Aha . . . hahaha . . ." he chortled. "So it's come to this. Of course, the Sorrows would try to make a play with the Deck. They're running out of moves."

"You were . . . part of this? Part of their house?"

"Mmhmm, I was their spy. The Spy of Light. More appropriately known as the Shining Savant."

The Deck glowed gently in Sierra's hands. She didn't even remember taking it out.

"You *have* it?" squealed Wick.

She unwrapped it and shuffled quickly through until she spotted the card with the sly-looking man in a bird mask and a feathered hat. He wore a golden cape and waved a bloodied cane blade as he glanced to the side. Behind him, rain fell over a dark city. "This," Sierra said, holding up the card.

Wick slid off the bed and landed on his knees. Sierra and Bennie stepped back. "Give," he pleaded. "Give . . . Just let me . . . let me see."

"So you can try to click with it again and get its powers? Nah." She pocketed the Deck.

"Stupid girl!" Wick spat. "You still don't even understand your own powers. So much you don't understand."

Sierra fought off the urge to kick him square in the face. *Of course* there was so much she didn't understand. No one would frickin' *talk* about this stuff. "You think I want to be here, talking to your ass? Tell me what the Sorrows are up to."

"There's no more magic in me," Wick whispered. "*You* took care of that!"

"Well, you were trying to kill my family. And you killed Manny, and . . ."

"Manny the fat newspaper man?" Wick narrowed his eyes. "That one is not on me. He was gone when my haint showed up to collect his body."

"That's a lie!" Sierra yelled. Bennie nudged her to quiet down. "Your haint chased me from inside Manny's corpse!"

"Of course, of course, but we didn't remove his soul from his body, is all I'm saying. His body was there when we arrived, but his spirit was gone."

"What?" Bennie and Sierra said at the same time.

Wick shrugged, clearly enjoying having the upper hand. "He must've known we were coming and skittered off somehow, transplanted his spirit somewhere else. Or perhaps he just let it vanish into the ether . . ."

Sierra and Bennie traded a glance. Sierra had always wondered why Manny's spirit had never appeared, but there didn't seem to be much logic to who showed up after they died and who didn't. She'd figured the throng haint had probably destroyed his spirit when it took over his body.

"Or maybe the Hound of Light got to him first," Wick said. "I know they'd sent it out to find Manny."

"Was it — did you see the Hound?" Sierra asked.

Wick looked around as if it might be right there in the room, then seemed to return to himself. "I don't know. The Sorrows never let me see the other minions of light. But . . . there was a giant dog in that yard behind the church when Manny died — the beast from the Junklot — and we assumed he was the Hound."

Sierra had to keep herself from gasping. "Cojo? He can't be . . . No."

"I only know what I saw," Wick muttered.

"What does the spy card mean?" Bennie asked. "What powers did you get from it?"

"Think about it: What does a spy do?" Wick sneered.

Sierra and Bennie stared daggers at him.

He sighed. "The power of infiltration. It's how I was able to be initiated as a shadowshaper even though I belong . . . belonged originally to the House of Light. As the Spy, I could hide the light in me from Lázaro when he made me a shadowshaper."

"Hmph," Sierra said.

"But I was only with the Sorrows because they initiated me first, Sierra. You have to believe I only ever did what I did —"

"I don't *have* to do anything, Wick."

"I just . . . I only ever meant to help. I know I failed, but I tried. I . . . My intentions were pu —"

"You can put your intentions back in ya ass where you found 'em," Sierra said.

"Because they're shit," Bennie added unnecessarily.

They turned to the door and were halfway into the hall-way when Wick smirked: "That was always your problem, Sierra. You never stop to listen to anyone else."

Sierra stopped. Turned.

"No. *My* problem right now is that people are trying to kill my loved ones and take what's mine. That was *also* my problem back when it was you trying to do that, and I crushed you. If people'd just stay out my way, I'd be good."

Wick slid off the bed, landing on his knees. "Sierra, I'm so —!"

She slammed the door on his apology.

SEVENTEEN

"Yo, the *nerve*!" Bennie growled as they made their way through the ER, past writhing, moaning patients. "For *him* to tell *you*, of all people . . . Nah. I just . . . Nah!"

"I know," Sierra said. "But Manny . . . What you think?"

Bennie made a face. "Can we believe anything that maniac says, though?"

"Wick lies to himself more than anyone else," Sierra pointed out. "That denial runs deep. But I don't know why he'd bother making up something like *that*. And what if Manny's like . . . out there somewhere? Or trapped somehow — by the Sorrows, maybe? I mean, why else wouldn't he show up?"

"Beats me."

"And Cojo . . ." Sierra let her voice trail off. She didn't even want to contemplate the thought that the giant beast might somehow be spying on her for the Sorrows.

"Hey mama hey mama hey mama hey mama," some old guy called from his bed. He wore a disposable yellow gown and his eyes never settled. A cop stationed next to him just shook her head and went back to texting. "Hey mama hey mama."

Bennie waved. "Hello, my son."

"Can you *not*?" Sierra said, pushing away a laugh. "He gonna think you want to take him home with you."

Bennie flashed a winning smile.

"Hey," Sierra said, stopping in her tracks. "You shadow-shaped ya ass off back there, girl."

Bennie covered her face. "I mean . . . I'm still getting the swing of it!"

"No, B. You *got* the swing of it, clearly. And it ain't just electronics or mechanics, you come in digital too? What kinda magic is this?"

"I know, right? I could barely believe it myself!"

"Believe it, girl. You something brand-new in the streets. A techshaper or something. I don't even know!"

"Shoot," Bennie said. "Oh snap, there go Tee now."

They hurried to the far end of the emergency room, where Izzy, Jerome, and Robbie stood around a stretcher. Tee had one of those yellow nighties on. One hand had been cuffed to the fall guard. Her eyes were still bright red, and she looked miserable. A cop sat in a foldout chair across the aisle from her, mean-mugging everyone who passed.

"Tee!" Sierra yelled, wrapping around her. "You okay?"

"My face still burning like mad," Tee said. "They washed it like eighty times already, but ugh. And I don't know what the hell I'm doing here" — she cast a sharp side-eye at the cop, who shrugged and kept looking around — "but 'sides all that, I'm good."

"Yo, we gotta talk, y'all," Sierra said.

"I can go," Robbie said sullenly.

"No, I want you here too," Sierra said. "I'm glad you're here." She really was, although she wasn't sure how she felt about that. Plus, she would probably need his help for whatever was about to happen next.

"This haveta do with why you decided something in the psych ward was more important than seeing Tee?" Izzy demanded.

Tee put a hand on Izzy's. "Ease up, Iz. It's cool."

"Wick was there," Bennie said. "The one and only Wick."

"Wick the dick?" Jerome said, eyes bulging.

Izzy gawked. "Wick the useless pri —"

"Yes, you guys," Sierra cut her off. "*That* Wick. Like y'all know a buncha other Wicks. And he said Manny's spirit wasn't in Manny's body when he went to kill him."

"So?" Jerome said. "He still stole his body and used it to try'n get us!"

"I know," Sierra said. "I'm just saying, it might mean Manny's out there somewhere. And he might need our help."

"Damn," Tee said. "That's scary."

Sierra took out the Deck. "There's something else." She unwrapped it as Bennie drew the curtain around them.

"Hey," the cop on Tee-duty barked.

"Relax, Turner and Hooch," Bennie said. "We just

helping her change her pants, since y'all felt the need to use chemical weapons on a teenager."

When the curtain was closed, they gathered in a tight huddle around Tee. Sierra said, "I wanted to ignore the Deck, pretend it didn't exist, but like Old Crane said, we can not believe in it all we want, it will still believe in us. And he's right. Can't keep pretending everything's cool when it's not. It's not. Look what happened to Tee."

"What *did* happen to me?" Tee asked.

"Mina gave you the Warrior card — the Knight of Shadows, right? And it clicked. It did whatever it is the Deck cards do when they find someone they like. And now it's, like . . . part of you somehow. It gave you its powers."

"That's how I threw that security guy across the hall?" Tee gaped.

Sierra nodded. "I'm pretty sure. And the whole thing is — Shadowhouse, that's us, and according to Crane, we on top right now. Somehow when I initiated y'all, it put us there officially. And the Sorrows wanna get where we are, and throwing all kindsa hell our way to make that happen."

"How come we Shadowhouse," Jerome asked, "and they get to be House of Light?"

"Cuz no one wants to be called Lighthouse, dumbass," Izzy said. "That's already a thing."

Sierra narrowed her eyes. "Y'all done? We got some important stuff to do." She pulled the food tray open across

Tee's stretcher and put the Deck on it. "I'm not exactly sure how to do this," she said, "except to just go through the Shadowhouse cards and try, like, giving 'em to each of you and see if anything happens."

They all looked doubtful.

"I'll sort through the Deck and find 'em," Bennie said, and Sierra let out a little sigh of relief.

"Thanks. And look: I know this is weird. I don't fully get it myself. But . . . I don't think we have much choice at this point."

"Here." Bennie handed her the cards and then put the rest of the Deck on the table.

"Thing is," Izzy said, "none of 'em gonna be as dope as the Knight of Shadows, so this isn't really fair."

"Who you telling?" Sierra put her own card on the table, face up. "This me." It still made her cringe, this monster version of herself. She knew she shouldn't take it so personally — it had been drawn a hundred years before she was born, after all — but something about it seemed to echo through her in the worst way.

"Damn," Jerome said. "You win that round. You creepy as hell, Sierra."

"Yeah," Izzy conceded. "Can't get much worse'n that."

"Thanks."

Bennie nudged Sierra. "C'mon, let's divvy 'em up and see what's what. We prolly don't have much time before someone barges in."

"Word," Tee said. "You know the privacy laws don't apply to us mental patients."

Sierra placed the next card down: the Shadow Hound. The monstrous creature glared back at them, gnawing away at the pale, blue-eyed child.

"Didn't we decide that Cojo the Shadow Hound?" Tee said. "He showed up with the card tucked into his collar an' everything. Plus, why else would he be acting all extra loyal?"

Sierra told them about Wick, how the Sorrows had used the Hound of Light to track down Manny, and how Cojo had been there when they went for him.

"So you think . . ." Jerome said.

"Cojo could be playing us?" Izzy finished. "That's low. How a dog gonna . . . And *that* dog of all the . . . Uh-uh."

"I don't know if that's what I think," Sierra said. "I'm just saying we really don't know the deal. But if this card clicks with someone" — she held up the Shadow Hound — "then we'll know for sure something's up. Here." She handed it to Bennie.

Bennie took it, eyeing it with a frown. "What happens when it clicks?"

"I dunno," Sierra said. "Tee said she felt something when Mina gave her that card."

"True."

"And I definitely had some kinda tremors happen in me when I found the Deck that night in Von King, which must've been when the Mistress of Shadows card clicked with me. Notice anything weird?"

"Hospitals smell like pee," Bennie said.

"Great. Thanks, that's helpful. Give it to Jerome."

The card went all around their small circle without any bright lights shooting out or sudden revelations.

"Alright, then," Sierra said. "Pass the other two and we'll see what happens." She pulled out the Shadow Sorcerer — a rude depiction of an old medicine man, complete with a bone through his nose and a bubbling cauldron.

"This shit racist as hell," Izzy said when it came around to her. "Who made these?"

"That's a great question," Sierra said. "And here's the Shadow Spy." The figure had dingy, yellowish skin, a hook nose, and a pointy beard. Slanted eyes glared out from behind a masquerade mask. He lurked along a dark alley, clutching a dagger and a vial of something green.

"Charming," Bennie said, taking the card.

Robbie gasped and everyone looked at him.

"What happened?" Sierra asked.

"I think I — I think something happened."

"Spit it out, Painty McGee," Izzy said.

"When Jerome passed me the Sorcerer card, I . . . It was like a . . . I dunno, like a wave of something moved through me. And little flashes . . . up my arm."

"Cast a spell, Merlin," Jerome said.

Robbie just shook his head. "I'd heard about the Deck but never really believed in it. But whoa . . ."

"Caleb said the Sorcerer does healing and initiation,"

said Sierra. "So we gonna have to see what's what with that. Anybody get anything from the Spy?"

"Nah, that's creepy," Jerome said, eyeing it and then passing it to Robbie. "The name cool, though: Shadow Spy? Like . . . Imma change my government name to that. All the fine mamis will come running."

"If it takes you changing your name to Shadow Spy to get some," Tee advised, "perhaps you should rethink just about everything."

"You guys!" Sierra said. "This isn't about which card is cool. They're all jacked up."

"Except the Shadow Knight," Izzy pointed out.

"But what matters is what powers they grant. Otherwise . . . otherwise I dunno what's gonna happen. But it ain't good. We in the thick of something much bigger than us, and I'm not even sure how we got there."

"At least we on top," Jerome said. "Yeah, it means people come for us, but we where everyone else wanna be. Gotta be some good in that."

"I guess," Sierra said. She packed up the Deck. Paused. Frowned at it.

"What's wrong?" Bennie asked as Izzy put her forehead to Tee's and whispered softly to her.

"Something's maybe . . . off?" Sierra flipped the cards into her other hand one by one. "Twenty-two . . . twenty-three . . . twenty-four . . . Son of a bitch!"

"What?" Robbie said.

"Count these, please." Sierra handed Bennie the Deck.

Bennie shuffled through it in seconds and handed it back. "Twenty-four."

"Damn, you fast," Jerome said.

Sierra scowled. "We're short one. Someone . . . some-how . . . but . . ." She looked around as if the card might be dangling from the ceiling somehow. "Who? How?"

Everyone shook their heads.

"Can you figure out which one by sorting through it?" Jerome asked.

"I don't have 'em memorized," Sierra said. "Wouldn't even know . . . And half of 'em don't even have images."

"Yow, di King an' har crew!" Desmond Pocket's smiling face poked through the curtains.

"Gah!" Jerome yelled, stepping to the side. "You gotta learn to knock, man! She coulda been changing in here."

Sierra packed up the cards and tucked the Deck into her hoodie.

"Oh, zeen! Sorry 'bout dat." Desmond shrugged. "But curt'n nuh mek noise when yuh knock it still." He was wear-ing a tailored suit and carried a briefcase.

"Thanks for coming so fast," Izzy said, dapping him over Tee's stretcher.

"Yeah man, a nuh nuting big. Look, mi talk to the offi-cer dem and they know they're in the wrong." Desmond slid momentarily into what must've been his lawyerly courtroom voice. "There's no way a school safety cop suppose to have

Mace on 'em in New York City and anyway, the details of why it escalated are very suspect, if yuh get mi. So dem naa press no charges."

"*They* roughed *me* up!" Tee yelled. "*I'm* the one that should be pressing charges."

"Well, I figure that's their concern. Damage control and such. If you waan sue, we can talk 'bout dat lata. The good news is we 'ave nuff witnesses, and footage — I got Lil Aaleyah running around gathering folks' info right now. And Calyx finding out 'bout the hospital reports . . ." His voice trailed off.

"What's the bad news?" Sierra asked.

"They have to keep you for a few days' surveillance. Standard operating et cetera et cetera an' whatnot. In the psych ward."

"But I'm not . . ." Tee sighed. "I don't . . . !"

"I'm sorry, Trejean."

Tee dropped her head. Izzy rubbed her girlfriend's back and growled.

"I did di best I could," Desmond said. "They wanted to keep you a full week, but I got dem to reduce it. Anyway, lemme leave you be now. Izzy 'ave mi numba if yuh need me, any hour, yuh hear?"

Tee wiped her eyes and looked at Desmond. "Thanks, man. Means a lot. Thanks for everything."

"Yeah, man. Dis soon blow ova, you'll see."

The intercom burped as Desmond nodded his good-byes

and retreated, and then a staticky voice announced that visiting hours were over.

"You okay, Tee?" Sierra asked.

Tee shook her head. "I will be, though. You guys be careful out there, okay? I need you all in one piece when I get out."

Everyone gathered in close, reaching over the bed arms for an awkward group hug.

"Visiting hours over," the hop-cop called from the other side of the curtain. "Let's go!"

A light rain fell on the two dozen protesters still waiting outside Woodhull. Sully Bradwick had made good on his promise, and a group of about ten white students held up a banner that read, *White Kids Ain't Cool With This Shit Either.*

"Yo, y'all real literal!" Jerome laughed when he, Sierra, Bennie, Izzy, and Robbie walked through the sliding doors together. "Who gonna know what you even talking about?"

Sully shrugged.

"At least throw the word *Racist* in there before the *Shit*. You got a marker?"

"Where's everyone else?" Izzy asked no one in particular.

"A cop came outside about twenty minutes ago and said they weren't gonna press charges on Pitkin, and everyone cheered and folks started heading off."

"Right," Sierra grunted. "Never mind about Tee! Just go about your business!"

"Did I not just tell them that . . ." Izzy just shook her head. "I don't even know why I bother sometimes."

"How she doing?" Sully asked.

"She'll live," Izzy said.

Bennie grabbed Sierra's arm. "Yo." She nodded at something across the street. Sierra turned. Cojo stood outside the bodega beneath the train tracks. He was sitting on his haunches, staring at them. Passersby kept their distance.

Sierra shook her head. "I can't . . . Okay, I don't *want* to imagine that he's somehow . . . I mean, he's a *dog*, goddammit! How could . . . Ugh."

"C'mon," Bennie said. "Let's go over there."

They crossed Flushing Ave, stopping to let an ambulance whoosh past, and then walked carefully up to Cojo. The gigantic dog stood, his huge tongue dangling out as he panted, dripping dollops of saliva on the pavement.

"How do we figure this out?" Bennie asked.

Sierra eyed Cojo. She'd come to trust him without second-guessing it over the past few days. He seemed like he'd fight off any foe for her, and he let her know when enemies were around. At least, it seemed like it . . . "I have no damn idea."

Cojo barked so loudly it made both Sierra and Bennie jump.

"Y'all okay?" Izzy called from across the street.

"We good," Bennie yelled.

"What is it, Cojo?" Sierra said. "Wha — wait! Wick said . . . Wick said . . . What if . . ."

"Girl, speak!"

Sierra kneeled, took the dog's big, jowly face in her hands, and tried to look in his eyes. "If the dog is our Hound, he gotta be a shadowshaper, right?"

Cojo panted, seemed to be smiling somehow.

Bennie nodded. "Right, but how does a dog become a shadowshaper?"

"Exactly. What if . . . Wick said Manny's soul wasn't there when they came for him, but —"

"Cojo was!" Bennie finished. "You think . . . ?"

"I dunno. But Imma try'n check." She closed her eyes again and placed her forehead against Cojo's, ignoring his slobbery dog breath. Colorful splotches lava-lamped over the darkness. A feeling emerged — Sierra couldn't name it, but it was pure Manny, like his essence distilled into a sensation. The smell of Bustelo and those cheap bodega cigars he loved filled her nose, and a slight faraway chuckle seemed to echo through her. Sierra looked up at Bennie and wiped some tears away. "He's in there. But it's, like, just a piece of him. Hard to explain. It's like he left a little bit of his soul with Cojo, but most of it's Cojo."

"Enough to get the dog anointed as the Shadow Hound, I guess."

Without thinking about it, Sierra wrapped her arms

around Cojo and squeezed. She hadn't had a chance to say good-bye to Manny, and the last time she'd seen his body, it was chasing her across the beach at Coney Island, a nasty cluster of spirits inside. Cojo keened and nuzzled her. "I didn't realize . . ." Sierra started, but there were so many ways to finish that sentence. In the end, she just hugged Cojo harder, flushed with memories of Manny's great big smile, his excitement about whatever local news story he was working on, his trash-talking the other domino warriors in the Junklot. Manny had been there at the beginning of it all, when Sierra had first noticed that painted tear sliding down the mural of Papa Acevedo. Sure, he hadn't been the most forthcoming about shadowshaping, but at least he'd tried to help send her in the right direction.

And now he was here, kinda. Sierra smiled at Cojo, then stood, wiped a few more tears away, and pulled out her vibrating phone. It was Caleb.

"Wassup, man?"

"Sierra, have you talked to Old Crane since you guys were at the home?"

"Nuh-uh. Why?"

"He's . . . he's gone."

Sierra's heart pounded in her ears. "Gone? But . . . how?"

"What is it?" Bennie mouthed. Sierra held up a finger.

"I don't know," Caleb said. "The staff don't know either. I went by to check on him and they were all freaking out, blaming each other. Cops were there. One of the orderlies said a tall, ashen-faced priest came to visit him, and then when the nurses passed by to check a half hour later, both men had vanished. No Crane, no priest."

"The hell?" Sierra said. "A priest? I don't get it."

"I think the Sorrows took him," Caleb said. "I don't know who else coulda."

"Not whoever sent those whisper wraiths the other day?"

"That mighta been them too. Either way, I'm heading to that cathedral the Sorrows hole up in, see what's doin'."

"Caleb, wait . . . You can't . . ." Sierra closed her eyes for a moment, felt her pulse pounding through her. *Where was the Hound of Light?* In a cluttered living room, some talk show flickered across a bright flatscreen TV. There was a bag of chips on the coffee table, a soda, and a gun. *Damn*, Sierra thought. But there wasn't time to worry about that now. What mattered was the Hound was nowhere nearby and not with the Sorrows. "We'll meet you up there."

"Oh, yeah?" Caleb sounded impressed. And a little relieved.

"Yeah. I gotta talk to the Sorrows 'bout some stuff anyway."

"Bet."

"You wanna talk to the who now?" Bennie said as Sierra hung up the call and then stared at her phone. "Wait, who you callin'?"

"Neville, see if he'll give us a ride uptown. Caleb thinks the Sorrows kidnapped Old Crane."

"They what? But Sierra, if you wanna come at the Sorrows, we gotta roll deep. How we gonna fit you, me, Iz, Robbie, Jerome, *and* this monstrosity —"

Cojo's bark echoed out into the gray afternoon.

"This beautiful, loyal monstrosity," Bennie amended, "into Neville's Caddy?"

"We just checkin' to see if Crane there," Sierra said. "We don't need the whole army with us, B."

"Why don't you ask Juan if we can borrow the Culebramobile from Pulpo?"

Sierra looked at the ground a little too quickly as she said, "Nah." Getting Anthony anywhere near this mess was the last thing she wanted to do. Plus, what if he insisted on driving and then Robbie would be there and then and then and then —

"Why not?"

"Look, Tee already said we look like the Scooby Crew running after ghosts with this big-ass hound dog, now you wanna roll around in a *van* too? A rock band van, no less? No way."

"There's something you ain't tellin' me, Si. You think you cute right now, but you ain't."

"Anyway," Sierra said, dialing her phone, "we not going to war with the Sorrows, yet. Just having a little . . . conversation with 'em."

"Whaddup, goddaughter?" Neville sounded perky as ever.

Sierra smiled. "You busy?"

"In a manner of speaking — whatchu need?"

"Gotta bop around town some and check on some things."

"I can pick you up in an hour."

"Bet. Hey, you wouldn't happen to know where Nydia is, would you?"

Bennie punched Sierra's shoulder and widened her eyes at her.

"Hang on," Neville said. "Babe, Sierra lookin' for ya."

"Oh!" Sierra hollered. "Oh damn!"

"Neville!" Nydia's voice crackled.

"Ow!" Neville yelled. "Ow, babe! Easy, easy! Here, you talk to her!"

Nydia was panting when she got on the phone. "Sierra?"

"Hey, girl! Don't let me interrupt nothin'!"

"I mean, look, I was gonna tell you!"

Sierra couldn't stop laughing. "It's cool, sis, I'm happy for you! Get you some! Shoot. Just come along when he picks me up? We're gonna need your help on something. Sorrows mighta snatched Old Crane."

"Dammit. We're on the way."

EIGHTEEN

The dim TV room flashed through Sierra's mind, pistol still on the table. Her eyes flew open. The West Side Highway whizzed past, the strains of Neville's old funk jams blasting away on the radio.

"Checking on the Hound?" Bennie asked. Sierra nodded. "What'd you see?"

"Some creepy living room. The Hound likes bad daytime talk shows. And has a gun."

"Still think it's Mina?"

"If that's whose view I was seeing through before, then it's gotta be. But she was whisked off to the hospital . . . None of this makes sense."

"So how long y'all been hitting it?" Bennie asked as Uncle Neville zipped in and out of late afternoon traffic.

Neville glanced at Nydia, who sat in the passenger seat shaking her head. "I was totally gonna tell you guys," she said.

"Since that night at the Tower," Neville said.

"I *knew* it!" Sierra shrieked. "Y'all ain't slick."

"Listen," Nydia said, twisting around to face the back-seat and then recoiling when she got a face full of Cojo breath. "Ah! Why is Cujo in the middle seat though? Put him at the window!"

"It's Cojo," Bennie said.

"And he's . . . not like other dogs," Sierra added. She didn't feel like going into the whole Manny situation with them, even if Neville, the only non-shadowshaper in the car, would probably understand.

"We gotta talk strategy," Robbie said quietly. He'd been acting all kindsa sullen and serious and Sierra understood why — it'd been a messed-up day and he was probably over-thinking whatever was or wasn't going on between the two of them — but it bothered her anyway.

"That's what I was about to say when I got asphyxiated by Dogzilla," Nydia huffed. "Sierra, if you wanna roll up on the Sorrows *again* and this time they're even more pissed, you gotta roll heavy, as Neville would say."

"Neville always roll heavy," Neville said.

Nydia patted his knee. "We know, babe."

"Alright," Sierra said. "We put Neville, at the gate like before, but this time, Bennie gonna post up with him, keep things handled on the spirit side. You good with that, B?"

"Hold down the rear guard? We can swing it," Bennie said. Neville reached a fist back without taking his eyes off the road and Bennie dapped it.

"Nydia, you, me, and Robbie gonna 'shape some

shadows and saunter up in there with 'em so they know we not there to play."

"Thought you were just gonna talk to 'em," Bennie said. "That don't sound like an invitation to talk."

"We show up looking vulnerable," Nydia said, "they'll throw what they got at us and see if they can't sweep the field. They probably won't kill Sierra, but the rest of us . . . ? Just keep your guard up, is all I'm saying."

"Agreed," Sierra said as Neville pulled off the highway and into a series of grim backstreets near the river. The rain had eased off, but night was a deepening shadow around them. Sierra tried not to think about what would happen if anyone got hurt or died in the midst of this — the very notion was enough to make her want to call the whole thing off and go home. But she knew she couldn't just pretend everything was fine; more people would get hurt that way.

"Look," Sierra said. Neville slowed the Cadillac through a puddle and pulled up at the rusted gate. "Nobody has to do this, okay? I mean, if they won't kill me, maybe I should just go myself. I don't want . . . I don't want you guys feeling pressured to come with because . . ."

"Because you don't want whatever happens to be on your head," Bennie said. "We get it. We making our own decisions, Sierra, and we in." Everyone nodded.

"And anyway, there are much worse things they can do

to you than kill you," Nydia added as they bustled out of the Caddy.

"Great," Sierra said. "Thanks."

A cadre of shadow spirits waited in front of the gate. A few of them were Black Hoodies, their faces shadowed beneath their hoods. Maybe one was Vincent. Sierra recognized other spirits who had shown up repeatedly over the past few months. They would walk into battle with her; they would do what needed to be done. She tried to find a smile through her growing unease.

"You want the ax again?" Neville offered, nodding at his trunk.

"Nah, I'm good," Sierra said. "Thanks, though."

"Uh, the gate . . . Looks like they updated the lock since our last B&E adventure." A massive steel-reinforced dead bolt clasped the gate closed. "Damn, that looks like a triple cylinder." Neville scratched his chin, eyeing it like it might pounce on him at any moment. "I can work it, but it's gonna take a minute."

"Yo, B," Sierra called. "Whatchu think?"

Bennie mean-mugged the dead bolt, then drew her Sharpie and headed toward it. "I got this."

"Well, alright!" Neville backed away with his hands raised. "Guess I'll just stand over here then."

Sierra turned to Robbie and Nydia. "Can y'all make some shapes for us?"

Robbie started to dig into his pocket for chalk, but Sierra held out her shoulder bag. "No, man, use these."

He took it and peered in, then looked back at her. "Okay, Sierra!"

Sierra smirked. She'd bought the spray paint a few weeks back on a whim.

"We in," Bennie reported as the lock fell away and the chain slid off, allowing the gates to swing creakily open.

"Nice," Sierra said. "Throw me a can, Robbie?" He underhanded her the maroon and she uncapped it, shook it, and blasted a thick line onto the pavement. It curved upward into a hood shape and then swung back down to form long, thick arms ending in clenched fists. She quick-sketched two more hooded warriors and then stood. Robbie had formed a small army of grinning green demons, and Nydia had made some fierce-looking abstract shapes with arrows and blades projecting out in every direction.

"Damn, Nydia," Sierra said. "You don't play." Shadowshaping had come quickly to the Columbia archivist since Sierra had initiated her that day on the beach; she'd said it was probably from all those years immersed in books about spirits and conjuring, but Sierra suspected it was just innate to her.

Nydia winked at Sierra, then bent down to 'shape the spirits into her paintings. Robbie was already down on one knee, his hand raised. Sierra took a second to appreciate how badass her team was, then crouched and raised her arm, slapping the fresh graffiti as each spirit dove through her and brought the hooded warriors to life. "Bennie," Sierra called. "Sharpie." Bennie tossed her the marker and Sierra drew a series of thick lines along her left forearm. Then she pulled her hair back into a bun, kissed Uncle Neville on the cheek and traded a dap with Bennie, and walked through the gate and up the path beyond as Robbie, Nydia, and a whole colorful battalion of painted spirits fell into step alongside her. Cojo barked one time at Neville and then raced off to keep up.

───────

"You don't wanna send some spirits ahead and see what's what?" Robbie asked as they passed the run-down cathedral. Faceless statues guarded the massive, graffiti-scarred doors.

Sierra shook her head. "I don't think they're expecting us, and I wanna keep it that way until we right up on 'em. Keep an eye out for lookouts."

They moved along a path around one side of the old church. Trees shuddered and loose leaves blew through the air, skittered along the ground through weeds and scattered trash. It was hard to believe they were in Manhattan, that just a few blocks away some nightclub was probably getting ready for another long night of partying and an office building was shutting down and a million people were going about their normal everyday business.

"Up there," Sierra whispered. They paused beside the

charred remains of a Jeep, just where Sierra remembered it from when she'd come in June. Up ahead, the path led down a hill toward the churchyard, where golden light radiated from a grove of pines. "The three statues are inside that copse of trees. The Sorrows worship them; they freaked when I went at 'em with Neville's ax." She met Nydia's eyes, then Robbie's. "Y'all ready?"

They nodded and headed down the hill as the painted spirits rose around them, ready for war.

A flurry of motion erupted in the grove of trees as Sierra and her crew approached the fence around the churchyard. Twelve gold-tinged shadow spirits slid out, striding in long steps toward them. The collective bristle of the 'shapers' painted warriors roiled through Sierra and she whispered: "Easy now, easy."

They could handle these gold-glowing wraiths. The Sorrows' defenders weren't 'shaped into anything, and Sierra could feel the rising ferocity of her own strength channeled into the painted figures around her. They would not be deterred. And anyway, something about the way the Sorrows' spirits hovered, their rushed appearance, was prickling at Sierra's consciousness. *They're trying to hide something.* She saw the trees beyond them shudder, but it was hard to make out anything in the gold-tinged haze.

She hopped the short rusted fence, Robbie alongside her. Nydia creaked open the rickety gate to let Cojo in, then followed him. The painted spirits breached just behind them in a single, solid line.

Sierra smiled as the Sorrows' spirits flinched back at the sight of her small army advancing. "Out the way," she grunted, approaching the center of their line. "You can't win this."

The center spirit swung its head from side to side, conferring with the others, and then Sierra just shoved through them, pushing shadows out of her way like a shimmering curtain. Beyond the row of shimmering phantoms, the three Sorrows hovered in front of their statues, huge shrouds of bright golden light against the gloomy trees. To their right, a thickly muscled man in a jumpsuit with a wrinkled face and white hair stood smoking a cigarette and glaring out at Sierra. To their left, a tall figure moved hurriedly around, tending to a much shorter, bent-over figure —

"Crane!" Sierra yelled. "What are you . . . ?"

"Sierra, no!" Crane wheezed.

The man in the jumpsuit swung his hands to either side. "You said this wouldn't happen, Crane! You said we were clear! Dammit!"

"Easy, Bertram," Crane said. "Let me handle this."

A flurry erupted behind Sierra, her hooded warriors handling the golden shadows, and then Robbie was by her side, panting.

Crane raised one hand, shaking his head. "Sierra, it's not what you —"

Two of the Sorrows hurtled toward Sierra, shrieking. She raised her arms, inhaled, and was about to send those arm drawings shooting out at them when the painted forms of Vincent's Black Hoodies stepped in front of her, blocking the Sorrows' attack. The towering golden shrouds hissed, rearing back.

"Stop!" Sierra yelled, her spirit voice booming across the churchyard. Behind her, the rustling of combat ceased. "Nydia?"

"Handling 'em," Nydia said.

Sierra stepped past her hooded warrior bodyguards. The two Sorrows that had attacked hung in the air a few feet away; she could feel their glares on her. In the copse of trees, the third Sorrow hovered beside the muscled older man called Bertram.

The tall stranger stood in front of Crane as if to block an attack from any side. The man wore all black except for a small patch of white at his throat — a priest's clerical collar. He had brown hair and a sallow face, and Sierra realized what she first thought was a hunched back was really a ream of chain draped over the man's shoulders. It was immense, much bigger than someone of his frail stature should be able to carry. He clenched one end in his hands like he could hold off the Sorrow with it.

Beside him, Crane leaned over his walker and met Sierra's glare.

"You pretend to help me," Sierra said, the fury rising in her voice, "and then treat with the Sorrows behind my back?"

Crane shook his head sadly. "Sierra, no. It's —"

"And you were friends with my grandfather, came to his *wake*. And you betray me?"

"Sierra."

She reached into her hoodie pocket and pulled out the Deck. "Over *this*?"

The Sorrows sprung forward as one, their screech a shrill, dissonant whisper in Sierra's mind: *She has the Deck!* They stopped an arm's length from where she stood, towering over her. Sierra put out a hand to keep the Black Hoodies from jumping between them.

"Sierra," Crane gasped. "I didn't tell them you had the Deck, see? They didn't know. I was trying to protect you." He said something she couldn't hear to the lanky priest, then shook his head and hocked a nasty loogie of phlegm into the dirt.

"Of course you were," Sierra scowled. "Just like you were trying to protect me when you ganked one of the cards?"

"I . . ." Crane started.

"Don't bother," Sierra said. "I see you've already found your Warrior."

Ooh, one of the Sorrows cackled, swooping in front of the other two. *You mean the old metalworker didn't mention his affiliation to you, Little Lucera? How interesting . . .*

217

Sierra had forgotten how the Sorrows' whispers slithered through her like hissing worms. She repressed a shudder. "And let me find out y'all recruiting spirits of the dead to do your dirty work." She cast a side-eye at the gold-tinged spirits facing off against her own. "I thought that was purely a shadowshaper thing."

Sinestrati have been cleansed, the head Sorrow seethed. *They are not like your filthy dead. They are purified of sin, of death, of all except their allegiance to the House of Light.*

"Charming."

Someone approaches, one of the Sorrows said.

Bertram launched forward from the tree with astonishing speed and then stopped short when the Sorrow held up a long, shimmering hand. The man looked positively ready to destroy something, his whole thick body clenched like a fist. And seeing how fast he moved, Sierra had no doubt he could inflict his fair share of damage. Everyone turned as Caleb came running over the crest of the hill toward them. "What the hell is . . . Crane?" He looked truly surprised, but Sierra had given up on trusting anyone. She nodded at Robbie and he ran up, stopping Caleb in his tracks, arms outstretched.

"Robbie?" Caleb gasped. "What gives, man?"

Sierra allowed a tiny smile to open inside her — Robbie had moved without hesitation, and Caleb had done Robbie's tats; they were the youngest of the old-school shadowshapers.

"Just hold back," Robbie said. The paintings on his arms, Caleb's own work, swirled to life and crouched at the ready.

"Why is Crane here?" Caleb said, raising his hands. "Crane, what's the deal?"

"Just be still and stay quiet, Caleb," Sierra growled. "I'm trying to sort that out myself, and I don't trust nobody right now."

"If I could just —" Crane said, his voice frail and congested.

"You stay quiet too," Sierra snapped. She turned to the Sorrow closest to her. The swirling beauty of its shroud rendered Sierra momentarily speechless. Tiny specks of gold revolved in an endless, slo-mo tornado; occasional brighter orbs of light would flash and then disappear. Somewhere, beneath it all, Sierra thought she could make out the contours of a human form, arms reaching out.

Well? it hissed.

Sierra shook off the daze. "Without riddles or games, tell me straight up what it is you want so badly."

A beat passed, then the silence extended and Sierra wondered if they were going to reply to her at all. *Smarmy powerplays*, she thought. Their power had diminished since the last time she'd come, and hers had blossomed.

Somewhere inside the Sorrow's shroud, the human form stirred, and then it spoke: *We've already told you what we want. We want what's ours.*

"The Deck."

Of course! the Sorrow hissed. *But not only that. We told you long ago, when you first came to see us. We've never concealed our intentions.*

"All you do is speak in riddles and code."

You, Lucera, you, Sierra Santiago, child of the shadows.

Sierra shook her head. "Why?"

Because you are one of us, of course. Without you, the Order of Light, the Sisterhood of Sorrows, the quadrangle, is always incomplete. We have been broken for so long, a fragment of a family. Empty. The ancient creature's voice trembled with emotion.

"No," Sierra whispered. A cool drizzle sprinkled her face. Robbie and Nydia stood on guard beside her, the painted spirits ready. "I don't . . . No."

You didn't notice the shine of your grandmother's spirit when you raised her from the waves? She was golden like us, was she not?

Sierra shook her head, but it was true: Mama Carmen's spirit had glowed with a shimmering, golden glory just like the Sorrows.

We tried to tell you when you first came to us, Little Lucera, but you wouldn't listen. Too bent on destroying Wick to hear us out. Too bent on revenge. Typical. You are very young still, much younger than we. You have much to learn.

"But . . ."

The Deck of Worlds is your legacy too. We are your legacy too. We are a part of you, just as you are a part of us.

"No!" Sierra yelled. "I reject it."

The Sorrow let out a sneering guffaw. *How can you reject it? You don't even understand it! My mother, your great-great-great-grandmother, Doña Teresa María Avila de San Miguel, created the Order of Light with magic she brought from the Old World. She was a compassionate, benevolent woman, heaven sanctify her — perhaps too much so. When she anointed us, her three daughters, into the Order, she also included her fourth, bastard daughter, María Cantara, a filthy creature conceived when our mother's innocence was taken advantage of by one of the servants.*

"I'm so sure that's what happened," Sierra mumbled.

What? You again speak of that which you know nothing about! Listen, child, that you may know the truth! María Cantara rejected our mother's teaching, rejected the Order of Light, ran like a coward from the plantation on which they lived, and vanished into the wilds of El Yunque, into the darkness.

"But . . ."

It does not end there! The bastard child created a bastard cult, in direct opposition to the Order of Light, that which became Shadowhouse. She entered into the worship of the dead, commiserated and communed with them. Thus the rupture was born. From an act of noble charity, your ungrateful forebearers rent the House of Light, shattered it, since our mother had bonded us together in a way that we could never be whole without all of our powers coming together.

Sierra just shook her head again, speechless.

It was then that, in her waning years, heartbroken by this arrogant betrayal and act of rebellion, Doña Teresa inscribed our broken universe upon the Deck of Worlds. An act of self-defense! A system of divination and the allotment of power that would protect us from our own traitorous ilk, from one whom we embraced as a sister in spite of her unfortunate circumstances, whom we were raised with, played with, whose coarse hair we endeavored to comb and —

"Enough!" Sierra roared.

Just know that this is the context in which we have endeavored to broker a treaty with the King of Iron.

"King of Iron?" Caleb gasped.

Old Crane held up his hands. "I can explain!" But a burst of coughing canceled out whatever he was about to say.

"H-how . . . all this time?" Caleb stumbled through the crowd of spirits. Robbie shot a questioning glance at Sierra; she shook her head. The huge tattoo artist raised his arms. "We trusted you, Crane."

Sirah! shrieked all three Sorrows at once. Their gold-tinged Sinestrati burst forward, tearing into the line of Sierra's painted warriors.

"Push them back!" Sierra yelled, skittering away from the closest Sorrow as it raised two gigantic limbs over its head. A blast of color hurtled out of the sky, barreling into the Sorrow, then another and another, shoving it backward. Nydia's sharp-edged attack balls had been hovering above the fray when the golden spirits charged. A few more zipped and dove across the churchyard as the two sides grappled.

Over by the statues, the tall priest once again stepped in front of Old Crane, this time placing himself directly in the path of Caleb Jones. He loosened the length of chain as he adjusted his stance. Caleb yelled, breaking into a run, his arms outstretched, tats coiled to strike. The priest swung the chain over his head once and then cut it across the air in front of him, shattering the sudden onslaught of colorful body art Caleb had flung his way.

"Caleb!" Sierra called, breaking toward him with spirits at her side. Caleb paid her no mind; he charged ahead and caught the priest's next chain swing full across his torso. It sent him sprawling into the dirt; he landed in a heap a few feet from the statues. Sierra hurled her own arm drawings out as she ran, grunting as each spun forward. The priest had already flung Old Crane over his shoulder. He swatted one of the projectiles away with his chain but caught the other four in the chest. The final one etched into his face as he reeled back.

Suddenly, all Sierra saw was gold: those slowly spinning glints of light flickering like a faraway golden city. One of the Sorrows reared up over her, consuming the entire world with its majestic shroud. Sierra skidded to a halt a half second too late and was immersed in a warm, gelatinous-like universe. Everything slowed down, everything burned with a hazy, ephemeral glow. Before her, a slender form resolved into view as if rising from the murky depths of a stagnant lava pond. Two wide blue eyes opened as a petite mouth stretched like a sudden gash across a delicate porcelain face.

Aaiiiiii! The Sorrow's ear-rending shriek shredded through Sierra. *Unclean!*

Sierra pushed herself backward and, with a gasp of air, the world came to life again in all its color and speed. How much time had passed? She shook her head to clear it as she skittered away from the Sorrow and the Black Hoodies closed ranks around her.

Where were the lanky priest and Old Crane? Gone. Caleb still lay crumpled in the dirt, a group of Robbie's green demons standing over him protectively. Movement caught Sierra's eye at the far end of the yard, where bushes fluttered at the foot of the fence. There! Dressed in black, the tall, slender priest was practically camouflaged standing amongst the rusted iron bars. He was leaning over the fence, whispering something, with Crane and the huge chain still slung over his shoulders.

"Stop him!" Sierra yelled, but even as a cadre of painted demons and warriors broke from the fray toward him, the fence opened up of its own accord. The priest stepped through, careful not to bang Old Crane's head, and then vanished into the street. The fence closed behind him. "Go!" Sierra yelled. "Find them." Her spirits raced forward only to be flung back as soon as they touched the bars.

"What —?" They should've been able to breach through. Something was — the priest must've charged the fence with some magic. House Iron magic. Of course. They could probably breach it when they'd recovered, but no — there'd been enough fighting tonight.

The Sorrows' cackle erupted through her as she glanced around the churchyard. They had pulled back to their shrine and reined in their tattered, gold-tinged shadow army. Bertram stepped into the darkness of the trees and was gone.

"He okay?" Sierra called to Robbie, who was crouching over Caleb's huddled body.

"He's coming around," Robbie reported.

"We gotta get outta here. Can he move?"

"Not alone, probably. I'll help him."

She turned to Nydia, who looked harried and ready for anything. "You good?"

Nydia nodded.

Sierra felt a swell of relief that somehow made her want to collapse and disappear from the whole world. She followed her friends to the edge of the churchyard, Robbie helping Caleb limp along as Nydia watched on either side, arms out and ready to 'shape. The spirits formed a protective ring around them.

Sierra paused at the gate, shot a glare back at the Sorrows, whose shrill laughter still seared the night. "The hell's so funny?"

We have only ever offered you power, Little Lucera, and you have always rebuffed and disrespected us. So very like your tatarabuela, you are. We could've killed you, your whole family, many times over by now, but those days are behind us. We have chosen to diversify our ranks and reached out our hands to you, to include you, to honor you, you who have always spat upon us, you who have always rejected and waged war on us, we have opened ourselves to sanctify you with the power of light. We have waited a long time for the role of Lucera to be passed on to one who is enlightened enough to accept the power we offer. You are that one, though you may not know it yet. We shall continue to wait, but it won't be long now, it won't be . . .

Sierra let the gate clang shut and hurried up the hill to her friends without looking back.

NINETEEN

"Hospital?" Neville asked as he veered the crowded Caddy around a sharp turn. "I think Columbia Presby's the closest."

"Gone," Caleb groaned. "They gone."

"I don't think so, babe," Nydia said, glancing at the backseat, where Sierra, Robbie, and Bennie tried not to get crushed between the twin giants on either side of the car, Caleb and Cojo.

"No," Sierra said. She swatted Cojo's tail out of her face. "They're not gonna be able to help him, this is . . . something else. Let me look."

Robbie lifted Caleb's polo shirt. A chain-shaped bruise cut a canyon across the man's broad chest. It glowed with a slightly bluish hue.

"No doctor gonna know what to do with that," Bennie said. "Ow! Cojo, get off me!"

Neville hurled them around another corner and everyone flew to one side. "Where to, then? We got a lotta cargo in here, and the last thing we need is to get pulled over."

"Head to Brooklyn," Sierra said. "Caleb's place is in Crown Heights. We go there. Robbie?"

"Yeah?"

"Can you . . . I know you've never practiced your powers, but . . . you picked the Sorcerer card. Or, the Sorcerer card picked you, and that's supposed to be the healer. Think you can . . . work your magic?"

"I . . . I'll try," Robbie said. He furrowed his brow and adjusted himself so he could directly face Caleb's wound.

"Brooklyn it is!" Neville yelled.

"Lemme hop out," Nydia said. "I can walk home from here and y'all need more room anyway. Sierra, you good?" Neville pulled over.

Sierra nodded. "Yeah, you're right, it's prolly better. Thanks, Nydia, for everything. Say hi to your boys for me."

"I will." She smiled, blew a kiss at Neville, and shot a concerned frown at Caleb. "Take care of him."

The door slammed and Neville pulled a vicious U-turn as Bennie climbed into the front. "Just . . . trying not to die!" Bennie muttered, landing headfirst on the seat cushion. "Don't mind me."

They zipped up the on-ramp and then down the West Side Highway.

"Let me get closer," Sierra said, squeezing past Cojo.

"If Cujo there licks me," Neville said, "he has to get out and walk. Just FYI."

Robbie had his hands a few inches over Caleb's wound, his eyes closed. The tattoos on his arms churned.

"Keep going," Sierra said quietly. "I'm going to see if I can enhance your powers with my own."

"Gone," Caleb moaned again.

Robbie nodded without looking. She put her hands a few inches over his and tried to push away the mad world rushing around her. Caleb had said she could potentiate the others' powers. She imagined the shadow within her, felt it rise.

But what the hell had happened back in the churchyard? Flashes of the throwdown kept surfacing, no matter how hard she tried to concentrate on her magic. Who was that muscled dude they called Bertram? The Warrior of Light, Sierra figured. It had looked like a proper tableau when she'd walked in on them — the Sorrows and Old Crane in the center, the tall priest and Bertram on either side, almost like a . . . like a card spread. Sierra inhaled sharply, then shook her head.

"You with me?" Robbie asked, his eyes still closed.

"Yeah, sorry," Sierra mumbled. "Got caught up." She lowered her hands, letting them rest on top of his, and closed her eyes. Immediately, Robbie's new power seemed to glare out of the emptiness at her. It thrummed through her palms, jangled up her arms, through her chest. This was a whole new energy in Robbie, something beyond the shadowshaping. She added her own energy to it, letting the shadow within seep forward, down her arms, combining with his, and then into Caleb.

Caleb's wound pulsed a sickly blue in Sierra's mind's eye. She steadied herself as the car swerved — Uncle Neville passing some fool driving the actual speed limit, no doubt — and then refocused. Her own powers were still a little mysterious to her, months after attaining them. Shadowshaping had come naturally, but this added bonus of being Lucera seemed to come with an ever-expanding array of sorcery she couldn't quite wrap her head around. If nothing else, the Deck had given some semblance of shape and context to what that meant. She was Our Lady of the Shadows, and with that thought, the horrible death-grimace of the figure hovering over the swirling sea appeared in her mind.

Sierra cringed. Scrunched her face. Tried again. Caleb's wound still glowed, but now Robbie's energy moved over it, dampening its fervor. Sierra concentrated on the overlapping pulsing energies and slid her own ray of energy on top. The blue light quivered, then dispersed entirely. Sierra opened her eyes and sat back against Cojo. "Whoa."

Robbie looked at her with wonder, then peered at Caleb's chest. The wound just looked like a nasty bruise now, dark and slightly yellowed at the edges. The ill blue shimmer was gone. "We did that," he whispered.

Sierra smiled.

"How it lookin'? Lemme see," Bennie said, craning her

neck around and coming face-to-face with Cojo's slobbery maw. "Gah! Never mind. Just tell me."

"Looks like we handled whatever spirit-type mess the chain inflicted on him," Sierra said. "Still gonna take some work, but . . . it's a start." She glanced out the window, caught a glimpse of the huge prewar buildings flashing by as they raced along Eastern Parkway. "Neville, you know where —?"

"To the tattoo parlor!" Neville yelled.

———

Caleb's studio occupied the cluttered first floor of a row house down a back alley in the Hasidic part of Crown Heights. Christmas lights blinked gently on and off in the storefront window, casting their multicolored shine on statues of various anime characters, monsters, and saints. Inside, Sierra stood over a wooden table surrounded by plants and posters of intricate, sacred body art. Bennie was snoring on an old paisley couch, Cojo curled up in a gigantic ball of fur at her feet.

The cards lay splayed out in front of Sierra. She placed the Sisterhood of Sorrows card beside Crane's now fully emerged King of Iron one. The red wash on the card had faded away to show a figure sitting on a throne welded together from steel pipes, metal bars, and various rusty detritus. The king had his face concealed in one hand, as if lost in thought, or mourning. Crane must've touched it when he was flipping through the deck, which she'd handed over to him like an idiot.

And then he'd slipped out the Iron Knight card somehow; he'd probably used those whisper wraiths as a distraction. Sierra placed a metal fork beside the King of Iron in its place. And once he had the card, Crane must've activated that tall priest dude, who clearly had some freaky superhuman strength going on, besides wielding that chain like a maniac.

On the House of Light side, the Sorrows had the Warrior of Light — a figure in a glowing suit of armor atop a white steed — who Sierra figured had to be Bertram, however unlikely it seemed. She placed the card beside the Sisterhood of Sorrows. Then there was the Hound of Light. She put that card down. Mina? The girl still hadn't shown up, but could she really be the mysterious entity whose vision Sierra could see through? None of it added up.

The fourth House of Light card was the Illuminated Sorcerer. A bearded white man stood with arms outstretched; bright waves haloed out from his fingertips, forcing off an encroaching army of shadows. *Who could this be?* Sierra thought. *Could be anydamnone.*

The Shining Savant was the House of Light's spy card. The figure wore a long-nosed mask like the Shadow Spy, but his robes were elegant and golden, and he carried a whip and cane blade. Wick said that had been him, but there was probably a new one now, yet another that could be anyone.

She sighed, laying down the Five Hierophants beneath the spread.

What's wrong? Vincent Jackson's shimmering, hooded form stepped out of the darkness in front of Sierra.

She was about to say something snarky about popping out of nowhere like that, but it just wasn't in her. She scowled instead. "These cards. A never-ending puzzle."

How is he?

"I don't know. Robbie's with him in the back. Seems like he'll make it through, but . . . I'm not sure what happened. That chain has some very, very bad magic in it."

I saw. Didn't like it. Some of my folks went looking for the priest and Crane, but . . . He shook his head.

Movement in the corner of the room startled Sierra, and she remembered — a second too late — that Bennie had been sleeping on the couch.

"Vincent?" Bennie squinted at them, tears already welling up in her eyes.

B, Vincent said. *I . . .*

"You're . . . you . . ." She looked at Sierra. "And you . . . I don't . . ."

Sierra opened her mouth. Closed it again. Sighed. "Bennie."

"No!" Bennie stood up, face tight, eyes sharp. "Don't you speak to me. How . . ." She shook her head. "How *dare* you? Either of you? Why didn't you . . . ?" She closed her eyes, took a deep breath, and then stormed out.

The door slammed.

Vincent looked at Sierra. *What do I . . . ?*

"You go after her, man! I told you . . ." She bit back all her frustration, let it out in a sigh. "Talk to her, Vincent. I know it's hard, but you gotta. Tell her you don't remember. And if nothing else, make sure she safe. This ain't the night to be running around Brooklyn upset and alone."

He nodded once and was gone.

Sierra pulled both hands down her face and let out a deep groan, forcing away the flash of the grinning skull mask.

"What happened?" Robbie said, walking out of the backroom.

"Everything? I don't even know, man. Chaos and drama. How is he?"

"He's gonna be alright, but . . ."

"What?"

"His tats — you know how I told you when I use mine to attack, they fade from my arms but then reappear a little while later?"

A sinking feeling filled Sierra. "Yeah."

"Caleb's won't."

"What?"

"That's why he kept saying, 'They're gone.' Those spirits, the ones that have always been with him since he first became a shadowshaper back when he was, like, twelve? The chain crushed 'em. They gone. *Gone* gone. Not coming back."

"Shit." Sierra slid into the reclining chair Caleb had his

customers sit in while he worked on them. "I don't know what to say."

Robbie walked to her, stopped a few feet away. "He's pretty broken up. Are you okay?" He looked like he wasn't sure what to do with his body.

"Yeah. I guess." Sierra stood again. "You can hug me. It's okay."

He did, that familiar Robbie embrace, and Sierra was glad he didn't try to tease his fingers along her spine like he used to. This wasn't the time for all that. She stepped away and turned to the table. "I laid out the Deck. What we know, what we can guess. Still coming up with a lot more questions than answers."

"Like what?"

"Like who my spy is." She nodded at where she'd laid the Shadowhouse cards side by side. "I'm the creepy, death-faced Lady of Shadows."

"Of course." Robbie let a sly smile cross his lips. Sierra glared at him till it went away, then smiled herself.

"Tee the Warrior, you the Sorcerer. Cojo the Hound. Who my spy? It ain't any of the crew. I checked it on Nydia while we were on the way: no dice."

"Could be any of the other shadowshapers, right? Even the old ones. Gotta see 'bout Sunny and Delmond. Francis True."

"Yeah. This gonna take some work. And meanwhile, we got a full stack of Sorrows denizens to contend with. Still don't know for sure who most of their people are. They could have another spy in our crew by now."

Robbie shook his head. "You'll go crazy if you don't trust anyone."

"You think I don't know that?" Sierra's fist hit the table before she realized she'd clenched it. Some cold coffee splashed out of the paper cup she'd been drinking from. "I still have to . . . I can't trust, like . . . *anyone,* Robbie. Look what happened with Crane. My granddad knew him! He was supposed to be one of the original 'shapers. Now he the head of a whole other house. Meanwhile, I didn't trust Caleb, and he the one who loses his own spirits throwing himself in the line of fire for us. I don't . . . I don't know what I'm supposed to do."

Robbie's face was stricken. "I . . . I'm sorry."

"No." Sierra shook her head, closed her eyes. "It's not you. I didn't mean to blow up. And it's true. I can't distrust the whole world, I just . . . I don't know what else to do."

"You can trust *me.*"

She opened one eye. "So you say."

He shrugged. "Mad trustworthy, that's me."

Sierra wasn't sure where to look, so she focused back on the cards. She felt Robbie shift beside her and put his attention on them too. "So House of Iron is coming through. Any guess 'bout the other emerging house?"

Sierra picked up one of the mostly blank cards, held it to the light, and squinted at it. "I see a figure. Looks like it's rising from water. That's all I got. Don't even know enough about what the houses are or what they mean for it to matter. Crane's the expert, and now we can't even be sure anything he said is true."

"The Sorrows had the cards before, right?"

"Yeah, that's how they set their whole house up and got everybody activated. 'Cept me, apparently."

"So . . . why do they want the Deck back so badly?"

Sierra frowned. "Think they think of it as theirs cuz their mom made it. My freaky bisbisbisabuela or whatever."

Robbie started pacing. "That it, though? The way they flew at you when they saw it, seemed like it was about more than just it being an heirloom. They *want* that Deck back."

"To keep us from setting up our own house?" But Sierra was following Robbie's line of thought, and it did seem like there was more to it than that.

Robbie grunted, stroking the invisible wisps of his goatee.

"And Wick," Sierra went on. "He lit *up* when he saw we had his Spy card, man. Damn."

Robbie stopped pacing in front of Sierra. "They still need the Deck for something."

"We gotta find Mina."

"And if she is the Hound?"

Sierra shook her head. "I don't know. I don't." All she could think about was Mina's bloodied body lying still in the middle of Greene Avenue. Would she have to hurt her? Kill her? She shuddered. How had things gotten so serious so fast?

Robbie's hands touched her arms. Sierra looked up at him and saw him moving in for a kiss. She put her hand on his chest and pushed him lightly backward.

"I . . . Robbie." She looked away.

"Sorry," Robbie said. "It's just . . . We . . ."

"What?" She wanted to cry and had no idea why. So many reasons, really.

"We're so great together," Robbie said, throwing a hand in the air. "We're a team. Like, I feel like this whole thing is freaky as hell but we can do it because it's *us*, Sierra. Because we go together. Who else got what we got, you know? Who else can understand what we do?"

She grimaced, feeling a million miles away from her own body. He was right. This was special. They had each other, in the midst of all this mess. Her heart should've been overflowing with . . . with something. To have a partner in this, someone she could trust. And here they were alone in a cozy little tattoo studio . . .

He stared at her, and she could tell he saw through the half smile she'd dug up, straight into all her doubts and confusion.

"Sierra?"

His phone let out a sustained buzz. He rolled his eyes, checked the screen, then put it to his ear. "Hay, Manmi. Wi m' sòti ak kèk zanmi ankò. M pral rete kay Treme aswè a. Dakò'."

Sierra realized she hadn't looked at her own phone since

before they'd made their move on the Sorrows. And it had been on silent the whole time. She pulled it out, scrunching up her face in anticipation of the onslaught of messages.

Izzy and Jerome had been waging a vicious emoji war in the group chat for the past hour. Juan had jumped in once or twice with random memes of skeletons playing guitars just to annoy them.

Three missed calls from her mom, then a text asking if everything was alright, and . . . a text from a number she didn't have saved:

pandabutt

The next one said:

pandabuttpandabuttpandabuttpandabuttpanda buttpandabutt

It was from an hour ago. "Shit," Sierra muttered. Another had come in fifteen minutes later:

Callin ya bro am at the garage dont worry about me if ur busy imma be fine ok talk soon

Culebra rehearsed and hosted occasional parties at an emptied-out garage in Prospect Heights, not too far away. It was almost midnight.

"Wi, mwen pwomèt," Robbie was saying. "M' pap pran nan danje."

I have to go, Sierra mouthed, pointing at the door.

Robbie shook his head, holding up one finger. "Okay, Manmi. M' ale! N' a wè demen." He pocketed the phone. "My moms. Worrying as always."

"Can't really blame her," Sierra said. "Imma go. A friend needs some help." She felt her face scrunching up as she said it; it felt like a lie even though it wasn't. She'd already pissed off her best friend tonight by not being straight up with her, and now . . .

"Okay," Robbie said. His voice said otherwise, though.

Sierra tried to ignore it. "You gonna stay with Caleb?"

"Yeah."

"Alright."

"Okay."

"Later." She looked at Cojo. "I'm out, Cojo." The Shadow Hound squinted up at her and opted to return directly to his nap. Sierra closed the door behind her and took off down the street.

TWENTY

Bennie, Im sorry. I wanted to tell u. Plz let me kno u ok.

Sierra pocketed her phone and looked up at the graffiti-covered garage door. The block was quiet around her. Closed-down car repair shops and warehouses lined either side, and a tall brick church took up the far end. The Franklin Ave Shuttle rumbled not far away. The outside lights of the garage had been turned out, but when she tried the side door, it swung open with a high-pitched whine.

A trap? The thought teased endlessly.

Robbie'd had a point about going nuts if she couldn't trust anybody, but . . . The other side could leave her dead or worse. There had to be a way to balance the two impossible extremes, somehow. Either way, she believed Anthony in a place deep down inside her, somewhere beyond reasonable thought. She'd extended her hand to him and wasn't about to snatch it back just because . . . because rival sorcerous factions were trying to destroy her and everyone she cared about? She sighed. Why couldn't her problems be easier to explain?

A dusty chandelier lit Culebra's drum kits, mic stands, and amplifiers; they were set up and ready to go, like sleeping Transformers in the middle of the wide-open practice space. Culebra shared the spot with a few other bands, each contributing a chunk of money every month and pledging to keep it (relatively) clean and replace any broken equipment. Sierra took a step in, closed the door behind her.

She narrowed her eyes at the dark edges of the room. A few couches had been set up there, but no one was in them. No spirits churned in the corners. The place was empty. "Hello?" Sierra called.

Only a single, creepy echo and then silence replied. She walked past the band setup to the back wall, where a slightly open door let a sliver of light cut the shadows. Inside, wound-up cables covered the walls like sleeping snakes and more amplifiers cluttered the small floor space. Anthony lay on his back on the carpet, his eyes closed and mouth open, chest rising and falling with slow breaths. Juan sat in front of him with his arms resting on his knees and his head down, snoring.

Sierra tiptoed over to them and punched Juan in the shoulder.

His head shot up. "What happened?" His eyes widened. "Sierra? What you doing here?"

"What you doing sleeping on the job is the real question."

Juan shrugged. "He says I'm more helpful when I'm sleeping because I don't annoy him with a million questions he can't answer anyway."

"Makes an odd kind of sense, actually," Sierra said. "Anyway, I got it from here. Santiago tag team." She dapped him. "Oh! And . . ." She glanced down at Anthony, who still lay with his eyes closed. "I'm gonna give you something; tell me how you feel when I hand it to you."

"Uh . . ."

"Shut up and pay attention."

"To what?"

"Yourself, jackass. Now shush!" This had obviously been a stupid idea. Juan was the least discreet person she knew. It was too late now, though; she pulled the Shadow Spy from her hoodie pocket and handed it to him.

"Whoa, this is creepy! What is —"

"Juan!" Sierra hissed. "Anything . . . happen when you took it? Anything *at all*?"

Juan shook his head. "Nah. Why?"

She rolled her eyes and took the card back from him. "Never mind, man. Go home and tell Mom I'm okay and I'll be home a little later."

Juan got up, stretched. "What should I tell her when she asks why you're hanging out all by yourself with a tall and talented bass player?"

"She won't ask that."

"Why not?"

"Because she won't know that part of what I'm doing." Sierra settled into the spot Juan had been sitting in, allowing her back to touch Anthony's side.

Juan smirked. "Oh, *really*?"

"What do you want, Obi-Juan Kenobi?"

His face turned serious. "Put in a good word for me."

"Depends. With who?"

Juan suddenly got very interested in the guitar cords.

"Juan! With who?"

Finally, he looked directly at her. "Bennaldra."

Sierra's eyes got wide. "B-Bennie? Really? I had no idea! Since whe — you know what, never mind. I will, but I don't think my word holds much sway with her at the moment."

"Whatever," Juan said, heading out. "You're girls. Whatever it is you want to kill each other over now, you'll be LMAOing about on group chat in two hours. Trust me."

"I hope so," Sierra said as the door closed.

It opened again a few seconds later and Juan popped his head in. "Oh, and thanks, sis. For that, and" — he nodded at Anthony — "this."

She waved him off. "No thing. Go home, Juan of Arc."

"Later, Pulpo. Feel better, man."

Anthony raised a hand with two fingers up and dropped it again.

"Oh, you're up!" Sierra said as soon as the door closed again. Had he been awake the whole time? Had he heard her talk to Juan about the card? She shook away the thought. "Did you *know* that? About my brother and Bennie, I mean. I mean . . . Whoa! I had literally *no* idea. I feel so daft! It was right there in front of my face. Like, *right* there. Wow. I wonder what else I've missed. And can you imagine them as a couple? She's like eighty million times more mature than him even though she's what? Two years younger? I mean, obviously, because: girl, but still. Hmm. I could almost see it in a way. What Juan lacks in emotional maturity, he kinda makes up for in brutal honesty and talent. Maybe he'd step up his game for a girl like B. But whoa."

Anthony moaned.

"Oh my God!" Sierra gasped. "I'm doing the thing that Juan does, aren't I? I'm so sorry! I should just go to sleep like he does so I don't keep annoying you. God, it's not even like me to talk this much, I *swear,* Anthony. I'm so sorry. Shit, I'm doing it still, aren't I?"

"Mmhmm." Anthony nodded, but there was a smile on his face. "It's okay though."

"It is?"

"You're prettier than him."

"Y'all even try'n ball when you laid out," Sierra yelled. "Men!" She slapped his chest and he rasped out a cough. "Oh my God! I'm so sorry! I was . . . I didn't mean to! Ack! I'm the worst panic attack helper person ever! Who would've thought Juan would be better at taking care of people than me just by falling asleep!"

But Anthony's face was clenched with silent laughter. He held up a hand, his eyes closed.

"Imma shut up now," Sierra said. "I'm a terrible person."

Anthony took a few more seconds to get himself together. Then he held up one finger. "First of all, and I mean this in a nice way: It's not about you or who you are as a person."

Sierra swallowed. Nodded. "Okay, I may have been making it all about me."

Anthony's smile was wide now. "That's alright, it's cute. Secondly: It's different with each person. When you talk, it's more calming. Partly because you make me laugh, which makes me forget that the whole world is a tiny box that hates me. For a few seconds anyway."

Sierra wanted to cry but was positive this wasn't the time for that. She pushed it away and found a grin for him instead. "So it actually is about me, huh?"

Anthony rolled his eyes. "My panic attack, my rules."

"Fair enough. Is there a thirdly?"

"What was that thing you gave Juan?"

Sierra felt her stomach plummet and her body go cold. She imagined the Deck glowing in her pocket, burning a hole through her jeans, her leg, her whole life. "Nothing. Just a stupid game we play." That much was sort of true. It was stupid. And a game.

"Didn't seem like a game. You sounded . . . scared."

She shook her head. "Nope. It's like a scavenger hunt.

Juan and I been playing it since we were kids." Blatant lie. "Don't worry about it. Was that the thirdly?" Her voice sounded crisp, unfeeling, and she hated herself for it.

He shook his head, caught his breath again. "Thirdly: Yes, I knew. She's all he talks about."

A moment passed before Sierra caught up to what he was talking about. Then she yelled and smacked his chest again. "Bennaldra Jackson? Oh. My. God! Anthony! What? What what? You have to — you have to tell me! *All* he talks about? I can't even . . . What?"

Anthony sat up, chuckling through a cough. "Except music shit and when our next gig is, yeah. And no."

"No what?"

"No, I can't tell you what he says." He propped himself up on a huge bass amp behind her and pulled his legs around so they were on either side of Sierra's. "That's bro shit. There's a code."

Sierra leaned back against his chest. There was no logic to it. It just felt like the next thing to do. There she was and there he was, cocooned around her, and outside the city was empty and quiet and gigantic.

"I see how it is," she said, very quietly.

"Do you?" His arms wrapped around her chest. She was enwrapped in him. Something inside her that had been holding tight for months seemed to give, ever so slightly. She felt like if she let go, if she allowed herself to sink fully back, she'd just detach from the world and float off into space. It didn't seem like such a bad idea. Her head fell back against his shoulder.

"Nope," Sierra whispered. "You have to show me."

His lips were on her neck and her whole body was on fire. She moaned, craning her head to the side to give him even more neck to suck on. His arms trembled, gripping her tighter, pulling her into him, and again Sierra felt the gentle tug of some invisible, delicious force, beckoning her into the void.

But not in a bad way.

She didn't think.

"Slow," she whispered, as he started exploring her body with his hands. "Slow."

He nodded against her head so she felt it. "Slow as you want."

"Feeling better, I take it."

"Much. Nice work, doc."

"Ah, well . . ." Sierra let her voice trail off. Tiny lightning storms were erupting along her arms, through her chest and belly, and she couldn't concentrate on making words while it was happening. She shivered, willing her body to chill the hell out. "You know."

"Listen," Anthony said, serious now. "One thing." He leaned to the side a little so Sierra could look him in the face without straining her neck.

"Yeah?" Sierra's voice sounded breathy and urgent, not like she was listening at all, in fact. She tried to concentrate.

Anthony smiled at her obvious effort. "Sorry to switch gears so fast, it's just for a sec. The one rule about this — what happened earlier, I mean, not *this*."

Sierra nodded, finally settling on a suitably attentive face.

"Whatever we say when it's happening, it's a zone of total trust. Means I know nothing I say or do when it's happening will ever, ever, ever be spoken to another living being. Not Juan, not Bennie, nobody. And same for what you say and do. I swear it. And . . ." He looked away, scowled, bobbed his head once, looked back. Met Sierra's eyes directly. "We never, *never* lie to each other in this space. It's sacred."

She nodded, feeling a whole other kind of fire light inside her from the one just a few minutes ago.

"When I'm cool you can lie to me every which way you want." He tried to laugh it off, but she could tell he was dead serious. His laughter faded quickly. "But yeah, when I'm in it, I gotta know you'll give me the real deal, no matter what. Even if it's awful news, whatever. I need to know. Juan and I agreed on it a few years ago, and that's how it is. You feel me?"

Sierra closed her eyes, nodded. Opened them again. Found his piercing into her, inscrutable. "I feel you, Anthony," she whispered.

"Deal," he said. He put up a hand. She put hers in it. Her shadowshaping hand. Their fingers entwined easily.

María Santiago was knocked out on the couch when Sierra walked in a few hours before dawn. Sierra paused, taking in her mom's face, creased with worry even in sleep, mouth slightly open. María was such a well-put-together, precise woman, it was striking to see her even slightly out of sorts. She'd been playing one of those word games she used to calm down, and the book and pencil had slid to the floor, where they lay beside her phone and a mug of cold hot chocolate.

"Mami," Sierra said.

María Santiago sat up, looking around. "¿Qué pasó? Oh, Sierra. You're back. Good. You had fun with Bennie?"

How could Juan lie so easily? Sierra wondered, leaning in for a kiss. She shrugged her reply, looked away.

María put her glasses on and squinted up at her daughter. "What's wrong, m'ija?"

Sierra shook her head. Shrugged again. Felt tears trying to well up for no clear reason. Pushed them down again. "Just . . . I don't know. So much."

"Ven." María opened her arms, revealing a still life with two ducks on her gray sweater. Sierra smiled at it and curled up on the couch, resting her head on her mom's lap. María sank her fingers into Sierra's fro and rubbed, just like she used to do when Sierra was little.

"¡Oy!" María said suddenly. "Pero . . ." She sat up very straight.

"What?" Sierra's eyes shot open. "What happened, Mami?"

"I don't know. I felt something. Something like . . . I don't even know. Something inside me?"

Sierra sat up, facing her mom, as the truth dawned on her. She shook her head slowly from side to side. "Oh . . . no . . ."

"What, Sierra?"

Sierra took the Shadow Spy card out of her hoodie pocket, held it out to María. "This."

"¿Y eso?" She took the card, frowning at it.

Sierra didn't have it in her to explain everything. Didn't even know how. She laid herself back down in her mom's lap and let the sobs surface and spill over.

"Shhh, Sierra." María's fingers kneaded back through Sierra's hair. Sierra rocked back and forth as the past few days of horror blitzed through her mind. "Sacalo, mi vida. Get it all out."

Slowly, the sobs subsided. María reached over to the table and pulled some tissue for Sierra. Sierra wiped her nose and put the crumpled tissue on the floor.

"Don't forget to pick that up, m'ija."

"I know, I know, sheesh!"

"Did you figure out what your costume is going to be yet?"

"What?"

"Halloween, m'ija. It's tomorrow. Well, today now. Which means your birthday is right around the corner too. Where've you been?"

"Dang, I totally forgot. I don't think Imma trick-or-treat this year."

"But you love trick-or-treating, Sierra. This has always been your favorite —"

"I know," Sierra said. "I just . . . Too much happening right now. Mami?"

"Hm?"

"You okay? I mean, about Abuelo and all? I realized I never really stopped and asked you."

"No," María said. "You didn't. But yes, I am. I think I said good-bye to him over the course of this past year, bit by bit. And I know you're dealing with a lot right now, Sierra. You don't have to add feeling guilty to the mix. I'm fine."

"Thanks, Mami."

"You going to tell me what this card is or not?"

Sierra sat up, tucked one leg under the other, and wiped a few tears away. "Some sick game a long-dead ancestor of ours came up with. Doña Teresa or something? She was María Cantara's mom, I guess."

"Ah, my namesake. I never heard much about her mother."

"Yeah, well, she made a creepy deck of cards."

María raised one eyebrow. "¿Y . . . ?"

"And the shadowshapers are part of it, and the Sorrows are trying to, like . . . get us out of the way, and they say I'm . . . we're . . . part of them somehow . . . part of their . . ." — she nearly spat the word out — "family."

"Must be where your Tía Rosa gets it from."

"Mami! This is serious!"

María smiled and pulled Sierra back into her lap. Hands returned to hair.

"I know, m'ija. I know."

"And now you're caught up in it too. That thing you felt means the card clicked with you, the Shadow Spy. Means you get special powers and can infiltrate the other houses."

"Doesn't sound like such a bad thing, Sierra."

"No, Mami, listen . . ." Tears slid down Sierra's face again. "It's . . . They want to kill us. Well, they want me to join them, but it's so they can have ultimate power and wipe everybody else out. You can't . . . Mami, you can't get involved. This isn't your —"

"Isn't my *what*, Sierra? Isn't my fight? My daughter's in danger and it's not my fight? These creatures sent Wick to destroy my father's life, no? This isn't my fight? How, Sierra?"

Sierra bit her bottom lip and closed her eyes. "I know," she whispered. "I just don't want you to get hurt."

María laughed sadly. "Now you know how I feel every single day."

TWENTY-ONE

Sierra perched on the edge of her bed, gazing into the mirror on the other side of the room. Exhaustion had come and gone while she'd been talking to her mom and now all she felt was wired. A deep, nameless terror loomed beneath it all. It wasn't one thing or another; it was everything, all at once.

Or was it?

She stood, catching her own dark eyes reflected back at her, and stepped across the room to stand in front of the mirror. A grinning skull glared out for a half second and then resolved back into Sierra's face. She pushed down the scream rising in her, glancing away with a gasp. Met her own eyes again. Let them settle. It wasn't just the Sorrows or Crane's betrayal — she'd felt off since she saw that card in the nursing home. It was like the image had somehow leapt off the card and plastered itself across her face. And it had stayed, skulking just beneath the surface of her skin, waiting for her to let her guard down and then shimmering to life.

She hadn't really looked in the mirror since, not full on. The grinning skull face was always ready, always waiting.

Her burgundy hoodie lay slung across her bedpost, the Deck weighing down one of its pockets. Sierra lifted it, fished out the bundle. Unwrapped it, feeling very much like she was dreaming, and shuffled through until she found the Mistress of Shadows. Her card. Her.

She held the card up. It wasn't her, though. Just some terrified old woman's imagination making monsters of her own daughter. Sierra tried to picture Doña Teresa hunched over a drawing table in some castle out in the Puerto Rican wilderness, pouring all of her deep-seated fears into this little piece of paper and then electrifying it with magic.

How powerful must María Cantara have been to inspire such fear in a wealthy matron. Sierra let a slight smile open across her face. Her great-great-grandmother had run off to El Yunque, if the Sorrows could be believed, and wreaked havoc on Doña Teresa's whole existence. She'd messed with the Sorrows — hell, the whole Deck had been created for the sole purpose of fending off María Cantara's attacks, and one day uniting the two magics again. Doña Teresa couldn't be all bad if she'd also hobbled her favored daughters' power by binding them inextricably to their mortal enemy.

The skull face smiled back. Her great-great-grandmother's smile. Her smile. A wild woman of the ocean, keeper of the shadows. "Shit," Sierra said out loud. "I'll be that." And she had an army of her own. Sierra's smile got wider.

Outside, dawn broke across the city.

Sierra grabbed her phone.

*Yo B. Im sorry im sorry im sorry i didnt tell u. Takin
a sick day. Come over a lil later? . . . Need ur help.
Its a hair thing.*

She pushed play on her stereo, making sure not to blast
it too loud, and the first urgent chords of Culebra's newest
track filled the room. Her phone buzzed.

*Im coming but only bc I hate school and if I dont
help u with hair stuff youll embarrass us all. U r not
forgiven.*

Sierra smiled. She texted back *bet* and started going
through her closet.

Sierra was drawing elaborate skulls when her mom knocked
on the door and poked her head in without waiting for an
answer. "Sierra? Why are you up so early?"

"Mom!" She turned down Culebra's thrash. "What if I'd
been naked and doing yoga or something?"

"Naked yoga? This is a thing?"

"I'm just saying, why knock if . . . Bah — never mind.
Now I know where Juan gets it. Can I help you?"

"Watch your tone, young lady. I wanted to show you
this." She came in and sat on the unmade bed, patting the

mattress for Sierra to sit beside her. She had the family photo album clutched to her chest.

"Oh boy," Sierra said, smiling. "Memory lane."

"Well . . ." María opened the big leather album and flipped backward past Sierra's baby photos and then the early years in Brooklyn, Neville and the family hanging out at various clubs and events, family gatherings. "I figured since the past seems to be inserting itself into the present in a particularly violent way these days, you might want to know a little more about what's going on."

"You right, you right," Sierra said. "Whoa, is that Tío Angelo?" A burly man in a cap and guayabera squinted in the Caribbean sun. Forest mountains stretched out behind him. He had a machete in one hand, a rifle in the other.

"Mmhmm. He's still holed up in the mountains somewhere, last I heard. He was always my favorite uncle when I was little."

"I thought he was *my* uncle."

María laughed. "No, he's your *great*-uncle. Angelo is Mama Carmen's younger brother. Younger, but equally a pain in the ass, from what I hear."

Sierra studied the picture, caught a hint of her grandmother's face in Angelo's set chin and fierce eyes. "You think he's . . . you know . . . ?"

"A shadowshaper?" María bobbed her head from side to side, weighing it. "Wouldn't be surprised, now that you mention it. He was always close with your abuela. They wrote constantly. I should see if his letters are in storage somewhere." She flipped the page. "There's Mama Carmen when she was little, with Angelo, and that's Cantara Cebilín, your great-grandmother." An old woman glared out from under a straw hat in the faded sepia photo, the teenage Carmen and preteen Angelo on either side of her. Cantara Cebilín wore a handsome vest and leather cowboy pants. She looked ready for war. "Abuela," María said, putting her hand beside the picture.

"She could dress like that back then?" Sierra asked.

"Cantara Cebilín dressed however she damn felt," María said. "I'm told she passed for a man at times, would show up in cantinas, drink everyone under the table, start a fight, and then walk out with the finest women in the place. A true rebel."

"Wow. Did she ever marry?"

"Not that I heard of."

"Any pictures of María Cantara?"

"Her mother? No, sadly."

"Did you ever meet her?"

María gasped. "How old do you think I am? She died long before I was born."

"Sierra!" Juan called from downstairs. "Bennie's here to see you! And she looks pissed!"

María cut her eyes at Sierra. "¿Qué hiciste, m'ija?"

Sierra stood up and kissed her mom on the cheek. "Nothing! Sheesh! Thanks for showing me the pictures, Mami!"

"Hold still, I said."

Sierra ignored the chill in Bennie's voice. "My bad. Anyway, that's the long and short of it. I feel terrible, I tried to tell him to do right, but I also wasn't in any position to, you know, disrespect his secret. It wasn't mine to tell. And he promised to tell you, so I figured he would sooner rather than later, but then everything started happening really quickly and . . . I guess he just . . . So, yeah."

Sierra glanced in the mirror. They'd gone the first couple of hours in silence — Bennie had come into Sierra's bedroom, put her earbuds in, and simply gotten to work braiding the silvery extensions into Sierra's hair. Now about half of them were in. Sierra's fro still exploded lopsidedly out of the rest of her head. She'd caught a few glimpses of a nap but was woken each time by an overenthusiastic tug at her roots.

Finally, tired of the stony silence and faraway tinkle of Bennie's R&B, she'd tugged on her best friend's sleeve and, when the earbuds came out, began telling her side of the story.

"I guess what I'm trying to say is: I'm sorry. I know it's really messed up to have . . . for that to happen, and I get that I messed up by not telling you even though I really couldn't. It just sucks and I'm sorry, B. You're the best person I know in the world *and* my best friend, and I really need you to, like . . ." An unexpected sob cluttered up

259

Sierra's words. She grimaced and shook her head, trying not to let it out.

"Stop moving," Bennie said. "Ya big baby."

Sierra snorted with relief, wiping her eyes. "I need you to like forgive me and still be my best friend."

"Who said I wasn't your best friend?"

"Well, I —"

"You're so goddamn dramatic, Sierra. I'm here, aren't I?"

"I mean —"

"All up in ya fro and you *know* these extensions gonna take a minute, by which I mean many hours. Think I want to spend my entire day off playing hairdresser?"

"It wasn't really a day off until I texted —"

"Not the point, smartass!"

Sierra exhaled. "I know. Thank you. I appreciate it."

A moment passed. The tinny squeals of a love song jangled out of Bennie's dangling earbud.

"Can we listen to something good now?" Sierra asked.

"What, like Culebra?" Bennie fake gagged.

"You don't like Culebra?"

"I mean . . . not really. I support cuz they're our peeps and whatnot, but . . . it's really not my thing." She made an ugly-cry face and yelped a gravelly impression of Juan's metal guitar riffs.

"Funny thing about that," Sierra said, pushing her smile all the way to the far end of her face.

"What?"

"It's just . . . nothing. Ow!"

Bennie released her death grip on Sierra's braid. "Don't *nothing* me, sis. What?"

"Juan asked me to put in a word on his behalf."

Bennie made a puzzled face at Sierra in the mirror.

"With you."

Bennie's eyes went wide. "Like . . .

Sierra nodded. "*Like* like."

"Hold still. But . . . but . . . I don't even . . . and we . . . and . . . whoa."

"Bennaldra Jackson, are you smiling, girl?"

"No!" Bennie squealed. "Absolutely am not smiling! I'm just surprised."

The door swung open and Juan popped his head in. "Oh, hey," he said, way too casually.

"Leave," Sierra said. "And come back when you learn how to knock."

"I was just going to grab a sandwich at the bodega." He walked in and started looking absentmindedly at random papers on Sierra's desk. He was wearing a loose tank top and he'd clearly just touched up his spiky hair. "You ladies want anything?"

"I'm good," Bennie said. "Thanks."

Juan spun the chair at Sierra's desk around and sat in it backward. "Whatchy'all doin'?"

"Plotting world domination," Sierra said. "What's it look like?"

He rolled his eyes. "Speaking of world domination, any update on the card situation?"

"I'm embracing my role as Our Lady of the Shadows," Sierra said.

"So I see."

"And Mom's the Shadow Spy."

"What?" Juan stood up.

"Whoa," Bennie said.

"But Sierra . . . what does that even . . . mean?"

Sierra didn't bother feigning nonchalance. "It means she has the power to infiltrate another house and hide the fact that she's a shadowshaper. Like, she could be initiated into that other house. Wick was the House of Light's Spy, that's how he was able to become a shadowshaper without Lázaro knowing he was with the Sorrows."

"But . . . Mom can't, she can't . . . She'll be in danger."

"That's what I said. She said now I knew how she felt. And the thing is, if we're being real 'bout this: We're all in danger. All the time. Constantly. Like, at any given moment, the House Iron or the Sorrows could just get fed up and decide it's worth the risk to wipe us out, even though we're supposedly stronger than both of them. We're also young and don't fully understand our powers yet, so . . ."

Sierra looked up suddenly. Anthony stood in the doorway, his tall frame taking up the whole thing. She felt all her insides scrunch up.

Anthony's mouth hung slightly open, his head shook slowly back and forth. "Last night you said those cards were a stupid game y'all play. A scavenger hunt."

Sierra gulped. "I did."

"They're not, are they? Not at all."

"No," Sierra said. "They're not."

Anthony turned around and walked away.

"Anthony," Sierra said, jumping up and wrenching her hair out of Bennie's grasp. "Wait!"

———————

"Just one thing." Anthony stood on Sierra's stoop, facing the street, his arms crossed over his chest. "That's all I asked."

"I know." Sierra stood beside him, trying to quell the rising panic in her. A few early trick-or-treaters made their way along the block: two fairy princesses and a Spider-Man with an already weary-looking adult in tow. "I'm sorry."

Anthony shook his head. "I know it doesn't seem like a big thing —"

"No," Sierra said. "I get i —"

"Let me finish."

She nodded, frowning.

"I know it doesn't seem like a big thing. And really, I had no right to pry, I know that too. Long as we've known each other, I barely know you, really. But I trust you." He scowled. "Trusted you. For whatever reason."

Sierra felt her heart vanish over some faraway horizon. Completely out of reach. Gone.

"And I *know* that I told you the no lies thing *after* you'd already told me the cards or whatever were no big deal."

Sierra nodded again. She hadn't been sure how to raise that point; it seemed moot somehow anyway.

"I'm not trying to say you did anything so wrong — you don't owe me anything, Sierra. I just . . . Now . . . something's different, that's all."

She nodded once more. No words came.

Mrs. Middleton came out of the house next door, her four little ones jumping up and down with excitement around her. Their faces were painted green, and each had a turtle shell on their back and a different colored bandana around their forehead.

"Hey Aya! Hey Sheneeca! Hey Kelsey! Hey Shemar!" Sierra called out, digging up a smile for them.

"Hi Sierra!" they all screamed at once. "Trick or treat!"

"You're gonna have to pass by our house on the way back in, Mrs. Middleton. We ain't set up the candy and all that yet."

"Okay, dear," Mrs. Middleton said with a wave. "We got plenty of territory to cover first, not to worry. Which way, kids?"

A spat broke out over which direction to go, which Mrs. Middleton eventually solved by deciding herself, and the crew bustled off into Bed-Stuy.

"And anyway," Anthony said, still looking across the street. "It sounds like you're in danger. I mean . . . How am I supposed to . . . What if you'd gotten into trouble while you were helping me? If I don't know what's going on, how can I . . ."

"What?" Sierra snapped. "How could you save me?"

"I mean . . ."

"What makes you think you could save me, Anthony? From something you have no idea about?"

"That's exactly my point — I have no idea!"

"And you still feel like you could save me from it. You can't, Anthony. No one can. No one understands the mess I'm in. Not Juan, not my best friends, not my mom. No one. Do you hear me? And you think you're owed that knowledge because you asked?"

"No, I —"

"No, you let me finish. I'm on my own in this, man. It's bigger than me, bigger than you, bigger than what happened last night. I just wanted — I wanted to have something peaceful, something beautiful, away from all that." She turned to him finally, taking in his tense face. "Something not tainted by all this shit I'm neck deep in."

He nodded, blinking. "I can understand that."

Sierra spat a laugh and shook her head. "No, you can't. No one can. I gotta go inside, man. I have half a fro, and if I apologize any more times today, Imma punch someone in the face." She walked back in without looking back.

"What the actual hell?" Sierra said, glaring at the doorway of her room.

Izzy shrugged her shoulders. "What?" She wore blue-tinted librarian glasses, an orange turtleneck with a red skirt, and a brown wig shaped into a bowl cut.

Sierra let out a much-needed laugh. She'd spent the past three hours mostly in silence as Bennie painstakingly wove braid after braid into Sierra's hair.

"Epic," Bennie said. "Did you bring mine?"

"Of course," Izzy said, tossing an orange wig, purple dress, and green scarf onto Sierra's bed.

"What it do?" Jerome appeared in the doorway, a big, goofy grin plastered across his face. He gazed out from behind strands of a light brown wig. A green V-neck T-shirt hung way below his waist. Bennie applauded wildly.

"You guys are . . . the Scooby Crew?" Sierra blurted out. "No!"

Izzy sat on Sierra's desk, crossed her arms over her chest. "Got the idea when Tee pointed out how we look like that anyway what with Cojo rollin' around with us, ya know? Like . . . why not?"

"What about me? No one thought to invite me into the fold?"

"Hold still," Bennie said. "We almost done."

"If you took a peek at the group chat more than once every seventeen months," Izzy pointed out, "you'd be more in the fold. As it stands . . . we tried, Si."

"Anyway, those braids look fly as hell," Jerome said.

Juan poked his head in the doorway and Sierra screamed. He'd bleached his spikes and laid them flat against his head in a swirl. "Ay, it's the 'shaper squad!" Juan said in a corn-ball accent. He wore one of their dad's white polo shirts and blue bell-bottoms.

Everyone applauded.

"They got you too," Sierra sighed. "I can't deal."

Juan crossed his arms over his chest and raised one eyebrow. "Never fear! The Scooby Crew is here!"

Jerome let out a very Shaggy-like guffaw. Sierra put her head in her hands.

"Sierra!" Bennie growled.

"Sorry!" She sat back up.

"Hey, guys." Robbie skulked in, face morose. "Looking good." The smile he flashed looked like it hurt.

Everyone exchanged daps and whaddups.

"How's Caleb?" Sierra asked.

Robbie shook his head. "He's getting there, but still outta commission for now. Said he's sorry he couldn't make it."

"That's alright," Sierra said. "Just pass along what we talk about."

Robbie nodded, not making eye contact.

"¿Galleticas?" María Santiago stood in the doorway wearing a pointed witch hat and holding a tray of cookies.

"Yes!" Izzy yelled, jumping off the desk and relieving Sierra's mom of the tray.

Sierra rolled her eyes. "Everyone, I'd like you to meet the one and only Shadow Spy."

A chorus of "Whoa!" and "No way!" rose, followed by pounds and backslaps.

María took it in stride, nodding her head and waving off the excitement like she'd just won an award. She sat next to Bennie on the bed and helped herself to a cookie. "This is everyone?"

"This is all the active shadowshapers except Tee and Caleb," Sierra said. "Thanks for coming, everyone. I have a couple things to say. Gonna make it quick, though, I know y'all wanna get to trick-or-treatin' or whatever it is you hoodlums have planned."

"Hey!" Izzy said.

"Long and short is: We in trouble. I've caught everyone up on the details of what's been going on. So, we got to go into wartime procedures. That means first and foremost: Everyone on highest precaution. If you're out, you're paying attention. These cats could come at us in a whole lotta different ways — could be spirits, could be corpuscles again, could be something else entirely. We don't know, so we gotta watch out. And *everyone* gotta carry some kinda drawing implement on 'em at all times. Preferably a spray can but at least chalk. Something."

"'Cept me," Izzy said smugly.

Sierra nodded. "Right, 'cept Izzy cuz she got that . . . You know what, there's no way I can say this without opening myself to all kinds of dirty jokes from Izzy, so I'm just gonna say, Izzy's power is . . . Forget it. No, you don't have to carry no chalk."

"Bet."

"Second: The buddy system is in full effect. If you out, you out with a buddy. For now, y'all trick-or-treaters are in a band of four, so that's cool. But don't be peeling off running around all willy-nilly through the streets of Brooklyn by yaselves. Not tonight. Not till all this Sorrows mess cools off. Feel me?"

Everyone nodded. They looked dead serious; no one had even heckled her. *That's a first*, Sierra thought. *Most of them saw what the Sorrows are capable of. They know this is no joke.*

"Izzy and Jerome, you two buddy up. Juan, you and Bennie."

She raised an eyebrow as Juan and Bennie high-fived over María's head.

"And y'all gotta escort Robbie to the train on the way out. Thirdly: Those of you who correspond to cards — that's Robbie and Mom and Tee."

"And you," Juan said.

"Right. And me — and Cojo, as a matter of fact. We gotta be extra, extra cautious. Imma stick around here and monitor the spirit stuff, at least for a bit. Then we'll see. And finally, we gotta find Mina. I don't know where she's gotten to, I don't know if she's the Hound of Light or not, but we gotta get ahold of her. Imma be checking in with Cojo, but if nothing else, we making a trip to Staten Island in the next day or so to see what we can find out from her family. Any questions?"

"Is Tee safe?" Izzy asked, sounding very much like a little kid suddenly.

"I got spirits watching the hospital," Sierra said. "And all y'all's houses. Sorry, I know that's kinda creepy." No one seemed to mind. "But it's only for now, I promise. Alright, that's it, y'all."

"Good timing," Bennie said, standing and stretching her arms over her head. "I'm finally done with these braids and need to get out this room." Everyone started clattering out into the hallway, chatting about their costumes.

"Robbie, hang back a sec?" Sierra said. He stopped at the door, let Izzy squeeze past, and then turned to face Sierra.

"What's wrong?" she asked.

Robbie shook his head. "Nothin'."

"Can you — would you mind doing the face part for me?" She held up the Mistress of Shadows card and the plastic container of face paints Bennie had brought.

He shrugged and pulled the chair up in front of her. "Sure. But you better like what I do — those waterproof ones are hell to get off."

Twenty minutes later, Robbie and Sierra both said, "Look," at the exact same time.

Sierra sighed through a forced smile. Robbie just shook his head, putting the finishing touches on what she could feel must be a meticulous rendition of the skull mask.

"You go first," Sierra said.

He shook his head. "Uh-uh. Ladies first."

"Fine, fine." She took the Deck out of her pocket and held it out to Robbie. "Here."

"Huh?"

"I've thought this through, it's not an impulse thing. I need you to hold the Deck for now."

He eyed it. "Why?"

"Because they're coming, Robbie. One way or another. And they know I have it. And they want it. So whatever happens . . ." Her voice trailed away as images of her own lifeless corpse flashed across her mind. She shook it off. "Whatever happens, they can't get the Deck, Robbie."

"But why me?"

"You been shadowshaping longer than any of us. You

know the spirit world like you were born in it. You can fight. And . . ."

"And?"

"And I trust you, Robbie."

He frowned, then finally relented, taking the Deck from her. "I don't like it, but I'll do it."

"Thank you. Now what were you gonna say?"

Robbie squinted at her forehead, slid the yellow face-paint along her temple, and then sat back. "Thing is . . . I don't know how to do this."

"Paint my face? You're the best artist I know, man."

"No, Sierra, this . . ." He waved his hand back and forth in the empty space between them. "Us."

"Oh," Sierra said. "Me either."

"By which I mean — I can't do this."

"I . . . but . . . Do what?"

Robbie paused, looking away. "Be your friend."

"Oh."

"Be *just* your friend, I mean. I can't."

Sierra nodded, somewhere between anger and heartache. "So you're, what? Out? You're not gonna roll with us at all?"

"I'm not walking away from shadowshaping, nah. And I know I have a role now, and that matters. 'Specially with everything going down. I'm not gonna leave you hanging like that. Imma carry the Deck like you asked. And I'll do what needs to be done, but . . ."

"Not as my friend." Sierra tried to banish the bitterness from her voice, failed entirely.

Robbie finally met her eyes. "It just hurts too much."

He stood and walked out of the room.

The Mistress of Shadows still lay on the desk. Sierra picked it up, opened her mouth to call after Robbie, and then just shook her head and pocketed the card. She put the set of fangs Bennie had brought her over her own teeth. Then she turned to the mirror and was met by a terrifying skull, half her mouth painted into a vicious razor-toothed grin, the other half frowning.

TWENTY-TWO

Spirits surged through the darkening sky over Brooklyn. It was Halloween, All Saints' Eve, Samhain — a night that had been feared and celebrated for its mysterious powers for thousands of years. Down below, costumed revelers roamed the streets as the shadows danced among them, perhaps felt but mostly unseen.

The sight would normally have brought a smile to Sierra's face, but none came as she gazed out across the rising and falling brownstones and high-rises of Bed-Stuy from her rooftop. Instead, she let out a low grumble.

You too, huh, Vincent said, appearing beside her and pulling down his hoodie.

Sierra shook her head. "Man, listen."

For a few moments, they let the sounds of passing traffic and laughing trick-or-treaters fill the air around them.

"Y'all spoke?" Sierra asked.

Vincent scrunched up his nose, a habit he'd carried with him into death. *She didn't tell you?*

"Nah. We made up, but . . . I didn't want to ask."

We spoke. I explained myself. She understood but said it still hurt her feelings that I'd talk to you and not her and that she needed some time to process.

"Sorry, man," Sierra said. *Lo siento* in Spanish, which meant *I feel it,* but she wasn't totally sure she felt anything anymore. An eerie emptiness had been creeping over her since . . . for a while now. Everything seemed very, very far away, most of all her own heart.

Vincent winced, squeezing his lips together. *S'aight. I deserve it. I dunno how to make sense'a who I am in this afterlife thing, let alone me and somebody else, but . . . guess Imma haveta do better at figuring that out.*

"Me too," Sierra muttered. "And anyway —"

Something was on the rooftop with them — the sudden weight of its presence was a whisper against her spine. A soft jingling sound reached her, carried from far away by the night winds. Sierra whirled around. A card lay in the gravel a few feet in front of her. She ran over and picked it up. The Iron Knight.

What is it? Vincent asked from behind her.

"Go get ya peeps," Sierra said. "Something's about to happen."

Vincent grunted and took off into the night.

No, Sierra, Old Crane's voice whispered, *I come in peace.*

"Crane?"

The jingling sound got louder and a hunched-over form

limped toward her across the rooftop. It leaned on a tall, shimmering scepter and ambled along slowly, tiny glints of light dancing along its body.

We mean you no harm. I give my word. The card is a token of my sincerity.

"Fat lotta good it does me now that you've already ignited your creepy priest friend into his full strength."

Possessing the card gives you more power than you know, young shadowshaper. Even more so now that you'll have the full Deck once again.

As the figure drew closer, Sierra realized its entire form was made from slowly spinning pieces of silverware, just like in Crane's room. The dangling, luminous metal reflected splattered specks of the city lights in all directions like a manic, ghostly disco ball. A twisted crown sat on its hunched-over head.

"You're . . . you died," Sierra said.

Mmm, all that excitement in the churchyard wasn't good for this old heart. It was high time anyway.

"Don't come any closer."

The King of Iron stopped a few feet from Sierra, seemed to arch his shimmering head up at her. *I see you decided to embrace your role as Our Lady of the Shadows.*

Sierra stared him down.

I said I mean you no harm and I meant it. When a patron of House Iron gives their word, you may rest assured that it is true. We are unable to break oaths or tell lies, spiritually bound to the words we speak.

"Tuh," Sierra spat. "Says the man who deceived my grandfather into thinking you were a shadowshaper for however many years." The cool October wind whipped past her, carrying whispers of rain and, more distantly, winter. She stood with her legs firmly planted, combat boots laced tight, her braids, hoodie, and dark green dress fluttering behind her legs like wings. Maybe it was the makeup, or the wind, or the week she'd had, but the closeness of her own death felt like a friend. It seemed to hover just out of sight, teasing, insinuating, waiting. It should've terrified her, but instead an eerie calm had taken hold. She'd passed on the Deck. Shadowhouse would find a new leader if they needed to.

I never told him I was a shadowshaper. The old spirit's voice creaked through her mind. *And old Lázaro never asked. I suspect he was well aware of what I was. Your grandfather knew the value of keeping rivals close by.*

Sierra shook her head. Another detail about her abuelo she could've done without. "So lies of omission are cool, long as you don't say them out loud."

The shimmering spirit shrugged, sending a cacophonous jingle into the night. *We keep our word. Sierra, I know you are hurt by my actions. You feel betrayed, understandably. And you have every reason not to trust me, but I pledge to you that what I have just said, along with everything else I will say to you, is the absolute, unadulterated truth. We of Iron House hold the truth sacred above all else.*

"Why are you here?"

I came to deliver the card to you, as a token of trust, and to provide, I hope, some measure of advice in this challenging time for the Shadowhouse.

"Advice from my enemy," Sierra said. "Just what I need."

The House of Light is determined to undermine you at all costs. They will stop at nothing. They forged an alliance with House Iron to ensure your downfall, but it is not your death they seek —

"It's my allegiance. I get it."

The Sisterhood of Sorrows waited a long time for the role of Lucera to be passed on to someone they thought would be amenable to joining forces.

"If by 'waited,' you mean 'tried to manipulate things to get their own guy in the job,' I guess."

And they won't simply give up because you refuse them.

"Right. Why would my consent matter in the situation?"

They don't know who your players are, nor do I, but they will incapacitate your allies one by one until you are all alone and have no choice but to join them. Already, two members of Shadowhouse are out of commission at this all too crucial of junctures.

"A temporary setback," Sierra said, trying to believe it.

Anyone who is a shadowshaper is fair game to the

Sorrows, Little Lucera. Do you understand what I am say-ing to you?

My family, Sierra thought. Everyone she loved, everyone who loved her, she'd put in danger. That was her legacy. She'd initiated her friends and family into a world of shit and now they were all paying for her stupidity. She'd lied. Betrayed their trust. Hurt them. And now . . . "Why are you telling me this?"

Consider it fair warning. And because I don't trust the Sorrows any more than you do.

"Trust them enough to align with them against me, though, huh?"

Alliances are built on tactical necessity, not trust. As you will soon find out if you survive this.

"Alright, Sun Tzu. I'm not interested in your advice, or your alliance."

Then what will you do when the Sorrows crush your every loved one and you have nowhere to turn? Or do you think them incapable?

"It won't get to that," Sierra growled. Something glinted in the corner of her eye — something gold. She turned; it was far off in the gathering twilight but moving quickly toward the street below. One of the Sorrows' spirits. Then another. They streaked downward through the night like phantom comets.

Sierra spun back to face the King of Iron. "It's begun already, hasn't it?"

The shimmering silverware head nodded slightly.

"You just came here to . . . to distract me."

Nothing I have said to you is false, Little Lucera. When this is over, remember that. What appears to you a betrayal now may strike you as a peace offering tomorrow.

Behind him, a cadre of gold-lined spirits approached through the sky.

"I see you, Crane," Sierra said. "I see you."

She turned and ran, pocketing the card as she went.

Little Tolula Brown and the tall slender spirit named Alice zipped alongside Sierra as she ran, their hoods pushed back by the rushing wind. Other shadows dipped and swirled at the edges of Sierra's vision, a gathering cumulus of illuminated badassery by her side. She crossed onto a neighbor's roof, dodged around a water tower, almost got tangled in a satellite hookup, and then hopped the small wall onto the next brownstone.

Two guys in tuxedoes and half masks were making out on a fancy roof deck, and one guy peeled his lips away long enough to yell, "Hey!" as Sierra blasted past. "I'm calling the police!" Sierra ignored him, hurdling another small wall and sprinting harder.

The night suddenly seemed very quiet: just her pounding heartbeat, the clinking of spray cans in her shoulder bag as it slapped against her back, and the rhythmic crunch of her boots on gravel. Then asphalt.

Up ahead was only sky — the row of houses came to an end; four stories below, concrete waited to greet her falling body full force. Sierra didn't pause or think twice — she just launched into the empty air. The world became silent. She started to career toward the pavement, it seemed like in slo-mo. For a flickering moment, she wasn't sure if she minded. Then her stomach plummeted as her arms flailed to either side, grasping at nothing.

The spirits surrounded her, lifted her, just as they had once lifted her over the ocean, and she walked with long strides across the expanse of sky between one row of brown-stones and another, like some Brooklyn demigod, silver braids flowing in the wind behind her.

Lucera. Alice's voice a concerned whisper. *Part of you . . . has given up already?*

Sierra felt a stab of shame. Was she so easy to read? She forced a smile. "Nah, I knew y'all would catch me."

She landed easily on the gravel rooftop, a spray can in each hand, and ran forward, splattering two thick lines, one black, one red, on either side of her feet as she went. Alice and Tolula and the rest of the spirits converged. Sierra pivoted, turning a sharp circle so her double line resolved into a fierce hook. She dropped the cans and slapped her creation. Felt the cool slide of spirits through her chest and down her arm.

Five of the Sorrows' Sinestrati spirits landed on the roof and blitzed toward her without breaking stride. The black-and-red hook lashed forward, clobbering the front two gold-tinged shadows. The remaining three closed on her. Sierra threw her hand to one side and the hook swept low across the gravelly surface, swiping two more. The final Sinestratus flashed forward before she could swing again. Sierra spun, lifting her back foot into the air, and let the Sharpie markings she'd drawn earlier fly off her leg. The first went long but the second and third found their mark, splicing through the shimmering gold of the Sorrows' shadow spirit. It arched backward, howling, but recovered quickly and swung a long arm at Sierra. She backstepped, leaning hard out of the way just as her hook came hurtling back around and crashed full force into the last attacker, splattering him into ether.

Sierra stood panting, and scanned the skyline for more flashes of gold.

Nothing, Alice said, appearing beside her.

"Why would they even come after us knowing we're stronger than . . ." Sierra's voice trailed off.

A distraction, Alice said.

Sierra was already running toward the nearest fire escape.

———————

Cojo sat waiting for her at the bottom of the metal ladder. He stood up and barked as she clambered down the last rung and dropped to the street.

Isake! a tall spirit yelped as it whirled down the street past them. *Jerome!*

Sierra took off after it, Cojo running alongside her.

Bennaldra. More spirits joined them, long shadows striding frantically across Marcy Avenue and off into Bed-Stuy. *Juan.*

"No," Sierra muttered. "No . . ."

She crossed Marcy, dodging a group of white twenty-somethings dressed like zombified Star Wars characters. "What gives?" one yelled as she shoved him out of the way and rounded the corner onto Madison.

Sierra sprinted hard; the huge, cathedral-like school, the brownstones, the costumed revelers — they all seemed to blur past.

"Where are they?" she said aloud. There wasn't time to stop and try to see through a spirit's vision, and anyway, the fierce tide of shadows seemed to flush her forward.

We think they're by that open yard in front of the school on Bedford. Vincent was beside her, gliding along with smooth strides. *I'm trying to get more info now.*

"Bennie's there," Sierra panted. "Go. Get there. Help . . . them."

Vincent nodded and rushed ahead, cutting directly into oncoming traffic and around another corner up ahead.

For no reason she could name, Sierra's mind returned to that moment of serene abandon between the buildings, as she careened toward what could've been her own death. She was lonely, she realized. Even surrounded by spirits. Even with a bunch of amazing friends and a loving family, she was still somehow faraway from the world, unreachable. No one knew what she went through, the burden she carried. It made a crooked kind of sense now, Tee confiding in Ms. Rollins like that. Sierra would've never picked her of all people, but she could imagine what a relief it must have been to unload all the magic and strangeness of this new life onto some unknowing bystander.

And then (crossing Madison, turning down Nostrand, where traffic bustled along and kids screamed, "Trick or treat!" at every passerby), she remembered that an unknowing bystander had asked her what was going on and she'd lied to him.

A screeching car brake shook her back to the world. She'd been running along amidst the tide of spirits without paying attention, but spirits could run right through traffic with barely a flinch. The delivery truck stopped a few inches from Sierra's startled face. "What the hell?" the driver yelled.

Sierra took off running, past bodegas and jerk chicken spots, then down a quiet, tree-lined street, brownstones on either side. From somewhere up ahead, she heard Cojo's mournful howl fill the night. Then another howl rose up, intermingling with the Shadow Hound's — one Sierra hadn't heard since the night Mina had first tried to give her the card in Prospect Park.

TWENTY-THREE

"Put *down* what you're holding!" a stern voice yelled.

The Sorrows' gold-tinged Sinestrati were closing in on the darkened schoolyard from various streets, but Sierra couldn't make out what was going on at the far end. A few figures were huddled in a clump, and another single one stood a little farther off, arms raised toward the group.

"Down," a man's voice yelled. "Put it down, goddammit."

Sierra slowed to catch her breath as she entered the yard. She squinted into the darkness. Was that Bennie? Shadows poured in around her — her own spirits — but the golden ones had already surrounded the group of figures. She passed Cojo, who stood growling at the convergence.

"You have five seconds to drop that can and then I'm going to shoot, is that clear?"

Sierra got closer, saw the light glinting off the muzzle of a gun, the police uniform, the cop's young face, tensed with fear. Without thinking about it, she pulled out her cell phone and started filming. Ahead of him, Izzy, Bennie, and Juan had their hands up. Jerome was still holding his spray can in one hand, motioning to the cop with the other.

"You don't understand," Jerome was saying. He still wore his Shaggy outfit and looked totally ridiculous. "Just hold on, hold on."

"One," the cop said.

"Put the spray can down!" Izzy yelled. "He's not playing." The gold-tinged shadows closed in another step.

"Two!"

"Jerome!" Bennie screamed.

"Three!"

"Hey!" Sierra walked faster, holding the camera up ahead of her. "Hey!"

The cop turned, suddenly unsure where to point his gun. "Stop right there!" His alarmingly blue eyes were wide open. "Drop what you're carrying!"

"It's a phone," Sierra said. "Just a phone." She raised her hands over her head.

"Sierra!" the whole crew yelled at once.

"Get down," the cop yelled. "On your knees!"

Sierra looked at him in disbelief. "Excuse me?"

"You're under arrest. I said get" — he closed the distance between them with a single lunge and grabbed Sierra's wrist roughly — "on your knees." He wrenched her arm behind her back. She felt a sharp pain behind her knee, and then her legs gave out.

"What the —" was all Sierra could get out before she was flung forward, facedown on the pavement.

"Hey!" Jerome yelled.

"You can't do that!" someone else said.

The cop must've holstered his sidearm, because now both his hands fiddled with Sierra's as the cool touch of handcuffs clinked around her wrists.

"Ow!" Sierra tasted the tang of her own blood. Her arms felt like they were about to pop out of their sockets. "I just . . . What is the damn charge?"

"You shut up!" the cop yelled, shoving her harder against the ground. Something heavy pushed into the small of her back — his knee, she realized. "You don't get to speak!"

"Yes she does!" Bennie yelled. "Get off her!"

Sierra felt herself hoisted up and the night sky and buildings spun a wild carnival ride around her. "Let me go!"

The Sorrows' shadows swooshed forward as one toward her crew. "No!" Sierra yelled.

"Shut the hell up, I said!" the cop snarled, shoving her forward away from her friends.

Hooded shadows burst into the fray, shoving back the line of Sinestrati. Somewhere, Cojo was barking furiously.

"Where are you taking me?" Sierra yelled as she stumbled forward ahead of the officer.

"Speak again and I'll blow your head off." His voice was a hoarse whisper. They passed through the fence surrounding the park and then Sierra was shoved up against the side of an idling police cruiser.

"You have anything in your pockets that might poke me? Any syringes?" Rough hands groped up and down her body.

"Ow! No!"

"What about in your bag? Will I find anything incriminating in there?"

She didn't say anything.

"We'll see." He opened the car door and hurled her inside, then tossed her shoulder bag in the front seat. He was about to get in when he stopped and gazed at something up the block. "What the —?"

Cojo's barking got suddenly loud. Sierra caught a glimpse of a huge black shape galloping toward them. The cop grabbed the handle of his sidearm and then just fell backward into the car, slamming the door behind him as Cojo smashed full force against the driver's side window, cracking it.

"Jesus Christ," the cop said.

In the passenger seat, a man snarled: "Drive goddammit."

Someone was running toward them up the block; Sierra thought it was a shadow spirit at first, but then Mina Satorius barreled out of the darkness, her mouth open in a scream, arms outstretched.

"Mina?" Sierra gasped. She was yelling something Sierra couldn't make out. The cop revved the engine and peeled off with a screech of tires, Cojo's barks receding in the distance.

Sierra shook her head, trying to think past her aching body. Why was this cop acting so strange? It wasn't just how aggressive he was — that was nothing new — but he hadn't called for backup, hadn't bothered with any of her crew at all once Sierra showed up. Bed-Stuy sped past out the window. A group of white kids dressed as aliens were singing Halloween songs on the corner, carrying on like everything was just dandy. Which, for them, Sierra supposed, it was.

She closed her eyes. Tolula Brown was side by side with Vincent and Alice in the thick of the fighting with the Sorrows' spirits. It looked like they'd forced the Sinestrati out of the main schoolyard and into a small playground off to the side, where shadows scattered and smashed each other. Where were her friends? She couldn't tell — there was too much going on and all the spirits were in the midst of it. And where was the Hound of Light? If it was Mina, she might still be with the others. Sierra concentrated, shifting through her mind to the now familiar vision of her enemy.

Then she gasped. There she was looking at herself, sitting in the backseat of a police cruiser, eyes closed.

She opened them and stared into a vaguely familiar face. They'd stopped at a red light, and the man in the passenger seat had turned to look at her. Spiky blond hair and that smile that was trying way too hard. The lawyer who had intervened when Jerome got stopped outside Prospect Park. Garrett, his name was. Wayne Garrett. Sierra heard her own breath come in quick, shallow gasps. She tried to steady herself.

He flashed an all-American boy smile and said, "Hi, Sierra. I've been looking for you."

TWENTY-FOUR

Sierra narrowed her eyes, willed her breath back to normal. The pieces began clicking together.

"You . . ." she said.

The Hound of Light nodded, looking very pleased with himself. Wayne Garrett had the strained look of a man who'd hit middle age in his early thirties. His grin cleaved all the way across his face, forcing his eyes into tight, desperate slits.

"You had Mina hit with the cruiser, didn't you?"

He just kept smiling, staring directly at Sierra.

"Then you . . . you were there that night and . . . in the backseat. They . . . they made you go to the hospital, didn't they?"

He shrugged, smile growing ever wider.

"So you were in an ambulance at the same time Mina was. And you . . . then you were recovering, and you sat at home, watching TV . . ."

A car horn beeped tentatively behind them. The light had changed. The Hound stared at her for another ten seconds and then nodded at the cop, who accelerated through the intersection.

That cop in the front seat had been there outside Prospect Park too — Stevens, in the mirrored sunglasses. The Hound must've had him snooping around all along, doing his dirty work. He'd probably been driving the cruiser that hit Mina. And Sierra was pretty sure she'd seen him once before, emerging from the darkness of Manny's underground printing press the day that she and her friends found him dead. Yes! Stevens had been the responding officer. And Garrett must've been lurking nearby because . . .

They pulled into an enclosed lot, and the Hound grabbed Sierra's shoulder bag and started rooting through it. "Where's the Deck?" he hissed after a few moments of rustling.

Sierra smiled sweetly. "What deck?"

He let out a low, vicious growl. "The goddamn — never mind. It's gotta be on you somewhere. I'll find it. C'mon." He got out, taking her shoulder bag with him, and then opened her door and hauled her roughly from the car. "Get in there. Go."

The precinct was brightly lit and full of bored-looking people in stupid costumes waiting to file complaints. An orange-and-black banner hung over the intake desk with a picture of a ghost and a pumpkin, imploring the whole, unimpressed room to "Respect the law so you don't get BOOOked!!"

Sierra rolled her eyes. "You spelled *shot* wrong," she told the desk officer.

He ignored her. "What ya got, Officer?"

"Trespassing and resisting arrest," Stevens muttered, shoving Sierra past him and down a corridor. "This one her lawyer." He nodded at Garrett, who followed them.

They came to a small, ugly room with a single cell and a desk with a computer on it. "Stand over there," Garrett said while Stevens logged on to the computer. "Try anything, he'll shoot you in the face. And no, spirits can't come in here. Our friends in House Iron saw to that. So don't bother."

The place smelled like an expired armpit. She crossed the room and stood against the wall, facing the desk.

"Hold still," Stevens said.

It occurred to Sierra that she was about to take one of the most epic mug shots ever. Robbie's ornate blue-and-orange skull rendering still covered three-quarters of her face. A few of her silver extensions had come unpinned and dangled past her chin. Plus, she still had the plastic fangs in. She curled her mouth into a wide grin.

"Real nice," Stevens grumbled as the laptop emitted a click. "Turn."

She did, wondering if she'd ever be able to get a copy of the picture. Izzy would want to post it on Whamzit or whatever that app was called.

"Now get in there." He pointed to the cell.

Sierra disappeared her smile and glared at him.

Garrett stepped forward and put his hand around Sierra's throat. "You wanna act tough, Little Lucera? Okay." He squeezed, just enough to tighten Sierra's windpipe. She felt like she was breathing through a straw.

"Stevens," Garrett said. "I'd like to speak to my client alone."

The officer left without a word, the heavy metal door clanging shut and locking behind him. Garrett loosened his grip some. Sierra took in a full breath of air, fighting to keep the desperation from her face. Her eyes flicked up to the security camera in the top corner of the room.

Garrett smiled. "Oh, you think that's on? Ha. Let me explain something to you, Sierra Santiago. As of the moment I had those cuffs put on you, your life belonged to me. It's mine to do with as I please. You think fear of getting caught would stop me from hurting you? Ha. There was a struggle and you attacked me. Boom, I pushed you and you fell, shattering your skull. Your fault. You think Stevens is the only cop I own? Ha. You think video evidence will save you? Ha. You haven't been paying attention, I guess. I could kill you slowly, if I want to. Your family isn't safe. Your friends. Trust me. And if I do get caught and convicted, which won't happen, you'll still be dead, and do you think I'm worried about these fools? I serve a higher power. I'm a Son of Light. Do you understand me? My degrees, my license, my success: mean *nothing* to me. They're stepping-stones along the way. These idiots have no idea what's going on in the world." His voice was perfectly even, his smile smug. "The Sisterhood of Sorrows birthed a new power in me, aligned me with my destiny. I'm the hunter, the Hound. I have a mission, and it is every inch of me. Without it, I'm nothing — just another useless dreg at the courthouse. It's not a hobby like you shadowshifters. It *is* me. I *am* the light. And you are darkness, the shadow. I'm here to cleanse the world of evil, little girl. I'm here to bring justice, banish the dark. And I won't flinch from my duty. Do you doubt me?"

She shook her head.

"The good news is, *you* have been given an option. Most people aren't. You get to choose the light. Because you walk in the legacy of light. And I get it." He actually smiled, a kind, older-brother-type smile with a twinge of sadness. "I really do. I've been where you are, believe it or not. Well" — he chuckled — "not *exactly* where you are, but you know: close enough. And I was offered a choice. The Sorrows lifted me up out of the darkness and infused me with light. I thought *this* mattered more than anything else in the world. This physical shit — cases won and guild awards and all these petty, ultimately meaningless little trinkets of approval. Ha. The Sorrows filled me with *light*, Sierra. Light. This is meaningless, life is meaningless, compared to that. Trust me. You'll see."

Sierra opened her mouth and then closed it again.

"Speak."

"If you're the Hound, what's Mina?"

Garrett's left eye flinched, ever so slightly. "A traitorous bitch."

Sierra just stared at him.

"And the Illuminated Sorceress. Or she was. They'll find someone new once . . ."

Sierra raised her eyebrows and he shook his head. "Get. In. The. Cell." Without waiting for her to comply, he wrapped a thick hand around her forearm and flung her inside, slamming the metal door behind her.

Prisoners had scratched their nicknames into the peeling paint, amidst various epithets and declarations of love. Tyrus had been here, and MAC, Breaker, Dash, and Killa P. The overheads emitted a noxious buzz, and Sierra could just make out the quiet murmur of precinct chatter through the wall.

How was it that just an hour ago she'd thought death might be a welcome relief, and now fear of it flooded through her unabated? It had taken all of her inner strength not to break down sobbing when the Hound had closed his hand around her throat. She'd kept it in as much out of spite as anything else; she'd not show him fear. He didn't deserve that. And anyway, her calmness seemed to have put him on edge.

But now what?

She was utterly alone, and the sob burst out of her without warning. She shook her head, collapsing on the cell bench and rubbing a few tears from her eyes. No one was there to comfort her or give her advice. And what could they say anyway? Any variation of *Everything's gonna be alright* would feel like a lie. Were her friends looking for her? They probably still had their hands full with the Sorrows' spirits. If they were even okay . . . And what did it mean that Mina had betrayed the Sorrows? Was she still their Sorceress?

Sierra stood up. The Hound hadn't been bluffing about the place being fortified against spirits — she could feel its emptiness: a void that felt deeper than death seemed to seep into her, hollowing her out. She couldn't 'shape. She couldn't run. But maybe she could see outside. If there were spirits out there, maybe she could see through them . . . She closed her eyes, casting her mind outward in radiating circles through Bed-Stuy.

Where are you all?

Nothing. They were fighting off the Sorrows, probably. Who knew what other attacks they launched tonight? Surely with Sierra locked up, they'd leap at the opportunity to strike.

Suddenly, the shadowy trees of Von King Park emerged into focus. Some passing spirit — Sierra could feel its disinterested, lugubrious gait as it bumbled along through the treetops like a tiny, over-it blimp. A group of trick-or-treaters traversed the otherwise empty park. That was it.

Sierra sighed and slumped back onto the cool metal bench.

Angry voices woke her, and somewhere far off, the pulse of drums and growl of an electric guitar. Sierra sat up. How much time had passed?

The voices got louder. An argument, just outside the room. She peered between the cell bars, saw a Stetson hat through the bulletproof glass on the door leading to the hallway.

Uncle Neville.

Sierra almost burst out laughing with relief. Even if he couldn't get her out, he was here. He was nearby. She could almost touch him. The world instantly became that much less terrible and cold. His words were muffled, but whatever Uncle Neville was saying, he was *pissed*.

For all his unspoken ferocity, Uncle Neville had never so much as raised his voice, let alone yelled in her presence. Sierra almost felt bad for whoever was on the receiving end of that wrath. Almost.

Someone else was talking now, this voice calmer but with no less urgency. She could tell from its cadence that the man was letting loose on some legal matter, listing off violations and possible consequences. Desmond Pocket. Uncle Neville kept saying, "Uh-huh" and, "That's right" after every phrase Desmond spoke.

A third voice, conciliatory, kept repeating, "Yes, okay, yes, I understand."

The glass door clicked and then swung open. Sierra ran to the edge of her cell, put her hands on the bars. "Neville." Her voice a choked whisper. "Neville."

Neville walked into the room, followed by the mustached sergeant who'd been running things the day Tee got arrested, Valdez. Desmond Pocket came in behind them. Desmond was mid-rampage, by the look on Valdez's face. Neville shot Sierra a quick wink and wily smile, then turned back to the others.

". . . which has already gone viral, not for nothin', so again I ask you," Desmond was saying, "what is the charge? Because resisting arrest not gonna fly and we all know that."

"That's right," said Neville.

"Your officer has already been caught in one lie . . ."

"A lie!"

". . . and this hasn't even fully been opened up yet. Understand, Sergeant Valdez, that we will completely obliterate any attempt to defame my client" — Desmond's voice was low, unwavering, his usually strong Jamaican accent reduced to a soft lilt beneath his lawyerly gusto — "who has no criminal record and is a model citizen in every way."

"Of course," Valdez muttered. "We simply —"

"Mr. Pocket wasn't finished speaking," Neville growled.

"That's correct. Furthermore, unlawful arrest is itself a crime. Are you prepared to have your officer put on trial for kidnapping? We already have proof. The press already has proof. The kids outside have proof too. And that situation is about to spill completely out of your control, with all due respect."

Outside? Sierra closed her eyes, and immediately the swell of music and chanting voices surrounded her. The park was full! Costumed revelers were packed in shoulder to shoulder, fists raised in the air, voices unified in a single chant: *"Free! Si-erra! Free! Si-erra! Free! Si-erra!"* There were vampires and aliens, witches, pirates. The Incredible Hulk stood beside a cow in sunglasses. Shadows swooped through the crowd, clustering in the air above the park and then splitting off again. Somewhere behind all the raised fists, Culebra thrashed in time to the chant. Culebra! Sierra almost broke down in tears again. Juan was there, and . . . Anthony stepped up to the mic.

"FREEDOM!" he boomed amidst the crowd's yells of *"Free! Si-erra! Free! Si-erra!"*

"How long we known each other, man?" Neville was saying when Sierra snapped her vision back to the cell.

Valdez sighed. "Neville, man, listen —"

"Don't *Neville, man* me, Raymundo Alvarez Quintero Valdez. I was at your goddamn baptism. And the young woman your department just roughed up and unlawfully arrested is my goddaughter. She is *my* people. She is with *me*." His voice never quite reached a yell, but Neville's unmistakable promise of dire consequences rasped through it. His whole tall, lanky body was wound tight like a jack-in-the-box. Sierra was pretty sure if she was ever on the receiving end of that wrath, she'd just go ahead and turn to dust rather than face it. "Anything that happens to her, I consider to have happened to me. And something has already happened to her tonight. She has been abused and unlawfully detained. Which means *I* have been abused and unlawfully detained. And I *dislike* being abused. I do not *enjoy* this detainment, which is unlawful. Is that clear? Have I been ambiguous or vague in *any* way?"

To his credit, Valdez stared Neville directly in the face and, very slowly, shook his head. Then he walked out of the room.

"Mi raas," Desmond whispered.

Neville turned to Sierra once the door had shut and flashed the winningest of smiles. "You alright, baby girl?"

Sierra nodded, pushing away tears. "Y'all got me out of here?" Her voice shivered but she held it together.

"We tink so," Desmond said. "Neva clear till it happen, dwo."

"Thank you both so much. I don't know what to say."

"Di King upload de video of you getting arrested deh on dat lil social network she have. Shit blew up. Fifty thousand views and counting in just a few hours. Local news already pick it up, CNN called."

"Izzy filmed it? I didn't even realize."

Neville rolled his eyes. "Y'all done changed the world with them little pocket thingamajigs and all the smack y'all talk online. Who woulda thought?"

"How long Culebra been playing out there?"

"Oh, they just set up a few minutes ago," Neville said. "Once Izzy dropped the video, folks started gathering here. Everyone was already out and about trick-or-treatin' anyway. Then Culebra announced they were playin' a live impromptu show in the park and, well . . . the other half of the world showed up that wasn't already here. It really is abouta get outta control; I wasn't bluffin'."

"We a get yuh outta here fas', Sierra, don' worry."

Sierra managed a smile. "Thanks, guys. Can you tell Izzy . . ." She glanced up at the camera. Was it really off? Garrett could've been lying. She beckoned Neville to come closer. "Robbie has what they need. He gotta stay safe. They're looking for it. Okay? The lawyer hanging around is with the Sorrows. Don't let him know you know."

Neville's face went cold. His eyes narrowed, and for a second, Sierra thought he might go strangle the Hound right then and there. Then he smiled, touched Sierra's hand on the bar. "We got you, girl. We on it."

Ten minutes later, Garrett walked into the room and closed the door behind him. In a moment of wild panic, Sierra realized this could be it. Close as she'd come to freedom, with all her loved ones just on the other side of that wall, she could die at the hands of her enemy right here. It was true what he'd said earlier — at the end of the day, what did it matter if he was even brought up on charges? She'd still be dead. But the House of Light wanted her alive, right? She looked at him, knowing desperation shone clear through her wide eyes and hating herself for it.

"Your godfather is out front finishing up the paperwork. You're free to go," he said without moving away from the door.

She exhaled. Almost smiled but didn't.

He didn't even flinch, just stood there, staring with those icy eyes.

"Does being free to go involve you opening this door at any point? Cuz . . ."

"Listen to me," he said softly, taking a step toward her. "You think you've won?"

She shook her head, holding eye contact.

"You haven't. You slipped away right now. Consider it a jailbreak. You may be legally free to go, but I'm beyond the law. Understand? The law is shit. You think you're safe? You're not safe. You're never safe. How do you think this ends? It ends with death. Maybe not yours — the Sorrows, in their infinite patience, seem intent on keeping you around.

For now. But I'm their enforcer, their finder, and I will find out how to break you and bring you over to them. I will. So here's how it ends: with you crying over the body of one of your loved ones, cursing yourself for bringing about their death. Picture that. And then picture it with someone else you love. And then someone else. Understand that once they're in my grasp, they won't get out as easily as you did. And remember I know the law. I own the law. I am the law."

Sierra didn't budge, didn't blink.

"And then picture crawling to the Sorrows on your hands and knees, begging them for mercy and to let you in. Picture them anointing you as they did me, bathing you in light. Picture them asking you to accept the supreme power of light inside you, and you saying yes. See them asking if you renounce the devil, the darkness, the shadows. See yourself nodding, saying yes and meaning it, and letting go of that evil within. And picture your cleansing, picture yourself emerging brand-new, a child of light, just like me." He looked like he might cry for a second, then he tightened his face. "They are merciful, the Sorrows. Me? Not so much. That's why they made me their Hound. Know that I will stop at nothing."

He opened the barred door and stood out of the way.

Sierra walked out of the room without a glance in his direction.

TWENTY-FIVE

It seemed like the whole of Bed-Stuy had come out to protest and party at Von King Park that night. A roar erupted as Sierra stepped out of the precinct with Neville and Desmond on either side of her. She blinked, startled by the sudden rush of excitement and people after all that steel and silence.

Her mom reached her first. "¡M'ija!" María gasped, wrapping Sierra in her arms and squeezing. She still had her pointy witch hat on and green face paint. Sierra laughed as tears streamed down her face.

Off in the park, Culebra had gotten wind of her release and paused their thrashing. Juan's voice took over the night: "My sister is free!" The crowd cheered. "But she shoulda never been grabbed up in the first place!" Boos and jeers. "She shoulda never been abused by the people that're s'posta protect her! S'posta protect us!" Behind him, Kaz ripped into a fast-paced bolero beat on his congas. His brother Ruben punctuated it with shimmering cymbal taps. "We s'posta be free!" Juan yelled.

Sierra's dad pulled her and María into a tight hug. "We were so worried about you, Sierra."

"I'm okay," Sierra said into his shoulder. It felt like a lie, though. Nothing was okay, least of all her. But still — she was alive. And she was free, for now, even if the sorrowful images Garrett had forced into her mind kept cycling over and over. "I'm okay."

Dominic Santiago, for the first time Sierra could remember, was crying.

"Daddy, stop," Sierra cooed. "Please."

He shook his head, burying it in María's jacket. "We didn't know . . ." he whispered through gulps and sobs. "We didn't know what happened."

"I know, Daddy, but I'm out now."

"C'mon, Dom," María said softly.

He nodded, wiped his eyes, and sniffled back some snot, blinking away tears. "I'm alright. But listen to me — whatever it is that's going on . . . Whatever you have to do, Sierra — end it. We need you to be safe, that's the most important thing."

"Okay," Sierra said. "I will. I'm sorry I worried you."

He cast a foul glare at the precinct. "It's not your fault, Sierra. We know it's not your fault. We saw Izzy's video."

"Where are the others?" Sierra asked.

As if on cue, Izzy's voice rang out across the park. "We sick'a this shit, y'all."

The crowd went nuts. A heavy drone dropped and then rumbled into a relentless, driving strut. *Anthony*. Sierra tried not to yearn, but the thought of his hands moving up and down that wooden bass neck made her all weak inside.

"We ain't takin' it no mo', y'all! This far and no further!"

"NO FURTHER!" The crowd yelled.

"How far?"

"THIS FAR! AND NO FURTHER!"

"We fed up! We in the schools bein' herded like animals. Being stripped and searched and arrested! White kids in the suburbs get that kinda treatment?"

"NO!"

"Then why the hell do we?"

Behind her, the Wild Seeds, all of them dressed like zombies, fell into line and let out a horn blast of approval.

"Listen, my girl Tee still stuck up in Woodhull's psych ward," Izzy shouted, "and you wanna know why?"

"Tell us why, King!" one random dude yelled.

The horns fell into a rising flourish as the step squad moved into position at the front of stage.

"They say she hallucinates dead people. That she worship the dead. Like . . . do you know what day it is? We *all* of us walkin' around dressed like zombies and ghosts. Why we ain't all locked up? Y'all see dead people?"

"YAA!" The crowd roared.

"We get the day off for Columbus Day, y'all. He dead. We celebrate Christmas! Jesus ain't die? They got statues up for dead guys that owned people. Name buildings after 'em. Entire colleges that they bully us about getting accepted to. America don't worship the dead? C'mon now! America worship the dead! It's cool when white America do it, but we can't worship *our* dead?"

The horns crescendoed and then Juan released a vicious, staticky explosion from his Stratocaster, Anthony's bass rumbling underneath all the while. Sierra made her way through the crowd. She needed to gather everyone. Whatever the Sorrows had planned, it wasn't over. Not yet. And no one was safe. And *where* the hell was Robbie? She dug into her shoulder bag, pulled out her phone, and frowned at it. Battery dead.

"Crap," Sierra said out loud.

People cheered for her and patted her back as she moved toward the makeshift stage at the center of the park.

"The King came to show you / came to let you know, you / can't escape the flow, can't fake the fro / gotta break the bro, take the ho and go!" The zombie marching band wound through the crowd like a joyful dragon as the step squad kept feverish pace with Izzy's rap. "Let 'em know!" Izzy yelled, and Juan ripped into another solo.

"Sierra!" Bennie practically jumped out of the crowd on top of her, squeezing with all her might. "You're alive! We were so worried!"

"You were worried? *I* was worried! What the hell happened?"

"We came to get free, y'all!" Izzy boomed. "And we ain't stoppin' till we free, you feel me?" The crowd let her know they definitely felt her.

"We were just hanging out, doing the thing," Bennie said. "Decided to practice 'shaping in the schoolyard. Then those gold-looking ghosts roll up on us heavy, and just as we gettin' ready to 'shape and fight 'em off, the cop shows, gun drawn. And that's when you came."

"The Hound of Light was in the squad car," Sierra said. "He's a damn lawyer."

"Right — after you got busted, Mina came running up to us, talkin' 'bout the Sorrows were planning to make a move and all this mess. And you know, far as we knew, she was the Hound, right? So we were like, real skeptical, you know? Cuz where *she* been all this time while we running around tryna not get got? But then she was making sense too and . . . that's why we were all freakin' out, because she saying the cop is . . . And then Izzy uploaded the video —"

"Where is Mina? And where's Robbie? We need 'em. ASAP."

"Mina was over there dancing a second ago. She actually alright, ya know. I had my doubts, but she cool. And Robbie —" Bennie shrugged. "Haven't seen him."

"Can you try calling him? My phone's de —"

"There she is, y'all!" Izzy's voice seemed to become the sky, ringing out over the swirl of trumpets and Culebra's thrash. Sierra cringed. "The woman of the hour! Our girl free!" People clustered closer, screaming and cheering. Sierra tried to smile, shaking her head. "Come up here, Si! Say a word!"

"No, no . . ." Sierra said, not even trying to pretend she wasn't mortified at the thought. "I'm good!"

"*Si-er-RA! Si-er-RA!*" the crowd chanted.

"C'mon, Si. Just let 'em know you alright."

Anthony was up there. He stood perfectly still, head down, as his fingers danced across the bass strings. Sierra had been keeping him in the sides of her eyes because if he looked up and she was looking at him, she didn't know what would happen.

"*Si-er-RA! Si-er-RA!*"

"They not gonna let up," Bennie muttered. "Just get it over with."

Sierra closed her eyes, nodded, then dapped Bennie and walked onto the makeshift stage. The crowd lost their minds. Izzy gave her a huge hug and handed her the mic. Anthony kept looking at his bass. Juan leaned over, still strutting a mean *wukka-wukka* on the frets of his Strat, and kissed her on the cheek. "Love ya, sis!" he yelled over the uproar.

"Uh . . . Thank you all so much for coming out," Sierra said, her voice clanging across the whole night. The band fell into a chill vamp — Kaz cycling through two heavy slaps on the congas and then a series of light ones, Anthony walking out a rugged jazzy riff as Ruben chimed in on the cymbals. "It's not really about me, though. It's about all of us. I'm just a black girl with big hair who wanna be free, just like anyone else. And there's no reason we should haveta rally in a park to make that happen, ya know?"

Angry yells of agreement rang out. Sierra smiled at her dangling braids, remembering her costume. "Okay, maybe my hair's not that big right now, but you know what I mean!" The crowd laughed with her and for a moment, everything felt sort of okay, like it was just a happy gathering of folks for a late October festival in the park. There was Mr. O'Leary, standing beside Ms. Rollins, of all people. And Trey Washington had shown up along with the whole Butler varsity basketball team, even that annoying guy, Gary. Pitkin was talking to Big Jerome and Butt Jenny. Farther back, Nydia stood beside Uncle Neville, one little kid on her shoulders and another holding her and Neville's hands together.

Sierra saw the shimmering hooded shadow spirits moving toward the stage, their eyes turned to her, fists raised. There was Vincent, stepping up beside Bennie. Bennie looked at her brother and smiled, and then their raised fists, one flesh and blood, one barely there, intermingled. Sierra raised her fist. "Let's get free, y'all!"

Ruben pushed the beat harder and the marching band in front of Sierra let out a mournful, harmonious growl. Sierra waved at the crowd again, yelled, "Thank you, Brooklyn!" into the mic King Impervious–style, handed it back to Izzy, and turned around to walk off the stage. Her eyes met Anthony's. He smiled. Trying to pretend her knees didn't just get wobbly, she ducked around his bass and slid up beside him. "Hey, you," she said, lifting up on her tiptoes to whisper in his ear over the swell of trumpets.

His smile got wider. "Hey."

"I'm sorry," they both said at the same time. Then they laughed.

"I'll go first." He hit a long, low note on the bass as the horns blasted out syncopated blasts. "I got lost in my feelings about everything. We moved really fast and it caught me off guard and I didn't know what to do with all the things I felt." He paused, looked away. Looked back, directly into Sierra's eyes. "Feel."

She smiled, realized she must look ghastly with the skull painted over her face, tried to ignore it. "I hear you. And I'm sorry I lied. I won't . . ." She paused, let the deep moan of Anthony's bass tremble up through her. The brass band yelped back and forth in a staccato call and response that gathered in fury with each new round. "I won't do it again. I'll tell you everything." She met his eyes. "I promise."

He kissed her, leaning and holding the bass neck out of the way as he hit another note. The crowd let out an extended, collective, *"Aww!"*

Sierra had forgotten hundreds of people were watching them. She opened her mouth in a wide grin, letting her fangs show, and laughed.

"Sierra!" Bennie yelled from the crowd. "I found Mina! And Robbie's on the way."

Sierra blinked at her. The world came back into focus, with all its danger and gloom.

Bennie looked sheepishly at Sierra. "Sorry, guys. Buzzkill, I know! Also: whoa!"

Sierra shrugged and punched Anthony's shoulder. "After this, we'll talk?"

"I would love to."

"Let me hear you say *freedom*!" Izzy yelled into the mic as Sierra climbed down from the stage.

"FREEDOM!" the crowd roared.

"I said *freedom*!"

"FREEDOM!"

"Stop killing us!"

"FREEDOM!"

"Stop cuffin' us!"

"FREEDOM!"

"Stop beatin' us!"

"FREEDOM!"

"You can't defeat us or treat us like we less than / we bless them with our presence our essence / you can't lessen the lesson / you won't repress them or stress them."

"FREEDOM!"

Bennie grabbed Sierra's hand. "Mina's at the far end of the park. The others are heading there too, and Ro —" They both looked up. Something was happening. A yell came from the edge of the crowd near the precinct. Sierra saw dark blue helmets peering over the tops of thick plastic shields. Riot gear.

"Oh, no," she whispered.

"This is the New York City Police Department," a mechanical voice exclaimed over yells from the crowd and the blasting marching band. *"You are ordered to disperse immediately from the premises. This is an unlawful gathering."*

People jeered and hollered insults. Culebra thrashed harder and the marching band resumed their strut through the crowd as the steppers bounced back into formation.

"Whose park?" Izzy yelled.

"OUR PARK!"

The shiny helmets advanced a step, shoving onlookers out of their way. *"This is the New York City Police Department . . ."*

"I said *whose park?*"

"OUR PARK!"

"Whose goddamn park is this?"

"OUR PARK!"

"Disperse immediately from the premises. This is an unlawful gathering."

A few people started peeling off at the edges of the

crowd. Sierra and Bennie traded an uneasy glance. "This ain't gonna be good," Bennie said.

Sierra took her hand. "We gotta leave. The Hound is . . . If any of us get —"

"If you remain on the premises," the megaphone blared, *"you will be arrested."*

A stark light blasted down from above — a police helicopter swooped through the sky, its beam bouncing giddily over the crowd, the *thwump-thwump-thwump* of its propellers barely audible over the fray.

"This a public park or nah?" Izzy's voice sounded calm, like she was just going about her business and a small child was annoying her.

"OUR PARK!"

"Do we have the constitutional right to congregate or nah?"

"OUR PARK!"

Izzy nodded at Juan. Juan and Anthony exchanged a serious look, then they both smiled. Sierra saw what was about to happen, started pushing her way toward the stage. "Juan!" she yelled, but her voice was swallowed up beneath the chants and megaphone blast. Then Ruben hit a four count with his drumsticks and Culebra unleashed electric fire from the center of the park. Both Juan and Anthony leaned into their instruments, stance wide and knees bent: full thrasher mode. They echoed each others' escalating riffs, Juan blasting up the neck of his guitar in ever-sharper power chords while Anthony's bass lines jangled toward an ecstatic howl. Ruben crashed and smashed away at his kit, sweat pouring down his face. Izzy just muttered into the mic, her eyes closed.

Sierra could barely make out her friend's voice amidst all the ruckus; it was like a gentle spoken-word lullaby in a sonic apocalypse. Then it dawned on her: Izzy was 'shaping. Sierra whirled around to where the crowd was shoving back against the line of cops. The spirits had joined them — shiny shadows dotted the mass of protesters. They were getting larger and thicker as Sierra watched, bolstered by Izzy's words.

"This is the New York City Police Department. If you remain in the park, you will be arrested. This is your final warning."

For a few trembling seconds, it looked like Izzy's spirit reinforcements would give the protesters enough strength to withstand the police line's forward thrust. Then the riot cops broke through the center of the protesters, hurling people to either side and slamming their batons against their plastic shields with rhythmic clanks.

"No!" Izzy yelled into the mic as protesters turned and began running through the park. The cops moved in fast, clubs swinging.

Sierra felt a hand grab hers and spun around. "Sierra," Robbie said. "We gotta get out of here. It's not safe." Culebra's song hurtled toward some kind of world-ending climax, each new riff shriller and heavier than the last.

"They're gonna grab up my brother and Izzy," Sierra said. "The Hound of Light is . . . He's a lawyer, Robbie. And he's got the cops in his pocket. At least some of 'em. We gotta —" Someone brushed past them, bumping Sierra and almost slamming head-on into Robbie.

"Hey!" the guy yelled. "Look where you're going!"

"Sierra, c'mon," Robbie said. A cluster of people ran past. The cops advanced closer, then as if on cue, they closed ranks and made straight for the stage. Culebra thrashed on, defiant.

"We ain't leavin'!" Izzy yelled.

In seconds, burly dark blue forms blitzed the band, tackling them in clusters.

"No!" Sierra yelled as the music shrieked to a feedback-laced halt. "Stop!"

The cops hauled up Izzy first, her arms handcuffed behind her back. A group of people gathered around, phone cameras out. "Long live the King!" Izzy yelled, a big smile plastered across her face. "We still here! You ain't heard! We here!" She looked even tinier than usual, all wrapped up in the grip of four cops in full riot gear. "You can arrest us, but we still here! We ain't goin' no place, tho! You seen us walk away? Nah, we here, boo! Treme, upload that shit to my Hoozit, boo, aight? And someone call Desmond. We keep that Jamaican busy, man. Long live the King!"

Juan was next, then Anthony, both escorted out with

grave looks on their faces. Sierra tried to get close, but a cluster of cops surrounded them.

"Sierra," Robbie said from behind her. "We can't do anything for 'em. The others are at the edge of the park. Mina's there. Let's go."

Sierra took a deep breath as the Hound's promise cycled endlessly through her mind. Then she nodded and ran off with Robbie.

TWENTY-SIX

Around the corner and up the block, away from all the chaos of the park, an empty, weed-strewn lot sat between a row house and one of those fancy new high-rises they'd been building all over Bed-Stuy. Sierra's dragon mural still glared off the Tower wall, but all of Manny's junk had been cleared out of the lot after he died. It still gave Sierra a lump in her throat to see the place empty. Thumping chopper blades pulsed through the night air above them, but there were no cops here, no flashing lights, no screams.

Sierra followed Robbie through a hole in the rusty fence and into the shadows, where Bennie, Mina, Jerome, and María waited.

"Mom?" Sierra said as Cojo ran up to her and nuzzled against her legs for his ear scratches. "What are you doing here? You can't . . ."

"You said to gather the 'shapers," Bennie said. "And your mom's the Spy, we can't leave her out."

"I know, but —"

"You damn right, you can't," María growled. "I know

you want to protect me, Sierra, but we don't have time for all that. Whatever we have to do, we all have to be on board."

Sierra sighed. "You're right. I know. Is Dad okay?"

"He will be. He's at the precinct with Neville and Mr. Pocket, trying to find out what they're doing with Juan and the others." María's face was steel — that mask she wore when nothing was even remotely alright but she refused to let it show. "But this . . . whatever is going on, I know it's not just about the police. Bennie says the Sorrows have someone inside the precinct?"

"The Hound," Mina said. "And he's got cops working for him."

"Oh, it was you that told her?" María rounded on her. "And why should we trust you? Sierra, isn't she with the Sorrows too?"

"I'm not!" Mina squealed. "I was, but . . ." She shook her head. "I left that behind. I betrayed them." She turned her pleading eyes to Sierra. "That's why I brought you the Deck, Sierra. I knew they were up to something, and . . . I didn't want you guys to get hurt."

Sierra frowned. She was so tired of playing these games, of not knowing who to trust. It would be so much easier just to cast everyone away, to disappear. But there was too much at stake, especially now that Juan, Izzy, and Anthony were caught.

And it was true: If Mina hadn't gone against the Sorrows, they'd all be a lot worse off than they were, hard as that was to imagine. She'd probably saved their lives. And they'd need her on their side if they were going to make it out of this mess. Still . . .

"You weren't honest with me about the Deck when I tried to find out about it, were you?" Sierra said. "You knew more about it than you let on."

Mina looked like she was about to shatter, but she took a deep breath and kept it together. "No," she said with a sniffle. "I didn't know if I could trust you yet. I'm sorry."

"If you didn't know you could trust us," Jerome said, "why'd you give us the cards at all?"

"There wasn't much of a plan at first, I admit. I had the Deck, so I figured opening things up a little couldn't hurt. Look, I knew the Sorrows were coming for you, one way or the other." She looked away, made a face. "They already had once after the whole thing with Wick."

"I *knew* it!" Sierra growled. "Of course that creepy guy that came at me outside the Red Edge in September had something to do with the Sorrows!"

Mina nodded. "Yeah. It's a long story. For another time. But I'd seen what they were capable of and I saw how everything would play out. I was already trying to figure out how to slow their roll, but I didn't think they'd put the Hound on me. *The Hound?* I've never known such terror. They kept his identity hidden, even within the House of Light, but I saw him peering into my hospital room the night after he had them sideswipe me. He couldn't do anything because there was security everywhere, but . . ." She shuddered. "I snuck out that night and been laying low ever since, and look . . . All I know now is that this whole system has to fall." She looked at Sierra. "You're the only one who can make that happen."

Sierra patted Cojo's side and pushed him forward toward Mina. "Can't do it alone, though."

Cojo strutted through the weeds to Mina, walked a full circle, sniffing at her feet and clothes, and then returned to Sierra, apparently satisfied.

That'll have to do, Sierra thought. Anyway, they didn't have much choice at this point. "You're the Illuminated Sorceress, right?"

Mina nodded.

"Still?"

Another nod. "They can't take it away without —"

"The Deck," Sierra said. "Thought so. C'mere."

"Si, what you doin'?" Jerome said.

Mina's face tightened with determination. She stepped up to Sierra.

"Sierra?" Bennie said.

Sierra fixed her gaze on Mina's. "Raise your left hand." She did, and Sierra put her own hand against it, palm to palm. "Close your eyes," she said, closing her own. "Everyone stand guard." The shadowshapers grumbled, but she heard them spreading into a circle in the tall grass around her and Mina. Cojo stayed close by Sierra, panting against her leg.

And then the whole world became a series of colorful globs flashing past in the darkness. She was within Mina's spiritual essence, exploring her inner depths like a deep-sea diver of the soul. A warm golden glow caught Sierra's attention and she focused on it — the Sorrows' touch. *This is what Mina would've been able to conceal if she was the Spy,* Sierra thought. It burned like a vast inner sun, spreading its rays along the entirety of Mina's being. And, Sierra had to admit, it was beautiful. But she wasn't here to admire the scenery.

She concentrated, allowing just a touch of her own shadow essence to escape from her and enter Mina. It slid along Mina's inner pathways and canals of bright color and took root. Sierra smiled inside herself as the wild landscape trembled and fell away from her. When she opened her eyes, Mina's mouth hung slightly open, her own eyes still squeezed tightly shut.

"Do you know what to do?" Sierra said.

Mina's smile disappeared as she nodded. "I don't know if it'll work, though." She opened her eyes.

Sierra shrugged. "Me neither. Robbie has the Deck."

"Thank you. For trusting me."

Sierra rolled her eyes but managed a smile. "Didn't have much choice, did I?"

"Did you just —?" María said.

"Sierra, what's going on?" Robbie asked.

Everyone had turned toward them, hands on hips or arms crossed.

"I don't have time to explain," Sierra said. "You have to trust me. And Mina. And each other. I . . . I have to go. Now." She hugged each of them, but not for too long, lest she break down crying.

"See," María said, not letting go of the hug even when Sierra tried to wriggle away. "You want to protect your mami and then you run off as if I don't want to do the same for you."

"I'm sorry," Sierra said, holding back a sob. "For everything."

"You don't have anything to be sorry about, Sierra. Just stay alive, please. We need you."

"I promise." She nodded into her mom's shoulder and then pulled away. "And I need you too. All of you."

"Forty-Second Street, Times Square," the train conductor garbled over the intercom. *"Stand clear of the closing doors."*

Sierra blinked awake. Something wet was on her face. She looked around with a start, clutching her shoulder bag close. A guy dressed as Zorro sat across from her, smirking. Beside him, Dora la Exploradora stared at her phone, entranced. A group of loud white guys, all dressed like

Ghostbusters, spilled their raucous, vodka-tinged laughter across the train car.

Sierra wiped the wetness from her face. Her fingers came away smudged with face paint and . . . tears.

Once again, she'd lied to the people she loved the most. The people who loved her. She had no business promising she'd stay alive when she knew damn well that was not likely to happen. A trance-like beat simmered along through her headphones — DJ Tazacaz's new track. Those moaning voices and persistent bass drones had laid the foundation for her troubled dreams: a tower made from the screaming faces of everyone she knew, teetering against a hellish red sky.

Half the shadowshapers were out of commission — wounded or in hospitals or prisons. It had taken less than a week to hobble her team, and most of it hadn't even been intentional on the part of the Sorrows. And she was supposed to be the one with the upper hand. But Sierra was only barely beginning to grasp how everything worked. What good was the upper hand when the whole system was clearly rigged against her? It had been designed and drawn with her destruction in mind. She sighed.

The automated intercom blurped out a warning to stay alert and stay alive as the train barreled uptown.

The rain fell in heavy sheets as Sierra walked out of the station and cut right down the dark sidestreets near the Hudson River. It thrummed a steady rumba against car hoods and bodega awnings, sent the last few trick-or-treaters scrambling for shelter. Sierra was soaked by the time she'd made it a block.

You sure about this? Vincent said, sliding up alongside her as she strutted through the downpour.

Sierra shook her head, her eyes unwavering from the path in front of her.

Ay, girl. It was Alice, her long strides keeping pace with Sierra's. *We with you, even when we ain't. Feel me?*

Sierra nodded. Up ahead, little Tolula Brown flitted through the shadows, executing a tiny pirouette, and then vanished.

Sierra unpinned her remaining braids as she walked past the ornate metal gate at the edge of the Sorrows' churchyard. The silver plaits fell in front of her face, covering it. She drooped her head, pulled her hoodie up, and walked up the path.

TWENTY-SEVEN

The gold-tinged Sinestrati fell into step on either side of Sierra. She caught shuddering glimpses of their shine through her swaying hair and felt their wariness of her as they clustered around. She watched her boots clomp through the mud and trash as the rain sent a million tiny splashes rippling across the dark surface of each tiny puddle. Instead of cresting the hill to the copse of trees, the Sorrows' spirits led her along the path to the side of the cathedral. There, a battered wooden door hung open, revealing only gaping darkness within.

Sierra paused at the entrance, took a breath. The spirits around her trembled, hissed harsh unintelligible whispers to each other, and waited.

She could turn back. Run. She'd make it to the gate, maybe, if that far. They'd drag her back, screaming, and she'd be no better for it. And anyway: No. Her mind was made up, and though her whole body shivered with what would come, she stepped through the doorway into the darkness.

Her hands ahead of her, she made her way along a

narrow passageway, following the dim golden glow ahead. Through another doorway, and then the air changed and the light grew stronger. She'd entered the main chapel. It was still so dark she could barely make out her own boots, but the Sinestrati clustered close on either side again, lending their dim golden shine to her path. Up ahead, she felt the collective might of the Sorrows awaiting her.

Welcome, sister.

Bury the rage, bury the hate. No snappy comeback would do her any good right now. Put it all away.

We thought you might come tonight.

Somewhere, water dripped incessantly from the far-up rafters. Outside, the rain covered the night, pounded steadily against the dark stained glass windows. Sierra's footsteps echoed through the vast chapel.

"Is she alone?" a gruff voice said. That would be the burly older man from the throwdown in the churchyard, Bertram, the Warrior of Light.

"She better be," said another. Sierra stopped walking. Wayne Garrett. The Hound. She closed her eyes, swallowed back the explosive curse-out teasing the edges of her lips. Started walking again.

Garrett chuckled softly.

Silence, the Sorrows hissed in unison. *It is not for you two to question our sister as she steps forward into her destiny.*

Remember, one said, *that soon she will be one of us.*

And more powerful than either of you, added another.

Sierra let herself revel in the thought of that for a moment, then shook away the image of both men cowering before her. She walked up the three creaking steps to the dais.

The golden glow grew stronger around her; the Sorrows closed in. She felt their warmth, sensed the fizzle of excitement in each of them as they laid pale, shimmering hands on her and turned her to face the empty chapel.

She has come.

She is here.

We have waited so long.

They spoke in hushed voices, giddy with anticipation. The men on either side of her took heavy steps closer until she could hear their bated breath. She watched her feet, the water dripping from her silver braids and catching the golden shine of the Sorrows as it formed tiny puddles on the chapel floor.

We begin?

Do we begin?

Is everything in place?

"Wait," Bertram said. "Let me check her arms."

A hiss of irritation from the Sorrows. Bertram took one of Sierra's wrists and pulled her hoodie sleeve up. "Let me see the other." She did. "Alright, she's clean. Don't need her shooting those arrows out at us if things go sour, do we now? And remember . . ." He stood behind her and clenched both her arms in his massive hands. "I can literally crush you up like a piece of paper and throw you away." He squeezed. Sierra could tell it was just a fraction of his strength, but both of her arms exploded with pain. She was locked in place. The Warrior's grip tightened and Sierra let out a gasp.

Enough! the Sorrows cawed. *There will be no need for that.*

Bertram squeezed a second longer; Sierra felt like she might pass out from the pain. Then he let go and stepped away. She exhaled, blinking through the slowly receding burn.

Silence, sisters, silence.

We begin.

A moment passed; the whole world held its breath. Sierra wanted to scream. The glow grew strong against her soaking wet hoodie and dress, her brown legs and heavy black boots. The Sorrows hovered directly in front of her. Their hands reached out; she felt the gentle, trembling weight of them against her braids.

Luceraaa, they said as one, drawing out the name as if savoring a fine dessert. *Lucera.*

Ever so slightly, Sierra nodded.

Our lost sistren. Gone for generations while we waited. Gone.

And now, returned.

Over hallow and hall, through merciless waves and the lash, through the pillars and the piles, bemoaned and forgotten, forged anew.

Returned to us.

To us.

Lucera.

Their whispers entwined like writhing snakes in Sierra's mind. She lost track of which was speaking or where they were — the church, the pounding rain, the Hound and Warrior beside her, all seemed to slip away on the golden tide of the Sorrows' prayer.

We three are one.

One.

We three are one.

One.

We now become four.

One.

And four becomes one.

One.

One.

One.

ONE.

The hands on her head seemed to catch fire. Sierra closed her eyes, allowed the pulsing burn to flare and then simmer across her crown.

She didn't cry out.

She will learn.

She will grow.

She will burn, unendingly, as we do.

One.

Our sister.

One.

The sisterhood, at last.

One.

Quadrangle complete.

ONE.

The glow burned through Sierra's eyelids in flickering waves. They were moving, or two of them were anyway. Two Sorrows swooped tight circles around her while one held perfectly still, inches from Sierra.

Do you, Lucera, accept the power of the House of Light within you, and step into your rightful place as a Sister of the Sorrows, thus completing the quadrangle to rule the House of Light?

Sierra took a deep breath. The rain-soaked night and dank church air returned to her. The world. Her family and friends. She blocked it out again.

"I do."

A collective sigh went up from the Sorrows. The Warrior shifted on his feet and the Hound whispered, "Jesus, it's done," and rubbed his fingers together.

Sierra found that she was smiling and wasn't sure why; she felt tears in her eyes.

Then we shall begin.

The heat simmering along the crown of Sierra's head suddenly seeped down her brow and spread across her face like a slow lava flood. Her teeth chattered; the raw, burning energy sent dazzling razors dancing through Sierra's neck and shoulders, down her chest and along her arms as the onslaught of blinding heat gathered and spread. An ocean-deep silence overtook the world, broken only by an occasional high-pitched clicking and a soft feminine voice chuckling idly.

"Uh," she heard herself grunt. Then the rain, the city, the world returned to her.

Shhhhh, child. The burn is only the beginning, but it will soon pass.

The birth of light amidst the darkness.

Burn . . . burn . . .

Thick hands grabbed her arms from either side, and for a second Sierra's breath caught — even the burgeoning heat within her became a secondary concern. But the Hound and the Warrior were steadying her this time, not restraining her.

She was their sister now, after all. Their soon-to-be leader. And she had wavered.

For a moment, they stood there frozen as the light from the Sorrows deluged languidly through her. Then she straightened. The shaking she'd only half been conscious of stopped. The Hound and the Warrior released their holds and stepped back, their footsteps echoing.

It begins.

It has begun.

We are one.

The warm, golden light took hold somewhere deep inside Sierra and then erupted outward, blasting forth in a million tiny rays. Sierra inhaled sharply.

Yes, child.

Release and allow the light to live inside of you.

It is done.

The brand-new sun within Sierra cooled and she felt it settle, swallowing back its infinite bursts.

You feel it, don't you, child?

Sierra nodded.

You feel the power of light within.

The Sorrows were spinning again. She wasn't sure when they'd stopped, but as before, one remained still in front of her while the other two circled around them. Together, they said: *Do you embrace the power granted to you by the light?*

"I do," Sierra said, her voice unwavering.

Will you use it for good and never evil?

"I will."

And do you renounce the House of Shadow and all the powers of shadow within you?

Sierra let a moment pass. The wind and rain, the heavy breath of the two men beside her.

She snapped her head up, flipping her braids away from her face. She recognized the Sorrow called Septima staring back at her with wide eyes. "No," Sierra said. The Sorrows gasped as one. "Never."

TWENTY-EIGHT

Wha — was all Septima could get out before Sierra lunged at her. The whole world became a glorious golden ocean as Sierra went into the shroud, and then that slender porcelain face emerged, its mouth wide open in terror. Sierra's hands stretched out, wrapping around that long, immaculate neck. She felt the room spin as the two of them careened off the dais.

"Never," she said again. Then she bucked her head as the shadow inside her roared up her spine, and the dark blue paint burst across the shining emptiness between her own face and the Sorrow's. It was just the top right quarter of Robbie's painted skull that went, and it landed dead center on Septima's petite nose, splattering an ugly, dead-eyed continent from her top lip to her forehead. She screamed and reared back.

Septima was still alive, Sierra realized. This was a flesh and blood neck in her hands, not a phantom. The Sorrows must've used the power of light as some kind of fountain of youth.

It didn't matter. Sierra gave the shrieking woman one hard shake and then shoved her to the floor, spinning around just as the other two leapt at her from the dais.

They halted in their tracks when they saw her face, and then looked down at their fallen sister.

What have you done? they moaned. Septima whimpered from the ground.

The painted skull now covered exactly half of Sierra's face — the only half that was smiling. "I did what you always wanted me to do." She took a step toward them.

The Sorrows flushed back. *No . . .*

"Yes. I joined your little club. We're sisters now." She stepped closer, and then the two golden shrouds parted to either side and a burly form moved out from between them: the Hound of Light. He had a T-shirt on but was still wearing his suit pants. He reached one hand across his chest and pulled something from beneath his arm: a revolver. The same one from her vision.

Sierra stumbled backward, raising a hand. She'd known she would probably face down that gun eventually. She'd tried to imagine what that might feel like, but the truth was, nothing could've prepared her for the sight of Wayne Garrett raising its sleek muzzle as he stepped slowly and deliberately toward her down the aisle, his eyes on fire with the certainty of her death.

"No!" Sierra yelled, and something inside her flared. The light lifted up and outward from her core, eclipsed even the Sorrows' shine and threw stark shadows behind Garrett. His huge silhouette flashed against the suddenly illuminated crucifixion scene at the back wall of the dais, and his arm flew up over his face.

The Sinestrati closed in from either side. They moved cautiously, glancing back and forth between Sierra and the crumpled form of Septima at her feet. "Rah!" Sierra yelled, waving her arm at them and letting the light flare higher. They skittered back, and the ring around her held.

This wouldn't last long. Garrett was blinking his vision back to normal. She had no idea how this light thing worked, could barely control it. She had to get that gun away from Garrett and then maybe, just maybe, she'd have a chance to make a break for it, regroup and figure out what the hell to do next.

Up on the dais, Bertram must've seen her eyes focus on the revolver. He broke toward Garrett at the same time Sierra did. Neither one got to him. Something gigantic shoved Sierra to the side as it galloped past her — something furry. Sierra stumbled, regained her footing in time to look up and see Cojo's giant form launch into the air as Garrett raised his gun and screamed.

The blast seemed to become the whole world for a second. A chunk of wood flew up into the air from one of the dilapidated benches beside Sierra. The Sorrows shrieked. Cojo collided full force into Garrett and the two landed in a heap on the steps.

"Shit!" Bertram yelled, running toward them. He stopped, squinted into the darkness behind Sierra. "Shit." He pushed past her, rolling up the sleeves of his jumpsuit as he went. The man reeked of sweat and menthols.

As Sierra turned, something bright and colorful slammed into the crew of Sinestrati next to her, blasting a few of them into pieces and scattering the rest. It looked like . . .

"Nydia!" Sierra yelled, just as the Columbia librarian stepped out of the shadows at the far end of the cathedral.

María walked past her down the aisle, one finger in the air. "You estay *away* from my daughter," she yelled, rage thickening her accent.

"Mami, no!" Sierra gasped.

"Oh, okay, lady," Bertram grunted, breaking into a run toward María. He was short but thick, and Sierra could see the power of the Warrior of Light surging through him. "This should be fun."

"He's the —" was all Sierra could get out before María pulled back her fist and decked him across the face. The hit spun him all the way around, sent one tooth hurtling off into the darkness in a splash of blood from his split lip. Sierra knew instantly that whatever else happened, the look of utter shock on Bertram's face at that instant would never stop bringing her joy.

He caught himself before completely toppling, shook his head, eyebrows creased with confusion. And then María was on him again. She yanked him by the back of the shirt, whirling him to face her, then took his collar in one hand and proceeded to wail on him with the other.

Each hit sent sharp echoes through the cathedral, followed by pitiful grunts from Bertram. For a few seconds, no one moved. Sierra's mouth hung open as she watched her mom let loose on this once unstoppable force of a man. The only way her mom could best the Warrior was if . . . Somehow, her plan had actually worked. Mina had initiated each of the shadowshapers into the House of Light, and María had ended up the new Warrior. Sierra shook her head. Her mom administered one final, devastating blow to Bertram's face and then let him collapse in a bloody, whimpering heap.

The scream from behind Sierra was so sudden and shrill it nearly toppled her. She spun around. The two Sorrows still standing had their arms raised and their mouths wide open. The Sinestrati stood in battle formation on either side of them, poised to attack. Their collective glow was like a small sun; it illuminated the whole front of the chapel. Sierra took a step back.

"Shadowshapers," she said, knowing her friends were behind her. "Attack."

A blast of light flashed from the back of the room, matching the Sorrows' blaze. Then something bright green zoomed past and resolved into a figure — one of Robbie's green demons, Sierra realized. Another flew by; this one looked like a Mack truck but had long robotic arms that swung wildly at the Sinestrati, holding them at bay.

Sierra glanced behind her, saw Jerome with his hands raised, a huge smile on his face. "I did it!" he whispered. Robbie was beside him, eyes squinting with determination. Caleb, towering over everyone and still looking somewhat busted, sent wave after wave of bristling shards cascading out into the air. Mina was there too, trying her best to 'shape something she'd painted onto one of the benches, while Nydia egged her on. Bennie had her eyes closed and one hand raised. Sierra watched Vincent's shimmering form dive toward her and disappear, and then a spray-painted triangle spun into the air and zipped over Sierra's head.

Sierra turned just in time to see it slice into one of the Sinestrati, hurling it backward, and then curve a wide arc and clobber two more. The Sorrows screamed and the Sinestrati flushed forward past Sierra. She clobbered the two nearest her, watching her arms blaze bright with her fury, and then a wall of shadows rose up before them. The two spirit armies clashed with a vicious howl.

The Sorrows screeched and closed in on either side of Sierra and then froze, their golden shrouds flickering in the dim chapel.

You . . . killed us . . .

Sierra blinked at them, both her hands raised to strike. "I did?" She'd certainly been about to try, but . . .

House of Light is no . . . more . . . The Sorrows both slid toward the ground like two glowing slow-motion waterfalls. It was beautiful and terrifying. The House of Light must've been powering the magic keeping them alive. They shrieked as they went, flashes of light spinning away from them until they were just two emaciated women in elegant dresses. In seconds, their skin turned gray and flaky. Their teeth crumbled to dust and their legs gave out as their small bodies collapsed into two piles of bones and torn flesh amidst their empty gowns.

Sierra stared at them. The room had gone very still. The only sound was Septima's wailing from the ground, where she still lay huddled within an ever-dimming glow, and Bertram laboring to breathe through his broken face.

"No!" Garrett's yell came from the dais. Cojo stood off to the side, the gun gripped securely in his maw and thoroughly drooled on. Garrett clambered to his feet, tears streaming down his face. "What did you . . . what did you *do*?"

Sierra shook her head, speechless.

"It's *gone*! Gone! We're . . . we're nothing now! Don't you see . . ."

"What are you talking about?" María said.

"The light, you idiots! The light is gone! Do you not . . . How is this . . . *how*?" He stepped toward Sierra but Cojo got in front of him, his low growl filling the cathedral. Garrett looked down at the dog, and for a second Sierra thought he was about to hurl himself forward, just to let

Cojo devour him and put an end to it. Then Garrett shook his head, turned around, and ran.

"Stop him!" Jerome yelled.

"No," Sierra said. "Let him go."

"What?"

"He's . . ." She looked around. Septima writhed within a purplish glow. Bertram lay on his back, his chest rising and falling. The Sinestrati had lost their golden glow and were shrinking into the shadows. Sierra's friends looked at her expectantly. "It's over."

"But he's still out there," Jerome said. "He still got connects with the cops."

"He won't, though. He's broken. He has no more reason to come after us. Nothing to fight for."

Cojo placed the gun on the floor and trotted over to Sierra's side, nuzzling his head against her.

"Because the House of Light is no more," Caleb said.

Sierra nodded. "And Shadowhouse gone too."

"What?" Bennie, María, and Jerome said at the same time.

Sierra dug into her pocket and pulled out the one card she'd kept with her. It had changed. *OUR LADY of SHADOW and LIGHT,* it read now. The skull now ran straight down the middle of the woman's face, just like Sierra's. "There's a new house, the House of Shadow and Light. And we're all part of it."

Caleb stepped forward. He looked exhausted, but his

smile was as wide as Sierra had seen it. "You did this," he said. "You made this."

Sierra shook her head. She looked at Jerome and Bennie, Mina, Nydia. Robbie. Her mom, who still glared at Bertram like she had a few more thumps for him. Vincent and Alice stood amidst a crowd of shadow spirits; Tolula floated in the air above them. Sierra thought about Juan and Izzy and Anthony, sitting in a holding cell somewhere, just like she had been a few hours earlier. And Tee, waiting out her mandatory detention in the Woodhull psych ward. "We did this. All of us. This is ours. We made it together."

María reached her first, wrapping her arms around Sierra's neck and squeezing way too tight. "Are you okay, baby?"

Sierra laughed through tears. "Of course I am. Are *you* okay?"

María nodded.

"Here." Mina held the Deck of Worlds out to Sierra.

She stared at it for a few seconds. So much damage had been done, so many lives thrown into upheaval. She would have to figure out how to find balance with this unwieldy magic. She took the deck and pocketed it. "Thank you, Mina." She looked up at her friends. "Let's get the hell out of here."

TWENTY-NINE

Sierra stood perfectly still, her hands shoved into her hoodie pockets, fro out and swaying in the weirdly warm November breeze. Around her, the rooftops of Bed-Stuy looked like rolling hills, punctuated by a church steeple here, a glass high-rise there. A few spirits flitted through the early afternoon sky. Farther to the south, the dome of the Brooklyn Museum peeked over the brownstone horizon.

"Goodness," Caleb said from behind her. "I see why you come up here all the time. Amazing view and no corny douchebags yammering away about nonsense."

Sierra smiled. "What more could a girl ask for, really?"

Vincent, standing on her other side, chuckled. *We ghosts yammer plenty about nonsense up here, as a matter of fact.*

"Fair enough," Caleb said. "I find the dead tend to be better conversationalists than the living, though."

For a few seconds, they let the city fill the silence around them: passing cars, a plane overhead, shouts and giggles from the Middleton kids playing blob tag down below.

Then a gentle jingling of metal whispered in the breeze, the devil's off-key wind chime. *Happy birthday, Lucera.*

Sierra rolled her eyes. "No diminutive this time?"

You have surpassed all expectations, the King of Iron said as his hunched-over, sparkling form resolved, lurching slowly toward her on the rooftop.

"Funny how I keep doing that and the expectations keep being low. Might wanna check on that."

Fair enough. I see you've brought a second to the parley. Your Warrior of Shadow and Light, I presume. Good afternoon, Mr. Jones.

"Don't speak to me," Caleb said. He had drawn the Sorcerer card, in fact, but Sierra had brought him along in part because she figured Crane would presume him the Warrior.

The King of Iron bowed slightly. *I apologize if you feel slighted by my deception. I considered you a true friend during my time with the shadowshapers, for what it's worth.*

"Ain't worth shit."

"What do you want, Crane?" Sierra said.

I come with assurances, and I ask but one thing.

"No."

But I . . .

"The answer stands."

The Deck is reshuffling. You have seen it, I'm sure. There are new houses emerging. We are all in danger if they unite and make a play.

Sierra smirked. "Like you did with the Sorrows? Not interested."

The old phantom nodded. *Perhaps one day you will be. The offer stands. In the meantime, I present another token of my sincerity.*

"The last time you presented one of those, I ended up in jail and my friends almost died."

You still have the card, though, no? It was not a fake. Possession of that card gives you the upper hand on me more than anything else I could have given to you. It surpasses that silly trick.

Sierra just stared at him. He was right, but that didn't make him any more trustworthy.

Your comrades, for the duration of their internment, will be protected.

She raised her eyebrows. "Oh?"

The prison is, of course, the domain of House Iron. That's why the Sorrows sent their Hound to have your associates locked up in the first place. As long as the shadowshapers are within the prison system, they will be safe. I give you my word.

"Anthony too," Sierra said.

He isn't —

"It wasn't a question. Anthony. Too."

The King of Iron sighed. *So it shall be. I give my word.*

Sierra nodded. Neville had already arranged for his people on the inside to keep an eye on them, but the added spirit protection certainly wouldn't hurt. "Good. Now leave. It's my birthday, and I've spent enough time away from the people I love on your account."

Very well. One more question, though: Septima?

Best anyone could figure, the only surviving Sorrow had received some bit of Shadowhouse magic when Sierra bapped her with the splash of painted skull, and it had somehow kept her alive when the House of Light collapsed. Either way, she was essentially powerless. They'd sealed her in the cathedral until they could figure out what to do with her. "Noneya," Sierra said.

Old Crane shrugged and turned away. The jingling sound filled the air for a few seconds after he vanished into the afternoon sky.

"Y'all trust him?" Sierra said, facing Vincent and Caleb.

"No," Caleb said. "But I believe him. If he's pledged House Iron to protect Izzy, Juan, and Anthony, they are safe. Those Iron cats take 'word is bond' to a whole 'nother level, Sierra." He dug into his leather shoulder satchel and took out a cardboard box about the size of a photo album.

"What's this?"

"HBD, as the morons on my Facebook page say every September. Took me forever to figure out what the hell they were talking about. Lazy asses."

"Caleb, you didn't have to —" She opened the box. "Oh, wow." The last time she'd seen the *Almanac of the Deck of*

Worlds had been in Crane's silverware forest of a room. "You . . . you stole it?"

Caleb cocked his eyebrow. "I mean, he died, so . . . wasn't really his anymore. As far as the St. Agnes attendants were concerned, anyway."

"Brilliant, man. Thank you, this is . . ." She flipped through the old pages to the entry titled, "House of Shadow and Light." The half-skulled face grinned out from the page. Sierra smiled. "We did that shit."

You my hero, Si, Vincent said. *Ain't nobody like you.*

Sierra shook her head and closed the book. "Feel like I got us all into this mess. I gotta do something to get us out."

"You can't take this on yourself," Caleb said, starting toward the stairs. "You didn't bring this storm on. This storm was coming. You held it off. And you changed the whole Deck of Worlds in the process."

"Bah." Sierra shrugged off his words.

Robbie's head appeared at the top of the stairs. "Hey, can I have a word?"

Sierra felt an unexpected flush of relief at seeing him. They hadn't had a chance to talk since everything went down at the cathedral.

"I'll see you down there," Caleb said, nodding at Robbie as he passed. Vincent traded a dap with Robbie and then disappeared into the stairwell.

"Let me start," Sierra said. "I'm sorry, man. I shoulda

respected your feelings more. I knew how you felt, you were clear 'bout how you felt, even if it took you like eight years to tell me, and I still . . . I dunno, I still hurt you. I'm sorry."

Robbie waved her off. "You did, but . . . I'm not sure if you had any say in the matter. I walked right into my own trap."

"Damn," Sierra said quietly.

"You have feelings for that bass player, huh?"

She closed her eyes. Nodded. It didn't make sense — they barely knew each other — but really: What *did* make sense these days? And since when did liking someone have to make sense? She opened her eyes. "I do."

Robbie nodded, swallowing. "I know I said . . . that I couldn't do this. But . . . after everything that's happened, I can't just walk away either. I can't pretend everything's alright. What I'm trying to say is: I'm going to try and just be cool. I can't promise it'll work and I know it won't be easy, but I can promise to let you know what's going on with me — not too much, though! Of course!" He allowed himself a little chuckle and Sierra did too. "But yeah. I'm gonna stick around. Be your friend and stuff. Gonna try." He kicked the asphalt with his sneaker. "Happy birthday 'nshit."

Sierra managed a smile. "Thank you, Robbie. That . . . means a lot. I will . . . I will do whatever I can to be your friend and not make you miserable."

He grimaced. "Just be gentle with me right now. I'm kinda fragile."

"I can do that. You ready to spend some time with the gang of ruthless hooligans that we sometimes call my friends?"

The front door opened as Sierra and Robbie were coming down the stairs. Tee poked her head in. "Y'all started the party without me?"

Bennie, Jerome, and Caleb stood up from the kitchen and yelled, "Tee!" Everyone crowded around her, trading hugs and daps and jokes.

"You okay?" Sierra asked.

Tee shrugged. "I will be. Worried about Izzy."

"Whaa gwaan, people?" Desmond Pocket had walked in amidst the commotion. He put a comforting hand on Tee's shoulder. "We ago get yuh gyal friend free, yuh hear?"

"What's the word?" Bennie asked as they all gathered back around the kitchen table.

Desmond sighed. "Ah, it's complicated, you know. Oh, an' happy birthday, Sierra. Unu 'ave nuh cake?"

"Of course." Sierra went to the counter for the half-eaten cake her mom had made that morning. "You want ice cream too?"

"Nah, dat awright. Look, Juan had a clean record and good standing, so dey was gonna let him post bail and be off till the hearing, which is in three months . . ."

Sierra felt her stomach plummet as Desmond's voice trailed off. "But?" She put two slices of cake on the table.

"Anthony did 'ave one prior conviction, and it was for possession with intent, so there's no bail, and because he seventeen it won't be juvie, it'll be Rikers — the adult side. Till the hearing, that is."

"Shit," Jerome said.

"And Juan refused to post bail."

Bennie looked like she was about to burst into tears. "But why?"

"For Anthony," Sierra said, rubbing her eyes. Juan had always been kindhearted, but to voluntarily stay in lockup to help his friend . . . that was another level. But how to explain?

"Who the hell is Anthony?" Jerome demanded.

"Pulpo!" Tee and Bennie said at the same time. Tee rounded it off with, "Where you been, man?"

"Oh, the bass player? That's his name? All this time? Damn."

"It's not my business to tell," Sierra said. "But Anthony has a condition that only Juan and a few other people can be of any help with. Juan's like his anchor . . . when it happens."

"Is he a werewolf?" Jerome said. Tee smacked his arm. "Ow. It's not like that's such an unreasonable question considering . . . like . . . who *we* are."

Sierra's chuckle took the edge off the sorrow rising inside her. "He's right 'bout that, but nah, nothing so extra. Anyway, my brother's amazing." She hoped with everything in her that they'd be okay. Even with the sworn protection of House Iron *and* Neville's crew . . . things could get ugly in there. And Rikers . . . A creepy old island out in the East River somewhere, the cold seeping in through all those layers of metal and concrete, all those unfriendly faces and Anthony in the middle of it all, tall and beautiful and curled up in a ball on a hard pallet in some cell . . .

No. Sierra shook away the thought. Juan would be with him. Or nearby, at least. And he'd be safe. And she'd figure out a way to visit if she could.

She would.

"Hey," Bennie said, putting her hand on Sierra's. The others had started chatting among themselves while Sierra got lost in miserable fantasies.

She looked up, saw a flicker of her own worry in her best friend's eyes, and managed to smile. "You . . . you caught feelings that quick?" she said quietly.

Bennie scrunched up her face. "Shut up. It's not like we haven't known each other for ages, and . . . I mighta been feeling the same way for a while, I just . . . I guess I just didn't think he'd ever . . . and you know . . . we only had that one night when I knew he felt any kinda way and then . . ." She exhaled, blinking. "Whew, yeah. At least we got to go trick-or-treating together for like twenty minutes."

"Man . . ."

"And you!" Bennie shook a fist at Sierra. "You got some telling me things to do, missy."

"I do, I do," Sierra conceded. "I *really* do."

Bennie's eyes went wide. "Oh word?"

"Anyway," Desmond said, finishing off his last bite of cake and wiping his mouth, "yuh parents handling some business downtown with Neville. They was livid but they unnastand. They awright."

"What about Izzy?" Tee asked, her eyes already watery.

"Izzy still sixteen and a minor," Desmond said. "But the charge for alladem is inciting a riot, and criminal anarchy. That's a felony, so . . . they put the bail super high and her family say dey not sure dey can afford it, you know?"

"We'll get the money together," Sierra said, rubbing Tee's back. "Whatever we have to do."

"So, it's not the best news, but that's what I got. Everyone working overtime on this, yuh know, and look, there's a lotta video footage of what happened and the NYPD already fighting a public image battle on all fronts. Plus, Neville's in with Sergeant Valdez at the Seventy-nine don't hurt either. I believe we gonna get dem off, you know, dey just gotta hang in der till the hearing. But lemme get movin' and make sure all the gears in motion fi get these charges thrown out, okay?" He stood and made his way around the table, dapping everyone. "Sierra, happy birthday again, love. I'm sorry it couldn't be a happier one, but hope dis year will be fulla nuff blessings fi you."

"Thanks, Desmond," Sierra said, standing and hugging him.

———————

An hour later, they were all sitting around the table sipping coffee and rubbing full bellies. Mina had shown up and everyone greeted her with big smiles and waves. She seemed to be settling in nicely with the group.

"So tell me again how this made sense," Tee said, pouring the last of the coffee into her cup. "Sierra, you rolled up on the Sorrows like 'Ay!' and they initiated you into the House of Light —"

"Also known as the Lighthouse," Jerome put in.

"Hush. And then when they asked you to renounce Shadowhouse, you were like 'nah.' That about right?"

Sierra raised one shoulder up to her ear. "Pretty much? It sounds a lot cooler than it felt when you say it like that."

"And meanwhile Mina was over there initiating all these mofos?"

Mina nodded, smiling. "I realized what Sierra was planning when we met up in the Junklot and . . . I didn't know if it'd work, but I figured it was worth a try."

"It worked," Robbie said.

"I don't think anyone thought that a whole new house would come out of it, though," Mina said. "And the end of two old ones."

"Your mom still pissed she's not the Warrior of Light anymore?" Bennie asked.

Sierra rolled her eyes. "She'll get over it. She got to righteously whup someone's ass during her ten-minute tenure; feel like that's as much as anyone could ask for."

"Incoming!" María called from the doorway. Cojo barreled into the kitchen, a gigantic, excited blur of fur and tongue and saliva with a furiously wagging tail.

"He's allowed in the house now?" Sierra said as María and Dominic walked in and hung their coats up.

"Figured since he saved our lives and whatnot," María said. "And anyway, he was waiting outside when we got home and it started raining again, so . . ."

Dominic scoffed. "She says that now. But who's going to be the one walking him? This guy."

"Don't you guys have school today?" María put her hands on her hips and sharpened her glare.

"Nah," Tee said. "It's Sierra's birthday. That's a national holiday, far as I'm concerned."

"We heard about Juan," Bennie said, standing up from the table. "I'm so sorry." She crossed the room and gave María a huge hug. Both Santiagos nodded, faces somber.

"Yeah, well . . ." Dominic tried, but his voice just trailed off. "Sierra, can I talk to you a sec?"

"Sure, Dad." She scooted her chair back and followed him into the hallway. "You okay?"

Dominic nodded, then shook his head and coughed a shaky laugh. "Great question. No. I will be, though. We will be. Look . . . I know . . . I know there's a lot I don't know. And I know it's something you and your mother got going, a whole world, that I can't really know about, and I get that."

"Dad . . ."

"No, it's okay, Sierra, just listen. I just want to say: You can still come to me about stuff, okay? Maybe you can't tell me about the spooky whatever stuff you and Mami got going on, but you can talk to me about other stuff. I'm still your papi and I'm still here for you, whatever it is. Okay? No matter what."

"Thanks, Dad."

"Alright. Imma let you all talk. And look — Juan's gonna be okay, alright? He is. Neville . . . and . . . He is. And Gael said he's gonna try and get leave to come home for a little while until things cool off."

"Whoa!" Sierra hadn't seen her oldest brother in more than a year. "That'd be amazing."

Dominic smiled, wrapped an arm around Sierra, and squeezed tight. "Go talk about all that top secret stuff with your friends. I need a nap before work. And tell your mami I'm not walking that direwolf."

"I will," Sierra laughed.

Neville and Nydia showed up next, Nydia's two little ones hiding behind Neville's legs. "Happy birthday, baby girl," Neville said, handing Sierra a heavy briefcase.

"Should I open this?"

"What else you gonna do, stare at it?"

"It's legal," Nydia said. "I made sure."

"Mm-kay." Sierra set it on the table by the front door and popped the latches. An old-school Olivetti typewriter waited inside. "Whoa! This is amazing."

"I know you more of a painting-type girl," Neville said. "But with all this stuff going on, seemed like you'd want somewhere to put your thoughts into words. Somewhere that can't be hacked into like all y'all's little phone devices."

"You're the actual best ever," Sierra said, giving him a hug.

"And this is for when you want to take your mind off everything else," Nydia said, handing her a shiny gift bag. Sierra opened it and pulled out a rectangular wooden box with a chessboard carved into it. "The pieces are inside. I'll come by and teach you how to play if you don't know."

"Thanks, Nydia! And hey, guys!" Sierra waved at the two boys peeking out from behind Neville. "Come in and have some cake."

"Why the BloodHaüs gotta be all extra and Aryan with their shit, though?" Jerome asked as the cafetera burbled to life on the stove. The Deck of Worlds was spread out on the kitchen table and everyone was leaning over it, gazing at the cards. Sierra got up to turn off the burner.

"Cuz they're white nationalists," Caleb said. "According to the book anyway."

"Oh." Everyone was quiet for a moment. "Well, that makes sense, then."

The BloodHaüs Master was a pale, bare-chested figure emerging from an endless sea of blood, his shaved head bowed. The card had been giving Sierra the creeps since she first saw it start to appear at St. Agnes. Murky shadows still dominated the other emergent house; hunched-over forms and blurry, drooping trees were all anyone could make out.

The Five Hierophants were starker than ever. La Contessa Araña cast a furious glance over her shoulder, her whole face twisted with rage. "She look mad," Sierra said, pouring herself a steaming cup and putting the cafetera on a wooden cutting board on the table. "Like, real mad."

"Well, you killed her daughters," Caleb said.

"*That's* the . . . She . . . she made the Deck?"

He nodded.

"Whoa," Bennie said. "That's your great-great-great-grandma."

Sierra made a face and settled back into her chair. "You don't have to rub it in."

"She looks like an asshole," Jerome mused. "Old people, man. They stay jacking up things for the rest of us."

"They gonna come for us, huh?" Bennie said. "All of 'em."

"Yeah, but we on top now," Tee said. "And we know what we doing. We gonna be ready for 'em this time. Right, Sierra?"

Everyone turned to the head of the table, where Sierra sat sipping her cafecito. She met their gazes: Neville and Nydia, María. Jerome and Bennie and Tee. Mina. Caleb and Robbie. A few shadow spirits had gathered around — Vincent and Alice, little Tolula Brown. In some detention center downtown, Juan, Izzy, and Anthony awaited their hearings. Further off, the gears of the Deck were spinning once again, as new houses prepared for another battle to get on top.

"No," Sierra said, a slight smile on her face. She took a sip of coffee, felt the shadow and light churn within her, rise. "They're gonna have to be ready for *us*. Cuz this time, we're gonna hit 'em first."

ACKNOWLEDGMENTS

I'm deeply grateful to Cheryl Klein, who once again brought her deft hand and full, open heart to this project, as she always does. Working with her on anything is like a master class in everything. Many thanks to the whole amazing team at Scholastic, especially Lizette Serrano, Jennifer Abbots, Michelle Campbell, Antonio Gonzalez, and Weslie Turner. Thank you to my ridiculously awesome agent, Eddie Schneider, and everyone at JABberwocky Literary for all their hard work and always backing me up.

Thank you to the brilliant folks who first put their eyes on these words and helped me hone it into the book you're holding: Cameron Glover, Saraciea Fennell, Jud Esty-Kendall, Jason Reynolds, and Nastassian Brandon. I had the honor of trading manuscripts with two authors I admire while working on this: Brendan Kiely, whose gorgeous *The Last True Love Story* took me on an amazing journey; and Leigh Bardugo, whose *Crooked Kingdom* is magnificent — one of my favorite fantasy novels to date. Both brought so much wisdom and insight to this book, and in both cases for me, to beta read was to fanboy.

Thanks to Sandy Alexandre for help with Robbie's Creole and Nas B for help with Desmond Pocket's Patwa.

Thanks to the whole We Need Diverse Books crew — y'all keep me uplifted and smiling through it all. To Jacqueline Woodson, who is like a fairy godmom to so many of us in the book community; I'm so grateful to walk this earth with you and all your compassion and badassness. Many thanks to the Voices of Our Nation Arts Foundation community, faculty, staff, and students — we doin' this! And thanks to An Na and all my fellow faculty and terrific students at the Vermont College of Fine Arts Writing for Children program and the Mile High MFA program.

Music is a huge part of my writing process, and there are too many artists on my essentials playlist to name here, but I do want to say that without the combined genius of Angel Haze's stellar album *Back to the Woods* and all three of Hans Zimmer's Dark Knight trilogy soundtracks, I never would've been able to finish that throwdown scene in the churchyard.

To everyone on Twitter, Tumblr, Facebook, and Instagram who has been cheering me on along the way, spreading the word, reading my stories, and finding yourselves in them: Thank you! I am where I am because you've had my back.

To Anika, for believing in the shadowshaper world from

way back when and bringing it to life. To Sorahya, for being there along the way. To Jud, Tina, and Aya for all their support.

Special thank you to Nastassian Brandon. To my amazing family, Dora, Marc, Malka, Lou, and Calyx, and of course to Nina. Thanks to Iya Lisa and Iya Ramona, Patrice, Darrell, and Emani, and Iyalocha Tima and my whole Ile Omi Toki family for their support; also thanks to Oba Nelson Rodriguez, Baba Craig, Baba Malik, and all the wonderful folks of Ile Ase. I give thanks to all those who came before us and lit the way. I give thanks to all my ancestors; to Yemonja, Mother of Waters; gbogbo Orisa, and Olodumare.

I wrote *Shadowhouse Fall* during a time that historians will look back on and describe as "tumultuous," although really, for many of us, most of this country's existence could bear that label. We marched, we chanted, we wrote. We lay down our bodies in intersections, highways, and bridges, in malls and jewelry stores, and we stopped business as usual, first just for a moment and then for many, many moments, to declare that Black Lives Matter. Thank you to those who led the way both in the streets and in the tweets, and especially to the young people at the forefront of this movement; there is so much power in what you've done and the world you are creating, so much courage and wisdom in your vision. This book is for you.

Author photo by Kevin Kane

Daniel José Older is the *New York Times* bestselling author of numerous books for readers of all ages. For middle grade, the Dactyl Hill Squad series, the first book of which was named to the *New York Times* Notable Book, NPR, and *Washington Post* Best Books of the Year lists; for young adults, the acclaimed Shadowshaper Cypher, winner of the International Latino Book Award; and for adults, *Star Wars: Last Shot*, the Bone Street Rumba urban fantasy series, and *The Book of Lost Saints*. He has worked as a bike messenger, a waiter, a teacher, and was a New York City paramedic for ten years. Daniel splits his time between Brooklyn and New Orleans.

You can find out more about him at danieljoseolder.net.

TURN THE PAGE FOR A
THRILLING LOOK AT

SHADOWSHAPER LEGACY

SHADOWSHAPER
CYPHER
BOOK 3

Once, a very, very long time ago, when the stars seemed so close and the trees and soil still sang songs of that first act of creation, a girl within the walls of a great palace made a deal with Death.

I know what you're thinking: These things never go well. And you're right — they don't. In some ways, this one was no exception. But of course, the truth is in the telling, and it all depends on whom you ask.

She was a small child with brown skin, curly black hair, and dark eyes, and she was fierce — the eighth born and most unexpected child of a magnificently gaudy and extremely powerful sorceress, who also happened to be a countess.

Of the seven who had come before her, three had died — one turned to stone soon after being born; one was too curious, scaled the palace tower when she was only five, and plummeted into the forest below; one went rooting around in La Contessa's potion cabinet, and they never even found the body.

But the reason this eighth child was so unexpected, you see, was that her father had died horribly two years before she was born. This of course meant that he wasn't her father at all, no matter how many times La Contessa insisted he had been to the guests at her lavish dinner parties.

The truth, which everyone around knew and almost no one dared to say out loud, was that one of the indentured servants, Santo Colibrí, was the real father. Santo Colibrí was a man known far and wide in the area as a healer and one of the greatest singers of all time, a man whose voice could call forth the gods from the heavens and persuade the trees to lower their branches when he passed so they could get a better listen to those sweet, sonorous melodies. His grandparents had been taken from the Congo, but they escaped when they reached this faraway island and found their freedom in the mountains.

No one was surprised that Santo Colibrí had made a baby with the powerful widow in the palace. Everyone was surprised that she'd let the baby live.

Ha!

Let the baby live. As if it were up to her.

The truth was, she'd done everything possible not to, but all her immeasurable powers, and they were great indeed, proved not to be enough to take on this small girl and her famous singing father.

Well, let's expand that circle a bit, shall we?

They may have been the final line of defense, but it was really the other servants — two cooks, a gardener, and one of the guards (of all people!) — who had sabotaged the first, oh, six or seven attempts.

You see, Santo Colibrí had a good handful of lovers and more than a few close friends on the palace grounds, and once it became clear what La Contessa was up to, which is to say, once she missed her first monthly, well, everyone got to work.

Selena the cleaning woman, also quite an herbalist in

her own right, switched out the potions in La Contessa's cabinet that she would've used to abort the fetus for ones that would help it gain access to the mother's powers.

When La Contessa sent scorpions skittering into the newborn's nursery, Parada, the gardener, picked them off one by one, and it was El Tuerco, one of the palace guards that La Contessa had brought all the way from Spain, who fought off a local drunk that had been paid to break onto the grounds and strangle the young girl in her bed.

On and on it went, and as the botched infanticides added up, La Contessa became enraged and paranoid (to be fair, she had every reason to be — at least half her staff was working against her). (To be even fairer, they had every reason to be — she was, after all, trying to murder her own daughter.)

The dinner parties became strained events, as La Contessa rattled on and on somewhat incoherently about vague goings-on in political events back in Europe — mostly failed assassination attempts and coups in places no one was sure really existed. One by one, all the high society expatriates stopped making the trek out into the woods to visit, and the palace became a kind of deserted hideaway, haunted by La Contessa; her four strange, pale daughters; her one unmurderable brown daughter; and the servants.

Of course, the townspeople made up stories about the palace: that it was cursed, that monsters lurked within, that those strange lights in the tower were La Contessa sending out signals to other witches around the world. Most of them would become true eventually, even if they weren't at the time.

But La Contessa was not one to give up easily. Or at all, really. Her tenacity and wit had earned her a place in the high court back in Spain, and that same tenacity and wit had gotten her exiled and nearly beheaded, and either way, she had no intention of stopping now. She'd been alive for a very long time, much longer than her moderately middle-aged appearance belied, and she'd studied under some of the greats, and she still had a few tricks up her ridiculous, puffy sleeves.

She stormed up to the tower one night in a fit of impatience and rage. At this point, it wasn't even about saving face or keeping secrets no one believed anyway — it was the principle of the thing. How dare a mere child resist death so many times, when death was La Contessa's will! It would not do to have her powers so challenged by one so small. The girl was six now, and had made friends with everyone in sight except her own sisters, and seemed to be charmingly oblivious to her powers.

There was, perhaps, a small seed of admiration in La Contessa's grim and twisted heart as she entered the tower room and set about her sorceries.

If the girl refused to die, then perhaps Death himself would have to be summoned to handle the matter. It was downright unnatural, after all. Who better to right such an egregious wrong?

It was a windy night, and everyone knows Death loves the wind. La Contessa prepared everything, and then waited till the clocktower in town struck midnight. Then she began to conjure, to pull, to sing and carry on with such a frightening cackle and howl that townspeople all over the Yunque looked around in terror and held their loved ones close.

Of course, nothing happened.

Not at first, anyway.

You don't just call up Death. Even if you're a wise and powerful sorceress — Death isn't one to just come when called. He's not some common street dog, after all. He's Death.

But La Contessa was, as you've seen, arrogant, and unwieldy, and probably more than a little bit lost in her own sauce by this point, if we're being honest. She didn't just believe the rumors about herself, she'd started most of them.

As the night wore on and on and on, and it became increasingly clear that not only was Death not coming, but none of his mighty denizens or fang-gnashing servants were either, well . . . you can imagine. An even more terrible clamor emerged from the tower, echoed through the valley over the treetops, and ricocheted across the forest-covered mountains, all the way to Aguadilla and as far east as Ceiba.

Then, because as anyone who has lived and died knows, Death has a sense of humor, as the sun began to rise over La Contessa's groveling, weeping form, a cool zephyr whipped through the room at the top of the tower. La Contessa looked up, and she must've looked something like Death herself — makeup smeared, her face twisted into an almost inhuman scowl of disappointment.

But there in the still gray twilight stood the towering empty visage of Death himself, that rictus grin just visible beneath the drooping cowl.

Please, La Contessa said, but it was really a demand. *Please, take that foul bitch who is my daughter! I beg you. I have been your devoted servant for so long, I remain so today. I ask only this of you, Death. Complete the work that I have started.*

Death, being Death, said nothing, only nodded very slightly and then was gone, with what La Contessa could've sworn was the slightest chuckle.

That morning, when La Contessa walked wearily down from her tower, the nursemaid Altragracia, one of the few palace servants who'd remained loyal, came running over in tears. It was Angelina, La Contessa's firstborn child — she had died in her sleep.

La Contessa sunk to her knees, raising both hands over her head. She ordered that the corpse be dressed in her finest gown and laid in state in the chapel, and then she stood, turned around without another word, and marched back up to the tower.

One must be specific when speaking to Death. La Contessa knew this. She had let her frustration and the long night get the best of her. She had made a terrible mistake. But that only strengthened her resolve. She would figure out what to do about Angelina later. Now, she needed revenge.

She spent the day preparing and mixing up new potions, and when midnight came around once again, La Contessa commenced another night of awful howling and carrying on, and the whole island of Puerto Rico trembled and looked off toward the dark rain forest, and wondered. Many nightmarish tales were conceived in those two terrible nights. Most of them would become true eventually, even if they weren't at the time.

Death seemed somehow proud of himself on that second daybreak. That smile seemed just a little wider, his back a little straighter.

La Contessa ignored it. What good would it do, getting mad at Death himself? None. The mistake had been hers, and hers alone.

La bastarda, La Contessa said. *Take her.* And then, because she knew the power of names and what they could do, she closed her eyes and whispered the words she hadn't spoken since the child was born: *María Cantara. Take her.*

When she opened her eyes, Death was gone, and the sun had just peaked over the tops of the palm trees. La Contessa allowed herself the slightest of smiles before beginning her slow descent to her living quarters.

Death came to María Cantara the next day at that yellow-blue hazy moment when late afternoon becomes evening, right as Old Salazar was making his rounds lighting the flickering lanterns throughout the palace.

It was María Cantara's favorite time of day; she loved to watch the forest grow dark and listen to the night birds begin their festivities. She would gaze out from one of the balconies and make up fantastic stories about the different creatures that lived in the Yunque. Most of them would become true eventually, even if they weren't at the time.

When Death appeared, María Cantara didn't fright or even cry like most people did. She smiled.

Death smiled back, but Death was always smiling, so that was neither here nor there.

Have you come to take me away? the little girl asked.

Death, ever smiling, nodded.

What if I don't want to go?

That empty stare was, even María Cantara had to admit, a little chilling.

What would it take for you to leave me?

Death, being Death, didn't talk, but he did raise one hand, palm up, as if to say, *And what do you have to offer, child?*

My mother, María Cantara said, and Death very nearly burst out laughing. That would never do, though. Too easy. And powerful as this young one was, if things came so easily for her, she would never come to learn the deeper secrets of life and death. He would've enjoyed complying, but it wasn't the way, it wasn't the way.

What then? the girl said, a little stubborn pout on her face.

Death, being Death, didn't talk, but he did slide three words in an icy whisper through María Cantara's mind: *Your firstborn child.*

Done, she said, with such finality and firmness that even Death himself was taken aback. She was, after all, only a child, and had little to no concept of what a firstborn was. Still . . . the speed with which she said it — the clarity — it was almost like she had something up her own sleeve.

Intriguing.

Death nodded once more, but then found that he wasn't quite ready to leave yet. The whole interaction had caught him off guard, and he wasn't used to feeling that way. He wasn't used to people looking him in the eye, or not crying and carrying on. And he hadn't spent any quality time with a flesh and blood mortal in a very, very long time.

So he stayed, and when María Cantara turned back to the darkening woods around them, she felt the icy presence of Death like a gentle breeze beside her, and together they stared out into the shadows, and made up stories of all that may have been and would probably soon come to pass.

The last streaks of a strange, greasy sunset slipped into darkness as night stretched across the cold New Jersey skies. Sierra Santiago grinned through chattering teeth and pulled her maroon hoodie up over her fro against a chilly breeze that swept across the field toward her, rustling the tall grass and sending tiny waves through a nearby puddle of murky water.

"You ain't nervous?" Bennie stepped up beside her.

"Excited, honestly," Sierra said.

She didn't have to look to know her best friend was rolling her eyes. "Okay, girl."

So much work had led up to this one moment, and Sierra was mostly relieved it was finally going to happen, regardless of how wrong it might go for them. Anyway, it had reached a point where it *had* to happen: It was simply, undeniably time, and if she'd tried to maneuver or predetermine the outcome any more than she already had, it would blow up in her face.

"You don't think they'll be mad that we, you know, lied to them and shattered the fragile peace and all that?"

Sierra smirked. "What peace? Ain't no peace that I can see." Since inadvertently destroying all but one of the Sorrows and becoming the House of Shadow and Light a month and a half earlier, Sierra's crew of shadowshapers had been getting threatening messages from whisper wraiths, catching strangely shaped figures that stalked them through the streets of Brooklyn, and fending off half-hearted attacks from random spirits. Clearly, someone was trying to rattle them. Old Crane and his House of Iron was probably behind it somehow, but he'd pledged neutrality until things calmed down, and had even sworn to protect Sierra's brother Juan, her crush Anthony, and Izzy while they were in lockup. Still: No one could be trusted. That much Sierra had learned. And anyway, Bloodhaüs was on the rise, clearly vying to knock the House of Shadow and Light out of the way so they could take over dominance. And allying with Old Crane on the low would be just the way of doing it.

Anyway, the Bloodhaüs was a bunch of raging skinheads, so regardless of whether they were behind the attacks, as far as Sierra was concerned, they had to go.

"You right," Bennie said. "I just mean . . . no one can prove it was Bloodhaüs that was coming at us."

"Ha."

"And they still gonna be mad."

"That only matters if they can do something about it."

Bennie shivered. "That mask you been painting on . . ."

"What about it?" Robbie had drawn it for her the first time. Halloween night, when everything had changed and she'd finally embraced her role as Lucera, Mistress of Shadows. It had felt right, and not just because everyone else was dressed up too. That face paint had saved her life when she'd squared off with the Sorrows later that night. It had been there for her when she'd needed it most, a form of art to channel spirits through, and ever since then it had felt like donning armor every time she applied the grinning skull over half of her face.

"Gives me the chills," Bennie said, raising her eyebrows. "But I guess that's the point, huh? You only paint it on when some shit's about to go down. What *are* you planning, Si?"

Sierra just let her grim smile speak for her.

It was a fair question, though, and usually she preferred having her people know the full score of what was gonna go down. But tonight was different. First of all, she wasn't totally sure how things would play. If Mina's intel was right, Bloodhaüs was every bit as ruthless as they'd projected themselves to be. And even if they were less powerful than the shadowshapers, they were more experienced and more desperate. They would play dirty, Mina had assured everyone at the planning meetup.

That's fine, Sierra thought, as Big Jerome rose from his position in the tall grass and signaled that someone was coming. She nodded at Bennie, and then crouched out of sight.

She had no intention of playing clean.